Discover the Passionate Dangers of
CHANNING HALL

I moved forward cautiously, the dankness filling my nostrils. With one hand I held up the hem of my gown and robe lest they trip me, with the other I held the candle whose flame was already burning low. . . .

Then, it was extinguished. A voice demanded, "Who goes there?" and my terror increased tenfold.

I gasped as strong male hands travelled my body and grasped my hair. I started as my captor murmured, "Damnation, Daphne! What are you doing here?"

A man's mouth covered mine, his lips demanding. I fought, pushing with all my might, but I was no match for him. I was shaking when his lips moved into the nape of my neck.

"You see, I knew how it would be *entre nous*," he murmured.

"My God, it is *you!*" I gasped in sudden and shocked realization. . . .

Berkley books by Ashley Allyn

CAMBERLEIGH*
MAYFAIR*
CHANNING HALL

published under the pseudonym of Evelyn Grey

CHANNING HALL

ASHLEY ALLYN

B

BERKLEY BOOKS, NEW YORK

CHANNING HALL

A Berkley Book/published by arrangement with
the author

PRINTING HISTORY
Berkley edition/December 1987

ISBN: 0-425-10498-2

A BERKLEY BOOK ® TM 757,375
Berkley Books are published by The Berkley Publishing Group,
200 Madison Avenue, New York, NY 10016
The name "BERKLEY" and the "B" logo
are trademarks belonging to Berkley Publishing Corporation.

PRINTED IN THE UNITED STATES OF AMERICA

10 9 8 7 6 5 4 3 2 1

DEDICATION

*To Evelyn Leslie
My greatest critic and my greatest champion*

Prologue
serena

August 12, 1830

Dear Diary,

I fear that I have not been an honorable companion lo' these many years, but my intent when I began sharing my intimacies with you was not to record day-by-day but rather on occasion to reflect at length. One day, I pray years hence, when I have passed to that nebulous realm that welcomes us all, I hope that you shall serve as a tangible reminiscence to Daphne and Alexander that I have lived and loved well if not always wisely.

It is eighteen years to the day that you and I entered on this journey. How young and naive I was when I first travelled with my beloved Jaspar to Camberleigh. Those were dark and brooding times, and I am ever thankful that I was protected from knowing that they were the first in a succession of same.

But, dear friend, as you well know, I have also been blessed with equivalent joy, which in these troubled times is something that few can say.

Justin has accused me of being moody as of late. I, of course, will not admit it, but I am certain that his perception is accurate. I know, if I am honest with my inner voices, that it is a growing sense of vulnerability on my part. One does not pass one's thirty-sixth birthday without fretting about one's denouement. I think that the fact that our Daphne's season is to begin in but a few weeks heightens the intensity of my awareness.

Do I sound jealous? I suppose, if I am to be honest, in a way I am. For she is about to launch her life, her womanhood, and mine is slowly ebbing from me.

If Justin were to read this, he would chastise me irreparably, for he tells me, nightly I might add, that I have grown more beautiful, more integral to him as the years have passed.

I rejoice in hearing that, but I cannot help but wonder as I look in the mirror each morning if the girl he fell in love with is the woman he loves today.

Admittedly I see little change in my visage. My hair, still a honey-amber, will be late, I sense, to be voided of its vibrancy. Like my dear, long-passed mother, the vestiges of time seem not to have awarded me furrows and lines for each period of worry or concern, and my figure, naturally tall and lean, has changed only minutely—Justin says appealingly.

I must wonder at times, though, if my green eyes deceive me. Does nature somehow protect us from acknowledging the ravages of time?

Perhaps. But I admit to you that even if I am lying to myself that my appearance is timeless, I assure you that my spirit is such. I look at Daphne and I think that we are in many ways far more sisters in attitude and response than mother and daughter.

How beautiful she is. Admittedly, she does look like a younger image of myself, except, of course, for her eyes, which harken back to Juliette, my maternal grandmother. There is a great sensitivity that lies behind those deep violet pools fringed with long, surprisingly dark lashes. Also I fear an impetuous nature, which Justin says she acquires naturally from her mother.

I have been more acutely aware of Daphne's inner self these past two years since welcoming Constance into our home. I took her in certainly against the better judgement of all who are close to me. But when I learned of the death of her mother, Clarissa, I simply could not bear the burden of abandoning the girl. Her mother and I were cousins, not by birth but by situation. That Richard was not truly Clarissa's father but that she had been borne by an illicit union between her mother, Maura, and some stable hand is a secret that we have protected these many years.

Justin tried to convince me that Constance should be sent to Camberleigh to live with Anne and Richard. Had other circumstances not intervened, I might have agreed, but my Uncle Richard has not been the same since his stroke four years ago, and poor Anne has little enough time for herself between looking after her husband and Camberleigh, not to mention her couturier business, which has become renowned throughout the continent.

Dear Anne, she, of course, volunteered to become Constance's guardian, but it seems much more logical that she come to Mayfair, where she might have the company of Daphne and Alexander.

I admit that sometimes within these past two years I have questioned the wisdom of my decision, but I am ever hopeful that with time her flighty, jealous ways will temper.

Her appearance was unsettling to me at first, for she truly is a replica of Clarissa—the same small bones and porcelain skin framed by a cascade of almost white-blond hair. Initially I found myself overly watchful for signs of her mother's deceptive and often cruel words and actions. It was actually Daphne who helped me overcome my tenuousness with her, for she accepted her so openly, so without suspicion, that I was forced to see Constance as Constance and not as some ghost of Clarissa.

In general I think all has been amicable enough. Alexander is hardly taken with her, but then he is less given to a gregarious nature than Daphne. It ever surprises me that my son, who is the image of his father, is so serious and such a loner by nature. Justin thinks I overdramatize the point, assuring me that he is simply a rather self-possessed young man who relishes his privacy, but I fear the explanation goes deeper.

That year after we thought Justin had died at sea and I had been duped into marrying Philip Taggart had, I feared, its greatest impact on Alexander. He had always been a quiet, cerebral child, but he had drawn even more into himself during that nightmarish year of our lives. Though but a child he had reacted quickly to Philip's manipulations of me, and it had bred a wariness in him that I feared would endure with him throughout his lifetime.

At first I thought that when we had discovered that Justin was indeed alive, his tendency to keep at arm's length would disappear. But brief though my marriage to Philip had been, it had cost him the freedom of adolescent naiveté.

Justin's opinion is that Alexander's being slow to trust may well stand him in good stead in adulthood. I know that it still haunts Justin that if he indeed had not been so trusting of Philip Taggart's railway venture, each of us would have been saved from months of pain and anguish.

It, of course, was not his fault. Philip was a clever and cunning opponent, and it was his very charm that deceived us all. Justin and I no longer talk of him, I think it is too painful for us both. When Philip died in that harrowing coach accident, it was as if we had to bury the memory of him while physically burying him.

The difficulty at first was that I insisted that Justin pursue the railway venture on his own. It had been a dream of his and one that I sensed would not, should not die with Philip Taggart.

It would have been easier not to continue his vision. After all, Justin essentially is an agriculturalist, and although we had lost fortunes in his gamble with Philip, we still had the Mayfair-Camberleigh estates, which continued to be the largest and certainly the most profitable in the county.

But I had a dreaded fear that if I did not encourage Justin to see through his beliefs in the necessity of railroads in England and the subsequent prosperity that they would bring, I would one day live to regret it. Justin is a man of passion, and when in years hence we were looking back instead of forward, I did not want him to hold me accountable for stifling his dream.

And so we have gone forward with it. Justin withstood the years of opposition from the anti-industrialists who saw the foray of the iron engines into the North as the beginning of the ruination of a healthy agriculture. Any doubts that I had had about the viability of this venture have long since disappeared. I now see that men like Justin who had the insight to perceive that the railways would bring not only a renewed prosperity but also a fluidity to England will become the champions of the next century.

We have yet to see any profits from this enterprise, but Justin assures me that by the time Alexander comes of age our wealth will be almost incalculable. 'Tis scarcely something that concerns me, for we are already blessed with the bounty of the Mayfair-Camberleigh estates.

A great part of that success can, over these past eight years, be attributed to Oliver. True to his promise when he returned from America with Rebecca, his new bride, he engrossed himself in learning about the farms, from managing the books through to acquainting himself with the various plights of the tenants. It has been a blessing for Justin, particularly since Richard's stroke, permitting him the time and freedom he needed to pursue the railroad venture.

Richard, who was never of a mind to direct the estates, is amazed, I think, that Oliver has shown such a passion for the land, but I know that he is tremendously proud of the innovations that his son has instituted.

Oliver credits Robbie with helping him in those early years to undertake the management of the farms. Justin worried at first that Robbie would resent Oliver's involvement, but I knew that it would not become an issue. Justin had brought Robbie along over the years from a mere stable hand to a position that ranked as his associate. But Robbie had never been comfortable with the economic responsibilities, and with Oliver's return he can now focus his attention once again on the tenants.

Robbie has never married, much to his mother's chagrin. Dear Charlotte, I think she still holds out some small hope that she will live to realize grandmotherhood, but secretly I doubt that that will happen in her lifetime.

She has aged greatly over these past years, being plagued with diseases of the joints, which leave her aching and infirmed most days. She continues in her official role as housekeeper of Mayfair, for I have not the heart to suggest that she retire and simply live out her last years without the thought of any responsibility.

I have subtly given Molly more of the physical duties over the past four years, and that Charlotte has seemingly not objected is perhaps the largest statement of how time is telling on her small frame.

There is not a day that passes that I do not think of my beloved Jaspar, lost to me now for over eight years. We had shared so much, my four-legged friend and I, and his faithfulness I shall always cherish. Justin, sensing what a loss his passing had been, surprised me the Christmas of his return with a puppy who could have, by markings and temperament, been bred of Jaspar. I named him Pluck, and although he shall never take Jaspar's place, his smile and ingenuous nature quickly won a large part of my heart.

Justin becomes very gruff with him sometimes late at night
when he, feeling ardor, turns our bed into the setting for our
lovemaking and Pluck, ever at my side, decides to angle his
brown and white haunches determinedly between us. Happily
Justin is always the victor.

We talked about having another child the first year after
Justin had come back. I had hoped that it would indeed happen, feeling that for us both it would be a renewal of our lives
and our vows. It simply was not to be. Perhaps it was for the
best, for certainly our lives are full enough with our family,
our work and our friends.

We are blessed with the latter. Richard and Anne, Monique
and, of course, Robin and Lilliane. Only our dear friend
William Cobbett did we lose some five years ago. I have
missed his quick mind and challenging treatises. There has
been none to replace his wit and intelligence at our frequent
balls and dinners. However, when I become melancholy about
his passing, I am refreshed by his memory and the knowledge
that his courageous steps towards social reform will be championed for years to come.

I suppose I envy him that his effect here on this earth will
not be finite to the years that he spent in the world as we know
it. I often wonder what it shall be that I will leave behind. Certainly our two wonderful children. And I suppose our heritage. I would like to think that Justin and I have returned to
the land as much as we have inherited from it.

I cannot be assured dear diary that Daphne, or Alexander,
will ever share the passion that Justin and I have for the Camberleigh-Mayfair estates. There is a part of me that prays that
one or both of them will choose to carry it on after we have
gone. But I shall never pressure them into it. I was raised with
a belief that I had the freedom to choose the path that my life
would take. That changed, of course, when I came to Camberleigh. But then I soon learned that that was my destiny.

If one can find happiness in one's own destiny, then I
should be thought of, as time passes, as a happy woman.

1
serena

I RECOGNIZED THE footsteps in the hallway and quickly closed my leather-bound companion, endeavoring to stash it back in the bottom drawer of my wardrobe before our privacy was intruded upon.

The door to the bedroom flung open as I straightened and smoothed the folds of my muslin gown.

"What, pray tell, are you doing, my love?" the resonant voice queried.

"Just organizing some of these drawers," I replied quickly, not wishing to share the penned intimacies of the past hours with him. "You look as if you have been riding," I pursued, thinking how handsome he looked in his chestnut breeches and billowing white shirt.

He nodded. "Oliver and I decided to give the horses a bit of a workout. If you are really determined to go to London, I want to exercise them as much as possible before we leave."

"What do you mean *if?*" I asked as he moved over to the wardrobe and withdrew a fresh shirt.

"Forgive me, darling, but I can scarcely put any importance on Daphne and Constance's season. They seem very well turned out to me without having to spend months primping and going to an endless array of balls."

"You men are all the same," I rebuked.

"Well, you did not have a season, and I would say that you

7

are certainly the finest specimen of womanhood I have ever seen," he replied, winking at me.

"You know perfectly well why I chose not to have a season," I argued, "and, besides, I married you shortly after the season was at a close."

"I suppose I should be grateful," Justin replied.

"And what does that mean?"

He strode over to me and took my chin in hand. "What that means, my lovely, is that if that barrage of maturing males had ever seen you, I doubt that I should ever have been able to call you my own."

I leaned up and kissed him lightly on the lips. "You know that is not true," I whispered.

His arm encircled my waist and he drew me tightly to him. "Show me," he murmured, his lips pressing into the nape of my neck.

I pushed him gently away. "You are incorrigible," I laughed. "You know I have but two days to get this family organized."

"Darling, you have been packing for weeks now," he replied, frowning at me. "If you won't let me bed you, then at least come and take a walk with me about the grounds. Channing Hall has its merits, but I shall miss the Mayfair lands these next few months."

"I suppose it would do no harm," I agreed. "Where is Pluck? He would like a romp as well I am certain."

Justin laughed. "The last time I saw him he was terrorizing Cook. He had gone into the pond and, tempted by her cinnamon buns, had maneuvered his way into the kitchen. She was fit to be tied."

"I best retrieve him," I replied. "I shall meet you out on the front lawn."

I left the wing that housed our bedroom suite and stepped out into the long hallway that led to the main staircase. I had done little to change the house since Justin and I had moved into it after our marriage. His parents, who had passed away before we met, had created in Mayfair one of the most magnificent manor houses in the North. Fashioned of limestone, its architectural details were oft commented on in historical journals. The staircase alone was worthy of note, spiraling in exaggerated sweeps to the lofty second floor. As my hand touched the highly polished balustrade, I could not help but think that Justin was right. We would indeed miss our Mayfair these next months.

As I reached the landing I was almost thrown over by Pluck, who ran full tilt to me from the rear hall.

Steadying myself I bent down to capture the wriggling brown and white body barking his greeting.

"I hear you gave Cook quite a turn this morning," I chastised as his cold nose nudged my hand for affection.

"Still in a snit she is," came a voice from the rear hall.

"I had not seen you there, Charlotte," I replied as her full figure hobbled into view.

"Aye, never seen the like of it," she replied, shaking her head." 'Twas like yer dear Jaspar's lookin' down at this one an' possessin' 'im te torture Cook."

I smiled at the thought. Jaspar and Cook had had a sparring relationship from the first, and it was uncanny that Pluck should have developed the same penchant for upsetting the kitchen routine.

"You look tired, Charlotte," I said as she approached, noting dark circles under eyes that even in age had not lost their twinkle.

"Well, the worst of it is over," she replied. "Gettin' those girls packed seems like 'tis takin' a month o' Sundays."

"There is no reason for you to be assuming that responsibility, Charlotte," I retorted. "Daphne and Constance are two strong young women. They are perfectly capable of packing on their own."

"Oh, aye know that, Serena, but if aye be leavin' them te their own devices, ye'll find we'll be gettin' te London with an odd lot in those trunks," she replied, pushing her madcap of grey curls back from her forehead.

I shook my head. "I keep thinking that I was so much more organized at their age, but then in truth I owned nothing to organize."

"I still kin remember that day ye arrived at Camberleigh with only a little satchel and yer Jaspar," she mused.

"Sometimes I look in the mirror and wonder if I was ever that young and innocent," I replied. "And then there are other days when I feel that journey was but yesterday."

"Well, they say the mirror never lies, Serena, an' if ye be seein' clearly, ye'll know that yer just as lovely as the day aye first laid eyes on ye. No, 'tis not true," she pursued. "Aye think ye've grown even more beautiful. There's a wisdom in yer eyes now. Aye've seen it growin' each year since Master Justin's return. 'Tis a calm it has added to yer beauty.''

I was about to thank her when Justin's voice boomed from on high. "Good grief, I thought I would have to go a spell to catch up with you," he called down as his steps assaulted the staircase as he descended.

"We are going out for a bit of a stroll," I offered. "We shall be back long before the dinner hour."

"Not if I have my way," Justin laughed, grabbing my hand.

Charlotte, who over the years had grown accustomed to my husband's playfulness, simply waved us on.

Justin flung open the massive oak doors that formed the entrance to Mayfair and pulled me after him onto the portico and onto the front lawn, while Pluck romped after us. I gathered the skirt of my peach muslin gown with its full petticoat and let Justin guide me across the verdant lawns that framed the drive. He slowed, finally realizing that my gown was impeding my ability to keep up his pace. His arm encircled my waist as he led me down along the lake, which at present was home for seeming hundreds of geese.

"Is Oliver staying the night?" I asked as we began to descend on the path leading to the chapel.

Justin shook his head. "I expect he has already departed. Rebecca was feeling poorly, and he thought he best return to Camberleigh."

" 'Tis nothing serious I hope," I replied.

He smiled. "I am scarcely an authority on these matters, but I sense her malaise is but a precursor to the pitter-patter of little feet."

I smiled. "I quite think Rebecca believes there should be a child in every bedroom at Camberleigh."

"That, my love, would be the most ambitious enterprise any of us have taken."

We had come within forty paces or so of the Mayfair chapel. Justin's father had had it built when he had met the woman who was to become his bride. They had, in fact, wed within its very walls, and it had become the site not only of Justin and Anne's baptismal ceremonies but also of our own children's as well.

Architecturally it represented an interesting disposition to Mayfair itself. As light and expansive as the main house, the chapel always made me think of Camberleigh with its heavy dark stones forming a seeming impenetrable mass.

Justin pulled at the heavy iron latch, which formed a cross against the arched doorway. The massive door emitted a low groan as it opened.

"It smells musty in here," I whispered as I stepped inside, my boots making a distinctive clicking sound as I moved forward on the granite floor.

"I really should tell Robbie to air it out this fall," Justin replied. "It would be a shame to see these old pews destroyed by the dampness."

Justin led me forward, while Pluck followed sniffing for the nests of mice that I was certain were secreted throughout. When we reached the front of the chapel, Justin eased me over to one of the ornately carved front pews, and the two of us knelt for a moment side by side.

After several moments of silence I offered, "Perhaps this small chapel shall be the host for several weddings within the year."

"If you are referring to Daphne," Justin argued, "I would counsel you that she is far too young. She has many years before her before she settles down with some unsuspecting husband."

I smiled to myself, thinking that for Justin Daphne would always be his little girl.

"You should know that I was only slightly older than Daphne when we married," I recollected.

"That has nothing to do with it," he volunteered. "You were more mature than Daphne."

"That is scarcely what you told me then," I posed. "If my memory serves me, you referred to me as stubborn, head-strong and impetuous."

"I still do," he replied, taking my hand and guiding me back to the aisle. "Which is even more reason to protect Daphne from those suitors, for she takes after her mother in character as well as appearance."

The sun had begun to set as we left the chapel arm in arm. Instead of returning by the lake, Justin led me up the high pathway north of the chapel through the fields where some sheep and cows grazed in the stillness of this late summer day.

"How do you expect the crops to be this year?" I asked, stooping to pick a few wild daisies from the field.

"A little shy of last year, but we experienced such a remarkable harvest twelve months ago that I would scarcely expect as great a bounty this year. Given any unforeseen problems we should be up again next year. Those new machines that Oliver ordered will permit us to plant far more extensively than we ever have before."

"I wish Alexander were coming with us to London," I offered.

"We have gone over that, Serena, and I simply will not have the boy fritter his time away at those silly balls. Besides, it is a perfect opportunity for Alexander under Oliver and Robbie's tutelage to learn more about the running of the estates."

"How can you be so certain that that is the kind of life he wants to pursue?" I challenged.

"I cannot," he replied quickly. "But these several months of exposure to the land and the tenants will serve to make him aware of the responsibilities. If, after, he chooses to pursue another existence, then it will not be for me to stand in his way."

I drew closer to Justin as the wind from the north bore down on the hollow we were in.

"You are cold," Justin advised.

"A bit," I admitted. "Perhaps we had best turn back," I added, looking about for Pluck, who I spied romping up ahead of us.

We strode in silence for a bit until Justin suddenly asked, "You shall not be bothered about returning to Channing Hall, will you, Serena?"

I knew he was referring to the fact that after Philip Taggart had died in the coach accident and Justin had come back to us, I had vowed that I would never again return to Channing Hall. It had been the locale of such a painful portion of my life that in those first years I could not bring myself to stay there even for the briefest time.

It was true that I had had a few uneasy moments contemplating our ensconcement there for the months to come, but I was determined to keep fresh in my mind that we were voyaging there for a happy occasion, not one to be fearful of.

"Serena?" Justin pressed.

"I am sorry, darling," I apologized. "To answer your question, I shall be fine."

Dusk had settled as we reached the main entrance to the

house. I turned back to Justin, giving him a light kiss. "I shall be down shortly. I want to change into something a bit warmer."

Justin nodded, saying that he would meet me in the library.

I returned to our bedroom and quickly selected an emerald-green silk taffeta gown, heavy ruching about the sleeves and skirt. Anne, who had fashioned all my gowns since those years past when I had first come to Camberleigh, always insisted that green was my best color since it seemed to intensify the green of my eyes.

She had indeed been generous with the girls, designing extravagant wardrobes for their coming season. I scarcely knew how we were going to transport all our trunks, but Justin had assured me that he was expanding the team to accommodate the extra weight.

I took one last look in the mirror, pulling the comb up higher on my head so that it emphasized the cascading effect of the tendrils falling down my back, and began my descent to the library.

2

daphne

I DREW BACK the heavy, red damask draperies and looked out of the north window. I smiled as my eyes cast downward and spied Mother and Father strolling arm in arm through the hedgerows towards the chapel.

I did not want to intrude on their privacy. They had little enough of it these days, what with Father's management of the estates and the burgeoning demands of the railroad. As much as I looked forward with some anticipation to the commencement of Constance's and my season, I could not help but feel somewhat guilty. Father, I knew, could scarce afford the time away from his work, not to mention that rounds of balls and galas scarcely suited his temperament. Mother had mustered enthusiasm enough for both, but I knew that was for our benefit. She loved Mayfair so, and to be displaced, even for three or four months was, I was certain, not a happy prospect.

I had qualms about leaving this house as well. It had been ten years since I had last resided at Channing Hall and that had scarcely been a joyous time—indeed it had been fraught with sadness and tragedy. I was in no way superstitious about returning there, it was far more that, like Mother, I would miss Mayfair dreadfully.

Constance accused me of being silly, but she had been raised in London. She was, I realized, accustomed to the people, the shops, the hustle and bustle of the city. I could not imagine looking out of the window and not seeing the endless rolling hills and glistening lakes, not to mention the woodlands beyond the glen where I oft rode my mare.

Some found it a solitary life here in the north country, but I had always revelled in it. I did not have many friends but that was due more to proximity than want. Of course, in the past few years I had had Constance's companionship, though admittedly at times that had proved more of a negative than a benefit. But that I knew was in part due to the losses she had experienced. It had to be painful and difficult to have had her father and then her mother pass away in such a short period of time. I had thought when she had first come to Mayfair that she might want to talk about it, to share her loss with someone her own age, but she had never murmured a word and indeed had appeared almost bored when I had broached the subject.

I actually had looked forward to her arrival at Mayfair, but the friendship I had envisioned we would develop had never come to fruition. We were friends, of course, not really intimates. That in part was natural, I suspected, since we were indeed so different. Constance could spend hours fussing with her hair, debating which gown to wear each day, while I invariably donned a riding habit and was down to the stables by the time the sun was full. Not that I did not care about the latest fashions. I was as excited about the new gowns Aunt Anne had sent as Constance. It simply was not a preoccupation of mine.

Even our physical appearance was totally different. I always thought she looked like a china doll, her delicate features seemingly painted against the clear ivory of her skin. Indeed I felt somewhat awkward when I stood next to her, for I clearly towered over her. But then the Barkhams were not a petite lot. I had never really given much thought to my height until Constance had arrived. It was true that frothy little gowns did not become me, but I did not mind my looks. Indeed Mother was considered one of the most beautiful women in all of England, and it could not be dismissed that save the color of our eyes, I was a replica of her. But there was something about Mother that I did not possess. I had oft studied myself in the mirror to try and determine where the difference lay. It was more a regard, a certain look. Where I saw myself as only average, she appeared breathtakingly glamorous.

I moved away from the window, realizing that I had best continue packing. I picked up a small leather-bound book of poems that Alexander had given me on my seventeenth birthday and tucked it into the side of the smallest valise. I could not hide my disappointment that he was not to come to London with us. Though Alexander was two, almost three, years my junior, I had always thought of him more as an older brother. We did not spend an inordinate amount of time together, for he was clearly a student and ever embroiled in his books, but the time we did spend was important time. He had a thirst for knowledge that seemed unquenchable. I had always enjoyed reading and my lessons, but I had never experienced the passion for prose that he had. Although he was generally quiet, it was that very passion that made him exciting. Constance found him a dreadful bore, but I heartily disagreed, for one could never leave a conversation with Alexander without realizing that one had learned something.

It scarce seemed possible that the time was upon us to leave for Channing Hall. I would never admit to Constance that I was nervous, for she was taking great delight in lording over me her knowledge of London. I did not want to appear the fool, not that I thought I would, but there was no question that I would be surrounded by more sophisticates than I was accustomed. Mother assured me that that was nonsense, for though we lived in the country, it was true we entertained frequently, including members of the royal family. I suspected it was more that this would be the first time that I would be meeting a series of eligible young men, and though I knew that Mother was in no way obsessed with seeing me married off, I could not deny that there was a chance that in the ensuing months I should meet my husband-to-be.

Constance and I had speculated, as I supposed all girls did, on who our mates would be. I found it for the most part an innocuous conversation, for how could one describe one's intended?

We had had such different familial experiences, she and I. Though it was never expressed, I sensed that her own parents had had less than a blissful experience. I could only hope that I would find but a part of what my own family shared. My father was a unique man. Though I was not obsessed with finding one who was his duplicate, I knew that his very presence in my life would give influence to my choice of a man to share my own life with.

I started at a knock at the door. "Come in," I called out.

Constance nearly flew into the room. "With all the help in this house, I cannot understand why Serena thinks that we should do the packing," she cried, flailing a large fan before her face. "I shall simply succumb if I have to do any more in this dreadful heat."

"Well, I am finished, I do believe," I replied, "save those few gowns that I shall save 'til morning."

"Is that all you are taking?" she said, amazed, her eyes scanning the numerous trunks and valises.

"All?" I gasped. "Father is going to be fit to be tied as it is."

"Oh, poo," she chastised. "You know you can do no wrong in his mind. In any event, if you are finished, then you would be a dear and help me. I cannot seem to do anything—'tis all such a bore."

I paused for a moment. "I was frankly about to take Her Fancy out for a run. 'Twill be some time before I might ride her again."

Her face darkened. "You and that horse. Well, if she means more to you than helping your poor cousin, then you go off and leave me to struggle on my own."

"I shall assist you," I replied wearily, "but only for a spell."

Her smug regard told me that she thought she would indeed inveigle me into doing all her work, but today she was greatly mistaken. I had only hours left to let my mount take me across the fields and pastures that I loved so well, and I wanted the scent of the land, of Mayfair, in my nostrils when we commenced our journey to London.

3

serena

As I ENTERED the ornately pine-panelled room, Justin was lighting the wood set in the fireplace. Alexander was seated on one of the twin love seats that framed the ornate mantle.

"Well, there are the two handsomest men in my life," I complimented. Justin straightened and, winking at Alexander, teased, "I think we should take exception to that statement since it implies that the lady has *other* men in her life."

"Only Pluck," I replied as I sat down and his warm body pressed against my feet.

I waved Justin off as his gesture questioned whether I should like to join him in a glass of port.

"You know, Alexander, your father and I were talking earlier about your spending the next few months at Camberleigh."

"What about it?" he asked, rubbing his hand through his dark waving hair.

"Well, I simply did not want you to think that we were banishing you there. I am certain your father would agree that if you would prefer to come to London, we might arrange it," I offered.

"Perish the thought," Alexander replied emphatically. "It is difficult enough to find some respite from those two here at Mayfair. I should expect at Channing Hall they would drive me quite mad."

I started to rebuke him for referring to Daphne and Con-

18

stance in such a manner but Justin's hearty laugh made me see the humor in his response.

"I expect that settles that issue," Justin concluded as there was a knock at the library door.

Giles entered saying, "Excuse me, Lady Barkham, but Charlotte asked me to tell you that dinner will be served shortly."

"Thank you," I replied to the elderly man who had butlered at Mayfair for almost half a century. "Oh, and would you ask Molly or one of the maids to fetch the girls?"

Justin downed his port and followed me and Alexander to the dining room, which was across the hall from the library. It was a massive room that dwarfed any gathering under thirty but one that I insisted on using, preferring it to the smaller breakfast room at the rear.

The first course of smoked salmon in a sorrel sauce was being served when the girls finally arrived.

"Before you chastise me," Daphne offered, "let me tell you that everything is packed."

"I sense that you are rather looking forward to the commencement of your season," I retorted.

"Well, I for one cannot wait to return to London," Constance insisted. "It is so dreary being stuck out in the country."

"Pardon us," Alexander exclaimed.

"You forget," I said quickly, not wishing an argument to ensue, "that Constance was raised in the city."

"Well, I hope that I shan't be found too provincial. They shall probably think me a country bumpkin," Daphne wailed.

"Oh, I should scarcely think that to be true," Justin assured her. "It is not as if you have not had privilege. And I should remind you that your mother is considered one of the most sophisticated hostesses in England. Of course, if you should carry on about this, I might advise you that it shall be your character and not your heritage that shall be rebuffed."

If Constance had intended to pursue her initial tack, she had been quelled by Justin's response. The girl had an annoying habit, which unfortunately persisted while she had remained in our care, of trying to lord over Daphne. Daphne was unquestionably brighter and, I thought prejudicedly, more beautiful than her cousin, but Constance was quick witted and had a cutting edge to her nature that seemed ever to penetrate Daphne's more gentle and gullible character.

There were times when I had been tempted over these past few years to protect Daphne from her cousin's taunting innuendos, but I had always held my tongue, for I was fearful of recalling my own experiences with Clarissa, Constance's mother, and imposing them on Constance herself.

Happily the conversation lightened as the girls eased into chatter about their gowns and their side comments to Alexander that he would be missing all the fun by not joining us in London.

I was curious as to how these next months would affect us all. It was an exciting time for the girls, and I enjoyed their enthusiasm about their season. For Alexander it would be the first time that he had been separated from Justin and myself for any length of time. I was loathe to admit it, but I doubted that he would be lonely. For his age he was a tremendously self-possessed young man. He was less gregarious than Justin but harkened after him in his seemingly innate desire for independence. Oliver, I sensed, would be a good influence on him. His raw sensitivity as a child had matured into a nature that was both quick and warm, and if there was any presence that I would trust Alexander to, it was Oliver.

In an odd way it was Justin whom I concerned myself most with. He had been borne to Mayfair, and though certainly a well-traveled gentleman of considerable exposure and means, it was Mayfair, I knew, that infused a certain passion and drive in him. He had often said that we could be happy anywhere, but at this moment I questioned the validity of his statement.

Channing Hall was an exquisite house, certainly one of the prettiest in London, but I did wonder if he should not feel trapped by its confines. There was a charming garden out back, but when one had been used to vast expanses of ever-changing land that one called one's own, the taut structure of a city environment I feared would prove stifling to him.

I had never truly been serious when I offered that he need not join us if he did not wish. We were separated once and I had vowed that never again would I permit spaces of time or distance to part us. I sensed that I would have to make a special effort not to plan his days too carefully in London.

His nights were another matter.

We dined languidly on following courses of roast pheasant with new squash and wild rice. I demurred to dessert, conscious that many of my new gowns were dangerously form-fitting and that food would scarcely be in short supply over these next months.

Justin and Alexander retired to the library after dinner, and I with Pluck at my heels begged off to the bedroom, where I began reviewing my packing of earlier hours.

I had already donned my nightdress and climbed into the soft, freshly changed sheets when Justin entered the bedroom. He tiptoed over to the heavily-carved bed, which we had imported from China shortly after our marriage, and knelt down brushing my forehead with his lips.

"I am not asleep," I murmured.

"Then I am in luck," he whispered as his weight pressed against the bed.

I opened my arms to him, and we lay quietly for a moment.

"Why do you not shed all these clothes and extinguish the candles?" I murmured.

"You have convinced me," he agreed.

I watched him as he rose and undressed, marvelling as I always did at the taut masculinity of his form.

Justin never bothered to don nightclothes. He always chided me that my own nightdresses were superfluous since they invariably wound up in a small pile at the base of the bed, but convention or modesty always prohibited my commencing our lovemaking in absolute nakedness.

I had never understood the disdain that my women acquaintances would on occasion impart about their husbands' advances. I was always obsequious in my own responses, being loathe to admit that I revelled in these moments when our bodies entwined desire and fulfillment was uppermost in my mind.

Having not had experience other than my own husband, save a nightmarish violation by Philip Taggart, I had no comparisons to make. But instinctively I knew that this man who lay with me as my husband possessed a sensuality that far exceeded the grasp of most men. I shuddered when after his long tender strokings of my body I felt his manliness insisting against me, spreading my legs and thrusting me up and to him.

It ever amazed me that Justin was able to make me spend all the frustrations and concerns of a day in either brief or languishing moments of the night. When we had first married, I had worried that he would tire of me one day, but his displays of affection seemed not to have lessened but perhaps intensified over the years.

I smiled to myself as Justin's slow rhythmic snoring, so characteristic of his drifting from the climax of our lovemaking, began to fill the room. I eased his head onto my breast, stroking his broad forehead, and drifted to my own peaceful reverie.

It was Charlotte who awakened me the next morning. I knew the moment I saw her with the breakfast tray that I had overslept.

"Master Justin said aye was te let ye be but aye know how ye dislike bein' abed too long so aye snuck this up the back stairs."

I propped myself up in bed and gratefully accepted the robe she handed me.

"You are a dear, Charlotte," I replied appreciatively, "but you should have had Molly or Elizabeth carry that tray up here."

"Nonsense," she argued. "Besides aye thought aye might be helpin' ye finish te pack."

"I do believe I have finished," I assured her, "but perhaps you can look things over while I partake of this feast. Cook must think I am going to starve in London by the looks of this tray."

As Charlotte began poring through my armoire and chest of drawers, I plunged eagerly into the eggs and kippers that Cook had prepared.

"Ye see 'tis a glad thing that aye'm lookin' over these trunks," Charlotte remanded. "Ye would 'ave fergotten all yer gloves. Not one pair do ye have packed."

I had not the heart to tell Charlotte that I was planning to put them in my small valise at the last moment, for she took such pride from mothering me.

"You know, Charlotte," I pursued, "I have been so involved with the children that I have not even asked you how you feel about leaving Robbie for these next months."

She paused, her hand kneading her left hip. "Aye'd be lyin' to ye Serena if aye said aye won't be missin' me boy but 'e's made a life fer 'imself 'ere now an' aye scarce think that havin' his mum gone fer a while will disturb the boy."

I smiled at her reference to Robbie, who was now in his late twenties, as a boy. I supposed it was simply a natural but motherly fault to think that our boys would always remain in that adolescent state.

"He will miss you dreadfully, of that I am certain," I assured her.

" 'Twouldn't be bad, I reckon," she retorted, her dark eyes gleaming. "Might spur the lad to seek a good woman fer his own. What with you, me an' the master gone, maybe he'll seek out a girl to make a life with."

"Do you think he is unhappy?" I ventured.

She shook her head. "Sometimes aye wish 'e were. No, ye an' the master 'ave given 'im everything. An' grateful aye am. 'Tis just that I'd like te see a wee babe around Mayfair again. An' aye guess cause I never had a regular life, I mean with a husband an' all, I'd like to see it different fer Robbie."

It was only on these occasions that I remembered that Charlotte had borne Robbie from a brief liaison with a farmhand who, even when he had learnt that she was with child, had abandoned his meager job and more importantly her. Charlotte, who had been a mere chambermaid at the time, had raised Robbie without the benefit of support, either financial or familial. Those early years, I knew, must have been nigh unto impossible, but she had endured. I had great respect for her for that. And for the son she had borne and raised. It was not an easy task, I knew that now, but Charlotte somehow had managed to see that baby grow into a man who commanded the respect of us all.

"Miss Constance is in one o' her snits this morning," Charlotte offered suddenly.

"What now?" I replied, moving the tray to begin my morning toilette.

"Determined she is that Lady Camberleigh made the nicer dresses fer Miss Daphne. Aye swear that girl can try yer soul at times," she replied.

"I think the best thing to do is ignore it," I cautioned. "Constance likes to test. I sense in that sense she takes after her mother."

Charlotte nodded. "Aye worry about our Daphne at times. She doesn't see her cousin clear-like all the time."

"Daphne will be fine," I assured her emphatically. "And so will Constance. If she takes after her mother, she will have a line of besotted suitors forming outside Channing Hall within weeks of our arrival."

"An' ye should hope that one of 'em will fancy 'er enough te wager his life with 'er."

"I want them both to be happy," I said emphatically. "Constance, I know, will have to marry someone of means. But Daphne, for Daphne I can only wish that she finds real love in her life."

My toilette finished, I donned a gingham dress with a large white pinafore overlay. Justin, I knew, would be spending the day with Robbie, handling last minute details before our departure. I decided to seek out Alexander since it would be some while before I would be able to spend any quiet time with him again. Begging Charlotte to get some rest before our journey, I ambled down to the library, where I knew that Alexander could invariably be found.

"So there you are," I greeted as Pluck came bounding forward. "I should have known, where your brother goeth, so go ye."

"I am a far second choice, you know that, Mother," Alexander insisted. "I am in his favor only when you are not available."

"Nonetheless, he will miss you while we are in London," I replied. "Of course he will not be alone in that."

"You will be busy enough," he countered. "And there are letters, you know."

"Am I intruding on you?" I asked suddenly, realizing that he had seemed to be deeply embroiled in some book when I had entered.

"Nonsense," he assured.

"What are you reading?" I queried.

"Oh, one of Cobbett's treatises. I regret that I never got to know him better. I sense I would have liked him."

I smiled as I poured a cup of tea, remembering my dear old friend. "He would have liked you," I offered. "He would have appreciated your mind, your curiosity."

"I should say that I inherited that from you, Mother."

I laughed. "You flatter me, but I suspect my curiosity has gotten me into some fine fixes over the years. You, and Cobbett for that matter, are far more cerebral in your quests."

"Sometimes I feel that bothers Father," Alexander posed.

"Why would you say that?"

He shrugged. "He is rather an awesome role model, you know. There are not many men who can manage the largest estates in the county, champion the building of the railroad, oversee a family, not to mention the sundry charities and projects he gets involved with."

"I admit at times that I do not know how he does it," I replied. "If truth be known, I oft wish he could abandon much of it, but that does not tell me why you feel that your, what shall I call it, your proclivity for issues, for matters of intellect, would prove troublesome to Justin?"

"Father is such an activist. He tends to plunge forward, while I ruminate about things, examining all sides."

"But surely that does not make him right and you wrong?" I speculated. "It simply is your approach that is different."

"I suppose," he agreed, "but having the perfect man as a father can prove intimidating at times."

"It should not," I countered, "for he is blessed with the perfect son. And though he is less demonstrative towards you, I know since you are grown, I can only tell you, Alexander, that he could not be prouder of you. And Daphne as well, of course, but there is a special bond between a man and his son."

He was quiet for a moment. "I think he is pleased that I am going to commence learning about the estates."

I nodded. "I just wish that I were convinced that it is truly something you want to do. I realize that you would not find the life in London amusing, but the last thing I want you to feel is that this apprenticeship, as it were, has been foisted on you."

"I do not, Mother. In an odd way I think the timing is perfect. If Father were about examining my every move, testing me, as we both know, want or not he would do, I suspect I would be so anxious that I would grow exasperated in short term. But this way I can learn in my own fashion."

I agreed. "But you must promise me that if you find you do not take to it, pride will not prevent you from being honest about it. I would hate to see you shackled to a profession simply by inheritance."

He nodded. "It has been a long spell since I have stayed at Camberleigh for any length of time. You do not think Anne would mind if I took my stallion? I know the grooms would exercise him but 'twould not be the same."

"Of course not," I assured, remembering back to the day when Anne and Richard had sent the horse to Alexander. We had thought then that Justin had died at sea and the foal had been sired by Justin's favorite horse, Medallion. Alexander had named the horse Justin in his father's memory.

He looked up at me frowning. "It still evokes unpleasant

memories for you, does it not?"

I paused for a moment and, summoning my courage, I asked him suddenly, "Alexander, do you harbor any dislike or resentment towards me for having married Philip Taggart?"

His strong brows knitted in a frown. "You do not truly believe that, do you?"

I shrugged. "Let us say that I have always hoped not."

"Mother, you were duped, we all know that," he assured quickly. "You thought Father was dead, and even though it was many years ago, I know how clever Philip was at his deceptions."

"I would do almost anything to undo that year," I reflected.

"I know that," he assured me. "When I was younger, I was confused. You must admit being told your father is dead, having your mother remarry and then having your father reappear fully alive, well, it was quite a shock."

"For us all," I said softly.

"Particularly for you," he replied.

I was very proud of Alexander. He likened himself to me, but his breadth of character, I knew, harkened more from his father. He was growing into a fine young man, and his assurances gave me a sense of relief. He was not one to volunteer his feelings, but having pressed I had received the answers I had hoped for.

"Well," I said, rising and straightening my gown, "I have intruded upon you long enough. Besides, I had best see to the girls. It frightens me to think what they have packed away in those valises."

I bade Pluck to stay behind with Alexander and went off to find Daphne and Constance. The two had adjoining rooms in the west wing. Daphne, who deeply cherished her privacy, had at first objected to her cousin's proximity, but I had not wanted to separate Constance from her. By bringing her to Mayfair I had in effect welcomed her into our family and I wanted from the first to ensure that she felt that she belonged.

Daphne had been quickly appeased, for I had allowed her to redecorate her own room. It was not difficult to discern which bedchambers belonged to which girl. Constance's was of the palest blue with a dainty trellised-patterned wallpaper encircling a tester and dressing table whose lines were almost hidden by the yards of gossamer which adorned them. Daphne's room by contrast was bold, almost daring, with a hand-drawn Chinese-motif paper of exotic birds and pagodas setting the stage for a great mixture of woods—yew, cherry and mahogany.

I knocked lightly at the door as I reached Daphne's room, surprised by the seeming tranquility from within.

"Come in," Daphne called out.

I entered to find her seated before her dressing table, her arms in the air holding her masses of coppery-gold hair high above her head.

She turned to me grimacing. "I should need some proper tiaras and combs if I am going to be acceptable in London."

"Oh, I should think you will be quite acceptable, Daphne, though I scarce think that pout is terribly alluring."

"Well, Constance has a full set," she retorted, "and I venture to say that she will not allow me to borrow them."

"Those were her mother's," I advised, "and I am certain that she feels a sentimentality towards them."

Daphne fell silent, and I knew that she was embarrassed by her display of envy. Secretly I had full intention of presenting Daphne with her late great-grandmother's tiara on the eve of her first ball. I was tempted to bestow it on her now, but it was a special piece and I wanted her receipt of it to be a memorable occasion.

We spent an hour or so reviewing the gowns she had selected to take to London. I wished that Constance were present, for I longed to help her with any last-minute decisions she might make, but I knew better than to search her out. I had been able to establish a friendship with the girl, but any word or move that came under what I categorized as motherly expression was rejected out of hand. The tumult that I had experienced in my own burgeoning womanhood helped me to empathize with her resistance, and so I interfered little in her day-to-day routine.

I admitted that I felt somewhat at a loss the remainder of the day. Charlotte had organized our trunks and the household so well that there was little for me to occupy my time with. I ambled through the house, drinking in the last images of Mayfair that I would hold for some months to come.

London had never held the same fascination for me as it did for Anne or, particularly, our dear friend Monique Kelston. I had grown up in the country, albeit in Cornwall, and though I still at times longed for the sound and smell of the sea, I had come to love these northern climes. There was a peacefulness in the country that I missed dreadfully when in London. But our sojourn would only be for three, four months at the most, and the anticipation of returning to our beloved home eased the sadness of leaving it.

We shared a quiet dinner, with Robbie and Charlotte joining the family. Cook prepared a particularly scrumptious meal. I was bemused by this, for I swore that she always made her most valiant efforts just before we departed so that our memory would only retain favorable impressions.

As Justin needed more time to review matters with Robbie, I retired early, Pluck staying close at my heels. The candles had burned well down by the time Justin joined me in bed, and we soon fell asleep, our bodies cradled in the form of the other.

When I awakened, Justin was already dressed, looking very dapper in a red cloth coat and paisley vest.

"What time is it?" I asked sleepily.

"Almost eight," he replied. "I asked Charlotte to bring you a tray, but I should like to be under way by nine."

I nodded, pulling myself up from under the heavy down covering. "Would you see to it that the girls are up and take Pluck for a bit of a romp?"

Justin agreed easily, calling a reluctant Pluck to him. Charlotte arrived moments later with a tray of hot porridge and cinnamon buns. I ate heartily, and when I had risen and finished my toilette, I donned the corsets that I loathed but were now very much in fashion. I accused romantics like Sir Walter Scott for having influenced the change in our mode of dress these past years. I preferred the simpler Empire styles of our regency, but there was little one could argue of change. I selected a carriage dress of silk brocaded with green and yellow fleurettes, full high-puffed sleeves adorned only by a lace pelisse and collar cuffs with solid-yellow satin bows at the neck and along the center skirt panel. Charlotte had offered to fix my hair, but as I was to coil it simply to accommodate my full-brimmed bonnet, I took the task myself.

It was almost nine-thirty when I descended to the library, where I found the girls dressed and in excited anticipation of the journey. Alexander entered and informed me that Justin had instructed the grooms to fetch the trunks and that we were to meet him in the front drive to await the carriage being brought round.

For the next ten minutes we were barraged by an entourage of staff, who all came to bid us well. I embraced Robbie warmly, bidding him to keep a special eye out for Alexander, whom he would take the following morning to Camberleigh.

There was an enormous lump in my throat when, learning that the barouche had been brought round and was fully loaded, we said our final goodbyes. I clung particularly long and hard to Alexander, trying as I did to suppress the tears that I found welling in my eyes.

"Now, you promise to write," I exacted from him as we finally pulled apart.

"Every week," he assured me.

Our driver, who had been with us for some years now, hoisted Pluck up to his seat. With five of us we were crowded within the carriage, but I had argued that it had seemed unnecessary to take two coaches, since it ensured that we could travel further distances by day. With little more ado the horses were moving us out of the cobblestoned courtyard and down the long drive away from Mayfair.

We could not have been more fortunate with the weather since, though the day was overcast, there was no hint of the precipitation which oft threatened the North at this time of year. It would soon be time for the full harvest and the fields along the main journeyways were dense with ripening grains. The sheep dotted the green undulating hillside beyond, their fleecy coats soon ready for shearing. I never tired of the landscape in Yorkshire, for it had a raw, wild beauty that ever seemed to challenge the eye.

Our driver moved at a swift pace, knowing that Justin wanted to press before we stopped for luncheon. Thus it was some three hours later when we arrived at the Horse and Hound, a small inn which we had frequented in our travels southward in years past. The accommodations and meals here were simple but hearty, certainly as good as any public house around.

The girls, who had chattered nonstop since our departure, ate scantily, insisting that they needed to watch their already trim figures. Justin seemed restless but I attributed that to his having been confined with four females, and thus I was not surprised when, as we returned to the carriage, he suggested that he should ride atop with our driver and Pluck.

It was exciting on this next stretch of our journey to see some evidence of Justin's long struggles with bringing the railways to fruition in England. It would be many years, I knew, before tracks were laid so that we might in fact travel by rail from county to county, but the work had begun and what had once been but a dream was now edging towards reality.

Dusk had settled upon the landscape as we arrived at the inn where we planned to stay the first night. We were all weary; even Pluck seemed to welcome the respite from the constant sway of the carriage. After partaking of a corn soup and mutton dinner, which was served by a bountifully-endowed serving girl who took a quick fancy to Justin, we retired to the cramped but clean and tidy rooms above.

I climbed wearily into the large bed, which sported taut muslin sheets and heavy wool blankets. Our routine today I knew would vary little over the next three. Though I longed to languish a bit with Justin, sleep was necessary for us all if both body and nerves were to be intact when we reached Channing Hall.

Blessedly, the remainder of our journey passed uneventfully, save some inclement weather that commenced in the early afternoon of our second day and followed us into London. Charlotte, who suffered from an inflammation of the joints and was prone to aches in damp weather, was perhaps the most relieved of us all when the carriage passed along the Thames to the small square that housed Channing Hall. Justin had troubled me some during the journey, appearing preoccupied most of the time, but as he helped us all alight from the carriage, his mood appeared cheerful, and I attributed his silent musings these past days to being his own way of escaping our female banter.

Though not by any means as grand or stately as Mayfair, in seeing it once again I had to admit that Channing Hall was still one of the most impressive homes in all of London. Crafted of polished white stone, its Ionic portico was raised on a terrace and flanked by many wings, fronted by Ionic columns. The house was set further back from the street than most, with high, ornately-carved iron gates framing the entrance. The heavy plantings of yews, foxwood and juniper, which helped soften the house's formed lines, had likely been pruned of recent in expectation of our arrival.

Before my feet had been firmly planted on the ground, Sidney, who had long served as both our driver and butler, came scurrying out to greet us. Justin extended his hand warmly as I straightened my dress and, edging the girls towards him, introduced them both.

"I would know ye any place," Sidney effused to Daphne, who was surprised at his recognition. "Ye be yer mother's daughter all over again."

"I am flattered," I interjected. "It certainly has been eight, no almost nine years since you have seen our Daphne."

"An' Master Alexander," he replied peering back to the coach, " 'e not be with ye?"

I shook my head. "He shall be residing at Camberleigh these next few months."

As Sidney picked up a few of the smaller valises, I joined step with him.

"Now, tell me, how is your Mary?" I asked.

"She be sendin' 'er apologies but 'er mum be ailin', an' she went te fetch the medicines fer 'er. But she'll be back by morn, don't ye be frettin'."

I smiled to myself with the realization that it had to be eight years since Sidney and Mary had married. They had lived together under the roof of Channing Hall for almost twenty years, but it had taken most of those to give Sidney the courage to ask Mary, our housekeeper at Channing Hall, to court.

As Charlotte alighted from the carriage, Sidney grinned broadly. "I was hopin' ye would be comin' with Lord and Lady Barkham," he called out.

Again I felt a smile spread my lips, remembering days gone by when Charlotte's presence had intimidated Sidney and certainly Mary. They had finally become fast friends, drawn together, as I suppose we all had been, by the wrongful news of Justin's death those many years ago. I knew that Charlotte and Mary exchanged letters on a regular basis, and though I was not privy to the contents, I suspected that, although theirs was an indelible friendship, each continued to try and emphasize their own importance with our family.

For myself, Charlotte had been like a mother to me, certainly my champion at the most unlikely times, and so there would ever be a bond there that only she and I might understand.

I tripped slightly as the sole of my boot caught against what I had forgotten was an uneven stone through the entrance gates. Quickly Justin was at my elbow.

"How quickly I forget," I muttered as I straightened my foot in its shoe.

"It has been a long time," he murmured as his strong arm slid under my own, supporting my full weight up the steps to the massive mahogany door that was our entrance. The door, which was already ajar, was swung open by Justin, and I entered with him into the center hallway, my spirits uplifted by the massive spray of flowers that had been arranged atop a Louis XV table.

"Oh, it is elegant," Daphne enthused as she and Constance joined us in the center hall. "Do you not think so?"

I spied Constance casting her eyes about I thought not without approval, but I was not surprised when she retorted, "Well, I find it pleasant, if not a bit small."

Clarissa and her husband's house had indeed seemed at first entry larger than Channing Hall, though admittedly I had always thought it one of the more grotesque great houses of London. Poor Constance could not know that her mother, once having commissioned Adam to create the ceilings, had had the nerve to try and instruct a master and had thuswise been abandoned. His, or should I say, her choice of a replacement had fashioned what was already untoward space into a melange that Monique referred to as "triste rococo."

Before I could make some comment, Pluck burst through the still open doorway, his large paws moving at a rapider pace than his body and barking at full tilt.

Sidney shook his head. "If I didn't be knowin' different, I would be thinkin' 'twas yer little Jaspar there."

"He is an amazing likeness, is he not?" I replied, realizing that this was Sidney's first exposure to Pluck, since in our prior trips to London he had always remained, unhappily I might add, at Mayfair.

"Will ye be wantin' the trunks taken te yer rooms, my Lady?" Sidney asked.

I nodded. "I think we are all a bit worse for wear for this travelling. Charlotte, you might show the girls their rooms, since I doubt that Daphne shall remember them well. And you might ask one of the maids to draw us all baths. I know I should like to refresh before dining. Is that agreeable to you, darling?" I concluded, turning to Justin.

As Justin seemed deep in thought, I repeated my question.

"Hmm, that would be fine," he replied absently, "whatever you say, Serena."

Sidney assured me that he would attend to everything, and Charlotte proceeded with the girls up the tall staircase. I moved towards the drawing room and opened the ornately molded double doors to it.

It was an unusual room for a city dwelling, pacing some thirty-five feet wide by forty feet in length. There were eight columns in the room, Corinthian in nature, which supported the half-domed ceiling designed by Adam. I had always thought the most appealing part of the room to be the architectural panels that host some wonderful paintings, including three Reynolds, all done in his youth.

The Waterford glass chandelier sporting some fifty candles had been lit for our arrival, and it cast a warm welcoming light to the room. I was pleased seeing the room again, for having redecorated it nine years ago, it was gratifying to see that it had stood the test of time. I had used bright floral chintzes and plenty of Worcester and hexagonal vases on scale bleu to continue the color. On either side of the fine chimney piece, which contained its original looking glass, stood a pair of Chippendale mahogany armchairs, the stuffed backs, seats and arm pads covered in light biscuit ground with gros- and petit-point needlework. I am particularly proud of those, since the handwork I did myself.

I moved forward to the arched windows, each with its own bow window seat of a deep rose brocade. I peered out the window facing the most northerly direction and thought my eyes to be deceiving me for the moment, for I swore that lights had just been extinguished in the house across the way. It would not have seemed so odd to me except that to my knowledge the building had been shuttered since the death of its owner, Viscount Penberthy, several years past. I pressed my face closer to the glass in anticipation of seeing some further movement or light, but when, after some minutes, I saw nothing, I determined that it must have been the reflection of our own chandelier or the mullioned windows.

The remainder of the day passed swiftly. Although refreshed by a leisurely bath, I was still tired. I sensed we all were and after dinner it did not take much encouragement to convince everyone to retire early. All except Justin, who opted to take a brandy in the library, allowing that there was some correspondence that he wished to catch up on.

The Dutch marquetry hall clock struck nine as I finally wound my way up the staircase to our bedroom. All the bedrooms in Channing Hall were panelled in pine. Justin's mother originally had them all painted white but I had preferred to add more color to the house, and when I had redecorated, I had done ours in a pale green. Our bed, a four-poster, had a particularly graceful carving of shell motif above the canopy. There was a double armoire in one corner, a French piece that I had purchased at Monique's insistence, and near it an inlaid mahogany dressing table with its toilet mirror and stand draped in muslin. The silver-backed brushes, tortoiseshell combs and silver ringstand that lay atop had been a gift from Justin on our first anniversary.

One of the maids had turned the bed down, and after changing into my nightdress and settling Pluck in front of the fireplace, I climbed into bed. I lay awake for a spell feeling the aches of travel ebb from my limbs, wishing that Justin would join me. He had been very quiet during dinner, and as we had not had an opportunity to have much privacy these past four days, I longed to be held by him.

I did not know what time Justin finally retired, for he had not awakened me and in fact had already dressed and was breakfasting downstairs when the maid arrived with my morning basin.

I smiled at the young girl, who was new to the staff since I had last been at Channing Hall.

"Might I ask your name?" I queried as she handed me my robe.

" 'Tis Jane, my Lady," she replied in a lilting voice.

"And how long have you been at Channing Hall, Jane?"

"Only a fortnight, my Lady," she replied, her gaze directed downwards.

"Well, I should hope that you will be happy here."

"Oh, I am certain I will," she replied. "Sidney an' Mary, I mean, Mister and Missus Bostwick been ever so kind te me."

I moved to the dressing table and, uncoiling my hair, began brushing it vigorously. "You might inform my husband that I shall join him for breakfast in the dining room."

Jane curtseyed sweetly. "I be leavin' ye then. Oh, an' 'ere I almost forgot. Mary told me te tell ye that Mister Bostwick took yer little fellow fer a walk."

I thanked her, took my toilette and selected a gown of

mauve and cream silk with a banded waist, high puffed sleeves and organdy and lace pelerine for the day. Not wanting to disturb Charlotte I dressed my own hair, forming it into two large braids, which I plaited high on my head, weaving a mauve ribbon of the same fabric as the dress through the elaborate coil. I fastened on an amethyst broach to the pelerine and matching earrings and, satisfied with my appearance, left the bedchamber to find Justin.

He smiled broadly as I entered the dining room and came quickly to me.

"You look delicious," he whispered as we embraced. "I should far have preferred to take breakfast upstairs, but you were sleeping so peacefully that I was loathe to disturb you."

"Just do not make a habit of it," I replied coyly as he guided me to one of the Chinese Chippendale chairs that complemented the oversized mahogany table.

"And what are you going to do today, my love?" Justin asked, returning to his chair.

"I suppose I need spend a bit of time getting the girls organized, but that shan't take me long, and frankly I thought we might spend the day together," I replied.

"I am afraid that that will not be possible, darling," Justin replied.

"Why not?" I asked, surprised by his response.

"There are simply several things I must tend to. Actually, I shall be out most of the day, just some business matters that need my attention."

I tried to hide my disappointment. I suppose selfishly I had thought that once Justin was away from Mayfair we might have more time to spend with one another, but my husband was hardly one to laze about, and I supposed that he had outlined numerous meetings and projects to occupy himself during our stay.

Sensing my chagrin Justin came over to me and kissed me on the nape of the neck. "I shall make it up to you, I promise," he assured.

I smiled up at him. "You were simply going to be my excuse for not tending to chores."

"Do not plan on me for luncheon, but I should be back well before the dinner hour," Justin said.

"I shall have organized the household three times over by then," I replied.

He gave me a swift kiss and left me to partake of the sumptuous breakfast, which was just being brought to my place.

I heard the front door close only moments later, and shortly thereafter Daphne joined me in the dining room.

"Good morning, Mother," she said brightly, giving me a swift kiss on the cheek.

"I must say you look refreshed," I said, thinking that the royal blue of her silk morning dress was particularly flattering. "Is Constance still asleep?"

Daphne shook her head. "She is fussing with her hair and fussing at the maids."

I frowned, realizing that I would have to address that later. Constance's mother had had a far different view of servants than I, and it was hard to discipline her overly demanding ways.

"Where do you think you are going?" I asked, suddenly aware that Daphne was pulling a bonnet over her head.

"Just to walk about a bit," she replied, tying the bonnet sashes under her chin.

"Darling, this is not Mayfair, you know," I chastised. "Young women simply do not go about London unescorted."

"Oh, Mother, do not be so provincial," Daphne accused. "I am perfectly capable of looking after myself, and it is not as though I am going to wander. I just need to get out and breathe some fresh air."

"Fine, you can do that directly on the front walk," I replied. "Just keep within the gates."

Daphne threw me a look of obvious displeasure. "You know, Mother, I am about to commence my season. I hope you are not going to treat me as a child."

"I shall treat you and Constance as young ladies as long as you act like young ladies," I replied.

Daphne shrugged. "I shall take Pluck out with me, and do not fret, I shall stay within the grounds."

As I watched Daphne leave the room, I thought that I would have to remind myself on occasion that she was indeed growing up. I had not been that much older than she when I had made that long journey alone from Cornwall to Camberleigh. In my case I had to grow up quickly. I did not want Daphne to lose the lightheartedness of youth sooner than the inevitable.

4
daphne

I OPENED THE door and stepped out into the cool of the morning. Pluck following close at my heels.

"Our mother does fret," I murmured, leaning down to pet the brown and white body that seemed entranced by all the new smells.

I could not believe that Mother had so little affinity for London and Channing Hall. Why, I had seen more elegant coaches and smartly dressed men and women since our arrival than I had for years' end at Mayfair. Of course, I did truly love Mayfair; it would be difficult not to, but our lives there were so placid. You could just feel a certain excitement here in London. I said a silent prayer that the men I should meet in the coming months should not find me dreary by contrast to the chic young women who had been born and bred in the city.

As a clatter of hoofs approached, I turned the latch and swung the heavy iron gates open to peer down the street. As I did, the carriage turned off to the left, and in that split second Pluck scampered through my legs and across the street to the house set opposite. I called to him, but he ignored my pleas, and I had no choice but to follow in pursuit. I could not tell where he had gotten to, as there was a brick wall that fronted the wings of the house. As the only entry seemed the front gate; I tried the handle and, noting that it was not locked, proceeded gingerly into the front courtyard.

I did not want to call out for him for fear that I might disturb someone, though I had to admit that the garden appeared immensely overgrown and untended, hinting that the house was perhaps not fully occupied.

I had just rounded a plot of yews that blocked my view of the back garden when a man's voice demanded to know what I was doing.

I whirled about to find myself face-to-face with a tall man, perhaps ten years my senior, obviously a gentleman by his dress.

"I repeat, what are you doing here?" demanded the deep resonant voice, which had a clear trace of an accent.

I looked up into a pair of dark, deeply-set eyes that examined me critically or quizzically, I knew not which.

"I do apologize," I insisted, flushing under his intense gaze. "I, we live across at Channing Hall, and our spaniel escaped over to your garden."

His eyes turned past me. "If he is brown and white, then he is there beyond," he replied, motioning by a large tree at the rear.

I swung around and called to Pluck, who came bounding towards me unaware of any embarrassment he had caused.

When he was in tow, I turned back to the dark stranger, who continued to study me intently. "I shall take my leave then," I said swiftly.

He bowed slightly at the waist. "The Count at your service," he replied, a small smile playing about his lips. As I began to move back towards the gates, he called out to me, "I would take some neighborly advice, fair damselle, and keep that spaniel of yours in tow henceforth. He might not have received such a welcome in other quarters hereabouts."

I did not pause but moved swiftly back to Channing Hall, chastising Pluck as I went. If I had expected Mother to be lying in wait, she was nowhere in evidence, and I crept steathily upstairs, praying that I should reach my bedchamber unnoticed. I had no longer reached my room than Constance burst into it.

"Who was that you were talking to?" she asked eagerly.

"I do not know what you mean," I replied.

"Oh, do not be such a silly goose," Constance moaned. "I saw you over there talking to some man. Who is he?"

"Some count," I replied.

"Count who?" she pursued.

I shrugged. "He obviously lives there."

"Is he attractive?" she pursued.

"I suppose in his fashion," I shrugged. "Quite rude, if you should ask me."

"You are dreary at times, Daphne," Constance reproached. "Here we are in London to meet young men, and you meet a count and all you can say is that he is rude."

"Well, he was," I insisted as Constance flounced down in front of my dressing table, toying with the blond ringlets that framed her face.

"I suppose since you have been out you have not talked to Serena," she mused.

"Not since earlier this morning."

"Well, then you have not heard that Monique Kelston is giving the first ball in our honor Saturday eve."

"That is just two days from now," I exclaimed.

"It cannot be soon enough for me," Constance insisted. "Your mother seems determined to keep us cooped up in this house. At least if we have some suitors, we should be able to experience a bit of London."

I had to admit that what she said was true, but I had no intention of accepting attentions from some gentleman just to be out from under my mother's watchful eye. I longed for freedom as well, but deceiving my family was too high a price to pay.

5

serena

I AWOKE TO find Justin leaning on his elbow, smiling down at me.

"And how is my beautiful bride this morning?" he murmured.

I smiled up at him. I had indeed felt like a bride the night before. Justin, who had seemed so preoccupied for days now, had suggested that we retire early. We had made love well into the morning hours and, finally spent of our physical and emotional selves, had fallen asleep entwined in each other's arms.

His lips covered mine before I could answer.

"What time is it?" I asked when he finally released me.

"Do you really care?" he teased.

"Darling, you have not forgotten that Monique's ball is tonight?"

"Monique's ball? Now, let me see . . ."

"You tease," I replied, nudging him.

"If you do not mind, I believe that I shall take myself out of the house today," he responded, pulling himself out of bed. "This is not man's business, you understand."

"Of course. Simply be back here in time to dress."

I stayed abed while Justin dressed, watching him don his striped britches and plaid waistcoat. If anything, he was a man who seemed to become more attractive with age. Only a sprinkling of grey at his temples gave hint that he was any older than when we had first met.

After he had departed, I dressed quickly and went upstairs

to see what state the girls were in.

Constance had decided on a pale-yellow silk taffeta gown whose heavily-pleated cap sleeves commenced just below the shoulder line. It was heavily crinolined with an overskirt bordered with a large drop of white French lace. I suggested that she wear her mother's pearls and matching pearl earrings with a simple spray of flowers wound about her hair.

Daphne's gown was of the palest ivory with dramatically arched sleeves that succeeded in accentuating her stature. It was relatively unadorned with only a sash of brown velvet bows encircling midskirt.

She looked surprised when I handed her the large blue velvet box.

"What is this?" she queried.

"It was your great-grandmother's," I replied quickly. "I am certain that Juliette would be proud to know that you shall be wearing it."

She opened the box slowly, her violet eyes, so like my grandmother's, growing wide as her fingers lifted out the tiara within.

"Oh, Mother, it is exquisite," she exlaimed. "And it shall be perfect with my gown."

I quickly withdrew the other box I had brought with me and handed it to Constance, who, I knew, would be coveting her cousin's good fortune at this moment.

She said nothing but opened the box, which revealed a fan of point de gaze mounted on gilded mother-of-pearl sticks. I knew by her expression that she was thrilled, though she only murmured a small thank you.

Satisfied that the girls were well in hand I took Pluck, who had accompanied me, and retired to the library, where I commenced my first letter to Alexander.

The day passed swiftly, and I must admit that I was becoming increasingly nervous when at six Charlotte had finished dressing my hair and was fastening the last of the buttons on my gown.

"Ye look beautiful, Serena," Charlotte complimented. "Lord Barkham better keep an eye on ye or those young gentlemen might fall all about ye."

"What was that about Lord Barkham, Charlotte?" Justin inquired as he strode into the room.

"Thank goodness you have returned," I sighed. "And not one moment too soon."

"Who is that goddess before me?" he asked, winking at Charlotte.

"You like it?" I asked, holding out the slim white silk skirt that fell from a high banded waist and neckline of gold braid.

"I know that my sister has a talented hand and eye, but I must agree that she has in you the perfect image for her designs."

Justin's comments heartened me. I was pleased with what I saw in the mirror, but it was always nice to have that confirmed, particularly by a man who I thought had a most discerning eye.

It seemed forever before our small entourage was finally in the carriage and on our way to Monique Kelston's. Some might have thought it odd that Monique and I had remained such close friends over the years, for it was scarcely a secret that she and Justin had once had a liaison. But that was before I had come to Camberleigh, and she had never given me any reason to doubt that she was my champion. In fact, it had been Monique who had first alerted me to the fact that I had fallen in love with Justin Barkham. I had at one time fancied myself as the bride of Monique's son, Robin, but though to this day I found him a charming and amusing companion, I would never have experienced the depths of expression with him that I had found with Justin.

"There is the house," I commented, pointing up ahead to the large brick facade that seemed to be fairly shimmering from the candlelight within.

The girls sat forward excitedly, seemingly overwhelmed by the line of carriages and smartly dressed men and women alighting from them.

"I knew this gown was all wrong," Constance moaned. "I should have worn the dark blue; it makes me look far older."

"You look absolutely exquisite," I replied, sensing that all she wanted was a reaffirmation. "You both do."

Sidney bade us to have a splendid evening as we made our way up the walk. The girls seemed particularly surprised but pleased that our circle of acquaintances seemed to be so broad. I feared that Daphne in particular thought our life in the country to be pleasing though provincial, and though we had hosted everyone, including the King and Queen, I do not believe she had any sense of her father's power and influence throughout all of England.

We had only entered the house and removed our wraps

when Monique pushed forward to us, exclaiming to the other people just arriving that the guests of honor had finally arrived.

I marvelled at Monique as she and Justin embraced. She seemed not to have aged at all since I had first met her. Her long black hair, which fell from a center part into a thick coil at the nape of her neck, was still unblemished by grey. The gold Chinese brocade gown accentuated her trim angular figure and picked up the flecks of light in her dark almond-shaped eyes.

"Serena, *ravissante comme toujours,*" she effused in her native tongue as we embraced.

"It was lovely of you to plan this for the girls," I replied. "They are beside themselves with excitement."

"*Charmant, absolument charmant,*" she enthused as I brought both girls forward. "There shall be many broken hearts before your season *est fini je pense. Maintenant,* you come with Monique, and I shall present you to some of London's most eligible young men."

"I suppose that leaves us to circulate on our own," Justin said as he closed my arm in his.

"I think that was Monique's subtle way of suggesting that we had best not hover over the girls," I whispered.

"Well, if she thinks I am going to stay out of earshot, she is mistaken," Justin replied, dogging Monique's passage into the drawing room.

I was amused by Justin suddenly assuming the role of the doting father. He, who had appeared to be uninterested in the girls' season, I sensed would be the one to participate most in it, if only to keep a watchful eye over Daphne.

We mingled amongst the throngs of elegantly dressed men and women whom Monique had gathered for the occasion, gratefully accepting their compliments on Daphne and Constance.

It was almost a half hour later when Monique, having settled the girls with four young men who seemed to be vying for their attentions, joined Justin and myself.

"Ah, to be young and beautiful again," she sighed, motioning over to Daphne and Constance.

"You are being overly modest," Justin assured.

Monique was about to reply when we were suddenly joined by a tall dark-haired gentleman whom I did not recognize from our circle of friends. I flushed as his gaze met mine, his dark-set eyes regarding me with unabashed intentness.

"You will pardon my interruption, but I wanted to bid my respects to my charming hostess," he offered in a deeply modulated voice that bore a heavy French accent.

I gathered that the two were old friends for their embrace hinted of a long familiarity.

"I am zo pleased you could come," Monique effused. "Allow me to present Lord and Lady Barkham, Count de la Brocher."

"Enchanté, madame," the Count greeted, his lips brushing my hand.

"Ze count ees your neighbor," Monique pursued. "He has purchased Viscount Penberthy's house just opposite Channing Hall."

"That explains the lights I saw the other night," I offered. "I had not known that the house was since occupied."

The count appeared puzzled momentarily, but I quickly realized that it was likely that he did not know that we had just arrived back in London.

"I am pleased that the house is being occupied again," I offered. "Though we have only been inside it several times in the last years, I always found it to be a handsome structure. The viscount had a rather exceptional collection of paintings, particularly those in the library."

"You have an obvious eye," the count replied with interest. "I was fortunate enough to have been able to purchase them will the estate, as he had no immediate heirs."

"And at a fair price as well," Monique offered. "But then the count has always been clever in the area of finances."

Before I could pursue his implied economic prowess, Daphne and Constance came bursting forward into our small gathering.

"Oh, Mama, it is all so thrilling, is it not," Daphne enthused, her violet eyes flashing with the excitement of the evening.

"You will pardon my daughter," I said quickly. "I fear that this is all very new to both our girls."

Constance threw me a look of unquestioned disdain at my reference to them as girls, since she had quickly taken note of the count and was regarding him with obvious fascination.

Monique placed her hand against the count's arm. *"Mon ami, puis-je presenter* Mademoiselle Constance—*et* Mademoiselle Daphne Barkham."*

Constance moved forward quickly, obviously thrilled when the count lowered his lips to her hand, keeping a respectable distance I noticed.

As he turned to Daphne, I was amazed to hear her utter, "Oh, the count and I have already met."

"That is quite impossible," Justin interrupted, seemingly as shocked as I by her outburst.

Daphne, pulling herself to her full height, exclaimed, "But we *did* meet, yesterday. In the garden. When Pluck ran off."

I remained silent, for I did not want to embarrass my daughter, who I realized must have disobeyed my heedings and roamed beyond the gates of Channing Hall.

The count appeared indeed perplexed as he honored the introduction of Daphne, saying, "You have me at a loss, mademoiselle, for though it seems extraordinarily impolite, I think that I should have remembered one of such incomparable beauty."

Daphne retracted her hand angrily. "You do not remember our meeting?" she demanded. "Why, you even chastised me for being on your property. It was scarce my fault, you know."

The count grew very silent.

Monique, who seemed to be uncomfortable from Daphne's remarks, interjected quickly, "Perhaps it is the champagne. Eet always goes to your head. I am certain he is only being temporarily forgetful."

Constance, whose face had drawn into a pout decidedly since she was not the center of attention, interjected, "Really, count, you must forgive my cousin. I am certain it is simply the excitement of the ball. She is not accustomed to our London society."

Before Daphne could respond, I suggested that the two girls retire to powder their noses, since I knew that dinner would shortly be served. Constance, I knew, would have preferred to remain, since she was obviously drawn to the count's dark good looks, but Justin echoed my suggestion and the girls excused themselves.

"You must forgive my daughter," I begged the count. "She is headstrong but not usually rude."

"Frankly, I find her quite charming," he mused, watching the girls as they moved out of the drawing room. "Though I cannot conceive why she thought that we had met before."

I wanted to pursue it a moment further, but dinner was announced, and Monique was anxious that we lead the way. I was disappointed to find that though Justin had been seated at Monique's right, my place was further down the table amidst several couples whose sons had been ogling Daphne and Constance earlier. The girls, who had been seated in and amongst several couples whose daughters were also commencing their season, looked uncommonly bored, wishing, I knew, that each could switch places with me.

I did not know whether I was getting old or whether the young men who chattered brightly about me seemed uncommonly young but though each made an effort to be pleasant, attempting to impress, I found them charming boys as opposed to charming men.

The dinner was delicious. Monique had a French cook who was artful in creating light sauces that complemented the fish and meat dishes.

Justin seemed to be enjoying himself thoroughly, his booming laughter carrying across the table at regular frequencies. Monique had always been able to amuse Justin. She had a quick wit and was not bashful about using language that men appreciated.

The count was seated beside Lady Amanda Ashburton, who although generally regarded as one of London's most fashionable hostesses, did not seem to be able to keep his undivided attention. I flushed as he caught my eye, embarrassed that he had found me staring at him. It was less than a half hour later when the strains of "The Dragoons," a popular waltz, were heard in the dining room and Monique encouraged the guests to take their dance cards into the ballroom.

I was pleased to see that Justin was to be my first partner and whispered the same to him as his arm slipped gently about my waist. We had barely commenced when Constance twirled by us, looking radiant in the arms of one of the young men I had spoken with during dinner.

"Is that not the count that our daughter is with?" I asked Justin as he continued to guide me about the marble floor.

"So it is," he replied, peering over my shoulder. "I cannot think why Monique would have paired the two."

"Well, she could not have known when she did that there would be some misunderstanding between them. But, after all, he is our neighbor."

6
daphne

As the guests commenced to excuse themselves from the table, I retrieved the folded dance card, which I had put aside during dinner, and opened it. As I did, Constance scurried to my side.

"Who is to be your partner for the first dance?"

I looked in horror at the name before me on the card. "How unfortunate can I be?" I murmured.

Constance took the card from my hand. "Count de la Brocher," she whispered, "Oh, Daphne, you *are* the lucky one. He is divinely handsome and so debonair. Why, it was all Lady Ashburton could do during dinner to keep her hands off him."

"Constance," I rebuked.

"Well, 'tis true," she replied, hardly looking mollified.

"Then she is scarce an arbiter of taste," I suggested. "Imagine that man denying that he had met me outside his house. He positively made me look the fool."

"You are being overly sensitive," Constance chided. "I cannot see why it is important. I wish it were I who had your card. Why do we not trade?"

"Cousin dear, you forget that the count has a card as well," I reminded her.

She shrugged. "Then we might as well proceed to the ballroom. But you need not look so dour or Serena will think you are ill and force us to leave, and I for one have no intention of allowing that to happen."

I followed her out of the dining room amongst the milling throng that was moving to the ballroom. I had no longer entered than I felt a hand at my elbow. I turned around to see the count smiling down at me.

"Miss Barkham, I do believe I have the pleasure," he said bowing slightly. "Whether 'twas planned or the luck of the draw, I must remember to thank my hostess for having paired me with the most beautiful woman in the room."

"I find your remark more than a bit effusive Count de la Brocher, given that a little while ago you did not even recall meeting me."

"I never pay a compliment to a woman without sincerity or intention, Miss Barkham, or might I call you Daphne?"

"Please yourself," I said, wishing that he would not ogle me so.

I was amazed at the strength of his arms as he guided me onto the dance floor, pulling me closer to him than I considered proper.

"Relax," he ordered, winking at me, "you shall find I won't bite."

"Neither will our dog unless provoked," I countered.

"Ah, we are back to that," he replied, a frown crossing his deeply set eyes. "And there are so many pleasant things we might discuss. When I purchased Viscount Penberthy's house, I had no idea I would find myself blessed with such pulchritude but a stone's throw away."

"We are only in London for the season," I replied quickly.

"More is the benefit, since I too shall be spending considerable time in the city this fall. I shall make certain that our paths cross frequently."

I misstepped suddenly and he caught me to him.

"I apologize," I murmured, feeling a flush creep to the base of my neck.

"*Cela ne fait rien,*" he replied. "Actually, I rather enjoyed it."

I could not believe the audacity of this man. He had not even made an attempt to apologize for his rudeness in refusing to recognize our encounter and yet his very regard now was suggestive, at the least.

"You see, when you relax a bit, you truly dance divinely,

Miss Barkham," he flattered, "but, then, I suspect that is not all you do well."

"I am not that accomplished," I replied quickly. "I loathe needlepoint and my pianoforte is less than inspired."

I was surprised to hear him laugh. "That is a good sign. I have never taken to women who amused themselves with needle and thread. 'Tis far too passive for my tastes."

"And what are your tastes?" I ventured, regretting the question as soon as I had asked it.

"I have a mare, at our château in France. She and I venture forth into the countryside. It is very beautiful, even now when the wood flowers are still in bloom."

"Your wife and children have remained in France then?" I pursued.

This time it was his turn to misstep. "My wife?" he gasped. "What caused you to think that I was married, much less a father?"

I flushed. "When you referred to the château, you used a plural noun . . . I only thought . . ."

He twirled me about the floor as he said, "*Au contraire.* I am unattached, which I hope is pleasing for you to hear. I only referred to my family's château."

When I did not reply, he continued, "Ah, perhaps it was my age that caused you to think that I should be keeping a wife, even children back in France. But, you know, Frenchmen do not marry as young as our English counterparts. We keep mistresses instead."

"I really think that is none of my concern," I blurted out.

The moment I reacted I regretted it, for I had not had the sense to see that he was goading me. He was clearly enjoying my faux pas, which infuriated me all the more.

"Do not tell me that I have shocked you, Daphne?" he mused. "You will pardon my saying so. I might have believed it of your cousin, but somehow I expect you are more, shall we say, experienced?"

I was unquestionably flustered.

"You English amaze me. You know, *les femmes françaises,* they can be shrewish, but they do not hide their passions. On the other hand you may be correct. It adds mystique. There is something fascinating, I suspect, in the unattainable. Or the thought of it."

I was at once incensed and embarrassed. That he clearly

thought me a woman of experience was an outrage but also frightened me. If he could but know, I thought, how protected I had been. I should have traded my card with Constance, for though I suspected that much of what she had related to me was more fiction than fact, she at least would have been clever in her responses. His remarks were far too provocative to dismiss and yet I could not risk creating a scene. I was angered with myself for my own vulnerability. There were smart responses, I was assured, but I seemed bereft of any, relying on my silence as my protector.

"You know, of course, that your eyes are the color of violets," he said as the music brought the waltz to a close.

I stiffened as his arm did not move from the small of my back. "The music has stopped," I said, cognizant of the breathiness of my voice.

"More is the pity," he replied. "But the next dance is open. We can continue this without reprimand."

"We can continue nothing," I advised, reminding myself to end the dance with the obligatory deep bow.

Again he laughed heartily. "My dear Miss Barkham, you could do far worse, you know. For example," he added, pointing to some squat perspiring young man directly opposite us.

"I will take my chances," I challenged, as I gathered my skirts in hand.

"Ah, you should always take chances, Miss Barkham, but 'tis always better to take educated chances. Nonetheless, this is only a beginning."

I spotted my family and began to move with determination across the floor as the count dogged my steps.

Just before I reached them, I whirled about. "*C'est dommage,* but you are very mistaken, Count. This is now at an end."

7
serena

JUSTIN SEEMED TO guide me purposefully over towards them as the dance came to a close. The count was smiling broadly as he delivered Daphne to her father's side.

"Your daughter dances divinely, Lord Barkham," he complimented, seemingly amused by Daphne's obvious discomfort. "Contrary to her insistence that she should prove a boring partner, I found her company to be most refreshing."

Justin laughed. "I have known my daughter to be many things, Count de la Brocher, but rarely so modest."

"Father," Daphne exclaimed, "that is hardly the truth and you know it."

"What is not the truth?" a voice intruded.

I twirled about to find Constance and her obviously besotted young dance partner behind her.

" 'Tis of no consequence," I said quickly.

"Well, then, since our dance cards indicate that this is an unassigned dance, perhaps I can inveigle the count to dance with me," Constance purred. "Do you polka?"

"I do and I shall be delighted," the count replied, quickly sensing my embarrassment that my cousin could have been so forward.

I did not think I had ever seen such disappointment as that reflected on the face of her initial dance partner as she tripped off on the count's arm, calling back gaily, "Do save a later dance for me, Harry dear."

"That man is insufferable," Daphne sputtered as she moved closer to me.

"Daphne, that is not like you," I chastised. "He seems quite charming, and he is our new neighbor. I do think you should at least try and be polite."

"Polite?" she gasped. "Why, first he ridicules me by insisting that we have never met before, and then as though nothing happened, he tells me I dance divinely. Well, Constance may find him fascinating, but I for one find him a deceitful boor."

Justin, who could not help but overhear her outburst, surprised me by saying, "Well, there is no reason to be involved with a Frenchman anyway. There are plenty of attractive Englishmen about. I agree with you, Daphne—he is best ignored."

"Darling, she is scarcely involved," I advised. "I cannot think why this man causes each of you to react so."

"I do not want you getting involved with that man, Daphne," he retorted almost angrily. "Do you hear me?"

Daphne, who had spent the last five minutes railing against the man, was as confused as I by his outburst. If she had hoped to turn to me for support, she was mistaken, for I was as befuddled by Justin's behavior as she was.

"Darling, I believe I need a spot of fresh air," Justin said suddenly. "Will you be all right on your own?"

"Of course," I replied, wondering if he was feeling poorly as he strode with deliberation across the room and out the double French doors at the end.

Aware suddenly that Constance's original dance partner was still in our midst shifting his weight awkwardly from foot to foot, I tried to discount my concern and quickly suggested that the two go and dance. I knew that Daphne resented being foisted suddenly into this young man's grasp, but I saw no solution but to put this little repartee aside and go off to find Justin in the garden.

I felt terribly conspicuous moving through the throngs to where Justin had exited, excusing myself politely as various gentlemen asked if I did not want to accompany them on the dance floor. I reached the back of the room and, seeing that the one set of French doors was open, slipped through them and out onto the stone terrace beyond.

"Justin," I called out in a low whisper. "Darling, are you out here?"

At the end of the terrace was a large stone balustrade that protected one from the gardens below. Though the steps to the lower area were broad, the pathways then narrowed into a series of mazes shaded by walnuts, plane and gingko straight ahead and topiary to the left and right.

I swore I heard voices from below. I strained to hear what they were saying, but I could only discern one man's voice, which I assumed was the count's, since though the words were not clear, they had an unmistakable French accent. I wanted to venture further into the garden but even with the reflection of the half-moon I did not trust my footing. I called Justin's name again, but seeing nothing and no longer hearing any voices, I made my way back into the ballroom. As I did, I ran almost full tilt into Monique, who drew me almost summarily inside, insisting that I would catch a chill if I stayed outside.

"Monique, wait," I insisted as she dragged me forward. "I am certain that Justin is out there. He has been acting most strangely this evening. I truly am quite concerned."

She threw her head back, laughing. "Ah, you are being silly, *mon amie*. Ees natural zat Justin would appear *un peu* strange. *Après tout* Daphne eeze his only daughter. You see how zat young viscount regards her. Eet is only *naturell* if Justin is jealous."

One look at the fair young man who propelled Daphne easily about the dance floor and I relaxed and gave Monique a quick embrace.

"You are right," I acknowledged. "But, then, you usually are, Monique. Some day you shall have to tell me how you became so wise."

"Only to you will I admit that eet eez experience," she whispered.

We chatted a moment longer, and I was surprised when I looked about the room to see that both Constance and Daphne had moved to other partners. The count, who seemed to have preoccupied the Barkham family earlier, had disappeared from the ballroom, and I wondered if he had decided to take his leave.

I was beginning to weary of making idle chatter with a group of women who were obviously ambitious for their sons, each trying to outdo the other for my benefit, when Justin reappeared as quickly as he had departed.

"You will pardon me, ladies," he pleaded in his most gallant fashion, "but I have hardly danced with my wife this evening."

"I hope I was not interrupting something," he murmured as we joined the other dancers.

"Scarcely," I replied. "I was thinking that you were never going to rescue me. I went out to find you earlier, but you must not have heard me call."

"You followed me outside?" he queried.

"Well, I was not following you, as you put it," I replied. "I simply was concerned. You may not have realized but you were gone for nearly half an hour. Was it you who was talking to the count?"

"The count?" he echoed.

"Count de la Brocher," I explained. "I hope you said nothing to embarrass him. I am certain his attentions to Daphne and Constance were only in the way of politeness."

"I encountered him quite by chance," he responded. "He was taking his leave. In truth I cannot recall what I said to him, but I can assure you that it was naught of import."

If I thought it odd that the count would depart by the back garden, I had not the chance to challenge it, for Daphne and Constance rejoined us as soon as the music ceased.

Constance, looking decidedly displeased, blurted out, "I cannot think why Daphne wishes to leave. The ball is not over and I understand there is to be a small supper later."

"I told you I am tired," Daphne insisted. "You stay if you wish, but I prefer to leave. Will you take me, Father?"

I was perplexed by Daphne's determination to leave, for she was generally gregarious by nature, but though I did not want to curtail Constance's evening, I sensed that we should return home. We were all still a bit weary from our journey to London, and there would be months of balls and dinners before us.

"You read my mind," Justin replied, obviously relieved by Daphne's request. "I shall collect your wraps and go and fetch Sidney to bring the carriage round."

I sought out Monique with the girls in tow to bid our good evening.

"You are not leaving zo soon," she exclaimed. "Ze young men zey shall be devastated."

"Well, it is not my idea. I am having a perfectly wonderful time," Constance exclaimed, fluttering her new fan boldly at one of the men she had danced with earlier.

"I think we are all just a bit weary," I interjected quickly. "But you could not have planned a more gala evening for the commencement of the girls' season."

I embraced her warmly, extracting a promise that she would come and dine with us in the near future.

I was troubled during one return to Channing Hall. Daphne was inordinately uncommunicative, and Justin again seemed preoccupied, almost remote. Save for Constance's animated chatter about the bevy of eligible young men who had been present, we were almost a dour group. It was not the ending I could have predicted for the girls' foray into society.

The only spark amongst us seemed to have arisen from Constance's sudden exclamation that by far the most attractive man on the premises was Count de la Brocher.

Daphne, who had been totally silent, suddenly burst out, "Well, there is no accounting for taste."

"That is my daughter," Justin suddenly chimed in. "I am relieved to see that you are entering this season of yours with some sensitivity."

"You think your precious Daphne can do no wrong," Constance interjected. "But I should be pleased to tell you that he spoke of her constantly while we danced."

As soon as she had uttered what I suspected she had meant as a retaliation, I knew that she had regretted it. Though the girls were compatible on the surface, there was an underlying jealousy evident on Constance's part that I had always prayed would not be laid bare, for it harbored emotions that I did not want to see surface.

Before I could comment, Daphne muttered, "Well, you are welcome to him if that is what you want, though I can not imagine why."

"You know I am not one to demand anything of you, Constance," Justin offered, "but I should stay far afield of that man if I were you. He is far too old, and besides, I am quite uncertain of his prospects."

I thought it an odd thing to say, since the count was likely closer in age to each of the girls than Justin and myself, not to consider that he had always been a proponent of the measure of the man and not his pocket.

It was almost midnight when we alighted from the carriage

and made our way into Channing Hall. The house was uncommonly quiet and I surmised that Charlotte must have stolen Pluck away to her room for the evening. The girls excused themselves quickly, for which I was relieved, for though tired, I looked forward to a languorous late evening with Justin. Hence I was particularly surprised when he pronounced that he was going to take a brandy in the library.

"Might I join you?" I asked, knowing that he oft liked to unwind a bit before settling down.

He shook his head. "I fear I shall be a boor this evening, Serena," he mused, pushing a lock back from my brow. "There are some things I must attend to, and I know full well that if I allow you to waylay me, I shall never tend to business."

I was disappointed but countered him not, for over the years I had come to know that he was not a man to be intruded upon when business matters surfaced.

"Will you join me shortly?" I queried.

"I might be late," he advised, his lips brushing my cheek.

I mounted the stairs admittedly dejected, but by the time I had settled into the soft down of our bed, I relished the slowly ebbing release of ache from my extremities. I fought to keep my eyes open as I felt sleep overtake me but, quickly realizing that I was indeed tired, drifted peacefully off to sleep.

Where I had accepted Justin's absence easily the night before, I awakened to find myself alone in the room, aware that he had left without even a perfunctory morning kiss.

I propped myself up in bed in response to a knock at the door.

It was Charlotte with Pluck in tow.

"I sorry to be disturbin' ye, Serena," she said as Pluck escaped her grasp and ran full tilt to where I lay, "but I could not contain the little one any longer."

"So, you missed me, did you?" I laughed as he leapt forward, bathing my cheeks with his tongue.

"Is Justin taking his breakfast downstairs?" I continued, pulling the long white robe about me.

"Lord Barkham left almost an hour ago," Charlotte replied.

"He left?" I exclaimed. "Did he say where he was going?"

Charlotte shook her head. "Not te me; maybe 'e said something te Sidney."

"I cannot think what has gotten into that husband of mine," I muttered as I selected a green plaid morning dress from the armoire.

"Ye not be 'avin' a row?" Charlotte queried.

"No," I emphasized as I struggled with the full petticoats. "It should sound odd, but I would almost prefer it if we *had* argued. At least then I might have some sense of what is troubling him."

"Oh, I think 'tis likely just the excitement o' seein' his little girl growin' up," Charlotte advised. "An' all this fussin' 'tis not a man's world. Lord Barkham 'es real comfortable sittin' a horse or workin' the lands. 'Twill take 'im a bit te rein in that energy."

"You sound like Monique," I retorted. "I wish I could dispel these doubts. Your logic makes me feel quite foolish."

Charlotte dressed my hair and I descended to the dining room, opting to take my own breakfast there. Mary informed me that the girls were still abed. Ordinarily I would have insisted that they rouse themselves, but a little indulgence after their first ball, I decided, was harmless.

The post had already arrived, and I occupied myself with opening the bevy of invitations that had been delivered. It was almost noon when I had responded to the last of them that I heard Justin's voice in the front hall. Pluck raced out to give him welcome.

"Well, how is the belle of the ball?" Justin greeted cheerily, striding over to me.

"A bit anxious," I admitted. "What took you out so early?"

He came and sat down next to me. "I am sorry if I worried you, Serena. You were sleeping so peacefully that I did not want to disturb you."

"Whatever it was, it must have been important," I pursued.

"Darling, I wish there was some better way of telling you this," he began slowly.

"There *is* something wrong then," I replied quickly. "I knew it. Monique and Charlotte said I was being foolish but I just couldn't dispel this feeling."

"What do Monique and Charlotte have to do with this?" he interrupted.

"Nothing. Just tell me what is wrong," I insisted.

"It is nothing as serious as all that," he assured me, placing his hand over mine. "But it does necessitate that I leave Channing Hall for a little while."

"Leave?" I exclaimed. "To go where? Why?"

"Something has come up with the railroad," he replied quietly. "I have to go up to Northallerton."

"When?" I queried.

"I fear I shall have to leave tomorrow."

"Tomorrow," I gasped. "Could it not be postponed for a spell?"

"Serena, you know I would not leave you and the girls if it was not a necessity," he argued.

"I know that," I answered quietly. "It is just it is so unexpected, and look at all these invitations," I continued, my hands leafing through the envelopes before me.

"Serena, simply because I have to be away is no reason for you to curtail any plans you have made," he insisted.

"How long will you be away?" I pursued.

"Two weeks if all goes well."

"What would you say if I suggested that I go with you?" I posed.

"That would be impossible," he replied quickly. "I shall be occupied day and night, not to mention that you could scarce leave the girls here unchaperoned."

"It is not as though Charlotte and Mary and Sidney are not in residence," I argued.

"Serena, I do not want to argue about this," Justin said emphatically. "Your place is here with the girls. It shan't be long before I return, and though I know you are disappointed, I do ask that you try to understand."

"I appear to have no choice," I replied resignedly.

"There, that is my girl," he cheered, leaning forward and giving me a quick kiss. "Now, if you will excuse me for a bit, I have some work to attend to before I leave."

I nodded and watched Justin as he strode out of the room. I knew that he wanted, perhaps even needed me to be understanding, but if I had commenced this day with doubts, they had only multiplied as it had progressed. Justin had always been a man who was committed to his work. Whether it was the overseeing of the Mayfair-Camberleigh estates or the railroad project, he had never been one to rest on the laurels of inherited wealth. I had always accepted that, indeed I took great pride in his accomplishments. But no matter how driven, how involved, Justin had always managed to make me feel that I and the children were the most important part of his life.

The part of the wifely shrew I had never played, and as devastated as I was about his impending departure, I knew that ultimately I would remain silent, bidding him well as he began his journey on the morrow. But that would not dismiss the uneasiness I felt.

I spent the large part of the afternoon with the girls. Daphne, who had been of a mood, I thought, these past few days, reacted to the news of her father's departure with the same disappointment as I. Constance was enraged but assuaged quickly when I explained that his absence would not affect the plans for their season.

Indeed, the second ball was to occur the following eve, leaving us little time to plan. The invitation was extended from the Baroness de Wycoff, whom I knew only slightly, but as she had two sons of marriageable age, it seemed likely that she was not overlooking that a suitable dowry would be an ideal combination to a suitable companion.

We dined together that evening. I admittedly had taken special care with my toilette, selecting a gown of grey silk taffeta with a satin ball fringe on the skirt and a beige lace collar bordering the slightly dropped neckline. Justin seemed more ebullient than he had in days, even weeks, but I could not suppress the sense that he was making a concerted effort to keep conversations light and pleasant.

When Justin suggested after dinner that he would take a brandy in the library and be up shortly, my spirits dropped, for I feared that once again he was avoiding any closeness between us. Happily I was mistaken, for I had only climbed into bed when he entered the room.

He strode forward and, kneeling down, covered my lips with his own.

"I have not been a very good husband of late, have I?" he murmured as he smoothed the hair back from my forehead.

"I hope you intend to change your ways this evening," I whispered, a smile playing about my lips.

Perhaps it was that my need for him was great. Perhaps that I anticipated our separation these next weeks. But I took him to me with a passion and abandon that surprised even myself. When after all the fears and needs and desires had been spent from our bodies and we lay entwined in a delicious exhaustion, only then did I begin to believe that my doubts and concerns were unfounded.

"I shall hate leaving you," he assured, pulling my body closer to his own.

"It would seem almost innocuous to add that I shall miss you, Justin."

"Serena, it simply is something I must do," he replied. "Would I be able to abandon this scheme, but I cannot; it is too important to so many people."

"What an odd thing to say," I mused.

"Why do you say that?" he countered.

"Well, I have never heard you refer to the railroads as a scheme—a project, a commitment, but never a scheme."

He chuckled. "A poor choice of words, I suspect. I forget that my beautiful wife was once a governess. Perhaps my own tutor was not as exacting as you, darling."

Justin yawned, his leg stretching against mine, and I decided that we should both succumb to sleep since it was indeed far too late to commence a debate on the use of the King's English.

It was early when I awoke, and though I felt well rested, Justin's packing had obviously intruded on my senses.

"You *do* seem in a hurry to get away from here," I chided, watching him pull his vestments from the armoire.

"I know at least a hundred men in London who, seeing you there, would say that I must be mad to leave," he replied, throwing a pair of trousers down and coming over to me.

"Perhaps you should consider that before undertaking this journey," I teased.

I was surprised to see a look of concern darken his face. "You do not mean that. Or do you?"

His anxiousness, feigned or not, pleased me, and I continued the repartee. "Well, one shall not know until you return I expect."

He took me suddenly in his arms, so fiercely that I cried out as my breath seemed to leave me.

"I love you, Serena."

"And I you, Justin," I assured.

That morning before Justin's departure was an odd one. Though loving and solicitous, I could not dispel the sense again that something was troubling him. At one point I had a feeling that he wanted to speak to me beyond our bantering pleasantries, but unfortunately that moment, though brief, was interrupted by Sidney's announcing that he had readied the carriage.

Charlotte, ever sensitive to my moods and knowing that if allowed I would be preoccupied with Justin's departure, commenced almost immediately to divert not only my own but also the girls' attention to the ball that evening.

And so it was at six o'clock that she not only had managed to have us dressed but also coiffed and admittedly anticipating the evening.

I did not think that I had ever seen either girl look more beautiful. Daphne's scarlet red gown I had thought would prove too startling with her coloring, which was so like my own, but instead it seemed to emphasize it and the effect was breathtaking. Constance by contrast was a confection in a frothy marriage of pink and white, which served to heighten her porcelainlike skin tones. My own gown was black silk, its only ornaments a dropped waist and off the shoulder neckline, which gave an elegant symmetry to the dress.

Sidney, having obviously been instructed by Justin, was particularly solicitous as we alighted from the carriage, assuring us that he would be close at hand should we need him.

The Baroness de Wycoff was not the kind of woman I generally warmed to. She was intensely preoccupied with the London social scene, a great favorite amongst Royals but only, I surmised, because she catered to the whims of nobility. Her husband, who had been notorious as a fancier of women, had died several years past, I suspected, of overindulgence of the senses. It had been years since I had seen her sons. Albert, the younger, struck me as a rather insipid sort, lacking any strong or distinguishing feature that I favored in a man. Charles, on the other hand, though I suspected conceited to a fault, was a specimen of masculinity. I was amused that his composure seemed ruffled in Daphne's presence and suspected that her blasé attitude was not one that he oft encountered.

So preoccupied had the girls and I been with the de Wycoff young men that I had scarce noticed that the baroness had moved off and returned with an all-too-familiar face in tow.

"Serena, dear, I should like to present Count de la Brocher," she effused. "He is your new neighbor, having recently purchased Viscount Penberthy's house."

"Ah, but we met the other evening at Monique Kelston's,"

I replied quickly. "You will remember my daughter, Daphne, and cousin, Constance."

"One could not forget two of such beauty," he replied, bowing to each.

I wished that Constance would have suppressed her flirtatiousness, for her fascination with the count was both obvious and indelicate. On the other hand, it balanced out Daphne's response, which was less than welcoming.

"And your husband," he continued, "has he not joined you this evening?"

I shook my head. "He was called away from London on business for a few weeks."

A dark frown crossed his brow.

"His absence appears to trouble you," I ventured.

His face relaxed. "Not at all," he assured. "I simply was thinking that I must invite you to dine with me. I should be less than neighborly if I did not extend the hospitality of my house, particularly while your husband is away."

"That is very kind of you," I replied, "but our schedules appear to be very full these next weeks."

"I am having a small gathering for dinner tomorrow evening," he pursued, ignoring my apology, "and I would be delighted if you and your cousin and your daughter could join us."

Seeing Daphne's look, I replied quickly, "That is very kind of you, but I fear we are otherwise occupied."

"Oh, Serena, we are not," Constance reproached. "I happen to know full well that we have nary a thing planned for tomorrow evening."

"Constance, really," I rebuked, feeling a deep flush on my neck. "You must forgive my cousin, Count de la Brocher. I fear her enthusiasm is a bit unbridled."

"There is no need to apologize, Lady Barkham," he replied quickly. "I find your cousin's frankness to be utterly charming."

I felt absolutely trapped. Constance had placed me in an untenable position, and I saw no way of declining without being rude. Besides I knew Constance when she got into these moods. She had a defiant streak and could easily turn a simple invitation into an unpleasant situation.

"You must forgive me, Count," I entreated. "I had thought that we were otherwise occupied, but I do believe my cousin is correct. And thus we shall be delighted to join you for dinner.''

I dared not look at Daphne, who I knew was seething. She had made her dislike of the count abundantly clear, and I knew that during the course of the evening she would express her anger at my acceptance of the invitation.

As it turned out, I did not have to wait very long, for as dinner was announced, Daphne took me aside and announced that she had no intention of accompanying us to the count's the following evening. The elder de Wycoff son proved my salvation, for he continued to dog Daphne's steps, and our discourse was fortunately halted.

For the most part I found the remainder of the evening to be exceedingly dull. There were many gentlemen who asked me to dance, but though I did not consider myself conceited, I was not so naive as not to realize that their conversations were far too familiar to be exchanged with a married woman.

Daphne and Constance certainly never needed to have feared that they would not measure up to their female counterparts, for each was never without a selection of partners. It troubled me that the one Constance seemed to favor was the count. I would have sworn from the other evening at Monique's that it had been Daphne who had piqued his interest, but as she had made her response embarrassingly clear, it was not surprising that he addressed his attentions elsewhere. I only wished it had been to one other than Constance.

The following day passed quickly. Once I had made it clear to Daphne that I was not about to cede her whims and that save being on her deathbed she would indeed go to dinner with us that evening, all was quiet at Channing Hall.

I had no call to anticipate it but I was hopeful that the count had included Monique in the evening's festivities. I did not know whether it was Pluck or Daphne who sported the more woebegone look as we gathered in the front hall. Sidney had insisted on accompanying us across the street, but Constance, who had been aflutter all day, ran ahead, reaching the door moments before us.

We were greeted at the door by a rather surly character, obviously of French descent, who took our wraps and ushered us into the drawing room. The count came forward immediately.

"The evening is now complete," he flattered us as he lowered his lips to my extended hand. "And the young ladies, *ravissantes* as always. Come let me introduce you to my other guests.''

His hand at Constance's elbow, he moved us into the room.

"The furnishings are exquisite," I overheard her say. "I do think the French have so much more style than we English. I have always preferred a more formal atmosphere."

"I do not believe she said that," Daphne whispered.

Actually, I had seen nothing untoward about her comment. The furnishings were indeed exquisite, mostly gold-leaf salon pieces with rich tapestry upholstery. With the viscount's paintings, which still graced the walls, the rich drapery hangings and an Aubusson carpet with some of the most exquisite colors I had ever seen, the setting was one of opulence.

There appeared to be only one female guest other than ourselves, a Madame Eugénie Truemont.

I was surprised to hear her say that she was acquainted with Justin, since our circle of friends were almost exclusively English.

Seeing my confusion she said quickly, "*Mais naturellement* only by reputation. The Barkham name is known even on the continent."

"You do not live here in London, then?" I ventured.

"*De temps en temps,*" she replied. "But it is France that is my home."

"You are from Paris?" I pursued.

"*Non, non,* far from there, in the Ariege, do you know it?"

I shook my head. "I fear my husband and myself have only visited in Paris."

She studied me speculatively. "I would have thought that your husband would have spent more time *dans la campagne.*"

"Why would you say that?" I queried.

"Oh, *je pense seulement . . .*" She broke off.

"No, please continue," I assured, allowing that she would not suspect that I was indeed fluent in French.

Before she could respond, dinner was announced and we were all ushered into the dining room.

Awkwardness was not a situation that visited me frequently but I had to admit that it was the feeling that overwhelmed me that evening.

That I knew none present save the count was not the matter. But I felt the conversation going around me instead of including me. The gentleman to my right, Etienne de Lefebre, was indeed charming, certainly attractive, but I was left with the impression that his queries were more in the form of inquisition than interest. But then the French as a nationality have always proved more curious than the English.

The count, who had seated Constance to his right, managed to continue in lively conversation throughout the evening. I was fascinated, for my cousin, though exquisite in her porcelainlike quality, was scarce a conversationalist. It amused me that Daphne, who had dreaded the evening, appeared obsessed by her cousin's entre nous with the count.

When after dinner Daphne and I had adjourned to the toilette, I could not help but be amused by her comment.

"Really, Mother," she suggested as she raised the comb higher in her hair. "Constance can only be deemed a trifle. Have you noticed how she is attentive to his every word? The man is clearly a scoundrel."

"I think the lady doth protest too much," I advised.

"I cannot believe that you of all people would say that," she countered.

Having added a bit of rouge to my lips, I turned to my daughter.

"Might I suggest that you sound a bit jealous?" I suggested.

"Jealous?" she decried. "I cannot believe that you would even suggest that, Mother."

"Well, the count seemed, shall we say, preoccupied with you at Monique's, but his attentions have altered, not surprisingly I might add, since you were not exactly receptive to him at Monique's."

"I believe Father was right," she finalized.

"Meaning?"

"One should focus on our countrymen," she replied. "I have come to believe those Frenchmen have no discretion—no morals."

We returned to the drawing room, myself intent on making excuses for an early departure to the count. I thought that Constance was looking a bit flushed but sensed that she was simply flattered by the count's attentiveness.

"Will you take some brandy with us, Lady Barkham?" the count offered as we entered the room.

I shook my head. "Actually, I was just thinking that we should be going."

"Certainly not so soon," he entreated. "I have just been getting to know your charming cousin better. She has been telling us of your home in the country. It sounds even more beautiful than I had imagined."

"It is very lovely," I replied, quietly wondering whether he would be so entranced with Constance if he knew that any dowry she might have would be that provided by Justin and myself.

"The count, he is being modest about his own property," Madame Truemont interjected. "Hischâteau *c'est magnifique avec beaucoup d' hectares.*"

"It is near Paris?" I pursued.

"Quite distant from there," he replied. "Do you know La Basticle or St. Girons?"

I shook my head.

"It is *dans le sud, près d'Espagne.* We know it in France as the Ariege."

I knew my face showed surprise.

"You seem puzzled," he pursued.

"No," I said quickly, "it is just unusual that all of you seem to be from the same area. We are accustomed to your countrymen here in England, but my experience, I expect, has been limited to Parisians."

"Well, as you are not limited to London, we are not limited to Paris," he retorted.

I was about to reply when suddenly I heard music playing and looked about to see Daphne holding up a small music box.

"How charming," she exclaimed, her fingers outlining the Sevres porcelain bird atop the case that rotated as the tune played.

I was about to rise to examine it more closely when the count lunged in front of me and snatched the box from Daphne's hands, shouting, "That, Miss Barkham, is not to be trifled with."

Daphne was so shocked that her hands hung in midair as the count removed the box to the far side of the room.

I did not know whether to be furious at the way he had lunged at Daphne or embarrassed that she had unwittingly disturbed what was obviously a prized possession.

"You must forgive my daughter," I said quickly, hoping to mollify the situation. "Daphne has always had a passion for music boxes since she was a child. I am certain that she meant no harm."

He rejoined the group, and although his face looked very agitated, he said quickly, "You must forgive me, Miss Barkham. I am certain that you meant no harm. It is only that that particular piece has a sentimental value, and I fear I am overly protective of it."

Daphne, I knew, was seething, and before she could reply, I rose quickly, saying, "It truly is late and we must be going."

"Now I shall feel that it is my bad manners that have driven you off," he replied.

"Nonsense," I retorted. "You were very kind to invite us here this evening, but I should not care to test your hospitality further."

"I will have my man see you home," he offered.

"That will not be necessary," I said, thinking that I would almost be more comfortable on our own.

He, however, insisted and we bade our good eves and were escorted back to Channing Hall.

The door had only closed when Daphne exclaimed, "I have never been so insulted in my life. How dare that man . . ." She broke off.

"Oh, do not be such a child," Constance countered. "He apologized, though I scarce think it was necessary."

"You would not be so charitable if it had been you that he had affronted," Daphne retorted, "or perhaps you would, since you spent the entire evening batting your eyes at that, that boor."

"That is enough—from both of you," I demanded. "To bed," I said, pointing up the stairs.

"I will not be treated like a child," Constance retorted, flinging her wrap on the hall chair.

"Then stop acting like one," I retorted.

"Are you coming to bed, Mother?" Daphne asked.

"Shortly," I replied. "I just want to check the fireplace in the drawing room. The house feels a bit cool."

The girls went on upstairs, and I moved to the drawing room, where seeing that the fire was indeed low, I added a few logs from the freshly stocked bin.

The fire rekindled quickly, and I was just about to replace the firescreen when I heard a sound seeming to emanate from the front hall. Thinking that one of the girls had forgotten something, I went to investigate. I looked about but no one was there, in fact the house seemed particularly quiet. I crossed over to the library, thinking that perhaps the noise I had heard had been Sidney or one of the maids who had forgotten to extinguish the candles.

The room was dark, save the embers glowing in the fireplace. I moved forward with the sense that I was looking for something but I knew not what. My eyes suddenly came to rest on a Staffordshire figurine on the floor beside the fireplace. I picked it up, puzzling as to what it was doing there. The light was poor, but turning it over in my hand, it seemed not to have broken and I realized that the carpet must have cushioned the fall. I replaced it to the left center of the mantle where it always rested, puzzling as to how that particular piece had fallen. Satisfied that nothing else was out of place, I gathered my skirts and wound my way back into the front hall and up to our bedroom.

Pluck, who was curled up on the bed, eyed me sleepily, his tail beating a welcome. It had only been two days since Justin had departed, but I already felt it was an eternity. He would disapprove, I suspected, of my accepting the count's invitation for this evening, having not found him a likely suitor for Daphne. Little would he know that it appeared that it was Constance who had, in fact, caught his fancy. It did not trouble me too greatly, for I thought it unlikely that he would be included in many of our upcoming engagements and by Justin's return Constance's coquettishness would have toyed with many other gentlemen of eligibility.

8

daphne

"DAPHNE, ARE YOU awake?"

I sat up in bed and pulled the covers about me.

"Well, if I was not, then you have remedied that," I replied as Constance crept forward, the candle she held lighting her way.

"Oh, do not be so tiresome," she whispered as she sat on the edge of the bed.

"What is it that you want?"

"What I want is for you to stop being so negative about Count de la Brocher," she replied.

"First off, I have the right to express anything I want to about Count de la Brocher or anyone else," I retorted. "Secondly, it would do you well to follow my lead. That man is a cad—he's insufferably rude, quite taken with himself, though for what reason I cannot imagine, and as evidenced tonight, he appears to have an ugly temper."

"I do believe you are jealous," she retorted.

"This is a silly conversation," I concluded. "Go back to bed."

"Do you not want to know a secret?" Constance queried.

I did not reply.

"Well, I shall tell you, but I will have your tongue if you repeat any of this to Serena."

My curiosity piqued, I replied, "You might as well tell me, since you are bent on it."

"Do you remember after dinner when you and Serena went to do your toilette?"

I nodded.

"Well, I excused myself to do same, though I never did," she replied.

"And . . ." I pursued.

"The reason I did not was that the count followed me into the hallway and right there at the back of the staircase he kissed me," she replied.

I pulled myself back up in bed facing her. "He did what?" I exclaimed.

"You heard me, silly," she whispered. "He kissed me."

"Well, I hope you slapped him—and hard."

"Oh, I knew you would say something like that," she moaned.

"What else would you have me say, Constance?" I argued. "That man insulted you, and it was incumbent upon you to set him straight."

She giggled. "You truly are such a prude, Daphne. If you continue your high and mighty attitude, it will not matter how many seasons you have, for you shall wind up an old maid."

"Well, if I do, at least I will know that I have not been trifled with by some count of no account."

"The trouble with you, Daphne, is that you have no passion, no sense of romance," she countered. "I want some excitement, some adventure in my life, and the count can offer me that. You heard Madame Truemont refer to his château . . . and he is *so* handsome, so debonair."

"You are a fool, Constance," I reproached. "One stolen kiss means nothing. I suspect you are not the first nor shall you be the last."

"Promise me that you will not say anything to Serena," she beseeched.

"For your own good I should tell her straightaway," I retorted, "but it will not be I who tells my mother of your indiscretion, though I think it is my father's wrath that you should fear most."

She sighed in relief. "It would be awfully decent of you if you would not go into a snit every time the count's name is mentioned. For some reason your mother thinks you have good sense. If she thinks that you like him, she might take more kindly to his courting me."

"You would do well to get this nonsense out of your head," I advised.

"You needn't extoll his virtues," she insisted. "Just try and be civil about him."

"Since I do not expect to be seeing Count de la Brocher, that should not be too difficult," I wagered.

She leaned forward and embraced me. "You can be quite decent when you try."

I shrugged. "Now go back to your room and let me get some sleep," I insisted.

Constance scurried off and I lay abed thinking upon what she had said. Was I really passionless, a prude as she suggested? I had not had the heart to tell her that the count had flattered me unabashedly at Monique's and that if I had not sensed him as a scoundrel, it would likely have been myself from whom he had stolen a kiss. He was not a man, I sensed, who would take rejection gracefully, and a small part of me wondered whether his attempted conquest of Constance was his way of spiting me.

Well, if that had been his intent, he would be sorely disappointed, for I cared not, excepting that I did not want to see Constance hurt. We were not that close, but she was my cousin, and we now were her only family.

9
serena

THE NEXT TWO days were blissfully quiet. Constance was piqued that nothing fashionable had been planned and sat most of the time gazing across the street until I suggested that she would be most embarrassed if the count knew that she was spying on him. I was surprised that Daphne, who had been so vociferous in her opinions of the man, had not seconded my heedings, but then, in truth, I was appreciative of the tranquility of those days.

It was on the third that a footman arrived with a note from Monique inviting us all for tea. It was a dreary day and I asked Charlotte to fetch the girls and tell them to dress appropriately. I went to my room to select a bonnet and was pleased to see Daphne waiting for me when I descended to the front hall.

"I hope Constance does not fuss too much or we shall be late," I commented, pulling on my gloves.

Daphne looked surprised. "Mother, Constance will not be going with us."

"For heaven's sake, why not?" I retorted. "I always thought she liked Monique."

"I thought you knew; Constance went out a little earlier," Daphne replied, her eyes lowered.

"She went out," I exclaimed. "Where? With whom?"

"I do not know," Daphne replied. "Only that a carriage called for her shortly after luncheon."

"I thought Constance had finally come to know the rules of this house," I fumed. "I have a right mind when she returns to instruct Sidney to take her back to be with your brother at Camberleigh."

"Do you not think that is a bit harsh, Mother?" Daphne challenged. "Constance does not exactly get along with Uncle Richard."

That was true I knew, but the reasons for same were unknown to Daphne.

"Well, we can not leave the house now," I observed. "Now when she is out galavanting who knows where."

"I am certain she will return safe and sound," she reassured me. "I think we should go on to Monique's."

"Not that I would allow it, but I would feel much better if it was you that was out there."

"Am I so dull that you do not think me capable of seeking some adventure?" Daphne questioned.

I stood back and looked at her, shocked at the serious expression on her face.

"Darling, how could anyone suggest that you would be dull," I exclaimed. "You have only to turn around and look in the mirror."

"I am not referring to my appearance," she retorted.

"Independent, spirited, yes, my dear Daphne, but hardly dull," I laughed.

Seemingly satisfied with my response, she pressed for us to go to Monique's so strenuously that I finally gave in, though my combination of fury and concern over Constance did not abate.

The large Dutch marquetry case clock had just struck four when we settled into Monique's library to take some tea. Her response to Constance's absence was to remind me that she was likely to take after her mother, who certainly had been flighty in her day, and then to reproach me for worrying too much.

"Monique, would you mind if I took a tour of your house?" Daphne asked suddenly. "I have never seen other than the public rooms."

"*Mais naturellement, chérie,*" Monique agreed. "You can show yourself about?"

Daphne left and Monique turned to me with a wink. "She eez a great beauty that one, like her mama."

"I can scarcely remember being that young," I sighed.

"*Je pense* that my friend Count de la Brocher was quite taken with her."

"It is odd that you mention him," I replied, rising and moving towards something that had caught my eye on the far side of the room. My hand reached out and grasped the porcelain bird that sat atop a box that was almost a twin of the one the count had snatched from Daphne's hands.

"Where did you get this?" I queried, opening it and instantly recognizing that it played the same strange little melody as the one at the count's.

"I scarce remember," Monique replied quickly. "In truth I had rather forgotten it was there."

"It is a most unusual piece," I said.

"Scarcely of great value," she replied. "Now, come back and sit with me. I have been longing for someone to talk to."

I replaced the music box and, crossing back to Monique, said, "I am sorry I seem so entranced with it. It is simply that it *is* unusual, and I saw its duplicate at the count's the other evening."

"At the count's? You do not refer to Count de la Brocher, Serena?" she countered.

I laughed. "I must admit he is the only count of my acquaintance. I should explain that he invited us, the girls and myself to dinner the other evening."

"*Mais ce n'est pas possible,*" she argued.

I was puzzled. "Well, I assure you we were there. Actually, that was my fascination with your small music box—the count had one identical to it. It would ordinarily not be something I would remember except that Daphne admired it and he literally wrested it from her hands."

"*C'est* strange," Monique murmured. "I could have sworn zat he told me he was returning to France for a spell."

Before I could retort, she added, "Obviously I am mistaken. Might I ask who else was at theeze soirée?"

I paused for a moment. "A Madame Truemont. A quite attractive gentleman, Etienne de Lefebre." I rambled off several other names and then added, "Oh, and a very quiet, older man, Antoine DeMarcier."

"DeMarcier?" she gasped.

"You obviously know him," I replied.

"Not really," she replied somewhat absentmindedly. "My

late husband had dealings with him at one time.''

"Frankly, I was surprised not to see you at the dinner," I replied.

She studied me for a moment. "Allowing that DeMarcier was present, I should have been, how you say, out of place."

"Why would you say that?"

"He is not a friend of the Ariege. His is a seigneurial family —*un ami de l'état et de Marot un avocat* from St. Girons. And meanwhile the peasants starve, they have no wood for fuel . . . *mais* this is of no interest to you."

I had not seen Monique become so vehement about something for many years.

"It is not that it is not of interest," I assured, "but you know Justin and me. We are so entrenched with what is happening right here in England that I fear we have become naive to the strifes of other countries."

Monique poured another cup of tea for us both.

"Well, eet has been years since I have lived in France, but eet eez my country *après tout*. And there are many injustices— the common people, zey are so heavily taxed, zey have no liberty no matter what Charles X and his minister Polignac proclaim."

I smoothed the ruffled inset of my gown. "I must say it surprises me that you and the count are friendly," I mused. "Although I do not begin to fully understand this conflict in the Ariege, you are clearly of opposite minds politically and socially."

Monique rose suddenly and moved about the room, obviously agitated, spewing French phrases that I knew would only be said by one out of extreme anger or frustration. Suddenly she whirled about and studied me so long and hard that I became anxious that I had said or done something to offend her.

And as quickly as she seemed to have been carried away by her temper, she threw up her arms, exclaiming, "You must forgive me, Serena, *c'est ridicule* this conversation. Let us talk of other things."

She returned to the couch and, picking up her teacup, addressed me, "Now, tell me about Constance."

I was puzzled by her sudden shift of mood and conversation, but I was glad to have an opportunity to discuss Constance with her.

"I think what is most difficult," I began, "is that I cannot help but compare Constance to Daphne. Not, mind you, that I do not think I shall have my hands full with my own daughter, for she has a strong, independent nature . . ."

"*Comme maman*," Monique interjected.

I smiled. "Perhaps. But Constance is such a flighty creature. There are times that I wonder if there is any sense in that head of hers, but then I wondered the same thing about Clarissa."

Monique looked at me thoughtfully. "Do you think eet eez the flightiness you refer to or do you think eet eez *peut-être* something more?"

"What do you mean?"

Monique leaned closer to me. "Serena, you cannot overlook Constance's past. Her grandmother—*complètement folle* —you above all people suffered at her hands. Zees things, we do not know why they happen, but they do. Constance eez of Maura's blood. If indeed zees waywardness of the mind eez carried in families eet could manifest itself in Constance as well."

"That is not fair, Monique," I retorted angrily. "Yes, Maura was mad, but Clarissa, her daughter, though insensitive and conniving, was as sane as you or I. There is no reason to believe that Constance should carry the ill seeds that destroyed Maura's mind within her."

"I disagree, *chérie*," Monique entreated. "Eet eeze as possible as eet eez impossible."

"I will not have Constance live under the veil of the past," I insisted. "She knows none of this, and I shall be passionate about protecting her from it."

Monique shook her head. "Serena, I . . ."

She broke off as I leaned forward and clasped my hand about her wrist.

"What, may I ask, are you two being so conspiratorial about?"

Monique, realizing that I had silenced her because Daphne had suddenly returned, withdrew her arm and laughingly motioned Daphne to come sit beside her.

"Ah, *votre maman*, she was simply telling me of how you are turning all the young men's heads at these soirees," Monique replied, "*mais* zat eez hardly a surprise."

Monique tried to pursue the subject of the upcoming balls,

but Daphne preferred to admire the house, I think for fear that she might get on the subject of the count.

It was almost six when the driver returned us to Channing Hall. I had made a concerted effort not to muddle over where Constance had gone earlier, trying to reassure myself that she would not have done anything untoward.

We had no more than set foot in the front hallway when Charlotte, Pluck at her heels, came scurrying to greet us.

"Saints be praised ye've returned," she exclaimed.

My heart sank. "What is it, Charlotte? Is it Constance?" I begged.

"Miss Constance?" she replied confusedly. "No, no, she be up in 'er room. No 'tis the Hall—there has been an intruder."

"An intruder?" I gasped.

She nodded. "I was up seein' te one o' the new maids with Mary, an' when I came down te fetch somethin' I be noticin' that the door te the library was ajar. Well, in I went, an', Serena, ye would not believe what I found."

"Go on," I encouraged.

"It looked like a storm had hit us," she replied, wringing her hands, "books, ledgers everywhere. Ye could barely get into the room fer the shambles."

I did not bother to remove my wrap but moved quickly over to the library. As I did, Charlotte called out, "I do not know if I did right, but I had the staff put it to rights."

I stepped through the door somewhat gingerly and moved slowly about the room, my eyes focusing on the familiar objects, which at first glance seemed to be in place. Daphne and Charlotte had followed me in, and we were joined only moments later by Sidney. They watched as I continued to appraise what damage there might be.

"At first I thought it was one o' the staff, maybe one o' the new girls," Charlotte offered, "but there was no reason te suspect that. I be thinkin' I just did not want te believe that someone 'ad gotten in 'ere."

"The odd thing about it, Lady Barkham," Sidney added, "is that when Charlotte fetched me, straight away I was puzzled."

"Why is that, Sidney?"

"From the time ye an' Miss Daphne left, I was out front seeing over the gas lighters, puttin' in the new carriage lights. Te come through the door they woulda had te pass me."

"What of the tradesmen?" I asked.

"Never out o' my sight," he replied.

"And the other doors and windows?"

"Mary checked them all," Charlotte replied. "Fer the life o' me I can't be thinkin' how they got in."

"You think it was more than one person?"

"If ye'd be seein' the mess 'ere," Sidney replied, shaking his head.

"Will ye be wantin' me te fetch the constable, Lady Barkham?"

"Considering that nothing seems to have been taken," I mused, my voice trailing off.

"Surely you are going to notify the authorities," Daphne, who had obviously been frightened by the situation, exclaimed.

"I do not feel any more comfortable than you," I conceded, "at the thought of strangers prowling about the house, but I suspect that it was likely some street urchins who slipped in through the back entrance. The lock on that door has never really been sound. I really think it the only explanation."

If Sidney was uncomfortable with my decision, he said nothing but agreed to have a locksmith fetched the next morning to resecure the back entrance. I went off to find Constance, musing as I did whether the disturbance I had heard the other night could have been related in any manner. I had not mentioned it, simply by oversight, to any of the staff, and in retrospect I was relieved I had not, for it would only have served to heighten an uneasiness present in the house.

Constance was primping at her dressing table when I reached her room. I studied her reflection in the mirror, searching for some sense of how to approach her.

"I suppose I am now to be interrogated or chastised or both," she exclaimed before I could address her.

"Perhaps you should tell me which," I replied, quickly closing the door behind me.

"What did Daphne tell you?" she demanded, her eyes narrowed.

So Daphne did indeed know something, I mused. "Daphne? She only said that you had taken a carriage."

There was no question that she appeared relieved. "And is that something to breed your scorn?" she challenged.

"You know I do not approve of either you or Daphne going

about unescorted,'' I replied. "Since I do not allow it at Mayfair, there is even more reason for me to hold fast to that here in London."

"What you forget, Serena," she replied testily, "is that until you ferreted me away to the country two years ago, London was my home. I have friends here. My mother, until she became so ill, was a great favorite of many of the shopkeepers. I do not see why I must be a prisoner here."

Selecting my words carefully I responded, "It is odd because I do not think that Daphne feels a prisoner here, and you are certainly afforded no less privileges than she."

"Daphne is different than I," she pouted. "She is happy to play the piano and read and speculate about these dreary young men with damp palms we have been meeting, one of whom she will likely marry. Well, I find that too boring for words."

"I would not be so quick to judge your cousin," I posed. "She may be less experienced, but I would not underestimate her. I suspect that Daphne will marry as I did—for love and with her father as an example, I would be amazed if she married a fop."

She shrugged. " 'Tis of no import."

"It may surprise you, but I am not going to press you to tell me where you were today," I offered. "That is if you will promise me that there shall not be a repeat performance."

Constance eyed me suspiciously but agreed quickly.

I began to take my leave. "By the way, you did not see or hear anything that might shed light on the intrusion we have had in the library?"

She shook her head. "I already told Sidney that I heard nothing."

Five days passed with little of event, except that Constance was abed with a bad cold, causing me to cancel two dinner parties. I had offered to attend but, whether out of loyalty to Constance or simply a lack of interest, Daphne bade me to send our regrets.

Happily there were no further disturbances, which further convinced me that it had indeed been street urchins, who likely not realizing the value of the paintings or porcelains in the library, had abandoned their search with little reward.

10
daphne

"HOW ARE YOU feeling?" I asked, entering Constance's room.

"Daphne, I think I shall rot if I lie here one more day."

"Dubious," I replied, seating myself on the small boudoir chair beside her bed.

"You simply *must* convince Serena that I am fully recovered," she pleaded. "There is a ball at the Foxcrofts's two nights hence, and it is crucial that I attend."

"You know my mother will not succumb to any pressure from me," I counselled. "Besides, what is so important about the Foxcrofts's ball?"

She did not respond.

"Well?" I pursued.

"Oh, I might as well tell you since you know part of it anyway," she conceded. "I happen to know firsthand that Count de la Brocher has been invited."

"Not that again," I sighed.

"Do you not want to know how I know that he has been invited?"

"How?" I pursued.

"He told me the other afternoon," she replied smugly.

"You do not mean to tell me that you met that man?" I gasped.

"Keep your voice down," she demanded.

"So that is where you went when you took the carriage," I concluded.

"I do so wish I could have told you, Daphne, but I could not chance that you would tell Serena, even if unintentionally."

I threw up my hands in despair. "You are even more a fool than I thought," I chided. "Running off to have a tryst with this, this womanizer."

She giggled. "You are so dramatic at times, cousin. It was scarcely a tryst, as you call it. He asked me to meet him in the park. We strolled along the river, it was ever so innocent."

Somehow I did not believe her, but I did not want to hear any indelicacy that she might reveal.

"Oh, do not be angry with me," Constance pleaded, twisting a long blond tendril that fell over her shoulder.

"You had best pray that my father never discovers what you are about," I counselled. "I cannot imagine what he would do."

She looked troubled. "When Justin returns, I expect that Count de la Brocher shall ask him if he might court me."

"If indeed that is true, I should not expect my father to look too favorably on it," I replied. "Besides the count's being a Frenchman, I am certain that my father will find that he is far too old for you."

She laughed. "Justin would be hard pressed to argue either point."

"Why would you say that?" I asked, trying to read a rather bemused look that crossed her face.

"Simply because there is the same separation in age between your father and mother and the count and myself, give or take a few years."

"That still does not address the fact that he is French," I pursued.

"That never bothered him with Monique," she accused.

"What does Monique have to do with it?"

Her eyes widened. "Surely you are not going to tell me that you do not know about your father and Monique?"

"What about my father and Monique?"

" 'Tis common knowledge that they have been, shall we say, intimate," she offered.

"That is a lie," I charged angrily.

"Daphne, dear, you are not so naive as to believe that your precious mother is the only woman that Justin Barkham ever slept with."

I was shocked to the point of being speechless. I suppose that I knew that he was not the kind of man to have been celibate before he married my mother, but I had never suspected that there had ever been any alliance between my father and Monique Kelston.

"Oh, do not look so shocked," Constance whined. "You truly are so naive. I mean, she is older, but you have to admit that she is an attractive woman. And not without admirers."

I felt suddenly as if I was going to be ill or likely that I would not be able to stem the tears I felt welling in my eyes. I gathered my skirts and, rising quickly, excused myself. Constance called out to me to stay, but I did not want to give her the satisfaction of knowing that she had upset me deeply. Whether she had done so maliciously or not, I did not know. That was not what mattered. The inference about my father's association with Monique, who had always been like an aunt to me, did.

I withdrew to my room and threw myself down on the bed. At first I thought that Constance had pulled something out of the air just to prove her oft-repeated point that I was a prude. She would know that I would not chance going to my mother. If it were true, I could never suffer her embarrassment. The more I thought about it the more I concluded that she must have spoken the truth. Constance was capable of being capricious, but she was not imaginative enough to have concocted this story. If Constance knew, then I concluded that Mother must have some inkling as well. If my father's involvement with Monique had been before his marriage to my mother, then I supposed I could scarce condemn him. Contrary to Constance's belief, I was not so sheltered as to believe that men, like women, came to the marital bed as virgins. But I could not dismiss the question that lingered in my mind. Did his involvement end when he married Mother? Or was there still some relationship beyond the bounds of friendship between them?

It was two hours later when I realized that I was torturing myself over something that might have little or no credence. My father worshipped my mother. Sometimes it embarrassed me seeing them fawn over each other, but I always had felt so secure in their love.

My time was better spent, I decided, trying to figure out how I could protect Constance from her obsession with Count de la Brocher. Something told me that that man, if he chose, could hurt deeply. And Constance I did not want to become another of what I suspected were numerous cast-off conquests.

11

serena

I WAS IN the library finishing a letter to Anne and Richard when I heard Justin's voice in the front hall. I jumped up, almost tumbling over Pluck, who was curled at my feet.

The doors flung open suddenly, and before I could steady myself, he had taken me in his arms.

"God, how I have missed you," he whispered as he covered my face with his kisses, holding me fast to him.

"No more than I, you," I replied. "I had not hoped, I thought at the earliest, 'twould be the morrow before you returned."

"I admit I pushed the team harder than the driver would have liked, but now that I am here with you I have no regrets."

He had stepped back from me, and it was only then that I noticed that his left hand was heavily bandaged.

"My God, you are hurt," I gasped.

He tweaked my nose with his good hand. "Nothing serious," he assured. "Simply some equipment that fell. The doctor said I should be right in no time."

"Are you certain?" I persisted, knowing that he was a man who would slough off anything that might trouble me.

"Absolutely," he assured, pulling me to him again. "And you will be happy to know that it in no way will impede our lovemaking."

"Justin," I exclaimed, putting my fingers to his lips, "someone might overhear."

He laughed, giving a swift pat to my derriere. "And what if they do, my love? Do you think that anyone would be abashed by one so besotted by his own wife?"

Had Pluck not wriggled his warm brown and white body between us, I think that Justin would have carried me forthwith up to the bedroom. And if the truth be known I would not have objected.

"I would be hard pressed to explain that our dog is jealous of my intentions towards his mistress," he muttered as he leant down to ruffle Pluck, who by now had rolled to his back, putting himself in full display.

I grabbed Justin's good hand and pulled him to the couch in front of the fireplace.

"Tell me everything," I entreated.

"You first," he replied.

"I fear I shall prove dull by contrast," I admonished. "Let me see, there was a ball at the de Wycoffs."

"At which you were devoured, I suspect, by men of my acquaintance who would deny it emphatically."

I smiled.

"And the girls? Did they match your popularity?" he pursued.

"Let us say it is quite clear that they shall not be devoid of suitors," I replied.

"And then we had dinner with Count de la Brocher," I pursued. "A strange evening admittedly, but I did not want to appear unneighborly."

Justin sat bolt upright. "You say you had dinner at Count de la Brocher's?" he demanded.

"Darling, I know that you are scarce enamored of the man, but I did not think that your reaction would be so, well, so impassioned," I replied.

"When was this?" he demanded.

I thought for a moment. "One, perhaps two nights after you left."

I jumped as he slammed his fist onto the table before us.

"That swine," he murmured under his breath.

I did not know how to respond. It was uncommon for Justin to utter such disparaging remarks in my presence.

"I must apologize," he said quickly, rubbing his forehead.

I did not respond.

"You should not have gone there, Serena," he said decidedly.

"If I had known that you would react so, I would not," I replied, piqued at his tone. "But when you take off as you did, I should remind you that all decisions are left to me. It would have been awkward for me to refuse." I did not add that I had also been coerced by Constance.

"I am loathe to ask what else has happened in my absence," he retorted.

"Well, I do not know why you should trouble yourself about our dinner with the count. Frankly, a far more disturbing incident was that the house was broken into about a week back."

His eyes narrowed. "Someone broke in here, to this house?"

I nodded. "We were at Monique's, for tea. When we returned, Charlotte and Sidney were in a tizzy. Somehow, someone got into the library. But by the time I returned, the maids had put everything to right."

"What was taken?" he asked, his eyes roving about the room.

I shrugged. "That was the odd thing—nothing seemed to be missing."

"I expect the constable was called," he replied.

"You may be angry with me, but, no, I did not notify the authorities. When there appeared nothing to have been taken, I suspected it was some street urchins who would have no idea of the value of some of the pieces. Either that or they were frightened off before they could collect their prize."

Justin said nothing for the longest time. While I had expected him to be annoyed with me, his attitude was one almost of relief.

We had no further chance to discuss the incident, as Daphne and Constance, alerted to Justin's return, had come down to greet him. We all spent the remainder of the day together. Constance appeared to be feeling rather spritely—indeed, fully recovered. If anyone seemed under the weather it was Daphne. She was unusually quiet and seemed ever watchful of Justin, studying him as though she were looking at him for the first time. I finally decided that I was being silly. She adored her father, and like myself, I was certain, had missed him dreadfully those past weeks.

One thing he had been right about. His wounded hand in no

way impeded our lovemaking. I knew that he had been ever in my thoughts when we had been apart, but Justin that night made me realize how my entire body had ached for him.

I was disappointed the next morning to find that Justin had already dressed and left, but I appreciated his letting me sleep, given the lateness of when, finally spent, we had drifted off in each other's arms.

I dressed quickly, telling Charlotte to save her talents with my hair for later in the day, as there was a large ball that evening. She helped me select the gown I would wear, and we finally settled on a cream silk with coffee-colored satin ribbons running the full length of the dress down to the three tiers of ruffles that fell from the knee to the hemline.

I left the bedroom, Pluck in tow, to find the girls, who were taking breakfast in the dining room.

"Where is your father?" I asked, noting his place had not been set.

"He had to go out," Daphne replied.

"Goodness, he only returns and he is off again," I commented.

"Well, you cannot shackle him, Serena," Constance advised.

"Not that it is any business of yours, Constance, but you should know that I not only cannot but would not shackle my husband," I replied tersely, placing the napkin on my lap.

"Mother, are you not going to open your gift?" Daphne asked as my eyes spotted the black velvet box before me.

I unfolded the small note and read, "A small reward for your patience. My love, Justin."

Inside the box lay a pin—a perfect circle of sapphires and diamonds set in yellow gold. I took it in my hand, murmuring how exquisite it was.

"Well, you can never accuse Justin of not having good taste," Constance purred. "Look what he brought for me," she continued, holding up a shawl of alençon lace.

"It is indeed lovely," I said, pleased that Justin had remembered the girls.

"But Daphne's gift is by far the most interesting," she continued. "Are you not going to show it to your mother?"

I watched as Daphne withdrew her gift from its box. At first I thought my eyes deceived me, for there was a near duplicate of the music box that had caused such a furor at the count's. and its twin, which I had discovered at Monique's.

"Coincidental, is it not?" Constance mused, watching my reaction. "Not only that, but open it, Daphne."

As she did, I was startled by the now familiar strains of the lifting though somehow haunting tune. I did not know why, but I felt troubled. Was it coincidence? It, of course, must be, I assured myself, but I could not quell my unrest. I supposed if the count had not reacted so dramatically, I might never have even recalled the piece. Music boxes were scarcely a phenomenon. It was simply that the design of this one was so distinctive, not something that one found regularly in the shops.

"It is akin to the one I opened at the count's," Daphne mused, watching me closely.

"You are right," I responded brightly, trying to conceal my own puzzlement. "Well, it is a lovely piece."

"Do you not think it odd . . ." Daphne pursued.

"Odd? No," I assured. "Though I would scarce tell your father of our little fracas at Count de la Brocher's. I do not want to take the edge off his gift."

Daphne, if not mollified, I knew, sensed that I was right. Her silence told me that she would only express her appreciation to her father.

"Well, if you have stopped this chitchat, I should like to talk about the ball tonight," Constance entreated.

"Have you decided what you are to wear?" I pursued, grateful at the change of subject.

"The midnight-blue," she announced decisively.

"And you, Daphne?"

She took a drink of coffee. "Oh, I do not know."

"Why do you not wear the pink faille," Constance offered.

I was amused, for the gown that Constance had decided upon was perhaps the most dramatic of her wardrobe, yet the pink faille that she encouraged Daphne to wear was, in my opinion, the least impressive of the dresses that she possessed.

"Have you forgotten that Oliver is arriving today?" I offered.

"Today?" Daphne replied. "I had not thought it was 'til two weeks next. Oh, it shall be wonderful to have him here. And he will have news of Alexander."

I nodded. " 'Tis a pity that Rebecca cannot join him, but if your father is right, she is again with child and never travels well in those times. And, of course, Anne will not leave Richard. It must be difficult for her; she always did love a gala."

Constance excused herself, as did Daphne, and I was left to finish my breakfast. I lingered over the post, wondering when Justin would return so that I might thank him for his extravagance.

There were several epistles that needed my attention, and so, ruffling Pluck's ears, I encouraged him to follow me to the library. I had opened the drawer to the French marquetry desk and was just withdrawing some sheaths of paper when I was distracted by a sudden low growl from Pluck.

I turned about and found him sniffing by the fireplace.

"What is it?" I asked as he again growled his obvious displeasure at something.

When he persisted, I rose to where he crouched low, seemingly transfixed at the grate within the ornately carved aperture.

"There is nothing there," I assured, passing my hand in front of the fire screen as he watched my movements intently.

My actions did not seem to mollify him, which puzzled me, for in the years that I had had him, I could only recall him growling once before, when he had taken a dislike to one of the stable hands, dislike which I later learned was justified.

"Come now," I encouraged, " 'tis likely nothing but a mouse, and he is by now decidedly more frightened than you."

Finally able to divert his attention I returned to my correspondence, wondering as the clock chimed eleven where Justin could have gone to. I was beginning to be a bit exasperated about his absence when Sidney entered the library and announced that Master Oliver had arrived.

We almost ran into each other full tilt as he swept into the library and, throwing his arms about me, spun me round and round.

"Oh, it *is* good to see you," I greeted as my feet touched the floor. "Come, let me look at you."

We moved over to the couch hand in hand. I never stopped marvelling at what a fine man Oliver had grown to be. The pale sickliness of his childhood was nowhere evidenced in his finely chiseled features and taut frame.

He brushed his flaxen hair back off his forehead, his pale blue eyes twinkling at me.

"If it is possible, you only grow more beautiful, Serena," he complimented.

"I fear I have grown pale by contrast to those two damsels

upstairs, but then you shall see that for yourself."

"How are they?" he asked.

"A great success," I replied, "though that should be of no surprise. In truth, Daphne has seemed a bit remote from it all, for which I am secretly thankful, for I do not know what I would do if they were both so unbridled, shall we say."

He smiled. "Cousin Constance has not been behaving, I presume."

"Oh, I do not think she means ill, but she has allowed herself to become entranced with a Frenchman, who lives just opposite. I am quite certain that Justin would not approve, and I am not certain that the count is as smitten as Constance might think. Anyway, all that aside, tell me about Alexander, how is Richard feeling? Is Anne well?"

Before he could reply, Sidney entered announcing that luncheon was served and that he had instructed the girls to meet us in the dining room.

"I do apologize that Justin was not here to greet you," I murmured. "I cannot think what is keeping him. He is not even back twenty-four hours and he is off again."

"Serena, I have never known Justin to stay put for any length of time," he replied. "It is of no concern; I shall see him later."

As Oliver seated me at the head of the table, the girls arrived. Daphne, who had worshipped her cousin Oliver since she was a young child, ran forward into his arms.

They drew apart, he holding her at arm's length. "Now, come and tell me how many hearts you have been breaking."

I was disappointed when Constance moved quickly to her place at the table, clearly avoiding any intimacy with her cousin. I was not surprised, for there had always been a coolness between the two, which I suspected had been created by Constance's mother, Clarissa, who had always resented Oliver. In turn, Oliver had never had any real love for his halfsister, which was easily understandable since she had been less than kind to him as a child. It saddened me but I was wise enough not to push. Perhaps in time a closeness would develop there.

"Before you ask me anything," Oliver advised, taking a sip of wine, "Alexander says you are not to be angered with him for not writing."

I was warmed by Oliver's brotherly protection of him.

"In truth, I have kept him busy morning 'til night."

"How does he seem to be taking to it?" I pursued.

He was thoughtful for a moment. "You know, Serena, he has surprised me. I would never have thought that Alexander would take to managing the estates. He is a loner, smart as a whip, but his mind takes its own directions. I should never have left him at Camberleigh so soon if I did not believe that he had quickly taken such a firm grasp to it all."

"I was tentative about this apprenticeship at Camberleigh," I admitted. "Alexander has never shown a particular interest in the estates before, and the last thing I wanted was for him to feel he had no option but to be involved. Particularly since he seems to have such a fear of being a disappointment to Justin, which as we both know, could not be further from the truth."

"You need not worry about that, Serena," Oliver assured. "This zeal of his, this enthusiasm is indeed genuine. It has particularly delighted me how well he has gotten on with the tenants," he pursued. "I always knew he would be able to run rings around me in all business aspects, but I never dreamt that the more personal part of the estates would appeal to him. I do not think he is consciously trying to emulate Justin, but it looks like he is his father's son after all."

"And Anne, how is she?"

He shrugged. "You know Anne, she never complains, and I know the situation cannot be easy on her since Father's stroke."

"She is a strong woman, Oliver," I advised, "but then I think that runs in the Barkham blood."

"Well, she certainly did not help me to travel light on my journey from Camberleigh," Oliver added, winking at me.

Constance, who had been particularly quiet, asked eagerly, "Does that mean that Anne has sent some new gowns?"

"I cannot be certain, but I suspect that is what is inside those boxes. I asked Sidney to take them up to your rooms."

"Oh, Serena, might we be excused?" Constance pleaded. "I may change my mind about what I am to wear this evening after all."

I agreed, and after Oliver and I spoke a while longer, I suggested that he rest a spell before the evening. He said he would welcome some sleep after his journey, and I decided to take advantage of the relative quiet and retire to my room as well.

I must have been more tired than I had thought, for I had

no longer lain down on the bed than sleep o'ertook me. The
room was dark when I awakened, and I was truly disturbed
that Justin, if he indeed had returned, had not come in search
of me.

Rising, I made my way downstairs. I was heading towards
the drawing room when I thought I heard voices coming from
the library. I crossed the hallway, and my hand had lighted on
the door handle when I heard Oliver's voice saying, "Then
you are sure she knows nothing?"

"Nothing," came Justin's voice in reply. "But believe me,
his being here in London, it worries me."

I opened the door and demanded, "What worries you?"

Justin was openly unsettled by my intrusion.

"Serena, I did not hear you."

"What are you worried about?"

Regaining his composure, he replied, "Oh, nothing, just
more nonsense on this railroad project."

I studied Justin intently. I had a dreaded sense that he was
not being fully truthful with me. Honesty had always been an
absolute between Justin and myself, and I was hurt to even
suspect that I was not privy to it at that moment. But I was
scarcely one to challenge him, particularly in front of Oliver,
who seemed embarrassed already by my silence.

"I hate to break up this reunion, for I am certain you have a
great deal to catch up on, but it *is* getting late."

Justin nodded. "You go on up, darling. I shall join you momentarily."

As I left the room, there was a part of me that wanted to remain at the door that I closed behind me, but I had never spied
on my husband, and though his behavior disturbed me, I was
not about to start now.

Charlotte was in the bedroom fixing a small tear in the hem,
which I had caused when selecting the gown earlier.

"I drew yer water just seconds ago," she advised. "So ye
pop in while 'tis still warm."

I thanked her and lingered a bit longer than usual, trying to
suppress what I overheard in the library earlier. It promised to
be a grand ball, being given at one of London's truly great
houses, and I did not want my insecurities to mar the evening
for the girls.

"Ye should see the gowns Lady Camberleigh sent along,"
Charlotte enthused as she twisted my hair high atop my head,
allowing only one heavy coil to fall back from the crown.

"I should have investigated, I suppose," I replied, rouging the bones above my cheeks. "Constance was encouraging Daphne to wear that pink taffeta. 'Tis a lovely gown but somehow too frothy for her."

"Well, then ye'll be pleased fer Miss Daphne is wearin' a lavender dress sent from Lady Anne. Matches her eyes, it does."

I leaned forward as Charlotte fastened a spray of feathers centered by a large topaz into my hair.

"Would you do me a favor and look in on the girls," I requested. "I would feel better if your trained eye was on them."

She laughed. "Fer sure, this is, if ye kin be handlin' the gown by yerself."

"If she cannot, then I will gladly be of assistance," Justin called out as he entered the room.

Charlotte left, bidding us a lovely evening, and Justin came forward and wrapped his arms about my bare shoulders, studying me in the mirror. His eyes caught sight of the box that contained the pin he had left for me.

"Am I to take it that you will wear it this evening?"

"My only disappointment is that you have not been about for me to thank you," I replied. "It is truly beautiful."

"I am glad you like it," he replied, burying a kiss on the nape of my neck.

"It was kind of you to remember the girls as well."

"My father always counselled me to avoid any jealousies amongst women, even if they are your own family."

I placed some perfume on my earlobes.

"The music box you gave Daphne," I mused, "it is most unusual."

"I hope she liked it," he replied as he moved towards the armoire and commenced removing his attire for the evening.

"You know, it is odd," I began slowly. "I saw almost a duplicate of it at Monique's." I did not add that that was the third one I had seen in the space of a few weeks.

"Hmm," he replied absently. "That is a coincidence."

Justin dressed quickly. He appeared, where strained earlier, now to be in a somewhat ebullient mood, and I was so happy to see him in good spirits that I kept the conversation, which he directed, light and amusing.

If Constance looked a radiant confection, I do not think that I had ever seen Daphne more beautiful. The lavender of the gown so intensified the violet color of her eyes that the effect was breathtaking.

"How does it feel, Justin, to be escorting the three most ravishing women in London to the ball?" Oliver exclaimed as he came down the stairs.

Justin laughed. "I expect I shall have my hands full."

Earl and Lady Foxcroft lived near Monique off Queen Anne Street. Their daughter, Kathryn, a dark, diminutive beauty, was also having her season, and it was in her honor that the ball was being given.

I was somewhat aghast at how many people had been invited, realizing that we would be expected to reciprocate in kind later this winter.

Had it not been for Monique, I fear I should have felt quite ignored as we partook of one sumptuous course after another in the large dining room. The girls had quickly been surrounded by a bevy of young men, one in particular, a Lord Peter Sanderson, an acquaintance of Oliver's, who seemed particularly taken with Daphne. Justin, usually attentive at these affairs, had, within moments of our arrival and a perfunctory greeting of other guests, removed himself to a corner of the drawing room with Oliver. I knew that he would undoubtedly be anxious for word on the estates and Alexander's progress, but I wished that he would have waylaid it to a more appropriate time.

When the dessert had at last been served and the strains of the music had commenced in the ballroom, Justin, who had been seated at an opposite end of the table, came to retrieve me.

"I was wondering when I might spend some time with you," I murmured as his hand took my arm.

He tweaked my nose. "I do believe my bride is feeling neglected."

If he had seemed preoccupied earlier in the evening, he now turned his attentions to me fully. I was always so proud to dance with Justin. He looked so smart in his grey waistcoat and britches. I always marvelled at how agile he was, whereas the other gentlemen invariably left their footprints on my dancing slippers, Justin never misstepped.

A waltz had just begun, and my eyes searched the room for Constance and Daphne. Both seemed to be having a wonderful time, though Constance appeared preoccupied, casting her eyes rarely on her partners but often towards the doorway.

It was but fifteen minutes later, when having taken a spin about the floor with Oliver, that I understood Constance's lack of attentiveness. For there, framed in the doorway, stood Count de la Brocher. The evening had been progressing so nicely, and somehow the appearance of this man put my nerves on edge. I had to admit that he looked particularly handsome this evening, but I could not dismiss the distinct impression, as I turned back to Constance, that she was not only not surprised to see him there but indeed had anticipated it. Watching her smile ever too brightly and raise her fan as if in a signal, I was outraged by her lack of decorum. Therefore, it was particularly shocking when the count, seemingly blind to her presence, strode deliberately over to where Daphne stood chatting with Lord Sanderson.

"Oh, Lord," I murmured, praying that I was not about to see some unpleasant scene unfold.

12

daphne

"MISS BARKHAM, MAY I say how exquisite you look this evening."

I turned about only to find Count de la Brocher smiling down on me.

"Count," I acknowledged, feeling a hot flush creep into my face.

"That color becomes you, it matches your eyes."

I could not believe the gall of this man. He had insulted me but a week ago, he was toying with my cousin's affections and yet one would think by his manner that we were more than mere acquaintances.

I started as Lord Sanderson stepped forward, his hand extended as he introduced himself. I was infuriated as the count, not taking his eyes off me, replied, "It was good of you to watch over my fiancee in my absence, Lord Sanderson."

"Your what?" I shrieked in disbelief.

"Now Daphne, dear, do not tell me that you were less than truthful with Lord Sanderson here," he admonished. "I cannot blame your entrancement, my Lord, but I fear our betrothal is so new to Miss Barkham, she does not realize that she can no longer, shall we say, encourage other suitors."

I was so dumbfounded that it took me several moments to find my voice. By the time I did, Lord Sanderson, obviously embarrassed by the incident, was spluttering an apology and moving away.

"Are you mad?" I exclaimed, whirling about to face the count.

He laughed, and before I could utter another word had taken me in his arms at the commencement of a waltz.

"My dear Daphne, I should lower your voice 'twere I you. I think your family would not be pleased if you created a scene."

"You *are* mad," I insisted as he held me in an almost vise-like grip leading me about the room.

He laughed. "Well, I do not think you need fear being bothered by that young chap again. Pleasant enough sort but scarcely your type, Miss Barkham."

"How dare you tell me what my sort is," I spat back.

Instead of rebuking him, my anger seemed to amuse him further. "There, now, there is the fire in your eyes I saw the day we met. You should become agitated more often Daphne, it becomes you."

I would have slapped this man right there on the dance floor if I had not been painfully aware that it would not only embarrass my parents but also bring the ball to a sudden halt.

"You must know how attractive I find you, Daphne," he whispered. "I could think of nothing save seeing you here again tonight."

"I despise you," I retorted, taking care to keep my voice low.

"Be careful, Daphne," he cautioned, his eyes burning into mine. "It has been said that there is a fine line between love and hate. I suspect that one day you will find that what is troubling you is not a distaste for me but an attraction to me that even you shall not be able to suppress."

"What you may not have suspected, Count de la Brocher, is that my cousin has been more than candid with me. Do you really think that you can be a rude boor with me and, I suspect, a scoundrel with Constance and believe that I should have anything but loathing for you?"

As tightly as he had held me to him, he released me suddenly, his face darkening with a frown.

"What are you implying?" he asked, his eyes searching mine.

"You know perfectly well," I charged. "What you do not realize is that you may insult me all you wish, but my cousin, who does not seem to perceive your true character, I promise you, I shall protect. I should warn you Count de la Brocher that it will only take one word to my father. He is a powerful man, as I am certain you know, and would not take this lightly."

Though my words were far stronger than my nerve at that moment, I was pleased for indeed the count seemed suddenly nonplussed.

I whirled about and began to walk away when I felt his hand grab at my arm.

"What are you talking about, Daphne?" he insisted.

"You know perfectly well what I mean," I retorted, trying to steady my voice.

His hand relaxed and I strode through the milling crowd and out of the ballroom. I was utterly mortified, and though I had managed to keep some composure during my exit, my guard dissolved as I raced to one of the upper bedrooms. I had no more than exited from the water closet and sat down on the petite chaise in front of the dressing table when the door swung open and Constance stormed in.

"How dare you," she accused, slamming the door behind her.

"You do not know what you are talking about," I admonished.

"Oh come, cousin dear, let us not mince our words. You know perfectly well that I have been seeing the count. We arranged to meet here this evening, and you had the audacity to flaunt yourself before him, not to mention monopolizing his time. How could you?" she demanded stamping her foot. "You know I find him a likely suitor."

"Constance, I resent your talking to me this way. If the truth be known, that man interrupted a perfectly pleasant time that I was having with Lord Sanderson. He, well, there is no point in repeating what he said to discourage any further attention from Peter, Lord Sanderson. But I *shall* tell you one thing and that is that Count de la Brocher is not only loathsome but I sense quite mad. If you have any pride, you will stay as far away from him as possible. Believe me, you will only be hurt in the end."

"I do not know why you are being so cruel," Constance

replied, her voice quavering. "Furthermore, I do not know what you are about, Daphne Barkham, but I shall tell you that I do not believe one word you are saying. You want the count for yourself, and you think by saying these things that you will dissuade me. Well, this time you shall not have your way."

I was not about to argue with her any longer. To have told her everything that was said between the count and myself would only have hurt her even further, and I was still seething over his insult.

13

serena

I HAD WATCHED as Daphne whirled about and left the ballroom, her eyes directed straight ahead. And almost as if by cue Constance had followed her cousin.

I knew that I should excuse myself and see to where they had gone, for I sensed that all would be less than amicable between the two. I had been at once perplexed and fascinated for this past half hour since the arrival of the count. For, while I had been certain that his dalliance had been with Constance, the man clearly seemed to have eyes only for Daphne this evening. It was clear to me that whatever had transpired between the two had proved distasteful to Daphne, for her face was almost stony the whole while the two had talked and danced. I was sorry that the count had chosen that precise moment to cut in, for Daphne had appeared to be thoroughly enjoying the company of the young man Oliver had introduced her to earlier.

Although Justin made no comment of the two being together, I noticed that he too was watchful. Were I to have been truthful with him about what had been going on in his absence, I suspected he would not have been reticent about separating the two.

If I had hoped that the count would turn his attentions elsewhere, I was to be sorely disappointed, for he purposefully sought Justin and myself out.

I forced a smile as he greeted us, Justin being quick to introduce him to Oliver, who had rejoined us.

"I cannot think what I might have said to your charming daughter," the count offered. "I did not think I was that poor a dance partner."

I suspected that she had had good reason but replied, "I am certain it was not your dancing, Count de la Brocher. My daughter tends to be high spirited at times."

The count laughed. "It is but one of the things that I find so attractive about her."

Justin, who remained oddly silent, suddenly turned to Oliver, exclaiming, "This is your last chance to dance with my bride this evening, old chap. I should suggest you take advantage of it."

If Oliver was surprised by his suggestion, he recovered quickly and, taking my hand, said, "I am not allowing him to change his mind for one minute."

I could hardly refuse and yet I felt that Justin had purposefully wanted me out of earshot, for as quickly as we had commenced our dance Justin and the count had removed themselves to the back of the room and appeared intent in conversation.

"Serena?" Oliver pressed. "I do not believe you have heard a word I have said."

I shook my head. "I apologize if I seem preoccupied."

"Is something troubling you?"

"Quite honestly there is. You know I am not one usually to pry, but might I ask what you and Justin were talking about earlier in the library?"

"It was just as he told you, just some problems with the railroads."

"You are certain," I persisted.

Oliver smiled down at me. "You know, Serena, you are commencing to be a worrier. Do you not know that if something was amiss, Justin would tell you?"

I agreed and scoffing at my own foolishness allowed Oliver to lead me in the next few dances. When Daphne and Constance had returned in tandem to the ballroom, I noted that while Daphne studiously avoided the corner where Justin and the count were talking, it was Constance who joined them immediately. Whether the count was indeed a good actor or whether he truly was mercurial, it was hard to know, but outwardly he showed no particular pleasure at the sight of Constance.

This was our cue. I decided to take our leave. If I had expected an argument from my cousin, I was pleasantly surprised, for she seemed almost relieved when I urged our departure.

It was not a particularly pleasant return to Channing Hall. Whatever had transpired between Daphne and Constance, it had created an obvious hostility, and although neither uttered a word, it was not difficult to perceive the tension between the two.

Blessedly Oliver chattered on about Alexander and the estates, keeping Justin from prying into the girls' evening. I was eager to learn what Justin had been discussing with Count de la Brocher for such a long time but decided it would be best to pursue in the confines of our bedroom, since the very mention of the man's name would likely incite difficulty with Daphne and Constance.

When we finally arrived back at Channing Hall, both girls retired immediately. Justin entreated Oliver to take a brandy with him in the library, but I was thankful when he begged off, sensing, I suspected, that he had already taken a good deal of Justin's time that day.

The soft sheets felt cool against my skin, but I warmed quickly as Justin cradled me in his arms.

"Have I told you how pleased I am that you have returned?" I whispered.

"No more than I, Serena."

I placed my hand over his, which was still bandaged. "Is it bothering you?"

"What?"

"Your hand, of course," I pursued.

"That is the least of it," he murmured.

I pulled away from him, trying to study his face in the shadows of the night. "What is wrong, Justin?" I proceeded cautiously.

"Why would you think there is something wrong, dear heart?"

"Well, you just said . . ."

"Just a bad turn of phrase," he interrupted. "I forget that I must choose my words more carefully."

"Is it the railroads?" I pursued, an anxiousness overtaking

me. " 'Tis not anything with Alexander? Are you and Oliver keeping something from me?"

He put his arm about me, drawing me back down to him. "Darling, you have heard Oliver yourself. Our son is not only well but seems to be doing brilliantly."

I relaxed a bit. I was not convinced that something was not troubling Justin deeply, but in my heart I knew that if something were untoward with Alexander, Oliver would not keep it from me. I wanted to pursue the matter further but, realizing that Justin's breathing had quieted, I knew that he had drifted off to sleep.

Try as I did I could not dismiss the sense that something was awry. Happiness had been robbed from me once at Channing Hall, and though I scarce thought that a house could breed evil, I longed for the safety and security that Mayfair offered us.

14

daphne

I UNDRESSED AS soon as I returned to my room, eager to retire before Contance descended on me again. She had left only moments earlier close to tears and vowing that she would retaliate for what I had supposedly done to her that evening. I had allowed her to spew those spiteful phrases at me, as arguing with her, I knew, would accomplish nothing. I was furious that she should verbally accost me, even more angered that Count de la Brocher had insulted me so. But at the same time there was a part of me that felt sorry for Constance. I had at first thought that his dalliance was just a passing whim, and I did not know whether her fascination was mere infatuation or whether she truly had developed some feelings for the count. But the man was clearly up to no good. He had scarce seemed to notice her this evening, when, just days earlier, he had led her to believe that his interest was sincere. For one moment I had wondered if he might not have staged that little performance with me just to incite jealousy on Constance's part. But if that were true, having piqued her fury or curiosity or both, he would, I sensed, have turned to her after he had played out his game with me.

I pulled my robe closer about me and picked up a book on my night table, turning to where I had last left off. When all the words seemed but a blur, I slammed it shut. This had been the first evening since our arrival in London that I had met someone whom I sensed I might have more than a passing interest in. And Lord Sanderson, I thought, had not seemed to find me distasteful. He had to be a gentleman of character, for my cousin Oliver would not have befriended him were he not. What he must have thought of me, I wondered, when Count de la Brocher suggested that we were engaged. Well, whatever hopes I had had there appeared to have been dashed. Lord Sanderson had scurried off before I could recover my composure enough to explain. And I had noticed that when later I had returned to the ballroom, he seemed totally preoccupied with Kathryn Foxcroft. I could not blame him truly, for though I wished his attentions had been focused on me, I had to admit that she was a pretty and seemingly pleasant young woman.

When after a few moments I found that I had been pacing about the room like some trapped animal, I decided to go down to the library. I had been less than sisterly, and though I had promised Alexander that I would keep him abreast of all our doings, I had not penned one word since our arrival.

There was a definite chill in the air as the candle lighted my way to the floors below. Happily, a fire still burned brightly in the library, and I quickly set about searching out the crested manila writing paper that I knew my mother kept in the desk drawer.

I knew that I should return to bed, but since sleep would not come to me easily, I decided to commence my letter there in the library. I smiled to myself thinking that Alexander would hardly be enthralled by my regalement of the various parties and balls we had attended. I had missed hm these past weeks. We had always been close, and though he could at times be a terrible tease, I knew that there was not a malicious bone in his body.

I had just picked up the second sheaf of paper when I started suddenly at a sound that seemed to be emanating from the fireplace. I rose quickly, and went over to it fearful that perhaps some embers had sparked forth through the fire screen. I studied the carpet carefully in front of the hearth, assuring myself that no embers smoldered there.

I was just about to return to the desk when I suddenly heard what sounded like a man's voice. I whirled about, not knowing what to expect, but was even further puzzled when I saw no one in the room. Yet it was clear to me that I heard not one but several voices. Indeed they were muffled but I was not mistaken. I pulled my robe closed about me and pressed closer to the fireplace, pressing my ear towards the cavernous opening. If it had indeed been voices I had heard, they had quieted as quickly as they had commenced, leaving only the crackle of the fire in my ears.

Not being one given to hallucinations, I moved deliberately to the bookcases that flanked each side of the fireplace and began removing books and placing them on the floor below. I did not know what I thought I was looking for, but I would not be dissuaded that I had indeed heard voices from somewhere beyond this wall. When I had cleared almost four shelves I paused again, listening for the voices I had heard earlier, but all was silent. Wearily I replaced those volumes I had withdrawn and moved over to the bookcases on the righthand side. With some effort, I pulled the library steps over and climbing up commenced again to withdraw the heavy leatherbound volumes. After proceeding through two more shelves I was commencing to be discouraged. Should anyone suddenly find me here at this late hour pulling the library apart, they would think me quite mad, but I was not about to cease until I had satisfied my curiosity.

I again replaced the books to their proper shelves and commenced on the third below, noting as I pulled the first forward that it was entitled *L'Histoire de la Fin du Siècle*. The book had scarce been full in my palm when suddenly the entire bookcase wall opened towards me. I jumped back, almost falling over the library steps. I shuddered as a rush of air blew past me, fortunately not extinguishing the candle that I had placed atop the mantle.

Shock was the only way to describe my reaction. Though I had not lived at Channing Hall since I was a child, and then only briefly, I could in no way assume to be as fully acquainted with it as I was with Mayfair. But I indeed thought it odd that neither of my parents had ever mentioned what seemed a secret doorway to me.

The bookcase was remarkably intact and though it had swung several measures from the wall, its movement had disturbed none of the books that I had so diligently replaced earlier. Recovering my composure I moved forward, taking the candle from the mantle above and peering into the blackened space beyond.

At first I thought that it was simply a false wall, for all that seemed before me was a blackened cavern. But on closer inspection I realized that commencing at the back rim of the bookcase there was a series of stairs leading downwards.

In my heart I knew that were I to be sensible I would leave things as they were and inquire to my father about this strange discovery in the morning. Channing Hall had been his family's home in London, and I expected that if he knew about this, he simply had thought it too dangerous for one to pursue. But I could not dismiss the surety that I had heard voices from beyond these walls, and my fascination o'ertook any trepidation I was feeling.

I moved forward cautiously as a dankness filled my nostrils. My slipper tested the first step and I gained confidence as I realized it was crafted of stone. I stretched my hand out hopeful of finding some rail or balustrade that would guide me as I descended, but the walls too were crafted of rough-cut stone.

The steps appeared unusually wide, and though my candle cast some light, it was not sufficient to make me sure-footed. I progressed cautiously, allowing my foot to reach out to discover each step's end before dropping it to the next. 'Twould have been wiser I knew to use my free hand to guide me along the right wall, but the hem of my gown and robe were long and I feared they would likely trip up my feet did I not support them above my ankles.

I had counted eight steps when I paused, struck suddenly by the audacity of my adventure. Temerity had never been part of my nature, but I was not so daft as to admit that I was foraging into unknown territory without the slightest thought that it might not only be unwise but also dangerous.

Thrusting the candle out before me, I could see that only four steps remained. I had come this far, and though a part of me longed to return to the sanctuary of the library, I was not about to abandon my search now.

It was with relief that, when having reached even ground, I knew that my descent was behind me. As I stepped gingerly forward, I covered the flame of the candle, which was already burning low. Whatever light had emanated from the library was lost to me at this point.

I did not really know what possessed me to move forward along what now seemed a passageway, for I was cold and the sound of my own heart was resounding in my ears. But having come this far I could not turn back. I had gone perhaps twenty or thirty paces when suddenly my foot slipped on what appeared, on examination, to be a rock that had dislodged from the ground surface.

"Damnation," I muttered, as upon straightening I realized that my candle had extinguished. I chastised myself for not having counted my steps from the crude staircase, for though the passageway appeared to have only one direction, the absence of light made the prospect of inching my way back a terrifying one indeed.

I stood transfixed for a moment, silently willing myself to muster courage enough to wend my way back.

I had turned myself about, placing my hand against the wall so that it might guide my way, when suddenly a voice demanded, "Who goes there?"

Whatever terror I had felt to that moment suddenly increased tenfold. I remained frozen in place as the voice again challenged, "Who goes there?"

"I mean no harm," I whispered, trying to find my voice. "Truly, I am lost."

I waited as I listened to footsteps that approached me, praying that whoever it was would prove friend and not foe. I jumped back against the wall as hands grasped my shoulders, and with the candle holder I struck out against my unseen enemy. I moaned as the heavy brass implement fell from my hand chinking as it struck the ground below.

"Please do not hurt me," I gasped as strong male hands travelled my body and grasped my hair. "I swear I mean no harm."

I started as my captor murmured, "Damnation, Daphne, what are you doing here?"

"How do you know . . ."

Before I could proceed any further the hands that held my shoulders in a vicelike grip enveloped me and a man's mouth covered mine, his lips demanding in their response. I fought, pushing with all my might against the broad chest, but I was no match for my captor, whose senses seemed heightened by the brandy he had recently drunk.

I was shaking when his lips finally moved from my own, pressing now into the nape of my neck.

"You see, I knew how it would be *entre nous*," he murmured.

"My God, it is *you*," I gasped with the sudden realization that I was in the arms of Count de la Brocher.

Taking my foot I struck with all my might against his lower leg, pain crippling my toes. Instead of angering him my fighting appeared to humor him, for he laughingly replied, "I sensed from the moment I saw you that you would be a fire-brand, but the passion in you is even greater than I had suspected. But then given that Serena Barkham is your mother, I should have known."

He had relaxed his grip on me enough that I was able to raise my arm, my hand stinging as it made contact with his face. "How dare you insult my mother! You are even more odious than I dared think."

"*Au contraire*, Daphne. You are too quick to judge. I meant only that your mother is *sûrement* the most beautiful and charming woman on the Continent. But she is clearly in love with her husband, so that makes her daughter the second most appealing, though I admit you are a close second."

"I beg you to let me go," I beseeched. "If you do, I shan't tell anyone I . . ."

Before I could conclude, his mouth covered mine again, his hands pressing at the small of my back. I tore at the fabric of his shirt, my nails clawing against his shoulders.

"Daphne, do not fight this," he whispered. "You may think that what you want is to have me release you, but trust me, I know better. If I knew that you would come to me willingly, but you are young and confused I know by the attraction you feel towards me."

"You flatter yourself," I spat at him. "You disgust me, and I warn you, if you violate me any further, I shall see you hanged."

"Dramatic, my dear Daphne, but I think you protest too much. Look at how you shudder when my hands caress that exquisite body of yours, how your breath quickens at my kiss."

"If I am shuddering," I moaned, "it is from repulsion."

He drew me closer. "Has no man ever caressed you, brought you to that place where you wanted him as much as he you?"

I did not know how I had been able to fight the tears, but now they cascaded down my cheeks as I choked out my pleas for the count to leave me be. I felt as though I were in a whirl-wind. I felt dirty and abused, but even worse I felt so naive. If I had had more experience, I might have been a match for him. And most of all I was frightened, not only because I sensed that he would not heed my opposition but also because some small part of me questioned whether his accusations had some merit. My mind was screaming for him to stop but my body seemed distant from me, as though I could not control it.

His breathing had become more labored, and as he pressed against me, I was aware of a great swelling in his abdomen. "What you do not understand, Daphne, is that the last thing I want is to hurt you," he whispered. "But I want you, and I know that if I do not make you mine here and now, it will be harmful for us both."

I felt close to collapse as his hands pulled open my robe, exploring my body over my nightdress. I prayed that I would wake up from this nightmare, but this, I knew, was far too real to be a bad dream. I gasped as I felt his hand fumbling with the buttons on his britches, his masculinity-thrusting force against me like a knife.

"For the last time I beg you," I choked, "if you say you care for me, then do not violate me."

"Even if I would, I could not turn back now," he groaned, dragging my body down to the ground with his own.

Later I would wonder how long he kept me there, how long it had actually taken him to enter me, to take me until he was fully spent. There had been one instant where a searing pain had spread through my body, and as I had cried out, he muffled my anguish with his mouth. Although we were in total darkness, I kept my eyes pressed shut, partially to stem the tears that continued to flow. My greatest struggle was in my brain, sensing somehow that though he might take my body, I could not allow him to ravage my mind. I remember when it struck me suddenly that the pain was gone. I had a distinct sense of climbing, of reaching for something I knew not what. And when I thought I could tolerate this no longer, there was one moment where my mind and body seemed to divide, the latter taking on a breath and being of its own. And still I climbed higher and higher, and then, just as I thought I could go no further, I felt myself falling into some warm indescribable abyss.

He lay atop of me, and though a man of considerable size I was surprised at how light he appeared. But whatever fight I had had seemed now robbed from me. I shuddered as his fingers smoothed the dampness from my cheeks.

"I swear to you I did not know, Daphne," he whispered. "I did not really imagine that I would be the first. I do not know if that would have changed anything, but on my life I promise you I mean you no harm. Next time it will be better for you. These tears shall become tears of joy."

"Next time?" I challenged. "Oh, no, Count de la Brocher, it is there *you* are mistaken. An eye for an eye. You have ruined me and left me no provocation but to see to your demise."

"Daphne, there is much you do not understand," he retorted, "but I swear to you that one day you will be mine and you, though you cannot now conceive of it, will come to me freely of your own intent."

"Never," I spat back. "Never. I would see myself dead first."

He released me suddenly, and though I knew that he was staring at me, I took some relief that he could not read my expression.

"Would that I could keep you here. I would but for many reasons I must return you to your house," he replied as his arms lifted me up.

I was about to protest but found myself too weak to flail against him. He lighted the candle that I had tried to assault him with earlier and made his way slowly back towards the steps that would return me to Channing Hall. I was silent, fearful that should I strike out against him, he might change his mind and leave me in this cavernous structure to fend for myself.

"We are at the stairs now," he said. "I will give you the candle and wait until I am certain that you have reached the top. When you do, push the bookcase closed. You will find it moves easily, and replace the volume where you discovered it."

"You must be mad," I retorted. "What makes you think I will do as you demand?"

"Because you *must*, Daphne. It was careless of me to have been down here at this hour. I never dreamt . . . in any event it is imperative that no one know you have discovered this passageway."

"Ah, so you do fear the recriminations from my family," I assaulted. "And well you should. You are naive to think you can threaten me any further. How could you even suggest that I would do anything you say."

"Believe me, that is scarcely why I entreat you to keep silent. Were it only so simple."

"You know me not, Count de la Brocher," I accused. "Perhaps my cousin Constance would keep silent but not I. I would rather bear the shame and see you exposed for what you are. I should tell the world, if I thought it could be your undoing."

He set me down, his hand grasping my forearm. "Daphne, this is no time for heroic measures. Let me put it this way. If you want to protect your father, you will not mention your discovery or this night to anyone."

My bravery was halted for a moment. "What does my father have to do with this?"

He paused and from the candlelight I saw his face had drawn into a deep frown. "I cannot tell you that. I can only assure you that it would be a mistake, a very costly mistake if you do not do as I tell you. This indignation you now feel, it will pass. You will see things differently between us. But you have to believe that your father would be in grave danger if you made mention of this. I know I cannot extract a promise from you, but I can warn you. And if you have anywhere near the wisdom I think you do, you will heed my warning, Daphne. Now here, take the candle and watch your way on the stairs. They can be treacherous if you are not careful."

He thrust the cold brass holder into my hand, which I tried desperately to steady for fear of extinguishing the flame. I dragged myself up the stone steps, biting my lip to keep the tears back. I nearly fell into the room and propped myself against the marble inset flanking the fireplace, praying for the strength to somehow get back to my room.

The house was quiet, but I knew I could not dally, for I could not risk being discovered in this state. I did not need a mirror to know that my appearance could scarce be explained away even to one of the servants. Taking a deep breath I methodically picked up the volume from the floor, wondering as I did why I was indeed doing as he had bade. The bookcase, as he had promised, moved effortlessly back against the fireplace wall. Before replacing the book I knelt with the candle, exploring the space at the back. It was difficult to discern in this low light but it was clear that the book fitted into a latch-like configuration. I moved it back somewhat gingerly, fearful that too strenuous a motion might release the bookcase again. Satisfied after a moment that it had not, I moved out of the library.

I had only made it halfway up the staircase when a wave of nausea swept over me, causing me to sink to my knees, my body afire with flashes of prickly heat. I pressed my hand to my mouth, praying for some inner strength to see me to the confines of my room.

How I managed it I did not know, but I said a prayer of thanks as I closed the door to my bedroom behind me.

When I finally saw my reflection in the mirror on my dressing table, I gasped at my appearance, for not only was I dishevelled but also my clothes and body were covered with dirt. Willing myself to stay calm I methodically removed my gown. My undergarments, I realized with horror, I would have to burn, because I could never think of donning them again. The embers were still live in the fireplace, and it was with some relief when the at-first smoldering cloth burst into flame.

The water in my basin was icy cold, but I cared not, for I could not wait until morning to try to wash away the devastation of this night. I scrubbed myself until my skin was raw, realizing as I did that I could wash away the grime but that I could not cleanse the misery from my soul.

When at last I donned my nightdress and climbed into bed, whatever energy I had mustered in this past half hour was thoroughly spent. I moved my hand gently across my stomach, trying to soothe the dull ache that persisted.

My fingers clenched about the wool covers as I fought to keep my senses. A part of me wanted to run to my mother and beseech her to hold me as she had done when I was a child, promising me that the hurt would go away. But I was afraid. Afraid of what? I wondered. Did I take the count's threats to heart? Did I believe that if I did not remain silent, I might truly injure my father? The count was a cunning man. It would not surprise me if his threat was simply a ploy to insure that I would not expose him. Then, why could I not dismiss it? I knew the answer, of course. It had to do with those many years ago when father had indeed been victim to the scheme of Lord Taggart's. But Philip Taggart was long dead, and though I knew the events of that time still occasionally haunted my mother, he could no longer torment us. But was there another who wished my father ill? If there were even the slightest chance that his threats were not veiled, I could scarce chance putting either of my parents in danger.

I felt totally trapped. Something told me that at any cost I must not put my family at risk. But in doing so, was I putting my own sanity at stake? I knew not the answer and prayed that God would give me the relief of sleep, for I should need my strength, both physical and mental, in these weeks to come.

serena

I AWAKENED THE next morning disturbed by a pattern that seemed to be forming. Once again Justin was not by my side. We had both been tired the night before, and though I would have been content to have just lain in his arms and talked for a while, even conversation seemed to prove trying.

But with Oliver about I knew that I would have to give over on monopolizing his time. The round of galas we had to attend were less than scintillating for Justin, and I was grateful that he appeared to accompany us willingly if not joyfully.

One of the maids had left my basin, and feeling newly refreshed I donned a morning dress of sea-blue taffeta. I longed for Charlotte to dress my hair but had not the heart to call her out when indeed a few simple coils were all that was needed.

When I had finished vigorously brushing my hair, I searched my dressing table for one of the silver combs that usually lay there. Puzzled at not finding one, I moved over to Justin's dresser, thinking that one of the maids might unwittingly have misplaced them.

I smiled to myself as I muddled through the clutter on his dresser. Neatness had never been one of his virtues. Finding one of my combs, I pulled it out, noticing as I did that a note had fallen to the floor.

Picking it up I was startled recognizing Monique's handwriting. Though it was scarcely my want to read my husband's correspondence, I could not help but be intrigued. I told myself that, had it been a letter of some length, I should have replaced it immediately, but it was clearly only a brief message.

Holding it closer I read. "Serena is becoming suspicious. I think you should tell her. *Maintenant.* In any event we must meet."

The note was unsigned, but having received more letters than I could number from Monique over the years, I knew it was penned by her hand. I reread the note two or three times, my heart pounding as I did. I longed to believe that only innocence lay behind it, but I could not reconcile that easily. Suspicious? Had I been exhibiting a suspicious nature of late? It was true there had been an uneasiness about me. But Justin and Monique? Once, years ago, there admittedly had been twinges of jealousy, but there had never been any cause for me to distrust either of them. Many women would say that I was being ridiculous, that Monique was a woman years Justin's senior, but I discounted that, for she not only did not look her age but also even in maturity she had not lost a certain appeal, a joie de vivre, that was truly unique. Could it be that Justin and Monique had rekindled the passion they had shared years ago?

Replacing the note on the dresser under some other papers, I moved to my dressing table and sank down on the skirted seat before it. "You are a foolish woman, Serena Barkham," I murmured to myself. Justin had never given me reason to doubt him. And Monique was my dear friend. I had always been confident in our love and in my own sense of self. It was not my nature to invent problems or be suspicious, so why was I permitting any doubt to unsettle me? I wanted to dismiss it and knew that I should. There was likely the simplest of explanations. I would not have given it a second thought had I not had this gnawing feeling since we left Mayfair that something was troubling Justin. He had seemed preoccupied. That was the only word for it. If nothing else, our intimate moments should have been sufficient reassurance. But then it had been months, it seemed, since he had lingered with me on a morning.

Oliver had assured me I was worrying too much. Oliver and Monique. I could not bear to think that they were conspirators in this. But in what? I asked myself. Was it possible that there was some thread of truth to these fears I could not dispel? What of Justin's sudden trip? Had his explanation of trouble with the railroads been a lie? I shook my head. That did not make sense, for I knew full well that Monique had been in London the whole of when he was away. That, of course, did not prove that they were not together. Justin could have been anywhere in London, even ensconced at Monique's, I thought with horror.

My fingers shook as I worked furiously to coil my hair. What was I to do? Should I confront Justin, tell him that I found the note? What if I were mistaken? Had I jumped to a false conclusion? But what else would I be suspicious about and what did Monique implore Justin to tell me?

Were I wrong, I should indeed feel foolish. Whatever anger and hurt I now felt, I could not dismiss that Monique was my friend. If indeed Justin had turned to her, the blame could not really be placed with the two of them. Perhaps over these past months I had become too absorbed with the girls and plans for their season. Certainly we had spent less time together than we had in the past.

I knew, as I prepared to leave the confines of our bedroom, that I would remain silent, at least for the time being. I could not chance being mistaken, nor could I chance the anguish that might come from any admission. I simply had to have faith that I was suffering from an overactive imagination.

Charlotte was working with young Jane in the front hall when I descended. "Where are the girls?" I asked.

"Miss Constance had Sidney take 'er out shoppin', tho' with that rain peltin' out there, I cannot think why she had te go out."

My heart sank, fearing at first that she was up to something again, but I relaxed, knowing that Sidney was driving, for knowing how loyal he was to the family she would not chance his revealing her.

"And Daphne?" I asked.

Charlotte shook her head. "Up in 'er room she is, an' I not be thinkin' she looks too good."

I turned on my heels and quickly reclimbed the staircase to Daphne's room. I knocked lightly at her door, saying, "Daphne, it is Mother."

As I entered and strode over towards her bed, I was shocked at how pale she looked.

"Darling, what is it?" I begged, placing my hand against her forehead.

" 'Tis nothing, Mother, truly," she replied weakly. "I expect I am just tired from all the festivities."

"Perhaps," I replied, looking at her more closely, "but I do not like those dark circles under your eyes. I should think it wise to send for the doctor, if only as a precaution."

"Mother, truly, I am all right," she assured, "just a bit weary. I would feel ridiculous if you called out the doctor, particularly in this weather. I need only rest a day or two and I shall be fine."

I studied her intently. "If you insist, then I shall waylay calling the doctor, but if I do not find you improved by tomorrow morning, I shall have to take matters in hand."

16
daphne

As Mother closed the door, I pulled the sheet about my mouth, attempting to muffle the sobs that racked my body. God how I longed to blurt out the torment that possessed every fiber of my being. I had never endured a longer night. My mind had been like a tightly wound clock. Try as I did to shut out the horror of last evening, there was no solace, no sense of reason that I could summon within myself.

For all I had scrubbed, I knew that I could never cleanse myself of the devastation of my soul. I felt dirty, as though my body carried some permanent stain. Though I knew in my heart that guilt was the last thing I should be feeling, I could not dismiss the thought that somehow I could have said something or fought harder to fend him off.

If only I had never gone down to that library. My curiosity had always gotten me into trouble, but the incidents of my youth paled by contrast. As dawn had brought the morning I had prayed for sleep, hopeful that I would awaken to find it had all been a nightmare, that I was still the young, unblemished girl I had been.

If I could have run away before the house awakened, I would have, but beyond feeling that I was spent of all energy, I knew not where to go. It had been painful to see my mother, and I had struggled with the urge to confess the despair that overwhelmed me. I wanted her arms about me, reassuring me that my life was not indeed ruined, that I would be able to look in the mirror again without cringing at what I saw. But as much as I yearned to be cloaked in the protective warmth of her arms, I could not bring myself to confess the travesty on the night prior.

The damage was done, no words, no retribution could make me whole again. I knew that he should not be allowed to get away with this, and that indeed if I were to expose him, he would likely have to face the highest courts of the land. Though I rarely thought of it, I was not naive to the fact that the Barkham name summoned respect and, if need be, power in England. A Frenchman, though a count, would have little recourse against mere accusation. And I knew full well that if I bared my soul to Mother, with or without Father's presence, she would unflailingly see to his ruin.

Knowing this, it was even more perplexing to me why I had a sense of foreboding about revealing Count de la Brocher. Did I indeed give any credence to his warning? Likely it was an artifice. But he had been so vociferous about my remaining silent lest it would bring harm to my father that an inner voice told me to proceed with caution until I might learn more.

Did anyone else know of the passageway? I wondered. I was dubious that my mother or any of the servants did, for I was certain that they would have made mention of it, if only to caution us of the dangers of foraging below.

My thoughts were a whirlwind of confusion. Assuming that the passageway had been there for some time, perhaps even from the original building of Channing Hall, for what purpose had it been used? And more importantly, where did it lead?

I knew that I had not covered it in its entirety before the count had discovered me there. It was not uncommon for houses such as ours to have wine cellars of considerable size, but even though I had had only the candle to light my way, I could not recall seeing any bottles or casings that would hint of that particular use.

How did Count de la Brocher come to be there? It was unlikely that he could have entered through Channing Hall, since after the house had been broken into, all the locks had been replaced; even the windows had been more fully secured.

I gasped at a sudden thought. Could it have been Count de la Brocher who had been the intruder? Was he the one who had ransacked the library? But why, what was he looking for?

Mother had been assured that nothing was taken.

I mused for a moment, wondering if it indeed had been Count de la Brocher. Had he overturned the library perhaps as a ruse? What if he had entered from the bookcase wall, worried somehow that he might be discovered and had created the chaos simply to insure that no suspicion would be cast his way. As enthused as I was that I was on to something, I as quickly abandoned my conclusion, since there would be no reason to even consider the count's involvement.

My focus needed to be on what I knew—that Count de la Brocher had access to the passageway, that he knew how to enter it from Channing Hall. That did not mean that entry was limited through the library below. Perhaps at the other end there was a bookcase with a hidden latch that matched the one downstairs.

"That is it," I whispered to myself, suddenly excited by where my thoughts had led me. The passageway could conceivably lead through to the count's house. Viscount Penberthy had been a close friend of my father's father, who had unfortunately passed away long before I was born. The houses had been built, I knew, around the same time. Perhaps for some reason the passageway had been planned by the viscount and my grandfather. Perhaps as a refuge should there have been an insurrection.

I knew somehow that my answer lay in the passageway. I had to know why the count was there and if it was indeed he himself who meant our family harm. I shuddered at the thought of venturing down there once again. I could not chance it. But if I were to enlist Oliver's aid, might I be able to resolve this puzzle without the count knowing?

Resolve would not come to me that morning. I was too tired and indeed too emotionally overwrought to make any sound decision. For the moment I only prayed that the ache in my body and heart would ease with time.

17

serena

I WAS TROUBLED when I returned downstairs to take breakfast in the dining room. First, there was that note. I wished I had never seen it, for though I knew that I must struggle to put it out of my mind, I found it impossible to do so. And then there was Daphne. She had not seemed to have a fever, but she had indeed not looked well. No matter how much she had assured me I felt that she was in far less fettle than she allowed. Her eyes had been red and puffy, almost as though she had been crying. Something had happened last night at the ball, of that I was certain. I knew better, however, than to press Daphne. Since she had been a small child, she had always retreated from any prying. If something were bothering her, she would come to me, of that I felt certain, but it would be when *she* wanted to.

The day seemed endless in its passing. I tried to read, to review the post, to pen a letter to Anne, but my preoccupation was with listening to the chimes of the clock in the front hall. I checked on Daphne at noon, thinking that I might take a luncheon with her in her room, but finding her asleep, I decided, rest being what she needed, to return to the library.

In some ways I was relieved that Sidney was out with Constance, for there were several moments when my resolve abandoned me and I thought the only course was to go to Monique's and confront her with the note I had found. But with Sidney gone and Justin or Oliver having taken the backup driver and carriage, I was stranded, save taking a public coach.

When Charlotte brought me early afternoon tea, I was surprised when studying me closely, she said, "Ye wouldn't be comin' down with somethin', too, would ye, Serena?"

I looked up as she poured the steaming liquid into the porcelain cup. "Why would you say that?"

"Cause truth has it, ye be not actin' yerself," she replied. "Nervous as a cat ye seem."

"Nonsense," I quickly dismissed.

"Even the little one there looks worried about ye," she replied, pointing to Pluck, who was indeed seated by my side with his ears perked up and his soulful eyes studying me intently.

I leaned down and ruffled his ears. "You are all imagining things," I insisted, trying to make light of it.

"Well, ye kin always talk te yer old Charlotte," she offered.

I smiled up at her, taking her hand and giving it a squeeze. "I know that and I promise I shall take advantage of that if there ever be a need."

Charlotte left muttering something to herself, and I tried to allow the hot brew to calm my senses.

It was but a few moments later when, hearing a commotion in the front hall, I realized that Constance had returned.

I called out to her, and she joined me in the library, sporting such an array of packages that one would have thought the holidays were upon us.

"Now, Serena, before you chastise me," she said, removing her wrap, "I can assure you that my outing was totally innocent, and if you do not believe me, you can ask Sidney."

"I have accused you of nothing, Constance," I replied quietly, "though I do resent your going off without informing me first."

"What harm did that cause?" she challenged.

"Since Justin and your cousin are out, it left me without any driver."

She frowned. "Were you planning to go somewhere?"

"Not really," I admitted.

Relieved, she replied, "Well, then, you see no harm has come of it. Now let me show you what I have purchased."

I watched as she opened one box after the other. There were several pairs of new boots, dress gloves and some four or five new hats.

"I think this one is particularly fetching," she enthused, donning a broad-brimmed chapeau with small pleats about the inside that framed her face like a picture.

"They are very nice, but I cannot think what you need them for," I mused.

"It is not a matter of need, cousin dear," she replied gaily. "In any event you cannot guess who I encountered in Belgrave Square."

"And who was that?"

"None other than Count de la Brocher," she replied.

"That man seems to be everywhere," I sighed.

"He was there with that Monsieur DeMarcier that we met at his dinner party. He could not have been more charming. And he has asked if he could call one day soon. I could see no reason to deny him that. Oh, Serena, is it not exciting to think that I may have a suitor?"

I must admit that I was thoroughly puzzled, for I should have sworn that the focus of the count's attentions the evening before had clearly been Daphne. In fact he had seemed scarcely enamored by Constance, who had been so brazen with her flirtations. To comment on same I feared would only increase whatever animosity there already was between the two girls. I prayed that the count was only being polite, for I had no doubt that Constance had been more forward than she ought.

"Well, I shall take these up to show Daphne," Constance continued, gathering the packages.

"I should not disturb her were I you," I said quickly. "She has been feeling poorly all day."

"Perhaps she is remorseful after all," she replied.

"That is an odd comment. What do you mean by that?"

"Oh, 'tis nothing," Constance replied gaily. "Where is Justin, by the way?"

"He and Oliver are out," I replied quietly.

She studied me for a moment. "He seems to be out a great deal these days. Perhaps you should follow my lead and do a bit of shopping, lest your husband is straying a bit too often from home."

Without another word Constance flounced out of the room, leaving me shocked by her pronouncement and angered that I should let her disturb me so.

Both Daphne and Constance asked to have trays sent to their respective rooms that evening, and since I could see no reason to argue it, I agreed. I admit that I was almost beside myself with worry when Justin, with Oliver in tow, returned near six.

"Serena, it is freezing in here," Justin boomed as he strode into the library, moving directly to the fireplace, where he added fuel to the dying fire. Oliver came forward and embraced me, saying, "Good Lord, Justin is right, your hands are like blocks of ice."

I felt a lump in my throat and shut my eyes, trying to will away the tears I felt forming there.

When Justin came over to me and pulled me into his arms, I felt myself stiffen at his touch. He pulled away from me, studying me intently. I could not look at him for fear I would break down.

He tucked his hand under my chin. "This is not like you, Serena," he murmured. "What troubles you?"

"Nothing," I lied.

"Ah, I should not let you off so easily, my sweet. Now tell me what distresses you."

I commenced to reply but was furious with myself when all that escaped from my mouth was a broken sob.

"My God, something *is* wrong," he exclaimed. "Oliver, fetch a brandy."

"No," I burst out. "I am fine, truly. I just did not know where you had gone to and with Daphne ill . . ."

"Daphne? What is wrong?"

I shook my head. "In truth I think it is not anything serious, but she is not herself."

"Too much partying, no doubt," Oliver chided.

"That may be," I said, calming some. "But she does not look well."

"I fear you worry too much," Justin said releasing me. "She is a strong girl and will be in full fettle in no time, I suspect."

"I do wish that you and everyone else would stop telling me that I worry too much," I blurted out.

The looks that passed between Justin and Oliver could not go unnoticed. I knew that I was on edge, and my voice and likely my countenance reflected that, and I was wholly relieved when Mary entered and announced that dinner was served.

It was not without difficulty that I tackled the pike in chestnut sauce, served as the first course. I do not know what I expected of Justin, but I thought, were he hiding something from me, he was indeed doing a champion job of covering up. Whether for me or just naturally, he seemed happy, almost ebullient, chattering about our good luck that Alexander had taken so well to learning of the estates, of the progress the railways were making.

Oliver joined in, deferring to me from time to time, and in truth by the time we had been served dessert of raisin cake with a luscious cream sauce, I was beginning to doubt any and all of my earlier suspicions.

Justin and Oliver decided to take port in the library, both encouraging me to join them, but the solitary emotionalism of my day had left me spent of all energies.

I did not ask Justin if he would be retiring shortly when I left the two, soon deep in conversation. I was also frightened of what my response might be if Justin approached me this evening. I wanted him. I needed his love and assurance, but I would not feign in lovemaking. And tonight that was what I would have to do for I could not, even with these last hours, put my mind at rest.

When I had undressed and changed to my nightdress, I stood up from my dressing table and began to cross towards the bed. As I passed Justin's dresser, where I had replaced the note so carefully, some obsession o'ertook me and I moved methodically towards the stately mahogany structure. My fingers sifted through the papers, knowing almost precisely where I had replaced the note.

I started suddenly as Pluck, who was curled in his favorite spot before the hearth, whined.

"I know," I whispered. "I should not be doing this, but do not chastise me, dear friend."

I withdrew the note, and carrying it over to where he lay, reread the words that were indelibly imbued upon my memory.

"Serena is becoming suspicious. I think you should tell her. *Maintenant.* In any event we must meet."

Hardly a note of passion, I considered. But then if there indeed was a renewed involvement, I suspected one would be careful. Then why had he placed it upon his dresser? That was easy. There was no reason for a man to suspect that one of the maids would have mislaid the combs, thus leading me there by happenstance.

Though one never truly knows another, I thought I understood Monique. She would not be one of those women satisfied with surreptitious trysts. With others perhaps, but not with Justin. And in an odd way she would consider me. Monique was many things, but she was not a malicious woman. If indeed their relationship had been rekindled, she would in her own way find it more honorable to be revelatory than to live under a veil of secrecy. She was also clever, and perhaps Justin, for whatever reason, was wavering, and she had decided by confrontation that she would force the issue.

The issue. If only I knew more—if only I truly was certain. And even if I was, what would I do then? Would I concede easily, finding any altercation too troublesome, or would I fight? Certainly Justin, our life, was worth fighting for, but how far would I go? How far would pride allow me to go?

I replaced the note nervously, aware that Justin might return at any moment, and climbed into bed, finding brief solace in the softness of the sheets. Another night I might have tried to fight my exhaustion, but tonight I succumbed gratefully.

If I were to have been able to summon the courage to have confronted Justin over the next few days, I had not the opportunity. Save for evening meals, he and Oliver were not about, leaving early each morning before I had arisen. This, of course, did little to calm my worst fears, and I found myself, when we would gather each night in the dining room, watchful for some sign, some clue to Justin's behavior.

By the second night I concluded that Justin was either a superb actor or that I had been conjuring something that did not exist, for he appeared not only in good cheer but also very attentive, more so than he had in weeks.

It was Daphne where my concern was largely now focused. She was pale and listless and, though assuring me that there was no cause to call for the doctor, remained privated off in her room. I queried Constance, hopeful that if there was something troubling Daphne, she might have shared it with her, but whatever the cause of the rift between them, the silence between the two persisted.

Constance herself was scarcely in high spirits, and I sensed Count de la Brocher was at the base of it. She had been so enthused about his asking to call on her, and when there was no sign of him, I think she began to sense that his was less interest than mere politeness. I was just as well relieved, for sensing that Justin would not approve, it saved me from having to argue on her behalf.

Pluck shadowed me those days, sensing, I suspect, that I was not able to concentrate on anything for too great a period of time.

It was in the early afternoon of the third day that Sidney, finding me in the library, announced that a Lord Peter Sanderson had come to call.

"Lord Sanderson?" I mused, trying to fix the name with a face. "Oh, yes, Oliver's friend," I replied, remembering that we had met at the Foxcroft ball. "Of course, Sidney, show him in."

I rose as Sidney ushered him into the room, thinking what a nice-looking young man he was with a slightly crooked smile that proved most beguiling.

"Lord Sanderson," I greeted, extending my hand.

"It was kind of you to receive me with no prior notice, Lady Barkham."

I motioned him to sit down. "I was just about to take some tea. Would you join me?"

"That is very kind of you."

I could not help but be amused at his nervousness. The tea-cup nearly shook from his hand as I handed it to him.

"You are perhaps wondering why I have called," he offered.

"Unfortunately, Oliver and my husband are not about at present."

"Actually, it was your daughter, Daphne, whom I was hoping I might have your permission to call on."

I was scarcely surprised, for he had clearly been dazzled by her at the ball the other evening, at least until the count had monopolized her time.

"Well, for my part I can not see any reason to object," I assured.

He sat forward. "Do you suggest that your daughter may be of a different mind?"

I shook my head. "It is just that she has been a bit under the weather these past few days."

"Nothing serious, I hope."

"I think not. Actually this series of balls and dinners prove somewhat exhausting on us all."

"Perhaps I might return on some future day," he offered.

I shook my head. "No, actually, I think it might do her good. If you will just give me a few moments, I shall inform her that you are here."

He looked pleased, and as I climbed the stairs to Daphne's room, I prayed that I would not have to disappoint him.

I found Daphne gazing out of the window.

"I have a surprise for you," I said gaily as I entered.

She looked puzzled. "And what is that?"

"You, my lovely daughter, have a caller, a gentleman caller."

I could have sworn that for a moment there was a look of fear in her eyes. "Who is it?" she murmured in a voice so low it was almost inaudible.

"That nice young friend of Oliver's, Lord Sanderson."

"Lord Sanderson?" she repeated. "Why would . . ."

"Why would he call? Well, I think that is rather obvious. He is taken with you."

"But . . ."

"But what?" I puzzled.

She shook her head. "Oh, nothing, I am surprised, that is all."

"I won't press you, darling, but I do hope you will come down. He seems such a pleasant young man. I would hate to disappoint him."

"Why not ask Constance to visit with him, Mother? I really am not up to it."

"Daphne, I can scarcely do that. He came here to call on you. It would be most awkward if I simply replaced you with Constance."

When she did not reply, I persisted. "Come down for a bit. It will do you good."

She threw up her hands. "Look at me. I can not receive anyone looking like this."

That she was concerned about her appearance was an encouraging sign. "I shall explain that you were resting and will be down shortly."

"What shall I wear?"

I strode over to the armoire and pulled out a blue and white gown. "This is perfect, and with a few brush strokes to your hair and a bit of rouge on your cheeks, he will never know that you have been feeling peaked these last few days."

Once I was assured that Daphne would indeed descend to greet Lord Sanderson, I returned to the library to inform him of same, only to find that he and Pluck had become fast friends in my absence.

Ordinarily I would have remained with Daphne and her caller, but as Lord Sanderson was a friend of Oliver's, I saw no reason to act as chaperone. As I took Pluck with me to the drawing room, I wondered whether this call would be the commencement of something important in Daphne's life. Contrary to most of my counterparts, I had never viewed a season as an absolute precursor to marriage. Many mothers, and fathers for that matter, were devastated if the series of balls did not lead to at least one proposal. But for myself, although I had to acknowledge that both Constance and Daphne were of marriageable age, I viewed this time in their lives as one of gay abandon. Lord knows there were enough pressures and problems to be faced in life, and this would, I hoped, prove a light and entertaining period for both girls, not to mention a time when both would form friendships that would hopefully endure throughout their lives.

I stroked the head of Pluck, who regarded me pensively. Suppressing an urge to go and see how Daphne was progressing, I picked up some needlepoint that I had scarce been disciplined to work on these past weeks. I knew not which of us was more nervous. I recalled the first ball at Camberleigh, when Robin Kelston had shown me such attention. I had been so nervous that I had thought I should faint, but then the circumstances were indeed different. I had not yet been recognized by my grandmother and thus resided at Camberleigh as a lowly governess. Not to mention that until travelling there I had lived a sheltered life, socially, that is. Daphne had been more exposed by age ten than I had at eighteen. And yet in matters of romance and courtship, we were all susceptible.

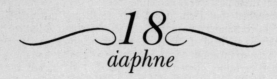

18
ðaphne

As I PULLED the blue and white gown over my head, I swore at myself for allowing Mother to have inveigled me into greeting Lord Sanderson. I had to admit that I was perplexed as to why he had come to call. After the incident at the Foxcrofts's, I had assumed that he had been quickly discouraged. How had he discovered, I wondered, that I was not affianced to. . .

I shuddered at the thought of him. I had spent the last days trying to rid my mind of the devastation of my body and soul. There was not an emotion that I had not endured through these days and nights. Anger, fear, revulsion, despair; I had come to live with them too well.

Fastening the silk frogs along the bodice of the gown, I sat down before my dressing table. I had sat here for hours studying myself, looking for some visible changes. It was as though I expected some mark to be emblazoned on my head or shoulder or some part of my body that lay doubt to my purity. In truth, I had seen none of these vestiges of change, save that my cheeks had hollowed some, which I knew was attributable to my scarce appetite. I uncoiled my hair, letting it fall about my shoulders, brushing tendrils about my fingers. I drew it back, though not so severely this time, realizing that the looseness softened the planes in my cheeks. Ordinarily I needed no rouge, since my color was high, but today it helped my pallor.

"I cannot do this," I muttered to myself. How could I descend and receive Lord Sanderson when in my heart I knew that I had been ruined for any man? He had liked me and I had sensed that. And in truth I had found him attractive as well. There was an openness about him. So many of the men I had met these past weeks had either been so shy or so painfully self-absorbed that I could not even feign any interest. But Peter, Lord Sanderson, he had seemed different. Admittedly, that he was a friend of Oliver's served to heighten my interest. I had been so infatuated with my cousin as a child, and though that had certainly abated over the years, I did indeed adore him and trust his judgement.

It was odd. Four days ago, I thought, I should have been aflutter with nerves and excitement if I had just been told that Lord Sanderson had come to call. Today all that was left were nerves. I was shaking, but not with anticipation. Indeed, I had had these little spasms since the other evening.

Willing my mind to get control of myself, I smoothed the skirt of my gown and proceeded out of my room to the staircase. As I descended, I did so determined that if Lord Sanderson perchance showed me any interest, I would remain polite but distant. There was no sense in encouraging something that could never be, for either of us.

I was relieved when I entered the library to find him alone. It was the first time I had been in the room since the other night, but I could only focus on the bookcase when Lord Sanderson rose and strode over to me.

"Miss Barkham, may I say how delightful you look," he effused warmly, his hand closed about mine, which I had extended. "It was kind of you to receive me, particularly when your mother explained that you had been unwell these past days."

I withdrew my hand and motioned for him to sit over by the sofa, noting as he did that he cut a fine figure in his grey waistcoat and plaid vest.

"I expect it is just all these parties and balls," I murmured, thinking to myself that were he to know the truth, he would scarce be regarding me so admiringly. "We are very quiet in the north by contrast."

He smiled. "Not to hear your cousin, Oliver, tell of it. Life sounds very full at Camberleigh and Mayfair, though 'tis hardly surprising since the estates of your family are indeed one of the most commanding within our country."

Spying the teapot in front of me, I offered him a cup. He shook his head. "Your mother was kind enough to provide me with refreshment when I arrived. I fear I should swim away if I took any more."

I was surprised to hear myself laughing. He had a nice manner about him, I decided. The openness I had sensed on our first meeting was indeed not forced, and there was a pleasant easiness about him. I took a sip of tea and relaxed back into the chair opposite him.

He studied me quietly. "I hope you will not think me rude, Miss Barkham, if I tell you that I was indeed nonplussed at the Foxcrofts's the other evening. I am not the sort of man to dally with another's fiancée."

I started to interrupt, but he silenced me.

"You need not explain. It was only later, in speaking with Oliver, that I realized that Count de la Brocher is indeed a clever chap but not one to whom you have pledged yourself. At least not as yet."

I felt a deep flush spread over my face. "I can assure you, Lord Sanderson, that that would be the last thing I should ever do."

He appeared relieved. "I cannot deny that I am pleased to hear that, Miss Barkham."

"Daphne," I corrected.

He grinned. "Daphne, and then I should hope you will call me Peter."

I nodded, replacing the cup on the silver tray.

"I have to give the count credit in that he quickly managed to dismiss me. Admittedly, I feel foolish for swallowing the bait."

"If you wish to give credit, Peter, then give it where it is due. And that is, I assure you, not to Count de la Brocher."

Noting that he eyed me curiously, I quickly changed the subject. "You have not told me where your home is, Lord Sanderson."

"Peter," he corrected. "My family home is in Devon, Eltshire Hall, though I spend more time at our London house these days. Much admittedly to my parents' chagrin."

"They, I gather, reside at Eltshire."

He nodded. "With my brother and sister, both of whom, were, shall we say, late additions to the family."

I was amazed at how calm I was, catching myself only occasionally when my eyes focused on the bookcases. We talked at great length of his family. I, in turn, spoke of Alexander and our life at Mayfair. His father was a barrister, which was indeed his own ambition, and though I knew little of that life, I knew of its importance to the court. I was admittedly amazed at the amount of time that had passed when Mother entered the library.

"I trust that I have given you time to visit," she enthused, looking, I thought, perhaps too closely between the two of us.

"Ample, Lady Barkham," Peter replied, nearly bolting from his seat. "I must apologize for the lateness of the hour, Lady Barkham."

"Nonsense, Lord Sanderson," she replied. "Indeed, I only came in to ask, though short notice as it is, if you would like to join us for dinner."

I must admit that I was astonished by my mother's invitation. Not that she was not a gracious hostess—there were none who could surpass her in that realm—but I knew that she preferred to plan. Spontaneity, socially, was not her wont.

It was therefore that I suspected she was greatly relieved when Peter apologized, saying that he had a prior engagement. I had to admit that I was disappointed, and a part of me did indeed wonder where he would be spending his evening. Before I knew what had possessed me, I had interrupted, suggesting that perhaps Peter might join us the following evening. Ordinarily I would never have been so forward, but Mother indeed seemed pleased at my suggestion, and when Peter accepted instantly, I relaxed.

Sidney had no sooner closed the door on Peter when my mother turned to me, her face expectant, and asked, "Well?"

"Well what?"

Obviously rebuffed, she paused for an instant. "Am I being overzealous, darling? Do forgive me if I am. But he seems such a nice young man and certainly interested in you. I only wondered if you found him appealing."

"Well, I have asked him for dinner tomorrow, have I not?" I retorted. As soon as the words were out of my mouth, I regretted them. My pain was my own. My poor mother had nothing to do with it. Indeed, I knew in my heart that she only meant well.

I excused myself, assuring Mother that I would return for dinner. I crossed the long hallway to my room as quietly as possible, for the last thing I wanted was a confrontation with Constance. She had looked in on me these past few days, more from boredom, I suspected, than solicitude, but each time I had feigned sleep. She would be intensely curious, I knew,

about Lord Sanderson's call, and though I felt somewhat
guilty about shutting her out, I was not emotionally prepared
for her inquisition.

I did not know how I had allowed Mother to cajole me into
meeting with Peter. Indeed, I had thought after the evening
at the Foxcrofts's that that was the last I would see of him.
Though, admittedly, I had scarce given him a thought these
past days. My mind had become my worst enemy. Try as I did,
I could not banish the horror of the other evening. Veritably I
had come to wonder whether I could ever feel whole again.

I had cried until there were simply no tears left. My palms
were raw from where I had dug my nails into them in the
middle of the night to stifle the audibility of my heartbreak. I
had come close on several occasions to breaking my silence.
Mother had been so concerned, and there were moments when
I thought I could no longer contain this agony unto myself.
But though I longed for her to soothe me, to reassure me that
all was not lost, I always stopped myself short of confession.
In part I could not bring myself to burden her. Not that I ever
doubted her strength, but Mother had borne a great deal in her
life and I had always been loathe to cause her concern. But the
real reason for my silence, I knew, lay more in the warning of
the count.

It was not that I gave credence to it, rather that I could not
disprove it. If it was a ploy on his part, it was indeed a clever
one. What nagged at me was why he would need to fabricate
such a threat. I now reasoned that if I were to accuse him, he
might well only deny the assault. No matter how important the
Barkham name was, it would still be his word against mine.
Though I had been beyond reason at the time, I knew that his
plea had been impassioned. But was it to save his own reputation or indeed to protect Father?

I was tormented by the thought. Would my silence guard
him from unknown dangers or would it in fact plunge him into
greater risk? I did not know if the answer lay in the passageway, but somehow I had to find out. If only I could enlist the
aid of someone. Surely Oliver would help me. But did I dare
involve him in something so insidious that I knew not its
bounds? No. If I were to ferret out the truth, I would have to
do it on my own.

But for the moment I had to concentrate on keeping my
emotions in check. Beyond courage I would need sensibility in
the weeks ahead.

19

serena

PERHAPS I HAD been overzealous asking Lord Sanderson to dinner. But I thought I knew my daughter well enough to know that she was indeed enjoying his company. That he was enthralled with her did not take a mother to perceive. He was a nice young man. There was a young, ingenuous quality about him. Terribly unlike Justin, but then Justin was an uncommon man. I had dealt, I thought, well these past few days pushing my fears and suspicions aside, but suddenly I felt vulnerable once again. Daphne's courter only seemed to sanctify my suspicions about Justin. I suddenly felt so old. My life, and rightly so, was centering about my daughter, but simultaneously I felt as though I was losing my own center. Were it not that this season, I sensed, was an integrally important aspect of life for both girls, I thought I could call on dear Charlotte to pack and return full speed to Mayfair.

Charlotte, how quiet she had been these last weeks. But she was in such pain I could not ask more of her than I already had. She would be the first to encourage that I share my fears, my anguish, but though committed emotionally, she had not the strength, I knew, to help me through this period.

It had been five when Lord Sanderson had left. The clock had now chimed six, and Justin had not returned. My palms were rubbed sore with the chafe of my nails against them. All I wanted to do was to retire to my room and search my soul for some answer to my queries. But that would not be. My responsibilities today extended far beyond myself. What Justin and I had to resolve, we had to do it together. What I owed the girls was something I would do, I sensed, on my own.

At six-thirty I instructed the cook to serve dinner. There had been no sign of Justin, but I could no longer pace that space between the library and drawing room. I instructed Mary to call both girls to the table at seven. Ordinarily I would have changed for the evening meal, but I was too preoccupied watching the street corridors before the house to even think of my appearance.

It was but a few minutes before seven when, hearing a carriage approach, I ran to the front hallway, almost colliding with Oliver who, dripping from the elements, had vaulted through the front door. I looked beyond him but seeing nothing, searched his face for an explanation.

"Lord, 'tis a terror out there," he effused as I took his cloak and instructed one of the maids to place it in the kitchen to dry.

"Justin is not with you then," I said quietly.

He ruffled his hand through his hair, the spray dampening my face. "Serena, he has been delayed unavoidably. But he shall return later. Unless you and the girls have eaten, he assures us to proceed."

I wanted to ask where he was, to plead of some knowledge as to what was happening, but whether not to visit my concern on Oliver or because I was muted by my own helplessness, I remained silent.

I suppose I should have applauded Oliver that evening, for if I was preoccupied and the girls were unusually silent, he was his most charming self. Ordinarily I would have been appreciative of his zest and ebullience, of his attempts at humor, but this night I did not seem to be able to rouse myself beyond myself.

I ate, aware that every morsel lodged dryly at the back of my throat, ever watchful of the dining room door, expectant of Justin's return. By the time the tart and coffee had been served, I had given up hope and had no further heart for amenities. My only thankfulness was that Constance and Daphne, though silent, were not bickering. If Constance was fascinated with Lord Sanderson's call, she was not about to impart same, likely, I supposed, because her hopes had thus far been dashed by her own suitor.

Certainly not from a physicality but after coffee had been served, I felt myself descend into an exhaustion that had haunted me most of the day. The girls, independently, seemed relieved to be excused from the dining room, and I cannot say that I was disappointed. Constance, though admirably silent, had, when she had communicated, been suggestive, pointedly so.

That was the first evening that I knew that Clarissa had shared more with her daughter than I had dared imagine. There was nothing specific—what was the word? Innuendo? Yes, that was it. I prayed that the drift would pass Daphne. She was an impressionable and, I knew, a passionate girl. No, woman. There had never been any reason to discuss her father's past. Mine was simple—more complicated, but that there were no intimacies of a male-female nature somehow lessened the complications.

When Oliver begged me to join him for a brandy in the library, I was tempted, but I was not feeling terribly emotionally stable, and I was loathe to break down in front of him. The simpler thing would have been to confront him, but I was too on edge to do same. I loved Oliver, trusted him. Perhaps I was fearful of the truth.

And so it was that the girls retired and Oliver excused himself to the library. It was Pluck who followed me judiciously up the stairs to the bedroom, watching my every move. I undressed methodically, willing myself to quiet my inner turmoil.

The room was cold, and though normally I would have stoked the fire, I had not the energy or perhaps heart to do more than climb amongst the cool, crisp sheets, with Pluck warming to my side. The rain pelted incessantly against the roof, and though I oft found it a soft, reassuring sound, this night it seemed to intensify my own malaise. I prayed for sleep as tears welled in my eyes, and I tried to stifle the sobs that o'ertook me. Pluck, ever sensitive to my moods, cuddled closer to me, his tongue lapping my hand in reassurance of those things sensed but not understood.

I had no idea how long I had lain there, but when the distant chimes of the hallway clock struck ten and the space in the bed next to me was still cold and empty, I decided to get up and search out some warm milk from the kitchen to soothe my nerves. I reached to the end of the bed, pulling my robe up about me, simultaneously assuring Pluck to lie still, as I did not want him to awaken the rest of the household.

The hallway was drafty, causing the flame of my candle to
flicker, and I cupped my hand to protect the glow. I had no
more reached the top of the staircase when I was certain that
I heard voices from below. Why it prompted me to move
stealthily I knew not, but I was quickly aware that I did not
want whoever was below to suspect my presence.

I paused midway down the stairs as one of the steps emitted
a sharp creak as it bore my full weight. Once assured that it
had not aroused anyone below, I proceeded with my descent.
The door to the library was closed, but as I crossed to it, I un-
mistakably heard Justin's voice. My first instinct was to enter,
but garbed merely in my robe, my hair flowing loosely about
my shoulders, I could hardly intrude were there other than
family members with him.

Pressing my ear close to the door, I heard, "Justin, you cannot. There is too much danger already." Oliver, that was
Oliver's voice, but what was he warning Justin about?

Before I could puzzle it further, Justin replied, "Trinqué
has been threatened again."

"And well he should be; he will give the people nothing,"
was the response from a new voice. "Where are they to go to
build their houses—to keep warm in the winter, to graze their
stock?" the man continued. "The pasturing of any *bêtes à
laine* is now forbidden."

"They should have accepted the royal decree," Oliver interrupted.

"Bah," a new voice argued. "A lot you know of it. If we
allow it to continue, the people of the Ariege will be ruined.
There have already been more than thirty separate incidents in
the arrondissement of St. Girons by the demoiselles. And it
shall become worse. You simply must continue to use your influence with the crown."

I could not have been more puzzled. My mind struggled to
make sense of the conversation, wondering as I did who these
men were and what, if anything, did Justin have to do with affairs in France? Monique, I thought suddenly—did this have
to do with Monique?

I started suddenly as I heard Justin say, "It is late; nothing
more can be settled tonight."

I looked quickly about me. I could not chance being caught
on the staircase. My eyes spied the pillar at the back of the

hall, and extinguishing the candle I scampered to safety behind it. My heart was pumping at twice its regular rate as I heard Justin and Oliver move into the hallway. I could not fathom why the other men had seemed not to follow them, for though I dared not peer out from where I was secreted, I had hoped to hear them speak again.

"What of that other matter, Justin?" I heard Oliver ask suddenly.

Justin's voice was barely audible as he replied. "It is sadly becoming more difficult. It was simple when the house was not full, but now I feel I am trapped. She watches me constantly when I am with her."

"Hopefully, it shan't be much longer," Oliver replied.

Justin paused for a moment and then added, "We shall talk more of this tomorrow. For my part I am going to retire."

Oliver appeared in concert, for within seconds the two were climbing the stairs, leaving me unnoticed in the darkened passageway. At this moment I was frantic, for I had heard nothing of the departure of the other two men. It was inconceivable that Justin should have retired leaving these strangers in the house, but unless they had tiptoed out, sworn to silence, they had, I reasoned, to still be in the library.

I was at wit's end, for I could not remain where I was, and though I could not chance being discovered by these strangers, I knew that Justin, once finding me absent from the bedroom, would come in search of me. I clutched my robe about me and scurried over to the library. The door was slightly ajar, and when after listening for a moment I heard nothing from within, I inched the door further into the room.

Peering into the room I was completely befuddled to find it empty. Only the hiss of hot coals remained in the fireplace. Glasses with traces of brandy were the only sign that indeed four had occupied the room but moments before. I longed to inspect the room, but I knew that I not dare dally, and closing the door as quietly as I could, I moved to the staircase and, grasping the balustrade, pulled myself to the landing above.

Justin and I almost collided as I fell into the room against the door he was opening.

"Good Lord, where have you been, Serena?" he demanded, putting his arms about me.

"I was looking in on Daphne," I lied. "She has been a tad out of sorts these past days."

"Nothing serious, I hope."

"I think not," I replied, pulling away.

He watched me warily as I strode quickly over to the bed, disrobed and climbed quickly in. Pluck wriggled against me in welcome.

"You are miffed with me," he said quietly. "And I do suppose you have a right to be, though I did send word via Oliver. Did he not inform you that I should be detained?"

"He apprised me."

"It truly could not be avoided," he advised as he changed to his nightclothes. "There are demands. Things that simply cannot be avoided; I have explained that."

Have you? I wondered, biting my tongue as he crawled into bed next to me.

His hand brushed the hair back from my forehead. "Darling, I know I have been difficult since our arrival in London. Believe me, it has not been pleasant for me either. But if you can just have a bit of patience. Sometimes there are things beyond our control."

I willed myself to remain silent, fearful that my emotional state was so near a breaking point that were I to try to speak, much less confront this man who was fast becoming a stranger to me, I should lose control.

I stiffened as Justin's arms encircled me, pulling me brusquely towards him.

"You do not have to do that," I said flatly.

"That is an odd comment," he retorted. "It is scarce what I *have* to do, 'tis what I *want* to do."

I could not bear to listen. "Justin, I am tired. It has been a long day and 'twill be again tomorrow."

Whether I wanted him to insist on closeness or not, I need not have worried, he lessened his grip on me, I knew not whether from relief or respect for my wishes.

I remained very still as moments later Justin whispered my name, asking if I were indeed asleep. I did not like this deception, but I needed time to think of all that I had heard earlier on. There had been enough for me to know that this was not a casual encounter. Both Justin and Oliver knew these men intimately. One thing I knew for certain. This had nothing to do with the railroad venture, or the Camberleigh-Mayfair estates, for that matter. But whatever it was, it was of a serious enough nature that Justin felt that he could not share it with me. Or was it less that he could not than he chose not?

I was not accustomed to being shut out. After the devastation we had experienced at the hands of Philip Taggart, we had sworn that we would never keep anything from one another, no matter how difficult or painful. Fortunately, over the years I had had no need to even consider harboring anything from him.

I struggled to bring focus to what I had heard. The key seemed to be this area of France called the Ariege. This was the third time that I had heard mention of it. The first was at the dinner party at Count de la Brocher's. The next at Monique's. But why or how was Justin involved? Not to mention Oliver. It was obvious that this area of the Ariege was one of political unrest, perhaps even of revolution. It was true that Justin was a man of not inconsequential influence, but I could not fathom what role he would play in this area closer indeed to Spain than Paris.

My mind drifted back to the evening of the ball at the Foxcrofts's. Prior to that time I had believed that Justin was as much of a stranger to Count de la Brocher as myself. I had discounted that episode in the garden, when recognizing the two in conversation I had puzzled why they would have removed themselves from the soiree to meet. But Justin had been very clever in brushing the incident aside. It now seemed likely that the meeting was far from chance, that there had been a specific reason that they had planned that encounter.

What was Monique's part in this? That she was linked, there seemed no doubt. But though indeed a passionate woman, I had, in all the years I had known her, never suspected that she had political interests in France. Had my fears these past weeks been unfounded? I wondered. Could the notes, the meetings, Justin's absences have naught to do with a reawakened intimacy between the two but have something to do with this involvement with the Ariege?

I might have been able to convince myself of same if I had not heard Justin say what he had in the hallway. The only person he could have referred to would have been myself. What had he said? "She watches me constantly"—that was it. If I had to look at it honestly, I expect what he said was true. I *had* been watchful of him, hopeful, I suspect, for some sign, some clue as to the strangeness of his behavior. I hated myself for that, but I was also angered that I had been made to appear so foolish. Oliver's involvement in all this was terribly painful. Oliver, whom I had helped raise, whom I loved as I would my own brother, whom I thought would ever be my champion, had in fact simply been a foil. He knew full well what Justin was about. How often had Justin inveigled him to lie for him? What a fool he must think me. I could not damn his loyalty to Justin. He worshipped him, and I suspect that if he had been forced to make a choice, a decision between us, it was more natural that his final loyalty would be to Justin. But that did not serve to lessen my own pain.

I had debated once before about confronting Justin, but this time I closed the thought quickly from my mind. I had no reason to believe that he would be truthful with me. My best recourse was to remain silent. The less suspicious he was about my knowledge of any of this, the better chance I had to discover the truth for myself.

It was in the wee hours of the morning when I had finally drifted off to sleep, exhausted by the machinations of my own mind.

Justin was almost fully dressed when I awoke.

"I was commencing to worry about you," he said, crossing over to the bed. "I have never known you to toss and turn so."

As he leaned down and brushed his lips against mine, I wanted to scream out for him to hold me, to assure me that everything was fine, that I was not, as my darkest fears warned, losing my husband to a woman or a cause I did not understand.

Pulling back from me, he studied me long and hard. "Still miffed with me, I suspect."

I shook my head, averting his gaze. " 'Tis not that. I expect I am simply preoccupied."

"With what, my pet?" he asked, smoothing the hair back from my forehead.

"We are having a guest for dinner this evening, and I was just realizing that I had not alerted Charlotte or the cook."

"Ah. And who, might I ask, are we entertaining?"

"Lord Sanderson," I replied. "But then if you had been here yesterday, you would have known."

As soon as the words were out of my mouth, I regretted them, for I had promised myself the night before to keep my equilibrium, not giving Justin any cause to suspect the knowledge, though obscure, that I had.

"What I meant," I added quickly, "was that Lord Sanderson came to call yesterday. You remember, he was that nice young man whom we met at the Foxcrofts's. Oliver's acquaintance.''

"He came to visit Oliver, then," he pursued.

I shook my head. "To the contrary. He came to call on Daphne."

"Daphne," he exclaimed. "Why would he do that?"

Despite my mental state I was amused.

"You seem to forget, my dear, that the girls are amidst their season. Perhaps you did not notice it, but Lord Sanderson seemed quite taken with Daphne at the ball. Lord Sanderson, I suspect, would like us to consider him a likely suitor for our daughter."

He rose suddenly and commenced pacing about the room. "And Daphne, what does she think of this?"

"Frankly, I was delighted. She has seemed so out of sorts these past few days. It was no small feat to get her to agree to receive him, I can assure you."

"Then this is far from serious," he speculated.

"I do not know," I replied. "But I would certainly say that she is not discouraging this young man. And for my part, I am pleased. He has a nice way about him. I suspect he is a very gentle and honorable young man. Certainly Oliver would not have befriended him were he not."

" 'Tis nothing to trouble over, I suspect," Justin mused. "Daphne will likely break many hearts before finding the one that is right for her."

I studied him. "Are you implying that you do not think that Lord Sanderson would be a good match for Daphne?"

He shrugged. "I scarce know the chap. Seemed pleasant enough I suppose, though a bit comely for Daphne. He does not strike me as one who might keep her interest for long. She is not unlike her mother, you know," he added, winking at me. "She is going to need a strong man at the helm."

I remained silent pondering what he had said. He was not altogether mistaken, but if we were indeed alike, she would also need a man of honor and commitment. Daphne might yearn for excitement, but what I wanted more for her was love.

"I think perhaps the father doth protest too much," I challenged. "Could it be that none would be completely right for your little girl, who, I shall remind you, is near a grown woman."

"I suspect, if I am truthful, there is an element of fact there.

But I think it truly is my instinct that Daphne should be with a stronger man. Perhaps Lord Sanderson *is* that man. Only time will tell.''

"Well, in any event he is joining us for dinner," I replied, "and I do expect you to join us, if only for Daphne's sake."

He looked surprised. "Of course I shall be there," he assured. "Actually, if you have not informed the cook, I might ask if I might ask another to join us."

"Certainly," I replied, wondering who our additional guest might be.

"I shall send word via Sidney to Count de la Brocher, then," he replied. "I will have him inform you of his response."

I do not know what he could have said that would have shocked me more.

"That is not disagreeable, is it?" he pursued.

"No, no, not at all," I retorted, trying to maintain my composure. "I am simply surprised, that is all. If anything, I sensed that you had little in common with him."

There was an awkward moment, but then he responded, "Well, I expect I have not been very neighborly. And he did entertain you and the girls in my absence. Frankly, as we seem to run into him at these functions, it has become awkward not to extend our hospitality."

"Will you be venturing out early this morning?" I asked.

"Just for a spell. But I should return by early afternoon."

"Should I have the cook count on you for luncheon?"

He shook his head. "And as Oliver shall be with me, you can avoid a place setting for him as well."

I purposefully stayed quiet as Justin took Pluck in hand, assuring me once again that he would return well before our guests were expected. As he departed, the maid arrived with hot water for my bath basin. I advised her that I would take breakfast in my room, and twenty minutes later, when refreshed from my toilette and Charlotte arrived with my tray, I felt ready to face the day ahead.

Noticing that Charlotte seemed to be muttering to herself, I inquired if everything was all right.

"Don't ye be botherin' 'bout me, Serena," she assured. "'Tis just Miss Constance. That girl kin try a soul, she can."

"What now?" I pursued.

"Oh she's playin' ever so grand again. Fer me 'twouldn't be matterin', but she orders the maids round so they not know whether they be comin' er goin'."

"I cannot think what possesses her," I replied.

"Oh, I think I be knowin' this time," Charlotte advised. " 'Tis a twinge o' jealousy, me thinks. With Miss Daphne 'avin' a caller yesterday, our Constance has 'er nose out a joint."

I knew that Charlotte was likely to be right. "Well, perhaps this evening shall appease that a bit."

As I moved over to the dressing table and Charlotte commenced dressing my hair, she asked, "She's te 'ave a caller, then?"

"Not exactly. But I have invited Lord Sanderson to dine with us, and Justin has asked that we include Count de la Brocher as well."

"So that is why Cook is fussin' so. Near bit me 'ead off earlier. She even snapped at Mary, an' ye know those two are like peas in a pod."

"I should like it to be an elegant, festive evening," I pursued as Charlotte deftly wound two coils up from the center part. "Perhaps you could ask Sidney to fetch some baskets of flowers. I shall do some arrangements this afternoon."

She agreed.

As she began to take her leave, I asked, "Do you know if Justin is still about?"

" 'E left before I brought yer tray. With Master Oliver."

I was quietly pleased, for I needed some time and I could not risk being intruded upon. I loathed doing what I was about to, but I could not weaken. Were I to uncover the truth about what Justin was involved in and Monique's part in it all, I had to be purposeful and clever.

Once assured that Charlotte was out of earshot, I crossed over to Justin's dresser and gingerly opened the small drawer at the top. My hands shook as my fingers sorted through the layers of handkerchiefs in search of some paper, some clue. I had almost become convinced that my efforts were futile when my hand closed about a small velvet box in the bottom drawer. I pulled it out, careful not to disturb the scarves and gloves that secreted it. It was a small box, one that would, I thought, be likely to contain jewelry. Pushing the small brass clasp aside, I lifted the top back. Inside lay a woman's ring, a sizable emerald surrounded by two rows of small though seemingly perfect diamonds.

I could not think what this ring was doing there. Justin did

from time to time bestow gifts upon me, though they would
far more likely be pins or necklaces or earrings, as he knew
that the only rings that I daily wore were our betrothal rings.
There had been an enormous collection of jewelry that
Justin's mother had left upon her death, but those pieces had
long been given to Anne, save those few that she had insisted
that I take upon my marriage to Justin. No, this, I was certain,
had not been Lady Barkham's. But then to whom did it
belong? Or to whom was it intended to be given? It was not inconceivable that it was intended as a gift for Daphne, but
Justin would never make a purchase of this magnitude without
first consulting me. I withdrew the ring and turned it over in
my hand. What troubled me more than the discovery of it was
that I had this strange feeling I had seen this ring before, and
yet logically I could not think of why it triggered my memory.
I replaced it in the box, thinking that it simply must be similar
to one that I had seen on another at some time.

I knelt down and carefully replaced the box in the exact
location I had discovered it. Thus far I had successfully been
able to subjugate the question that fought for an answer. Had
I in fact happened on some bauble, some gift that Justin intended for Monique?

I hated myself for what I was doing, but I was also angry at
Justin, angry that he had forced me to stoop into this action of
distrust. Clenching my fists I moved over to his armoire and,
turning the key, put my hands out to catch the opening doors.
Methodically my hands searched his wardrobe, hoping to find
some missive that would explain the unexplainable, yet relieved, as I neared end, that I had come up empty handed. I
was about to close the armoire when I remembered suddenly
that it contained a false bottom, where Justin occasionally
kept notes and coins, which he maintained were for emergency
use. I knelt down and felt for the board, which, if on my
recollection, slid back to reveal a small opening, enough for a
hand to close about what was within. Pushing against the
board I struggled to move it back. I winced as a splinter bore
into my index finger, withdrawing it quickly to see if it had
drawn blood. Extracting the upright sliver I attempted once
again to move the board. No amount of effort on my part
seemed to have influence. The only way that I could dislodge
it, I decided, would be to use some tool to pry it open, and I
could not chance that discovery.

Dejected, I pulled myself to my feet and turned the brass

key in the lock. I determined that, were something indeed ferreted there, it had likely been there for years, for though I was scarce possessed with brute strength, I sensed that, had this cache been opened in recent weeks, I would have been able to have maneuvered it.

I moved myself over by the fireplace and, warming my hands before it, tried to assess any and all information I had to date. The more I thought, the less clarity I had. There was the note from Monique, Justin's disappearances, the secret meeting below focusing on the Ariege, the involvement of Count de la Brocher and now the ring. There had been one other thing, which, in truth, I had dismissed since Justin's return. When he had assured me that nothing had been taken after intruders had broken into the house, I had decided that, indeed, my notion of street urchins had been likely. But now it gave me pause. I could not afford to overlook the slightest occurrence that was out of the norm.

It was late morning when I finally descended to check on how the household was progressing for the evening. Justin had indeed extended the invitation to Count de la Brocher, who, Sidney informed me, had responded eagerly. After checking with Cook I set about arranging the baskets of flowers Sidney had purchased earlier, while Pluck, who had been kept from me most of the morning, shadowed my every move.

I took luncheon by myself in the breakfast room, since Charlotte had informed me that the girls, who had had their hair washed, preferred to remain in the warmth of their respective rooms.

20
daphne

I WAS BRUSHING my hair, seated close to the fireplace, when there was a knock at the door.

"Who is it?"

" 'Tis I," I heard Constance respond. "Might I come in?"

The last thing I needed was a confrontation with my cousin today, but I could not disallow her entry.

I did not look up but continued to fluff the damp strands of my hair before the fire.

"Primping for your Lord Sanderson, I see," she said, coming to sit opposite me.

"I have only had my hair washed, as have you," I retorted. "And I cannot think what would cause you to refer to Lord Sanderson as though I had some claim on him."

"Oh, Daphne, you can be dreary at times," she sighed. "He called on you yesterday, he is coming to dine this evening. I should say it is very clear that he intends to be a suitor."

"I scarcely know the man," I argued. "And I hope you shall not make more of this than it is—someone coming to dinner."

"I shall have better things to occupy me," she replied coyly.

I threw my head back and once again commenced brushing the heavy mane about my shoulders.

"What did you two talk about yesterday?" she pursued.

"We merely exchanged pleasantries," I replied. "He told me a bit about his family."

"Kathryn Foxcroft told me that his family has great influence and that they are terribly wealthy. Mostly inheritance, I believe."

I wondered at how Miss Foxcroft seemed to be so well acquainted with Peter, Lord Sanderson, but I did not want to pursue it with Constance.

"Well, I should not be too blasé about his attentiveness. I mean, he is scarcely my type, but it is not as if he is unattractive, and then with all that money . . ."

"Constance, must you always be obsessed with material things? For myself they are unimportant, at least in matrimony. No amount of fineries would bring solace if it were an unhappy union."

She shrugged. " 'Tis easy for you to say, because you know that you shall never want for anything. Your dowry alone makes you the potential belle of the season."

I deemed it best to remain silent to her barb.

"Well, since you obviously do not want to share anything about Lord Sanderson with me, I might as well return to my room," she said, flouncing towards the door. "Is that what you are intending to wear this evening?" she continued, pointing to the red taffeta gown on the bed.

I shrugged. "In truth I have not decided."

"Well, I shall not wear red, just in case."

As Constance left, I could not help but be amused. She was aching, I knew, to discover more about Lord Sanderson. In truth, I was not being obsequious, for I myself had little more than a sense of him. I was fond of Constance in my own way, but I had also learned in those years since she had come to live with us that she rarely passed the time of day without some ulterior motive.

I could not chance her saying or doing something that would prove an embarrassment to Peter, not to mention to myself. I truly did not think she was a malicious girl—simply insensitive at times.

I had thought that the red gown would be appropriate, but as I looked at it now, it did not seem right. I went to the armoire and commenced sorting through the endless variety. My eyes narrowed on one that I had not worn before, an emerald green taffeta with high puff sleeves and a particularly full skirt with a scalloped hemline. I withdrew it and held it up to me before the mirror, swooping my hair back to see the effect.

As I stood there, sudden despair o'ertook me. "What am I doing?" I challenged to my own reflection. "I am fussing about here as though Peter truly is a suitor. Even if he were interested the slightest bit in me, how interested would he be if he knew . . . knew that I had been violated by another?"

I threw the gown against the chaise and sank down on the bed. What was I to do? I wondered. I could not in all conscience give Peter any encouragement. I had not the right to receive his attentions. But what was I to say to him? Do not waste your time with me, for I am soiled goods? What did I expect him to say? Oh, trouble yourself not, Daphne, it makes no difference. No, Lord Sanderson was a man who would demand a great deal of the woman he would marry, and her being uncompromised was an absolute.

Desperately I wished that this dinner was not to take place. If I feigned illness at this point, I knew that Mother would become suspicious. I had worried her too much already, and I could not risk that this time she would indeed fetch the doctor. No, I would have to make an appearance, and I would have to be amicable. But I would not give any encouragement.

I bit my lip, trying to suppress the tears. It was not fair. I was the innocent in this. My ruination had not been by my own provocation. I had been wantonly brutalized by some madman, spoiled for any other, and nothing that I might ever do or say could change that. Count de la Brocher would go about his ways, his associates and friends never suspecting that he was so evil. Of course, it was likely that there had been others, but I could not even think of it. It simply was too distasteful.

Happily, Constance stayed to herself the remainder of the afternoon. Seeking to get my mind off the evening, I commenced a letter to Alexander. I had not much to recount save the balls and dinners, but I tried to keep the tone as light as possible lest he should sense that something was awry with me. As different as we were, Alexander had always had an uncanny way of reading my moods, sometimes knowing that something was amiss even before I recognized it. I missed his presence here at Channing Hall, though I knew that he would quickly have become impatient with this season of ours. In that he was blameless, for in truth, if I had my druthers, I would be on the first coach back to Mayfair at dawn.

Charlotte came by in the late afternoon to help me with my hair. I was careful to appear more ebullient than I certainly felt, for Charlotte, as with Alexander, was not easily fooled. Seeing her move so slowly and in such obvious pain, I oft felt selfish when I welcomed her help, but Mother had assured me that it gave her great pleasure, and thus I did not object.

She dressed my hair high at the crown, with soft waves falling about my face and then cascading down my back from a knot that she fastened at the back. We debated the use of combs but settled in their stead for a ribbon that matched the dress, which she wove deftly through the heavy curls at the back.

It was almost six o'clock when I stood before the mirror critically studying my reflection. It was a lovely dress, and I had to admit that the color was good for me. Ordinarily I would be feeling great excitement at the anticipation of this evening, but right then I was only willing myself to struggle through it.

Mother had been very specific that Constance and I should be down in the drawing room by six, and knowing that my cousin was invariably late, I thought it best that I fetch her before descending.

I must say that I was taken aback when she permitted me entry to her room, for she had selected a gown that I found more appropriate for a ball than for a small dinner gathering at home.

"Do you like it?" she cooed, twirling the yards of sky-blue silk about her.

I nodded. "The color is lovely on you."

She looked pleased, and I swallowed my temptation to add that it was a bit much for the evening. I waited as she picked up the fan Mother had given her. With one last tug at the sleeves, which served to drop the neckline even further than it was, she turned to me and exclaimed, "I think this should prove a very interesting evening, cousin dear."

21

serena

IT WAS ALMOST three when, after having exhausted myself preparing endless bouquets and fussing over the table settings, I returned to the bedroom. It was still early, and I told myself not to fret that Justin had not returned. He *had* promised, and if not for me, he would not disapoint Daphne, much less insult the count, since he had made such a point of inviting him.

I did not know when I had drifted off to sleep, but I awoke with a start as Charlotte entered.

"I be thinkin' I best rouse ye," she said, lighting some candles.

"What time is it?" I replied, near jumping from the bed.

" 'Tis five by the chimes."

"I cannot believe Justin is doing this," I murmured angrily.

"What kin be the matter, Serena?"

I shook my head. "He promised that he would be home tonight. I cannot believe that he would embarrass me so."

"Well, ye 'ave naught te worry then, fer Lord Barkham is downstairs with Oliver. 'E looked in on ye earlier, but ye were sleepin' so soundly 'e told me 'twas better te let ye rest."

I felt foolish about my outburst, and relieved.

Charlotte helped me with my hair and was just fastening the velvet buttons at the back of my gown when Justin entered the bedroom.

He laughed as Pluck scampered forth barking his greeting.

"You were sleeping so soundly, darling, that I was loathe to disturb you earlier," he said as he came over and placed a kiss on the nape of my neck.

I reached up and clasped my hand about his. "I am just relieved to find you here."

"Is that gown new?" he asked.

I shook my head. "But I think I may have only worn it once before," I replied, smoothing the mauve velvet skirt.

"Well, it becomes you."

"Ye be needin' me fer anything else?" Charlotte asked.

"Just one thing," I replied. "If you would keep Pluck within your quarters tonight, I should appreciate it."

Pluck, hearing his name, came to me and pressed his full weight against my leg. I rubbed his ears and encouraged him to go with Charlotte, which he did grudgingly.

"Did you have a pleasant day?" I broached tenuously.

"I think a better word would be full," Justin replied as he commenced changing his attire.

"I expect that Sidney apprised you that Count de la Brocher shall be joining us this evening."

"What?" he said absently. "Oh, yes, the count, yes, I know he shall be dining with us."

I took a deep breath and ventured. "I had thought of asking Monique."

"Monique?" he exclaimed. "Why would you do that?"

"Why would I not?" I challenged, watching him carefully. "Particularly now that the count will be joining us."

He had turned away from me, so I could not watch his expression, but I had the distinct impression that my suggestion had made him uneasy. If indeed I might have at that point pressed and gleaned further reaction, I was fearful that it might put a pall on the evening.

Justin finished dressing in silence, but I waited for him so that we might descend together. I was delighted to see that Oliver and the girls were already in the drawing room. Admittedly, I was not as at ease as I would have liked. As determined as I was to maintain a sense of calm, I was watchful of Justin, though that was not at present my major concern. I had not informed the girls that Lord Sanderson was not to be our only guest this evening. Nonetheless there was something about Constance's demeanor that made me suspect that she knew that Count de la Brocher had been included, and though he had made no effort, to my knowledge, to call on her, I think she still fancied that he had taken a particular liking to her. Daphne, on the other hand, I knew had formed an almost immediate dislike for the man. I sensed that there was more there than I perhaps knew, for though he had been curt with her over the music box incident, he had clearly sought her out at the Foxcroft ball. I prayed that his presence would not mar the evening, for I indeed believed that she was more than a little pleasured by Lord Sanderson's attention.

Both girls, I admired, could not look more beautiful. Constance's gown I found inappropriate, but the color matched her eyes, and I had not the heart to suggest that she had overdressed for the evening. It was amazing what a contrast the two made. Daphne, tall and regal with an aura of still unbridled passion and adventure, and Constance, diminutive, a rosebud that one wondered if 'twould ever come to full flower.

Justin had only just offered us some refreshment when Sidney announced that Lord Sanderson had arrived.

I could not help noticing that Justin eyed him guardedly as his trim, smiling figure strode into the dining room, turning his first greeting to me. I was dearly grateful for Oliver's presence, for while Justin appeared a bit reticent in his welcome, Oliver made strides to make his friend feel welcome.

I could not help but notice that Constance was a bit more effusive than I thought necessary, but it helped to counter Daphne, who appeared oddly subdued.

"And how, might I ask, did you and Oliver here come to become acquainted?" Justin broached, handing him a glass of port.

"Actually 'twas in America," Lord Sanderson replied. "Well, that is not wholly true. It was several years ago, and we were returning on the same boat."

"Ah, that would have been when you took Rebecca back to visit her family," I recalled.

Oliver nodded. "And a rough journey that was. Rebecca was confined to bed for the most of it, and I, who suffer from cabin fever, took to prowling about the decks. Peter here became a welcome companion those days."

"Was this a voyage of pleasure, Lord Sanderson?" I pursued.

"I fear not, Lady Barkham. Indeed, my father has some business dealings there, and as my own mother had taken ill round the time of departure, he sent me in his stead."

"Oh, *do* tell us what it was like," Constance encouraged.

He had just commenced on a most interesting recounting of his travels when Sidney announced that Count de la Brocher had arrived.

There was a mixture of reaction that I had only seconds to notice before his tall frame appeared in the doorway. Daphne emitted a loud gasp, while Constance's face was wreathed in smiles, and I somehow knew then that his presence here was of no surprise to her. I met Lord Sanderson's gaze for only a moment but long enough to catch the obvious displeasure in his eyes.

Fortunately, before I had time to worry the situation, Count de la Brocher strode into the room, his hand extended to Justin. I watched the greeting between the two, looking for something, a look, a gesture that would give rise to my suspicion that each knew the other far better than they cared or dared admit.

I could not help think, as he took my hand, that there was a certain magnetism about the man. Like Justin, one could not overlook his presence in a room, and though I found Lord Sanderson to be genuinely attractive, I did have to admit that Count de la Brocher far overshadowed him.

I thought Constance's eyes would never stop fluttering as he complimented her on her gown. But it was to Daphne that he seemed most drawn, though in this case his admiration was silent.

"I think my daughter has lost her voice," Justin suggested as he gave the count a glass of port. "If that is true, it shall be the first time. My daughter is very like her mother—scarcely shy of her opinions."

"And very beautiful," the count replied, raising his glass in toast to myself and Daphne respectively.

"Oh, *do* come and sit over here by me," Constance urged. "It is so much cozier by the fire."

I was almost relieved by Constance's suggestion, for the count had barely taken his eyes off Daphne, whose sudden paleness was alarming. I hoped that I was the only one who had noticed it, but Lord Sanderson had too, for he sat forward suddenly, asking if he might get a glass of water or something for Daphne.

If I had not known better, I would have thought that she was in some sort of trance, for until Lord Sanderson repeated his question, she seemed not to have heard him.

I watched her carefully as she seemed to recover her composure.

"No, no, Peter, I am quite all right, truly," she assured.

I noticed that eyebrows raised round the room at her use of his given name, but he seemed truly cheered that, whatever the moment, it had passed.

I could have kissed Oliver, for he managed immediately to banish all awkwardness by regaling us all with tales of his ship's passage with Lord Sanderson. Justin managed to join in, though he was obviously circumspect about leaving the sordid details of his harrowing journey at the hands of Philip Taggart unspoken. There were few who knew us well who did not know the whole of the story, if not in detail, but with strangers there was no need to dredge the unpleasantness of the past. When Sidney announced that dinner was served, I was amused that Lord Sanderson nearly leapt to Daphne's side.

I had taken care to seat Daphne next to him at the table, with Constance between Oliver and Count de la Brocher at opposite. I had purposefully placed the count on Justin's end of the table, for I suspected that I would glean more from watching the interchange between the two than by monopolizing his attention.

Justin appeared to have warmed a bit to Lord Sanderson, and as the first course of smoked whitefish was served, I tried to relax a bit.

"You must miss your homeland, Count de la Brocher," I ventured, taking advantage of the break in conversation. "Do you plan to travel there soon?"

I noticed the quick look that passed between him and Justin before he replied.

"It is true that France is my home, Lady Barkham."

"Serena," I corrected.

"But for the present I am just as well pleased to reside here in London."

"Ah, that must be because of the problem in the Ariege," I ventured. "Are your lands threatened? If I recall, you have a château, sizable estates within the area."

"Let me just say that it is not safe at present for some seigneurial families presently in the area."

"Then the peasants continue to harass you?"

His eyebrow raised, he regarded me quizzically. "You misunderstand, Serena, my sympathies are with them.''

"More's the pity for them," Daphne, who had been strangely silent, exploded. "It appears you have changed your tune, Count de la Brocher. Why, at dinner with your friends— Monsieur DeMarcier, was it not—you quite sounded as though you would have them all shot. Or perhaps you would fancy doing that yourself.''

I was shocked speechless.

Before I could find my voice, Justin had thrown his napkin on the table, exclaiming Daphne's name.

"I cannot think what has come over my daughter, Count, but I must apologize for her outburst. As will she.''

Daphne's color was so high that I almost ran to her to see if she was all right. Constance started muttering something innocuous. Daphne suddenly burst into tears and, pushing herself back from the table, ran sobbing from the room.

"What in blazes?" Justin exclaimed, looking to me for some explanation.

"Let me go after her," Oliver said quickly.

But Count de la Brocher was already to his feet. "No, as it is obviously I who have provoked her, let me see to her.''

It scarcely seemed appropriate, but I was too confused and embarrassed to resist.

"You know now I am convinced of it," Constance piped up suddenly. "I *do* think Daphne is quite daft. She has been insulting to me for weeks now, and I could not think why, but now, well the poor dear is obviously not mentally sound. I mean . . .''

"That is enough, Constance," I advised sternly, wishing that she had kept silent, for at that moment Oliver had arisen and whispered something to Justin.

No one had given any thought to poor Lord Sanderson, who sat quietly thoughtful.

"Lord Sanderson, I must apologize," I said. "Believe me, this is not like Daphne. She has not seemed well this past week, and I chastise myself for not calling the doctor in. At her insistence I did not, but I suspect that she was merely trying not to concern me.''

He shook his head. "Please do not think you need apologize, Lady Barkham. I think I know what might have provoked this. Daphne, I know is a very reasonable young woman.''

"*You* think you know what incited this?" I pressed.

He paused for a moment, wiping his mouth with his napkin. " 'Tis a silly matter and perhaps indelicate to recount, but I am reminded that at the Foxcroft ball Count de la Brocher suggested to me that he was affianced to your daughter."

"That is not possible," Constance interrupted.

"I know that now, but it was a successful enough deception to discourage my pursuance of your daughter. I have to admit it angered me later, but simultaneously I had to give the chap his due."

I was incredulous that Justin was laughing.

"I scarce see the humor in this, my dear," I advised.

"Forgive me," he quieted. " 'Tis of no affront, Lord Sanderson, I assure you. But knowing my daughter and the count . . . well, it does amuse me."

In the most naive way of all he had admitted a fact that I had searched for for weeks. This was in no way a chance meeting. Somehow, somewhere, within some space that I still did not understand, Justin and Count de la Brocher were far more than merely acquainted.

"I can appreciate your position, Lord Barkham," Lord Sanderson replied. "But I trust, though a secondary one, that you can see mine."

Oliver now was the one borne to laughter. "She has been a rascal since she was knee high," he reminisced. " 'Tis not surprising that she should be the center of such controversy today."

"It is amazing, dear Oliver, that you like the rest continue to defend her so. I certainly do not wish my cousin ill, but instead of taking all this lightheartedly, I would suggest that each of you should realize that the poor dear is not sound of mind or perhaps even of body."

"Oh, Constance, please," I moaned. "This is becoming tiresome."

"You are all so blind," she retorted. "My evening is ruined. All our evenings are ruined, thank you, due to precious Daphne. Well, one day you shall see how mistaken you are. You mark my words."

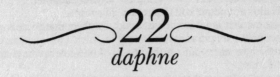

22
daphne

I HAD RUN from the dining room into the library not by intent, simply that in my despair I had escaped to the place of closest tranquility. I sank into the sofa, frightening myself as my hand pounded the plumpness of the pillow beneath.

"How could you?" I moaned.

My anger was directed wholly at my mother, and yet I knew in my heart that unwittingly she had constructed the entourage for this evening's dinner. In truth it was myself that I was angry with. I had made a fool of myself, of my family. The only one who would escape from this unblemished was the only one who should not.

I had not heard the door to the library open. He was before me before I was aware of his presence in the room.

"How dare you follow me here," I assaulted.

"Who better, Daphne, like it or not? I may be the one person who understands your turmoil at this moment."

I could not bear to look at him. "You?" I challenged. "Oh, yes, I suppose there is partial truth in that, for it is indeed you who have cast me in this state."

"It is regrettable that you appear so distressed. Believe me, Daphne, would if I could rescind what happened the other evening, I would. I desired you from the moment I first saw you. I cannot tell you that I regret our union, simply the fashion of its coming about, for instead of bringing you to realize

159

the passion that burns between us, it has left a bitterness within you that blinds you to the good."

"What nerve, what stretch of imagination, causes you to believe that there is or ever could be anything between us except loathing? I detest you, Count de la Brocher."

"I am certain you have heard it said, Daphne, that there is a fine line between love and hate."

"Just know which side of the line I fall on when it comes to you," I snapped.

I cast my eyes up to his face, surprised at how troubled his visage was. I felt a moment's exhilaration. If I had hurt him only slightly, it might help me dispel some of my own pain.

"Be that as you will it," he replied slowly. "I *am* thankful for one thing. That being that you have remained silent about the other night. I cannot emphasize to you enough how dangerous it might be should anyone know that you have knowledge of that passageway. Your silence is the only way you can protect Justin."

"You have bought my silence only because my humiliation is too great to share it with anyone. I have no cause to believe that these threats of yours have any substance. Likely 'tis just a ruse. But I shall uncover the truth, and when I do, I shall expose you for the beast you are. If there are secrets buried in that passageway, I shall uncover them at whatever cost to myself. And I forewarn you, that if and when I unravel this deception, you will best be far gone from England if you intend to continue to be a free man."

His eyes narrowed. "Do not be a fool, Daphne. You have it now in your power to cause untold harm, to all of us but primarily to Justin. Think what you will of me, but do not do something you will regret for a lifetime."

His vehemence momentarily gave me pause. I took a deep breath before responding. "It is you who shall have the regrets, Count de la Brocher. I do not know whether it shall take me a day or weeks, even months. But I shall be unfailing in my efforts to discover the truth. If it gives you any self-satisfaction, then know that in the interim I shall be silent. Not because you intimidate me, but because I cannot bring myself to inflict pain on my loved ones."

"And about Lord Sanderson?" he pursued.

"What has he to do with this?"

"It would take a fool not to see that he is ever so taken with you," he replied. "Not that I blame him."

"Peter, Lord Sanderson, is none of your business."

" 'Tis only my business if you were to tell me that you shared his interest."

"I shall tell you nothing," I snapped, "except to say that I find Peter to be charming and decent. He is very kind by nature, but then that is not a characteristic you would recognize."

He studied me for a moment. "I cannot deny that he seems a pleasant enough chap, but he is not for you, Daphne. You are a woman who needs adventure, excitement in your life. You would quickly become bored by Lord Sanderson. He is not enough of a man for you."

"And I suppose you think that by violating me you have expressed your male superiority? Let me assure you, you have only shown that you are less than a man."

He had not moved from his stance before me this whole time, but now suddenly he reached for me, grabbing my wrist. I wrenched away from him, putting him slightly off balance.

"Do not *ever* touch me again," I warned.

His eyes narrowed and he stepped fully back from me.

"Some day I fear you shall regret that, Daphne."

I did not know how I mustered the courage to return to the dining room, for I felt as though all emotions had been spent. As watchful as Mother and Father were of me upon my return, Peter, gentleman that he was, made a supreme effort to recoup the evening by being light and conversational. Constance's eyes bore daggers, but she seemed quickly assuaged when Count de la Brocher focused his attentions on her. He had no scruples, this man, and though I cared not what he said or did, I knew how vulnerable Constance was, and I did not want to see her hurt as well.

It seemed the longest evening of my life. When finally I retired to my room, I thought I would collapse from relief or despair, I knew not which. I had excused myself after dinner, feigning a headache, but from politeness or concern none had objected. Peter had taken his leave, and the rest had retired to the library for a brandy. Constance, I knew, was not about to let any moments pass while Count de la Brocher was under our roof. If only I might warn her, be honest with her. But I could not. For though I had no care, certainly no trust in the count, perhaps from fear I could not risk challenging his warnings.

I had told him that I would remain silent. And I would.

I had pulled the covers up about me when there came a knock at the door. I stayed silent, begging that whoever it was would disappear, believing that I was indeed fast asleep.

The door handle turned, and simply by her footsteps and scent I knew it was Mother.

She approached the bed quietly, saying nothing but laying her cool, slender hand to my forehead.

"I am not asleep," I whispered.

She sat down gently on the bed aside me. "I am not going to push or question, Daphne. I only want you to know that I know that something is troubling you. Lord Sanderson told me what Count de la Brocher had done the night of the Foxcroft ball, and though I cannot think what possessed the man, I think you are overreacting."

"Would you mind if we did not discuss this now, Mother?" I beseeched.

She rose patting my hand. "It is late and we all need our sleep. I only wanted you to know that I am here if you should care to speak of this, or any matter, for that reason."

She leaned down and kissed my forehead. I fought to hold back the tears and, worried that I might break down completely, murmured only a good night.

23

serena

I WAS TROUBLED as I made my way to our bedroom. There was
more to this rift between Daphne and Count de la Brocher
than anyone knew. Of that I was certain. But pressing her
would be senseless. Daphne was a very private person. If there
indeed was something more, the sharing of same would have
to be on her own initiative.

If I had to speculate, the count's interest in Daphne was
more than a passing fancy. Constance had deluded herself into
believing that he had intentions towards her. But save the evening of the dinner party at his home, his regard for her appeared polite but reserved. Unless my instincts deceived me, it
was Daphne that he wished to woo. He did not like seeing
Lord Sanderson as a rival, and a rival he was. There was no
question that he would pursue Daphne, and I could not say I
was displeased. If a bit reticent, he was a charming young
man, and when the count was absent, Daphne appeared to
genuinely enjoy his company.

There was one disturbing thought that I could not dismiss. I
remembered back through the years to when, as a young girl
of Daphne's age, I had reacted as ferociously against Justin. I
had spent so many months believing that I had never loathed
another as much. In my case it had taken a series of rather
drastic occurrences to bring me to the awareness that 'twas not
loathing but love that I felt for him. Could it be that history

was repeating itself? I wondered.

The evening had proved frustrating, for though I had watched and listened intently, there had been no exchange between Justin and the count that had brought me any further in understanding what the relationship between the two might truly be. I was a fool to have expected anything different. If there were some sort of collusion between the two, and perhaps Oliver as well, they would certainly have taken special care not to arouse my suspicions.

Pluck was curled by the fire when I entered the bedroom, and I strode over to him, ever delighted by his affectionate greeting. I had only been in the room for a moment when Justin joined me there.

"I take it Count de la Brocher has departed?" I queried.

He nodded, striding over to me. "It turned into quite a tempestuous evening, did it not, my love? I must say, though I listened to Lord Sanderson's speculation, I cannot see why Daphne should carry on so. I thought she could take a good tease."

"If it *was* a tease," I murmured.

"Surely you jest," he replied. "Luke would have no cause for seriousness with Daphne, not with me as her father."

Surprised, I looked up at him. Never before had he mentioned the count by his given name, and it had rolled off his lips as one who was not a mere acquaintance of this man.

He put his arms about me, his lips brushing my forehead. "In any event I am pleased that you are still up, for there is something that I must discuss with you."

"It sounds serious," I replied.

"Oh, I should not say serious, but I know that it shall not please you."

I sank into the chair before the fire, pulling Pluck close to my knees.

"Well?"

"It is going to be necessary for me to leave London again for a spell."

My heart sank. "Oh, Justin, no, not again, I beg of you."

"Serena, I swear to you I have no choice in this. Were it not of dire importance, I would not even consider it. Please try to be understanding."

"Understanding?" I choked. "I think my patience has been tried long enough, Justin. When you *are* here, you are never here save for the nights. I expect that I should be happy that you are at least sleeping in your own bedroom. But then you take off, for weeks on end, with some feeble story about problems with the railroad. You return expecting everything to go on as usual, and now you tell me that you must leave again? What excuse are you going to give me this time?"

I was shaking as Justin came forward and put his arms about me.

"Good Lord, Serena, I have never seen you like this."

I shrugged him off. "Do not think you can appease me with affection, Justin. Not unless you are prepared to tell me that you will cancel this trip or whatever you are planning."

"Well?" I pursued, noting the despair in his eyes.

He was silent.

"There you see—you have no intention of remaining here with me. What use is there my beseeching you to remain? I can see it in your face. You have determined to leave. Well, then, leave."

I rose and strode over to the armoire, where I commenced undressing.

"Serena, I beg you to have trust in me," he begged. "This is something that cannot be avoided. You know that I have responsibilities. This business needs my attention. Oliver shall accompany me, for I shall need his assistance. We should only be gone one, two weeks at most."

"I expect that you have forgotten, but we are hosting a ball the Saturday following next."

He rubbed the back of his neck. "In truth I had, though I swear to you that I shall return in plenty of time for it."

"You may not care about me, but you will disgrace Constance and your own daughter if you are not at my side to receive our guests."

"You have my word," he assured.

"I am not certain what that is worth these days," I mumbled to myself as I climbed into bed.

As Justin drew the covers back and slipped beside me, I could feel my whole body cry out in ache for him. I needed him, needed his passion to dispel my worst fears. But I fought my responses as his fingers brushed my shoulder.

"Do not draw away from me, darling," he pleaded. "I want you. I need to carry a sense of you with me when I am away."

I had never used our lovemaking as a wedge between us, but I could not welcome him to me this night. Not until somehow I could lay my suspicions to rest. Thankfully he did not press me, for I did not know if I could trust my body to be in concert with my mind. I turned over on my side, biting my lip as I heard Justin whisper, "I love you, Serena."

Justin was packing the next morning when I awakened. "Good morning," he said tentatively.

There was no use continuing our argument of the evening prior. I sensed that nothing I could say or do would dissuade him, and I had already said enough for him to wonder whether I was suspicious.

"I hope you won't leave without saying goodbye to the girls," I said quietly.

He smiled. "I have already tended to that."

"Were they upset?"

He shrugged. "One never knows with Constance. Though Daphne visited her own displeasure. I expect I am not a terribly popular fellow hereabouts this morning."

"Does that surprise you?" I charged.

"I wanted you to know that I have employed another coachman for the journey so the household will not be disturbed," he advised.

"Might I ask where you shall be heading?"

"Back up to Northallerton."

"I see."

He had pulled the last strap on his valises and turned to face me. "I hate leaving you like this," he said, his eyes searching my face.

"You know my answer to that."

He strode over to me, climbing over Pluck, who had put himself in his path. "One kiss for luck?"

I almost dissolved as he took me in his arms, holding me tight to his strong chest. One tear had managed to escape, and the salt of it I tasted as his lips pressed against mine.

"Promise me you will call on Mary and Charlotte and, of course, Sidney to help you these next weeks."

"Frankly, I am thankful that I shall have something to occupy my time."

He pulled me forward, gently kissing each eyelid.

"The time will pass quickly, you will see."

I nodded as he rose and collected his baggage.

"Justin?"

"Yes, darling."

"Be careful."

I watched him leave, wondering if I had done the right thing. Perhaps it would have been better to have laid bare all my suspicions, all my accusations, and demanded the answers I sought. With Justin and Oliver gone, I had little hope of learning anything further until their return.

The first week of Justin's absence passed surprisingly quickly. Acceptances to our invitation continued to arrive daily, making me wonder where I was going to put all the people. Mary and Charlotte were dear, spending each morning reviewing menus, arranging for the musicians, planning how the drawing room would be rearranged to open into the great room to accommodate the dancing.

It was during the evening of the second day that I came upon an idea that I chastised myself for not having thought of earlier. I went to the library, withdrew some paper from the drawer, and proceeded to invite Monique to luncheon two days hence, begging her assistance with plans for the ball.

As I sealed the note, I experienced a moment's hesitancy about actually sending it. It was pure deception on my part. I did not want Monique's assistance, though to her credit she was most adept at planning social functions. I wanted the time with her, hopeful that were I careful not to appear suspicious, I might elicit some information about the situation in France and indeed how Justin was involved in it. I could hardly confront her about her liaison, if indeed one had been renewed with my husband. But I knew Monique well, and though she was clever, I did not think she would be able to fool me. If only from instinct, I suspected that I would have my answer.

I gave the note to Sidney and bade him to take it straightaway to Monique, asking for an answer before returning. I felt foolish sending him off into the night at this hour, but I could not trust my nerve to the next morning.

The girls had asked if trays might be sent to their rooms, and though I would have preferred their company, I did not object. I took my own meal in the breakfast room, carefully penning the first lot of place cards for the ball.

It was there that Sidney found me. I took the manilla envelope he handed me and, assuring him that I would need him no longer that evening, set to opening it.

Dearest Serena, *I read.*

You know there is nothing that would make me happier than to help you *mais malheureusement* I have been suffering from some malaise this past week which has kept me to my bed. I should be well again by the time of your soiree if I do as the doctor advises. I am bored to tears but trust you understand. My love to you and girls.

                                                    Monique

I reread the note several times before replacing it in its envelope. I had no reason to suspect that she was indeed not ill, save one thing. She specifically sent her love to myself and the girls. There was no mention of Justin. That was not like Monique, unless she knew that Justin was not at Channing Hall. But how would she know that, unless Justin had told her. What proof did I have that Justin had indeed gone to Northallerton? For all I knew this was all a ruse, and he was ensconced at Monique's, revelling in how clever he had been.

I had to stop thinking like this. I was tormenting myself with these suspicions, and if I did not stop, it was I who would find myself ill in bed.

One thing gave me respite from the obsessive wanderings of my mind over the next few days. Lord Sanderson became a regular caller at Channing Hall. Although Daphne did not appear exactly aflutter in his presence, she was not without enthusiasm, and at the least his visits seemed to be taking her out of herself. I realized that this put Constance in a somewhat awkward position, for though she had the good sense not to intrude on the visits between her cousin and Lord Sanderson, it only served to obviate that Count de la Brocher's intentions towards her were less than serious.

Thus when she begged me to take the coach out to visit the shops, I had not the heart to deny her. Indeed she had given me no further cause for alarm since I had spoken to her weeks past.

It was on the afternoon of the sixth day after Justin's departure that, having taken a brief nap, I rose and with Pluck at my heels went down to the library intent on completing the place cards for the ball.

I had but closed the door to the library when I had a strange sense that something was amiss. I looked about the room, my eyes stopping on a variety of familiar objects. Nothing seemed to be misplaced, but I could not dismiss my air of apprehension. I would not have thought anything about it except that we had had intruders the month past, and I shuddered to think that it might have happened again.

Going in search of Charlotte, I found her in the kitchen. Not wishing to alarm the rest of the household, I asked her to join me in the library, where I had left Pluck.

"Somethin' seems te be troublin' ye, Serena," Charlotte noted.

"You will think me foolish perhaps, but I think something is amiss in here."

"What do ye mean?"

"I wish I knew," I replied, studying the room. "I know what it is. The steps, they have been moved."

"I cannot be thinkin' why," Charlotte replied. "Must a bin one o' the maids."

I shook my head. "They cannot possibly have budged them," I said, looking at the eight tiered steps crafted out of solid mahogany.

"Who would want te be movin' them?" Charlotte pursued.

"I do not know, but it gives me an uncomfortable feeling. Are you quite certain that those new locks are secure?"

" 'Tis odd that ye should mention it, but I checked them myself the other day an' they be fine."

"I would not say anything to the others," I advised. "I am likely making more of it than necessary."

"Ye can't be too careful, Serena. Particularly with the master gone an' all. I'll be feelin' a lot safer when 'e an' Oliver return."

I regretted now that I had troubled her and tried to lighten the conversation by asking her about Robbie, from whom I knew she had received a letter but days earlier.

"O' 'e be fine, thank the Lord. Te tell ye the truth I think 'e be a bit lonely though. I like te think 'e be missin' his mum, but I think 'tis Lord Barkham."

"There is no trouble, is there?"

"The weather's bin a bit harsh, but we kin be thankful the crops are in."

I nodded, petting Pluck, who had sided up to my knee.

"Ye miss it, don't ye, Serena?"

I looked up at her. "Mayfair?"

She nodded.

"Do I make it that obvious?"

She smiled. " 'Tis only that I be knowin' ye fer a long time now. This house has never bin a happy place fer ye."

"Do I appear so unhappy here?" I pursued.

She smiled. "Ye'll always make the best o' things. But in my heart I be knowin' that if 'tweren't fer the girls, ye'd be up north. 'Tis a quieter life, but ye've always loved the land. An' I know ye be missin' Lord Barkham. 'Tis not me place te be sayin', but I'm not approvin' of his goin' off like this an' leavin' ye 'ere. This place, it has not good memories fer ye."

How right Charlotte was, I thought. Scarce did she know that what troubled me today was not memories but the present. Could it be that Channing Hall somehow boded doom for me? I was not superstitious, but I could not quiet the thought. No matter how hard I tried, a feeling of unrest o'er-took me here.

Dismissing Charlotte I turned my thoughts back to plans for the ball. I had not realized how many hours I had been at same, until, in late afternoon, Constance, laden with packages, joined me in the library.

"Oh, Serena, you should have come with me," she effused. "I cannot think why Daphne did not want to go."

She commenced untying a box and withdrew an elaborate bonnet fashioned of velvet and fur.

"There is a new milliner just off Queen Anne's Street. Ever so chic run by a Madame Trissot," she effused. "And you would not believe whom I encountered there."

"I cannot suspect," trying to join in her enthusiasm.

"You remember Monsieur DeMarcier, whom we met at Count de la Brocher's?"

I nodded. "Well, I suspect that he is an intimate of Madame Trissot's."

"Constance," I cautioned, "beyond being an indelicate statement, I do not think such speculation is terribly lady-like."

She sighed. "Well, do you think he was there to buy a chapeau? In any event, far more interesting was that just when I was about to leave, Count de la Brocher arrived."

"Are you to tell me this was pure chance?" I asked, studying her carefully. "I find it uncanny that in all of London you should encounter him of a sudden for the second time."

"Serena, I swear it," she entreated. "Frankly, no one could

have been more surprised than I. In any event he could not have been more charming. Do you know that he invited us for dinner tomorrow night?''

"Well, we shall have to think of it," I replied.

"Serena, how can you say that? You *cannot*. I have accepted. 'Twould have been rude not to, and besides, it has been terribly dull this past week. We have not had one dinner, one ball to attend."

"Constance, it was not your place to accept such an invitation," I advised.

"Perhaps not, but now that I have accepted, we simply must go."

"I assume that the invitation was to include myself and Daphne."

She replaced the bonnet in the box. "Well, of course, though I do not understand why he would include Daphne, since she has been so atrocious to him. But obviously he harbors no ill will."

"I do not think your cousin will take well to this invitation," I advised.

"Oh, please, Serena, you must insist that she attend for my sake. 'Twould be such an affront if she were to refuse. And it *is* only one evening."

"We shall see. For now I would suggest you take all these boxes to your room and ask Daphne to come down to me here."

I helped her gather up the new finery and commenced a letter to Alexander while I awaited Daphne. It was not long before she joined me in the library.

"You wanted to see me, Mother?"

I turned and smiled up at her, thinking how young and innocent she looked with her hair flowing loosely about her shoulders.

I nodded. "Come sit with me by the fire."

She eyed me suspiciously. "You seem so serious. Nothing is wrong, is there?"

"No, no, 'tis nothing like that. Simply a favor I have to ask of you."

"Ask on."

"I gather that Constance has not shared news of the invitation with you."

"What invitation?"

"She swears 'twas by chance, and I must trust that. In any event she encountered Count de la Brocher while she was out shopping, and he has invited us all for dinner tomorrow night."

"You have not accepted?" she gasped.

"Darling, I fear I have no alternative since Constance took it upon herself to do just that. It would be terribly awkward if I should pen a refusal now."

"When is that man going to leave us be?" she wailed, jumping to her feet.

Her outburst alarmed me, but it was her words that left me troubled.

She spun about. "I do not care what you do, Mother, or Constance for that matter, but you cannot make me go. I will not set foot in that house again."

"Daphne, calm yourself," I advised. "I do not know what it is about Count de la Brocher that puts you into such a state, but whatever it is, I would advise you to overcome it."

"Mother, the man is odious, and I cannot see why you do not realize it for yourself. And to encourage Constance? Well, it is madness."

"Daphne, I admit that Constance's preoccupation with the man troubles me," I commenced slowly, "for I fear that she exaggerates his interest in her. But thus far she has no nice young men like your Lord Sanderson coming to call."

"He is not *my* Lord Sanderson," she interrupted.

"In any event she does not have anyone who has expressed more than cursory interest at these dinners and balls we have been attending. You know there would be no sense in discouraging her interest in the count. I suspect that when over time he makes no effort to seek her out, she will realize that he is only being pleasant and friendly in his own fashion. When we commenced this conversation, I asked you for a favor. I want you to go with us tomorrow evening. I am not asking you to feign pleasure at this invitation, but I do beg of you to join us. For my sake and Constance's."

She studied me for a moment. "Mother, you know I would refuse you nothing, but if you have any regard for me, I beg you not to press me on this issue. Believe me, Constance would be far better served by your sending our apologies."

"You may be right, Daphne, but in this case I am going to use my prerogative as a mother to insist that you accompany us. I do not ask you to be happy about it, only to make the best of the situation."

I could not bear the look she thrust at me. "If Father were here, he would listen," she accused as she gathered up her skirts and without another word fled from the room.

She was obviously so upset that I regretted being so insistent with her. My initial reaction was to chase after her and give in to her pleas. But that would only set about another rift with Constance, and so in the end I simply left her to her room to sort it out for herself.

Once Constance knew that I would indeed permit the dinner the night next, her spirits were ebullient. She joined me in the dining room that evening, and though I found her obsession with what she was to wear the night next to be a bit boring, I admittedly was cheered by her good humor. When Daphne had requested a tray in her room, I had not objected, sensing it was best to let her be.

I slept fitfully that night, and it was not until it was almost dawn when, with Pluck curled beside me, I fell asleep. I hated the lateness of the hour when I finally arose but was grateful for the rest. My exhaustion these days, I knew, had far more to do with my emotional than my physical state. In the recesses of my heart I knew that I had concluded that I must confront Justin fully upon his return, no matter what the outcome. But having decided that, I found each moment that he remained away more trying.

I was grateful for one thing that day. Lord Sanderson came to call on Daphne shortly after luncheon. His presence always seemed to have a positive effect on her, and I hoped that it would cause her to dwell less on the evening ahead.

A light snow had commenced falling when we gathered in the front hall, and I was pleased that I had selected a heavy velvet gown to don for the evening. While Constance looked a confection in a creamy silk taffeta, her hair piled high in tightly curled ringlets, Daphne looked particularly severe in a black taffeta gown whose high neckline accentuated the heavy coil at the nape of her neck. Her appearance was, in fact, too comely for the occasion, but I was loathe to say one word for fear we would have a repeat of yesterday's outburst.

Sidney insisted on accompanying us, and though it was a short distance on foot, I did not object, for I was still a bit uneasy about my experience in the library a few days past.

We had only been ushered into the front hall when Count de la Brocher appeared at the top of the staircase.

" 'Tis a nasty night to be bringing you out, but I must say this pulchritude of beauty brings warmth to this house," he called down as he descended.

"I trust we are not too early," I offered as he took my hand.

"Not at all," he assured. "There was simply something I had forgotten to attend to. Please come join us in the library."

Constance smiled broadly as he extended his arm to hers, leaving Daphne and myself to follow.

The man who rose as we entered I recognized immediately from the count's last dinner.

"You will remember Antoine DeMarcier," the count offered.

I nodded as his lips brushed my hand. "Of course. I trust you have been well since our last meeting."

"Indeed, Lady Barkham, and it is easy to see that you have been so as well. I was most pleased when we encountered your charming cousin by chance yesterday at Madame Trissot's, since I had already been invited for the evening. And though I think my friend de la Brocher here is charming, I admit your presence here makes the evening far more enjoyable."

I noticed that Daphne, who had been particularly silent, selected a chair at furthest distance from the count. Admittedly, he did not seem to noitce, for again surprisingly he was particularly attentive to Constance.

"I regret that your husband could not accompany you this evening," Monsieur DeMarcier offered. "I have heard a great deal about him and should like to meet him one day."

"He is away on business," I advised.

"Ah, in England, I presume."

I nodded. "Northallerton actually," I replied as the count handed me a glass of port.

"You have chosen to remain with us in England, then," I suggested.

He looked at me curiously. "What would cause you to think differently, Lady Barkham?"

"Only that when we last visited, you seemed quite passionate about your countrymen. They were in the Ariege, were they not?"

He nodded. "You have a good memory."

"Less that than, for an area I had not been acquainted with until several months ago, it has been the topic of numerous conversations since."

"Really," he said, obviously interested.

"Yes, I find it fascinating truly. You must share more with me of the events therein."

"*Malheureusement*, the situation has worsened. The incidents have spread to the cantons southeast of St. Girons. The peasants, they have disarmed and threatened one of Laffont-Sentenae's forest guards. Hundreds of them have come to Massat, the chef-lieu of the canton, chanting in support of the king. Trinqué himself has been threatened that if he does not give those bêtes right of pasturage, he should come to harm. The desmoiselles, they should be barricaded and shot."

"Really, Antoine, we do not want to bore these charming ladies with our problems at home."

The last thing I wanted to do was to let the conversation drop, but I was loathe to press, for I in no way wanted anyone to sense that my interest was more than passing. I had to admit, however, that I was puzzled. Antoine DeMarcier was clearly supportive of the wealthy landowners—vehemently so. When I had first met the count, I had believed that he shared his sympathy. Yet that evening when he had taken dinner at Channing Hall, he had clearly been in support of the peasants. I sensed that I was not the only one to be confused, for Daphne too seemed perplexed.

"Ah, then your sentiments have changed again, Count de la Brocher," she challenged, suddenly breaking her steely silence.

He flushed deeply. "No, not at all Miss Barkham. Antoine gets carried away. It really is not a matter that should be of any interest to you."

"I *do* think all these wars and revolutions are such a bore," Constance interrupted. "There are so many more pleasant things to discuss."

I sensed that Daphne was about to challenge the count once again, but she was silenced by the announcement that dinner was served.

For myself I was surprised that we were the only guests. I had hoped that some of the people who had been at the count's last dinner would be here this evening. The voices of the men I had overheard talking to Justin and Oliver that night in the library had clearly sported French accents. I hoped that if I heard them again, something would trigger recognition.

The count clearly was in control of the conversation during dinner. I could not fathom the reason, but he appeared almost purposefully to direct talk away from himself and his French roots, focusing on our own family background.

While Daphne was clearly uncomfortable during dinner, Constance was effusive and obviously entranced by the count's flattery. While, in times prior, I had taken his attentions toward her as mere politeness, tonight I had to wonder if I was mistaken, for he seemed visibly taken with her.

Dinner was satisfactory, though we were blessed with such exceptional cooks at both Mayfair and Channing Hall that all other presentations always fell short to my palate. A dessert of fresh berries and cream had just been placed before us when from somewhere in the bowels of the house came a scream so bloodcurdling that it caused me to drop the silver utensils to my plate. My heart was pounding as I looked over to the count, who was visibly shaken.

"What was that?" Constance murmured.

"Nothing to be concerned about," the count, who seemed to recover his composure, assured. "Cook is forever dropping something or scalding herself. I fear 'tis not an uncommon occurrence, but I do apologize if it frightened you."

"Perhaps we should see to her," I ventured.

He shook his head. "I am certain, if there was need, I would be fetched. Now where were we before our little interruption?"

I could tell from Daphne's expression that she, like I, thought his attitude a bit cavalier, for if a servant was injured in our home, we would respond as one would to a family member.

Try as one would, the light banter of earlier was difficult to regain after such a jarring incident, and when we retired to the library and the count offered us a brandy, I tried to beg off.

"Oh, 'tis early, Lady Barkham," he encouraged. "You would not deny Antoine and myself the pleasure of your company for a bit longer."

I started to object, but Constance's eyes beseeched me to remain a while longer, and I was, with some reticence, cajoled into remaining.

I had no more than agreed when Daphne rose suddenly and announced that she wished to take her leave.

I was concerned, for she did indeed appear pale and drawn.

"Well, then we all shall leave," I said quickly.

"No, Mother, you stay, truly," she replied. "I am only feeling a bit tired."

The count had risen. "Antoine, will you be so kind as to see Miss Barkham back to Channing Hall."

"Truly there is no need," Daphne retorted.

"Constance, gather your things," I said. "I do not feel right about Daphne returning without us."

"Mother, please do not make such a fuss," Daphne implored. "Monsieur DeMarcier will accompany me, and there is no reason for concern."

I did not feel right about letting her return alone, but she was so insistent that I permitted her to leave with Monsieur DeMarcier, who assured me that he would see her ensconced in the house before returning.

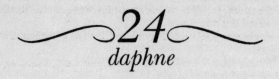

24
daphne

THE SNOW HAD continued to fall, and the night was silent, save for the crunch of my boots against the icy surface. I longed to run full flight towards Channing Hall, but Monsieur DeMarcier, holding my arm tightly within his, insisted that we proceed cautiously over the slickened cobblestones.

The house was well lighted, and as I tested the door handle, I was relieved that Sidney had left the door unlocked, for I had no wish to rouse the servants. True to his promise Monsieur DeMarcier saw me into the front hall, and only with my assurance that I would retire immediately, did he take his leave.

I removed my cloak, shaking the remaining white crystals from it as I did. I could not wait to reach the sanctity of my room, and after hanging up my cloak I gathered my still damp skirt and commenced climbing the stairs. I had only reached the sixth step when I was certain that I heard a noise from below. I paused, wondering if I had been mistaken, but there it came again, a low rumbling sound, almost like a moan.

I turned on the stairs and tiptoed gingerly down the stairs. The sound, I was certain, had emanated from the direction of the library. My heart was pounding as I crossed the cold marble floor. Something told me that I should not venture forward, but I tried to dismiss my fears by assuring myself that Count de la Brocher was ensconced in his house and there could be no threat of him to me here this night. My palms were clammy as they came in contact with the brassy cold of the door handle to the library.

I pushed the massive doors open gently, noting as I did that a fire still burned brightly in the fireplace. I took only one step into the room, my eyes roving about for some clue as to what had caused this odd sound.

It was in that split second that I saw him lying just beside the fireplace.

"Oh, my God," I called out as I ran forward, dropping to my knees as I reached him.

Blood was trickling from his temple as I turned him to me. "Oliver, 'tis Daphne. Talk to me please." I put his hand in mine, rubbing it vigorously as I called his name out repeatedly.

He squeezed my hand and whispered, "If all else fails, you can become a nurse, dear Daphne."

I was shaking as I tried to lift his head onto my lap. "Oliver, what happened? What are you doing here?"

"One question at a time," he whispered, his hand moving to the gash on his head.

"Let me get help," I pleaded.

His hand tightened against my wrist. "No, I shall be fine. Just give me a moment." He withdrew a handkerchief from his pocket, and I pressed it against his temple, which fortunately appeared not to have been cut so deeply that I would not be able to stay the bleeding.

He placed his hand against the floor and drew himself to a seated position.

"If you will lend me your arm, I think I should do better in that chair."

"Oliver, I do not think you should get up just as yet," I advised.

"Nonsense," he replied. "Now, come be a good girl and give your clumsy cousin a hand."

I bore as much of his weight as I could and helped him cross to the nearest chair, which he nearly collapsed in.

"Are you going to tell me that this was an accident?" I pursued, studying him closely.

"And what else would you imagine it to be?"

I shook my head. "I do not know. I just thought . . ."

"Well, trouble yourself no longer, dear heart. 'Tis simply that your cousin Oliver is not as nimble as he once was. I simply tripped on the rug there. I expect I struck my head against the hearth. Wherever it was, I know 'twas a nasty crack.''

"Can I fetch you something, some water or tea perhaps?''

He smiled. "You can, but I think this calls for something a bit stronger. A spot of brandy would do fine.''

I nodded and quickly crossed over to the decanter set, where I poured a full cup of the amber liquid into a glass.

After he took a few sips, he appeared to relax a bit.

"Serena, is she in bed?''

I shook my head. "Mother and Constance are still across the street at Count de la Brocher's.''

"They are *where*?'' he demanded.

"We were there for dinner. I returned just a short while ago. Thank goodness I did or I might not have found you.''

"Not that I do not appreciate your ministering, but I should have come round on my own. 'Twould take a great deal more to fell this hard head.''

"You still have not told me how you have come to return?'' I pursued. "Is Father here as well?''

He shook his head. "No, I returned on my own. Justin was concerned about you women here alone.''

"Are you saying that my father will not be returning shortly?''

"No, nothing of the sort. He shall be back well in time for the ball, if that is your concern.''

"To be truthful that has been the last thing on my mind. 'Tis simply that I miss him. We all do. Mother particularly. She has not seemed herself since you departed.''

He sat forward in the chair. "She is not unwell?''

I paused. "You know Mother. She would not tell us even if that were the case. But I do not think it to be physical. It is difficult to describe, but she seems preoccupied somehow.'' I shrugged. "Perhaps it is my imagination.''

He became thoughtful. "I see.''

"I would think that they should be home shortly. Mother will be ecstatic to see you, but she will fret as a mother hen when she sees what has befallen you.''

"Daphne, you must not tell her or anyone about this little accident,'' Oliver pleaded.

"Goodness, why not?''

"You know how Serena is. She will worry her head off, and

I know with the ball coming upon us that her mind is full of other things. I shall be right as rain by morning, and there is no sense in troubling the household over my clumsiness.''

"If you insist," I replied, finding his request more than a bit odd.

He downed the rest of his brandy. "And, now, if I can lean on you just bit more, I would be very grateful if you would see me upstairs. One performance a day is enough for me."

I agreed, and though he seemed less than steady on his feet, I supposed that getting to bed was the best thing for him.

I was relieved that Mother and Constance had not returned before I retired, as the last thing I wanted was to have to explain why I felt I had to get out of Count de la Brocher's, much less to feign some story about Oliver.

I changed hastily into my nightdress and, extinguishing the candle, climbed under the heavy covers. I had forgotten to draw the drapes, but the sight of the snow falling outside the window was somehow reassuring.

I never should have permitted Mother to insist on my going this evening, though without telling her the truth I was harboring in my soul, I did not see how I could have avoided it. Yet in some strange manner I was pleased that I had gone. I was now convinced that Count de la Brocher was even more odious than I had first thought. He had no shame and certainly cared none for mine. He had not avoided me, but it had been clear that he was not the least fazed by my presence. Indeed, instead he had flaunted his attentions on poor Constance, who, it appeared, was to be his next unwitting victim. Well, I for one would not permit that to happen.

Was he genuinely interested in her? I thought it unlikely. Could it be that he thought that his performance this evening would incite jealousy within me? Any rational person would know differently, but then Count de la Brocher was far from rational.

I would give him credit in one category—he was a brilliant actor. Save in one area. It seemed clear to me that though he had tried to deceive my father by purporting that he was a man of the people, there was little doubt that he was an elitist. I had not liked Monsieur DeMarcier from the first, and though I knew little of these scourges in the Ariege, my sympathies were clearly with the peasants, who were only fighting for fuel and shelter. That DeMarcier was obviously such a good friend of his only reinforced where the count's sentiments truly lay. The only puzzling thing was why he had taken such great pains to deceive my father.

If I would permit myself to believe Count de la Brocher's warnings about danger to my father, then where did this deception fit in? Where he had appeared to be protecting him, could it be that it was he, in fact, who should be feared? If there was a threat to Father, was Count de la Brocher the force behind it?

It was only moments later that I heard movement on the stairs and pausing, realized that Mother and Constance had returned. I knew that Mother would look in on me, and as I was in no mood to explain my earlier behavior, I closed my eyes pretending sleep as she opened the door to my room. Satisfied that I was resting comfortably she moved on.

I could not understand Oliver's not wanting her to know of his return, for it would be no small surprise to discover him ensconced in the house in the morning. Finding him there as I had earlier had been a shock. He had assured me that he was all right, but as with so much else these days, I found this incident to be troublesome. Oliver was many things but clumsy was not one of them. Oh, 'twas true anyone might take a spill but that gash on his forehead—it did not seem logical. But if it had not occurred in the fashion he had described, then how had he come by this blow? A shudder spread through my body, and I pulled the covers up tighter about my neck. I could not allow my mind to run on like this. I had never known Oliver to lie to me, and I could not suspect him of this now.

The snow had stopped when I awakened the next morning, leaving the trees and walkways blanketed in white. I was fully dressed and just fixing my hair with some tortoiseshell combs when there came a knock at the door.

"Come in," I called out.

"Oh, I am pleased you are up," Constance effused as she entered.

"Goodness, what has you up and about at this hour?" I asked, thinking it uncommon for her.

She sank down on the edge of the bed. "I simply could not sleep. I do believe last evening was one of the most exciting of my life."

I turned to face her. "Then you are easily excited, my dear, for 'twas only a small dinner party and not a terribly scintillating one at that.''

A pout formed on her face. "I do not know why you must be jealous, Daphne," she accused. "After all, you have Lord Sanderson. I find your attitude most uncharitable."

"Uncharitable?" I exploded.

"You resent the count's attentions towards me. Why can you not be happy for me? I, after all, am perfectly pleased that *you* have found a suitor."

"Again I remind you that Peter, Lord Sanderson, is not a suitor," I advised. "He is a friend and that is all."

She laughed. "You *are* naive, cousin dear. You have only to see how he ogles you to know that he is besotted. And he calls almost daily. And Serena approves. Of course, he is titled and wealthy, so why would she not?"

I studied her for a moment, watching her twist a ringlet that had fallen about her neck.

"I shall reemphasize, Constance, that Lord Sanderson is a friend. And that is all he ever can be."

She looked up at me. "What a curious thing to say," she mused. "You sound almost ominous."

"I only meant that your fantasies are running ahead of things," I replied cautiously. "Besides, what my relationship is or is not with Peter Sanderson has naught to do with this."

"But it does," she insisted. "I want you to be as happy for me as I am for you."

"What does that mean?" I pursued.

"Oh, Daphne, do not be so blind. You were there last evening, you saw how the count was, you cannot deny that he is taken with me. I know you have been suspicious of him before, but last night you could see it for yourself."

"I saw nothing of the same," I replied slowly. "Do not misunderstand. I am certain Count de la Brocher finds you attractive; he could scarce find you not. But I think you continue to mistake flattery for intentions."

"How can you be so cruel?" she cried out.

"Constance, believe that is the last thing I want," I replied. "Let me ask you something. Save pleasantries during these various soirees, has the count given you any reason to believe that he intends something further? You must admit he has not exactly been breaking the door down to call on you."

"He is a very busy man," she interrupted.

"Oh, yes, he is very busy indeed," I replied sardonically.

"You forget that he kissed me," she insisted, "and he nearly begged me to convince Serena to have us attend dinner last evening."

"Have you ever thought that he might have other motives?" I posed.

She eyed me suspiciously. "Motives? What motives?"

"That is unimportant," I replied carefully. "Constance, all I want is for you to see things as they are. Your image of Count de la Brocher and the man he really is are at opposites. I simply do not want to see you hurt."

She stood up suddenly, her hands on her hips. "What you do not want, Daphne Barkham, is for me to be happy. You *are* jealous no matter what you say. You may pretend dislike of Count de la Brocher, but I suspect you are as fascinated with him as I, and secretly you wish it was you to whom he showed attention. Well, I shall not have you ruin things for me. I warn you, he is mine, and I will not have you interfere in this any longer."

Before I could reply, she had gathered her skirts and flounced from the room. I turned back and studied my face in the mirror. I knew that I could never share the real truth with her, but I also knew that even if I did, she would never believe me.

25

serena

I AWAKENED TO the feel of Pluck's tongue lapping at my hand. I leaned over and kissed the soft white marking atop his head.

"Sensing I need some affection, are you?" I asked as his tail beat against the covers.

I pulled myself up as there came a knock at the door. It was Charlotte with my morning basin.

"Good morning, Serena," she greeted, her lips spread in a toothy smile.

"You should let one of the maids do that," I advised.

She shook her head. "Not this mornin. I wouldn't awanted one o' them to be spoilin' the surprise."

"Surprise? What surprise?"

" 'Twouldn't be a surprise if I be tellin' ye. Now come along an' get dressed. Ye'll be wantin' te take breakfast below this mornin'."

I did as she had bade and dressed hurriedly. With Pluck at my heels I nearly flew down the stairs to the breakfast room.

"Oliver," I exclaimed, rushing forward to embrace him. "When did you arrive? Where is Justin? My Lord, what has happened to your head?"

He laughed, hugging me to him. "Hold on, Serena, one thing at at time. I came in last night, and as it was late, I did not want to disturb you. Unfortunately, Justin is not with me,

185

but it really is because of him that I have returned a few days before I expected. He is worried about you and the girls here alone."

"Why this sudden concern?" I murmured.

"Pardon me?" he asked.

I waved him off. "Oh, 'tis nothing. And your head?"

"Simply having my head in the wrong place at the wrong time," he assured. "I fear it looks far worse than it is."

"And Rebecca, have you had news of her?"

He shook his head. "Actually, I rather hoped that a letter would await me here."

"I have had no word. I know 'twas silly of me, but I did somehow hope that Anne and Richard might come down for the ball. I feel it has been a lifetime since seeing them."

"And Alexander?"

"I had a long letter two days past. He seems well and certainly continues to be enthused in his responsibilities."

"Well, I know that Daphne is well," he said, taking a sip of tea. "For she was still up and about when I returned last evening."

"Daphne was up and about?" I queried.

"You seem surprised."

"Oh, it is too long to go into, but as she likely told you, we were at Count de la Brocher's. And she left early. I have not fathomed it completely, but there seems to be bad blood between the two. Perplexing, truly, for I could have sworn that the count had designs on Daphne. And now it appears his interest is in Constance."

Oliver looked troubled suddenly. "You have not encouraged this, I hope, Serena."

I shook my head. "Fortunately, 'tis not an issue, for although I think she fancies that he has intentions to court her, I suspect that Count de la Brocher is somewhat of an enigma and should like to keep it that way."

"Who else was present?"

"At the dinner?"

He nodded.

"Only a Monsieur DeMarcier. I believe we had mentioned him before. You know him perhaps?"

He smiled. "You know me, Serena. My roots are here in England. There would be no cause for me to be acquainted with the French. Other than Monique of course. There I should commit mind and body.''

I raised my eyes and studied him, abashed at what I had heard. That he would say that he would commit fully to Monique gave me suspicion if not proof that he, too, would indeed lie to me. Oliver, who I had believed could never betray me, could no longer be trusted by me. His allegiance was now to Justin, and I had only become a complication to be dealt with.

The next two days nearly flew by. I was grateful to have the ball to tend to, for it permitted me less time to dwell on the questions and fears that harbored within me. Oliver, when he was about, which was not often, appeared cheerful if preoccupied, and I wondered if the smiling face he showed to me was not a forced deception. That ultimately was less distressing than the stony silence that existed between Daphne and Constance. The two had not been best of friends when we were ensconced at Mayfair, but they had had an amicable and at times warm association. That they were at odds did not help the mood at Channing Hall. I sensed that somehow Count de la Brocher was at the root of this schism between them, but I had nary the time nor the energy to unravel this petty feud at present.

If I had had any doubt about Lord Sanderson's intentions, they had been dispelled these past weeks. He had become almost a fixture at Channing Hall. Daphne, though appearing to enjoy his company, was uncommonly circumspect about voicing her feelings. Though I continued to find him a most appealing young man, I found myself wishing that he would be a bit more reticent in his pursuit of Daphne. Justin had only had the opportunity to be acquainted with him on a cursory basis, and though I trusted my own instincts, I longed for his views as well. Lord Sanderson was the first real suitor that Daphne had known. Marriage was not easy under the best of circumstances, and when and if she took that step, I wanted it to be out of love and passion, never by convenience.

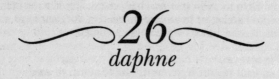

26

daphne

PETER HAD COME to call again. He broke into a broad smile as I crossed the threshold into the drawing room.

"You look wonderful, Daphne," he complimented as I seated myself opposite him.

"Take care, Peter, or your flattery shall go to my head," I replied.

He studied me for a moment. "I should doubt that. You are far too sensible for that."

I wondered. Would I describe myself as sensible? I supposed in a way I was but somehow I did not care to think that that was the trait I revealed most. Sometimes I wondered, when, like this morning, Peter and I visited, if he did not see in me what he sought to see versus myself as I truly was. He had such a gentle nature. I had not once seen him downcast or morose. And indeed there was something to be said for that. His character had a rather soothing effect and these days that was a welcome feeling. I no longer needed to wonder about his fondness for me, for he had spoken of same several times. There were moments when alone in my room I wondered of my feelings for Peter. I *was* fond of him. Fond of him in the same way that I was of Oliver. But was that not more of a brotherly love? Perhaps I thought this was what was intended. Someone in whom you had trust and admiration, someone who in turn championed your own beliefs and dreams.

I did not know why I even allowed myself to think this way. Even if Peter truly did have intentions, I had no right to encourage him. Count de la Brocher had dashed whatever hopes I had there. I felt guilty allowing Peter to continue to call, for I had no right to show him encouragement. But was my life to be ruined because of some cruel transgressions? The answer, I prayed, God would allow me to find within myself.

"Daphne? Are you quite well?" Peter asked, an alarmed look in his eyes.

I laughed. "I am sorry, Peter. I fear I was daydreaming."

"I hope that does not suggest that you find my company tedious," he suggested.

"Of course not," I assured. "I must simply be preoccupied with the ball set for tomorrow evening and all."

"I do hope that you shall save as many dances as possible for me. As I evidenced once before, I tend not to do well with too much competition."

He was referring, of course, to the incident with the count at the Foxcrofts's, but I saw no reason to dignify this with any comment.

Mother had been kind enough to invite him to join us for luncheon, but he begged off, sensing, I suspect, that with all the bustle about the house he might be intruding.

I saw him to the door, and then deciding that I should return to my bedroom to examine the gown I intended to wear the night next, I climbed the stairs. As I passed Constance's room, I paused for a moment, wondering if I should not try and mend the distance between us but decided that likely anything I would say would only serve to irritate her further.

I thought it curious, when I reached my room, to find the door slightly ajar. I distinctly remembered closing it tightly earlier, a habit we all adapted, since Mother was loathe of drafts. I had no longer pushed the door open than the sight in front of me sent me reeling. For there on the bed lay the gown, or remnants of the gown I had laid out on the bed only hours earlier. The ecru tissue faille had been so torn, or cut, I knew not which, that the gown was scarcely recognizable. Silver threads with which the fabric was spun and hundreds of silvery seed pearls were strewn about the floor.

I moved over to the bed simply incredulous at the devastation that lay before me. The yards of gossamer fabric had been desecrated, and tears welled in my eyes as I watched piece upon piece fall like feathers through my fingers.

Several moments had passed before the shock of finding my dress in this fashion passed enough to have the obvious question bore into my mind. Who could have done this?

As soon as my mind pursued this thought, I felt a shudder pass through me.

"How could she?" I murmured to myself.

She had warned me of vengeance, but never in my life did I imagine that it had been more than a threat expressed in anger. I could not fathom this cruelty. Constance knew that this was the gown that I had saved specifically for this occasion. Anne had sent it over to Mayfair just before our departure. I thought I had never seen anything so exquisite. She had not excluded Constance in her bounty, but this one gown had been special. Constance had coveted it from the first.

And now it lay in ruins before me. It frightened me to think that she would have gone to such lengths to hurt me. She was volatile and unthinking at times, but I could not imagine the rage that must have burned within her to have gone to such lengths to see my hopes for the evening dashed before they commenced.

I sat there as if mesmerized by the sight before me. I do not know how long it took, but I was suddenly aware that my feelings of hurt had become those of anger. I was too angered, in fact, to confront Constance at this moment. And what if by chance it was not indeed my cousin who did this? To wrongly accuse her would be a grave mistake. But if not Constance, then who? One of the maids? Oliver? No, there was only one to suspect.

I wondered, as I gathered pieces of the gown together, if she thought that miraculously somehow I would say nothing of this. If she were the least bit repentant, she would have come to me by now. More likely Constance was experiencing fear, for she knew that Mother's wrath would be great. On that score I was surprised she was not at this moment begging my forgiveness, for Constance, though verbally brazen, had always had a streak of cowardice.

I found my mother in the library, arranging a large spray of flowers. I said not a word but crossed over to her and dropped the debris onto the table before her.

She looked up at me, a puzzled expression on her face as her fingers filtered curiously through the scattered remnants.

"What on earth is this?" she asked.

"I am not surprised you do not recognize it," I cried. "It is the vestiges of my gown, the one Aunt Anne sent me that I was to wear tomorrow night.

"Oh, my Lord," she gasped.

"After Peter left, I returned directly to my room and there it was."

"Not again," my mother moaned.

I moved forward to her quickly, for she had paled so, her hands shaking suddenly, uncontrollably, that I was terrified for her.

"Mother, are you all right?"

Her hand was across her mouth, and I thought for a moment she was going to be ill.

I put my arm about her, begging her reassurance that she was all right.

Seeming to recover her composure, she asked me if I might fetch a glass of water, which I did immediately. By the time I had returned, she appeared somewhat more composed, though unless I imagined it, there was a distant, almost haunted look about her eyes.

"Mother, I apologize," I said quickly. "It was unthinking of me. I know what a shock it was for me finding it there. I should have forewarned you."

She waved me off, the color thankfully returning to her face. "I expect my nerves are a bit on edge these days. Anticipation of the ball and all."

I regarded her curiously. "Why did you say 'not again'?"

"Did I?" she shrugged. "Oh, I expect 'tis just one of those nonsensicals that one utters at a time of surprise."

"I know that she is miffed with me, but I cannot imagine that she would stoop to this," I muttered.

"You know who did this?" Mother queried.

"Let us call it a simple matter of deduction," I replied, gathering the fragments into a ball. "Can you understand that, though I am so angry with her, I still feel I am betraying her somehow by coming to you?"

She studied me for a moment.

"You think it is Constance, do you not?"

I nodded. "She is the only one that makes sense. I do not want to go into it, but you must have sensed a schism between us. Though I am totally abashed that she would resort to this.

In truth, though loathe to admit it, I think I came to you because I feared what I might do to her if I saw her."

My mother shored herself up in her seat. "Daphne, you must get hold of yourself. I know how much this gown meant to you, but it is just a dress after all. And you have no evidence, no admission that it was Constance who did this. I want you to promise me that you will leave this matter to me. Totally. There is, as you have suggested, already ill will between you two, and I want you to allow me to intervene here. There will be nothing gained by your confronting Constance. Particularly, if contrary to your suspicions, she is not the guilty party."

Begrudgingly I gave her my assurance. I knew she was right, but I also felt I needed a confrontation with Constance or whoever had done this to me.

"I suppose what you are going to tell me to address now is what alternate gown I will choose for tomorrow?"

She rose. "You read my mind. I want you to follow me."

I did so up the staircase to her bedroom, wondering what she intended. Mother instructed me to sit on the edge of her bed, while she moved methodically over to her armoire. I peered about as she withdrew a gown, which, even from a distance, shimmered in the light streaming through the windows. She moved towards me and placed it over my lap, holding the train up from the floor.

"There, by the mirror. Hold it up in front of you," she urged.

I took the gown, which was woven of what appeared solid gold threads in a diagonal across the bodice, moving to a horizontal weave at the waistline. The neckline was low, an inverted heart shape, and the sleeves, though long, I could quickly see would cling to one's figure.

"You may find it too sophisticated," Mother offered.

"It is divine," I replied, twirling about before the mirror.

She smiled. "I shall tell you a secret if you swear not to tell Anne."

I put my finger to my lips. "My silence is golden."

"Anne gave it to me a year ago, and though admittedly it still fits, it only does so if I do not take a deep breath. I suspect it will be perfect for you. And with your grandmother's tiara, well, you shall be the belle of the ball, not that I believe the dress makes the woman."

I ran forward and embraced her. "Are you certain?"

She nodded. "Though I think we shall keep this between us. At least until your unveiling."

I did not want to ask if she feared a repeat performance. At her insistence I tried the gown on, and indeed it looked as though it had been made for me. As I watched myself in the mirror, I was pleased with my reflection. The gown was by far the most elegant I had ever worn. I looked, no, felt different in it somehow. Older, more sophisticated. Yes. But there was something else. I could not decipher what, but I looked, yes, that was it. Different.

I had later to be amused by Mother's demand for secrecy from Aunt Anne. She was as svelte as I, even today, and though I would not have challenged her, I knew in my heart that the bestowal of this dress was out of love and generosity and not that she had outgrown its measure.

27

serena

I KEPT TO my room after Daphne had departed, trying to bring reason to something which I knew had no reason. Daphne, I knew, was hurt and angered by what had befallen her. For myself it was fear that wallowed in my soul.

What I had not told my daughter was that I, too, had experienced the same devastating experience when I was just about her age. Even the dress, though of a different style, evoked memories of the one I was to wear to a ball, for it, too, had been white and it, too, had been given by Anne. I too had returned to my room one afternoon to find the gown, which I had thought the prettiest I had ever seen, torn into obliteration. The assailant was unknown to me, though I think I always suspected it was Clarissa. When I discovered that she had indeed been my victimizer, I was no less hurt or shocked.

Coincidence? Perhaps. For there was no reason to believe that Constance had ever known of what her mother had wrought. Yet how could it come to pass that with so many elements being equal, Constance had enacted this crime on my daughter.

Many had warned me that by embracing Constance into our household I was taking a chance. But Clarissa, though volatile, certainly devious and acid of tongue, scarce to be trusted, never displayed the cunning and, in fact, madness of Maura, her mother. But then she had died at a relatively young age, so we would never know if she would have been spared a disease of the mind as that had taken her mother.

We had always kept silent about all of this, largely at my own insistence, for I had not wanted to see Clarissa hurt by revelations of her real heritage, nor did I ever want to see it cast a shadow over Constance's life.

I was stymied about where to turn. If only Justin were here, I thought, he might guide me. This was no petty spat. Chastisement would not suffice. I had to confront Constance, and if she, as we suspected, was the culprit, stern measures would have to be taken. I knew the one thing that would devastate her most would be if I disallowed her from attending tomorrow night's ball. Whatever punitive measures I took, they would not address the question of what kind of personality defect would cause one to take such drastic measures.

Gathering up the remnants of the gown that Daphne had left in my keeping, I bade Pluck to stay behind and wound through the hallway to Constance's room.

"Who is it?" was the reply to my knock at her door.

"Serena. Might I come in for a moment?"

When she opened the door, I was taken aback, for her mood certainly was cheerful for one anticipating my wrath.

"I was just trying this new comb," she said, pointing to the ostrich feather fanlike ornament that held her hair high atop her head. "What do you think?"

"I have not come here to talk about hair ornaments," I replied tersely.

"Goodness, Serena, you do seem agitated."

"I am."

"Well, I can understand that, with Justin going off as he does lately," she replied, placing the comb on the dressing table. "I mean, leaving you with all the responsibility of the ball and all."

"Justin has nothing to do with this," I argued. "What I wanted to see you about was this," I continued, taking the shredded fabric and placing it before her on the dressing table.

Her hands picked over the silky yardage. "What is this?"

I studied her carefully. Unless she was the consummate actress, her face showed no recognition of the pieces before her.

"Look at it more closely," I advised.

"Really, Serena, I have no idea what this is about," she insisted. "I mean, I can tell it is or was a gown. 'Tis the same fabric as the one Anne gave . . . you are not telling me this is Daphne's gown?''

"If this is an act, Constance, let me assure you I am not amused.''

"Serena, you are not making any sense.''

"This is, or shall I say was, Daphne's gown,'' I replied. "Someone went into her room this morning while she was visiting with Peter and cut or tore it into shreds.''

Her pale blue eyes widened. "You mean someone tore this gown like this?'' she murmured incredulously.

I nodded.

She was quiet for a moment, and then a cloud passed over her eyes. "And you have come here . . . you cannot think . . . you do, you think I did this,'' she cried.

"Did you?'' I asked, watching her carefully.

"Is that what Daphne told you?'' she demanded. "She hates me. How can you be so blind to that? Just because she is your daughter, you think she is perfect. If it had happened to me, you would scarcely accuse your precious Daphne,'' she sobbed.

"Constance, I am not accusing you. I am asking you. Are you responsible for this, and if you are, what in heaven's name possessed you?''

I had never seen Constance so impassioned nor so frightened. I knew that if I were to form my judgement at this very moment, I would swear that she was telling the truth. But if Constance had not been responsible, then who?

"You have to believe me, Serena,'' she beseeched. "I will not deny that I have been furious with Daphne, but I swear to you I did not do this.''

I studied her carefully. "I pray that you are telling me the truth, Constance, for if I find that it was you, it will only make things worse.''

"What are you going to do?'' she choked, dabbing a handkerchief to her eyes.

I commenced gathering the scattered fabric. "First, I am going to have a talk with Daphne and tell her what you have said. And next, I shall interview the staff. I am not going to let this pass without an answer. In the meantime I suggest you wash your face and rest a bit.''

I spent the rest of the afternoon doing as I had said, going first to Daphne and then, enlisting Charlotte's aid, talking to every member of the staff. I knew that Daphne was suspicious of her cousin's denials, but she agreed not to accuse her or harbor any resentment until I could uncover the truth.

Charlotte, who had been with me at Camberleigh those years ago when the same thing happened to me, was shocked, and I knew, as I, frightened by this bizarre recurrence. She and Mary gathered the staff, and one by one I questioned each. I suspected when I began that it would prove fruitless, for beyond there being no motive amongst any of the servants, each appeared more shocked than the next about what had happened here at Channing Hall.

When Oliver returned later that afternoon, he found me in the library still trying to fathom who might have done this.

"You certainly seem in a somber mood, Serena," he said, crossing to me and kissing my cheek.

"Do you have a moment?" I asked.

"My time is yours," he replied. "That is, if you will permit me to take a glass of port. Winter is upon us."

I waited until he had poured his drink and settled into the sofa opposite me.

"I am all ears."

"Something happened here today that has troubled me greatly," I began. I went on to explain the events of the day, taking care to keep calm so that I might impart what information I had as accurately as possible.

When I had finished, Oliver surprised me by rising and pouring himself another port. His reaction I found curious. If I expected him to be shocked, that is not what I read in his facial expression. He was troubled, that was clear, but he seemed at the same time preoccupied.

"I am at a loss to know where to go from here," I murmured. "I thought perhaps you might have a notion."

He rubbed the back of his head with his hand. "Would that I did," he said finally. "But I should not be too quick to accuse Constance. There is, as you point out, obviously a rift between the two girls, but I suspect we will find that Constance is innocent."

"What makes you say that?" I challenged, thinking it curious that he would champion Constance's cause.

He shrugged. "Nothing really. What I suppose I am advising is that you try to put this out of your mind. Until, of course, you have some proof of something."

I could not believe my ears. I do not know what I expected Oliver to say, but this certainly was not it. Oliver was not a man to sweep something under the carpet. From the time he had been a child, he had always tackled things directly, seeking answers, believing there were solutions.

He must have read my mind, for he quickly added, "What I meant was that I should temporarily not let this trouble you. Goodness, tomorrow evening you are hostessing one of the largest balls London has ever experienced. You do not need something like this to preoccupy you."

In that respect I could not deny that he was correct. But though it appeared that there was little else I could do at this moment, I was no less determined to get to the root of all this.

We all dined together that evening at my insistence. Save from Oliver, who made a special effort to uplift the mood, tension hung almost as a presence in the room. I was just as pleased to retire early, for Oliver had vowed that Justin would return by midmorning the next day, and his homecoming was to signal the commencement of my receiving the multitudinous answers I sought.

As I climbed into bed and Pluck nuzzled against my arm, I murmured, "There is not a corner of my life that is not troubled, save you, my dear friend." What I was determined to learn over these next days, I knew might cause me great pain, but it could not be worse than the pain of suspicion that had weighed on me this past month.

I awakened the next morning and was pleased when one of the maids brought me a breakfast tray, for 'twould only be a matter of hours before the tranquility of the hour would be lost to the day. It surprised me when she relayed that Constance had asked her to advise her when she might be able to come to my room. As this was curiously out of pattern, I had a darkening suspicion that perhaps she intended more than just pleasantries. Was she going to admit to me that it had, in fact, been she who had destroyed Daphne's gown? And if that was so, what then would be my recourse?

I told the maid to have her come to me straightaway, and she arrived only moments later. I watched her carefully as she crossed over to the bed and took a chair next to it.

"You wanted to talk to me?" I ventured.

She nodded. "I am not very good at this, but I did want to

thank you for believing me about Daphne's gown. I really did not do it, you know.''

I was completely nonplussed. Not only had my suspicions of her visit been totally wrong, but also I had never seen Constance appear contrite or sensitive about anything.

She appeared hurt by my silence. ''You still do not trust me, do you, Serena?'' she cried. ''I knew I should not have wasted my breath.''

I stretched my hand out to her. ''Constance, that is not true,'' I admonished. ''I want to believe you. Truly. I do. But it is very worrisome, you must appreciate that. Nonetheless, I have promised myself not to dwell on this today. Have you decided which gown you are to wear?''

''The green,'' she replied. ''Oh, Serena, I just know this is going to be a very special day for us. I knew 'twould be all along, but after last night, well, now I know it to be certain.''

''What pray tell was so important about last night?''

''You would not believe me were I to tell you.''

''One cannot be certain unless you do tell me.''

She paused. ''You shall think me quite daft, but last night, I know not the time for I had been sleeping, my mother came to me.''

''Your mother?'' I gasped.

She nodded. ''She stood right there at the end of my bed. And she told me that the ball would be a very important night for me. She said that she knows that Count de la Brocher finds me attractive.''

''What you mean is that in your dream she spoke to you,'' I suggested.

She shook her head. ''It was not a dream, Serena,'' she insisted. ''I was frightened at first but . . .''

''Constance, you must not allow these tricks to be played on your mind. It is only natural that you should miss your mother. Particularly now during your season. We will likely never understand the complexities of our minds and bodies, but do you not see that in your mind you have called up her spirit to share this time with you?''

''But it was so real,'' she insisted.

''I am certain it was. But it was very real to you. I shall share with you that it has been almost twenty years since my own mother died, and yet I too have had the same experience as you, where I have awakened knowing that I have sensed her presence. Though we physically lose our loved ones, we do not lose the memory of them."

"You really think it was a dream?"

"I *know* that is what it was, and I am certain you do, too."

"It just seemed so real, Serena," she replied, rising and straightening her gown.

As she commenced to take her leave, I called out to her. "Thank you for coming to me, Constance. I hope you feel that you can always talk to me. I can never replace your mother, nor would I try, but I can be a friend."

My emotions were terribly mixed at this point. I so desperately wanted to trust the girl and yet there were still nagging doubts. I knew what it was like to lose a loved one, and though she had rarely spoken of her mother since her death, her loss had obviously gone much deeper than even I had imagined. Count de la Brocher had been invited to the ball this evening, but I hoped that he would not display too much interest in Constance. She was in a fragile state at this time, and if, as she believed, he really was interested in her, I felt that she was not ready for a serious relationship.

I had but put the tray aside on the bed when I heard a clamoring from the house below. I had no more pulled my robe about me when the door to the bedroom was flung open and Justin strode into the room.

"Good Lord, you frightened me," I gasped as Pluck ran forward, barking his greeting.

"Is that the best welcome home my bride can muster?" Justin replied as he strode over to me and took me in his arms.

" 'Tis just, I did not expect . . ."

He put his finger to my lips. "Hush, darling. Let me just look at you. God, I have missed you."

I felt myself go rigid as his arms tightened about me, his lips covering the length of my neck.

"Serena, what is it?" he demanded, pushing me back to study my face.

"It is nothing," I choked, pulling away from him.

"Serena, do not tell me that," he retorted. "Look at you. You are shaking. You pull away from me as though my touch singes your skin, and you want me to believe it is nothing?"

"My nerves are on edge, that is all."

"Well, what happened to bring you to this state?"

I whirled to face him. "There are times when I do not think I know you any longer, Justin Barkham. You disappear for weeks on end, and then return suddenly and expect to pick up exactly where you left off, Well, life is not like that. Things happen, people change."

I pulled a handkerchief from my dresser, aware that his eyes had never left me.

"I suspect I am naive in that sense," Justin replied. "I have been so preoccupied these past weeks with returning to you that I suppose in a way time stopped for me."

I twisted the handkerchief in my hands, fearful of turning to face him lest I should break fully down.

"I know you think me insensitive for leaving you here, but as I explained before I left, it was not something I completely had a choice about. To be honest with you, the problems I left to solve are still not resolved, but I had sworn to you that I would return by this day and I have."

I whirled about. "And what do you expect, that I should be eternally grateful for this small token?"

He shook his head. "All I ask is that you talk to me about what is troubling you."

I took a deep breath. "We will talk, but not now, not to-day."

"Serena, this is obviously serious enough that we should not let this pass."

"Oh, I shall not let it pass, Justin," I assured. "But lest you have forgotten, we are hosting one of the year's largest social functions this evening. I cannot allow myself to be emotionally spent when I have to face our guests."

"You won't give me some clue as to what has upset you so?" he pursued.

I shook my head. "It is not just one thing, Justin, and that is what complicates it so."

"Damnation, Serena, do you not see how frustrating this is? I come back obsessed by the thought of you, aching to take you in my arms, longing to be a husband to you, and instead I find you obviously distressed, oblique and distant."

"I know, Justin, and for that I am sorry, but we will talk. Tomorrow or the next day. I swear once this ball has passed, we will talk."

Justin left me to go in search of Oliver, and I sank back down on the bed, aware that my heart and mind were in total conflict. On the one hand I longed for the feel of Justin's arms about me, longed for his lips pressed to mine, longed to take him to me. But I knew that if I were to do that I would never have the courage to confront him with my suspicions. And that I could not allow. Too much time had elapsed already.

With all my planning these past weeks I could not believe how many last-minute details needed tending. It was close to four when, giving one last survey of the public rooms, I returned to our bedroom to commence my toilette. Justin and I had shared luncheon together. He was particularly watchful of me, but I was determined to keep the conversation and mood as light as possible, sharing with him the last letter from Alexander and telling him about Lord Sanderson's persistent interest in Daphne. He appeared to dismiss the seriousness of the latter, but then he had not been about to experience the frequency or intensity of his visits. I had debated discussing the mystery of the torn gown with him but decided that that, too, would wait. I knew that he would be enraged that such an occurrence could have taken place under this roof, and I did not want to mar the evening for the girls.

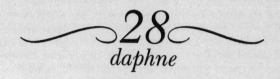

28
daphne

I FINGERED THE gold threads of the gown I would wear that evening. When I had found the gown I was to have worn in shreds on my bed, I thought that I would never be looking forward to this evening, but I had to admit that I could barely quell the excitement within me now.

I rouged my lips, studying myself in the mirror as I did. Charlotte had dressed my hair in the style I fancied suited me best, with deep waves framing my cheekbones and the hair cascading down my shoulders from a high knot at the crown. Mother had lent me a large gold filigreed comb, which secured the weight of my hair. We had tried a variety of feathered ornaments, but they somehow seemed excessive with the dress, which literally shimmered in the light.

Mother had extracted a promise from me that I would at least not make mention of the incident with the dress until the ball was over. It was not easy to put it out of my mind, for if Constance, as she had sworn to me and as Mother seemed to believe, had not done this deed, then how had it come to pass?

The only disappointment of the day was that, though I was thrilled by Father's return, I was troubled by a tension that seemed to exist between him and Mother. Likely it was simply the pressure of the ball. Mother usually seemed to take these things in stride. She was the consummate hostess, but these past weeks she had seemed preoccupied or troubled, I knew not which.

I stepped into the dress, taking care not to pull the fine threads as I slipped my arms into the slender sleeves. I smiled to myself, thinking of Peter's insistence that I promise most of the dances to him. It would scarce be a strain, since he was a superb dancer, but at the same time I thought I should make a special effort to mingle amongst the other guests this evening. I still did not feel right about encouraging Peter any further. It was odd that when I was with him, I was almost able to convince myself that there was no crime in encouraging his attentions. But when I was alone, doubts crept into my mind.

The one aspect of the evening that I dreaded was encountering Count de la Brocher. I could not have demanded that he be excluded from the guest list, but though I had hoped that he would not embarrass me with his presence, I knew those hopes were in vain.

I took one final look in the mirror before descending below. Candles shimmered at every corner of the house as I crossed from the front hall into the drawing room. I was surprised to find that a number of guests had already arrived, including Monique, who was deep in conversation with my father. She waved me to them, and I went, wondering where Mother had gone to.

"Daphne, *es si belle*. I have never seen you more elegant. That gown, it is *magnifique*," she effused as she kissed me on both cheeks.

"Truth be known, it was Mother's," I replied. "Speaking of whom, I do not see her about."

Father placed his hands on my shoulders and twirled me about. "There she is behind Oliver. They have been showing some of our guests about the house."

Mother looked radiant in a midnight-blue velvet gown with intricate lace insets about the bodice. I was about to cross over to her when a voice, which I recognized as Peter's, loomed behind me.

"I have been looking everywhere for you, Daphne," he said.

I turned about, thinking how handsome he looked in his black waistcoat.

"Peter, you know Lady Kelston and, of course, my father."

"I expect I should welcome you home, Lord Barkham," he said. "I trust your trip was successful?"

"In a fashion," my father replied. "I understand that you

have been a frequent visitor to Channing Hall during my absence."

I noticed Peter's flush. "Indeed I have, sir. Your wife has been most cordial by allowing me to monopolize some of your daughter's time."

"I suspect I should not have been so generous," Father replied.

It was now my turn to blush, but Monique saved the moment by adding, "You know, zees fathers, Peter, zay theenk zat no one ees correct for zere daughter."

"Do not be fooled, Lord Sanderson," my father advised. "Mothers can be just as protective. Let us just say, we are more direct about it."

"Peter, if I were you, I would ferret Daphne away from here," Monique advised, winking at him. "Zees eez a ball for the young."

Taking the hint, Peter suggested that we might go in search of some refreshment.

As he took my arm and guided me across the floor, I found myself wishing that I had stayed behind, for directly in our line of passage was Count de la Brocher, who appeared terribly amused by something Constance had just said. There was no avoiding them, though I sensed that Peter was acutely aware that Count de la Brocher was the last person I wanted to see.

"Miss Barkham," he said, bowing slightly from the waist. "Might I say you look ravishing this evening."

Constance eyed me warily.

I remained silent, fearing that my voice would divulge my nervousness.

"You will excuse us," Peter said. "We were on our way to take some refreshment." His arm tightened about mine, for which I was grateful, for I felt suddenly unsteady on my feet.

"You are shaking, Daphne," he murmured. "And your hands are like ice."

" 'Tis nothing," I assured. "The excitement of the ball and all."

"Not Count de la Brocher?"

"Why would you say that?" I snapped.

"Is it not obvious? He seems to have a powerful effect on you. I must say that I have found myself quite jealous of the man at times."

"Jealous?" I gasped. "You?"

He nodded, taking two glasses of champagne, handing one to me. "You must know how I feel about you, Daphne. How much I have come to care for you. And I have been moved to hope over these past weeks that you feel something for me as well. But every time I see you in the count's presence, I have my doubts."

"Peter, let me assure you of one thing," I said firmly. "The only thing that exists between Count de la Brocher and myself is loathing. The man is detestable beyond words. If he does cause me to react, it is only that I cannot tolerate being in the man's presence."

"I cannot think what it is that provokes you so about the man, but I must say I am relieved to hear it. I should not like to have to deal with him as a rival. Somehow I think Count de la Brocher is only satisfied as the victor."

It amazed me that Peter would seem so intimidated by him. I had thought he had greater confidence in himself.

He took a sip of champagne. "I must admit the chap does keep one off balance. One minute he seems intent on pursuing you, and the next he appears enthralled by your cousin, Constance. Unless my eyes deceive me, she is hardly opposed to his attentions."

I turned in the direction he was looking just in time to see the count whisper something in Constance's ear, something, I suspected, that was less than delicate, for a deep flush spread about her face and neck. The man had absolutely no scruples. How could he have thought that I would ever believe his professions of caring for me? What had he said? We were meant to be together? And then he had the nerve to romance Constance under my very eyes? What sort of fool did he take me for? Was he doing this for my benefit? I wondered. Was he flaunting his conquests in front of me, or was it simply that now that he had done with me, he would move on to the next victim? I knew not how but somehow I would make Constance see the count for the scoundrel he was.

The ball was an enormous success, and I was delighted for Mother, who was the center of compliments by the guests. Peter, who had not left me out of his sight, sat next to me during dinner, which was a feast of fish and fowl. I could not help but notice that several gentlemen eyed Constance with considerable interest, but Count de la Brocher appeared intent on monopolizing her time.

Only one thing troubled the mood of the dinner for me. I had looked down to the end of the table where my mother sat and been shocked by the expression on her face. Where she should have been ecstatic over the obvious success of the evening, she appeared troubled. I knew her well enough to know that this was more than just nervousness over the progress of the ball. She was looking down the expanse of the table where my father appeared deep in conversation with Monique. A casual acquaintance would likely not have suspected that something was amiss, but as I watched her, I saw pain, or was it sorrow, in Mother's eyes.

I looked back to my father again. I had noticed him with Monique earlier, and I had thought little of it. They had been friends for years. Why, then, would this prove so bothersome to my mother? I took a sip of wine as a sinking feeling o'ertook me. Was there some truth in what Constance had suggested? Had there been something beyond mere friendship between my father and Monique? Did my mother suspect some current liaison?

I tried to dispel my thoughts. After all, Monique was years older, though, I had to admit, she did not look it. I had always thought her not pretty but an interesting looking woman. This was silly, I thought. Father adored Mother, they had always been indelibly close. Then why did I see such despair in her face?

I had not time to ponder it further, for at that moment the musicians commenced their play, and Peter, taking my arm, urged me for the first dance. Though I suspect he resented that I felt that I must spend time with our other guests as well, Peter did not stray far from me. When at last the musicians paused for an intermission, he was immediately at my side.

"Might we move to someplace a bit quieter?" he asked. "There is something I should like to talk to you about."

"I can not leave, Peter. 'Twould be terribly rude, but we might move down there by the French doors."

He accepted two glasses of champagne, and I followed him through the milling crowd down to the end of the room.

"I suspect I know why no one else is down here," I murmured, accepting the glass he handed me. "There seems to be a considerable draft through these doors."

"Is the chill too great?" he asked.

I shook my head. "In truth I welcome the cool. Lord

Smythedon fancies himself quite a dancer, and I was feeling quite flushed after he twirled me about the floor."

He laughed. "Well, you appear none the worse for wear. I have never seen you as radiant as you are tonight."

"As I have said to you before, Peter, you are a great boost to a woman's ego."

"To *one* woman," he contradicted, "for as you have like noticed, I only have eyes for one. Which is what I wanted to talk to you about. I know this is scarce the time, Daphne, but if I do not speak of it now, I shall wonder when I should have the courage again."

I was silently fearful of what he was about to say.

"Daphne, you know of my caring for you," he pursued. "Though I have known you only a short time, it is difficult to explain, but I feel as though I have known you forever. I suppose what I want to speak to you about are my intentions."

"Perhaps this is not the time," I ventured.

"No, please let me continue," he beseeched. "I certainly cannot compare my credentials to, let us say, your father, but my family is one of means, and I am not without prospects. It is time for me to think of building my life, taking a wife and starting a family. Not that I have been a rogue, but I have experienced sufficient, I believe, to know what I want. I no longer wish to call on you without making my intentions known to you and your family."

He wiped beads of perspiration from his brow, saying as he did, "I am not doing this well. In any event, what I am trying to say is that I should like permission to pursue you with the intent of taking you as my bride."

I had sensed where the conversation was leading, but I had no idea how to divert it. His nervousness was obvious and to have silenced him midstream would only have insulted him. But now, having allowed him to conclude, I was faced with a major dilemma. Years before I had dreamed of this moment, when some young man stood before me, as Peter did now, talking of his fondness for me and his desire that I should be his bride. But that was when I had been young and naive, virginal in both mind and body. Today that seemed eons ago. What was I feeling at this moment? Confusion seemed to blur all other emotions. I was fond of Peter, that I knew. And though I cared less that he descended from a family of importance, indeed it made his acceptance less fraught with doubt. I would be the envy of many, I knew, were I to encourage his interest. I knew not what I should be feeling at this moment. Indeed I was flattered. But my heart was not soaring as I once dreamed it would be at this crossroad of my life. Likely that was because in the depths of my soul I had to ask myself if I had the right to allow Peter to pursue me with other than casual motives. I had too much regard for him to perpetrate some hoax upon him. But if I were to agree to allow him to become a suitor, was that not what I would be doing?

Peter was a man of character. Over these past weeks I had come to respect him, to like him. He did not deserve one who was less than an honest and complete woman. If I were indeed to encourage him, would it not end in great pain for us both?

There was one option I had. But I sensed I had not the courage to enact it. I could tell Peter the truth. But what would be the outcome? Hurt? Outrage? Would he take me into his arms, assuring me that it was of no matter, that he would love me anyway?

I suppose I wanted to believe that, but that would be demanding of him an understanding I thought too much to ask of anyone. And then where would I be left, except to suffer further embarrassment and pain?

"I know it was not a good time, Daphne," he ventured, "but cannot you say something, anything to give me hope, some inkling as to your response."

"Peter, I cannot," I whispered, taking a deep breath.

"I see," he replied. "I suppose it was too much to ask of you, but allow me to say, it will be difficult for me to hide my disappointment."

"Peter, please, you do not understand," I entreated. "I am very flattered by your interest, your intentions. There is not a woman here who would not envy me, were I to agree to what you ask. But I simply cannot permit it. It would not be fair to you."

"Fair? That is an odd thing to say."

"I suspect it is, but for reasons I choose not to go into, let me say it is the most accurate word I might use."

"Daphne, can you tell me that you truly feel nothing for me?"

I shook my head. "You know that is not true."

"Then give me some hope. Allow me to court you to proclaim my affection for you."

I did not know where to turn. I did not want to hurt Peter, but if I allowed him to pursue me, would that not be what I was doing? He cared about me. And I had come to care for him, but would I not be deceiving him if I allowed this? Could I keep this dark secret buried within me? Need it ruin my prospects, destroy my hopes for happiness for a full life that I might share with another?

"Daphne, I know I ought not press you, but I want your answer. Having declared myself, I think it is owed."

I nodded. "Peter, I need time. This has put me in a quandary of sorts, and I need time to think it through. I want to do the right thing, but at this very moment I do not know what the right thing is."

He smiled down at me. "I suppose I should be grateful for that. But I do ask that you do not take too much time, Daphne. I know 'tis selfish on my part, but I do not think I can go on like this, not knowing, and keep my wits about me. I cannot deny that it is a decision I want, and I forewarn you that I shall press you until I have one. And now, as the orchestra has commenced once again, might I ask, Miss Barkham, if you would permit this hopeful suitor to twirl you about the floor? I promise that I shall do so a tad less vigorously than Lord Smythedon."

"Peter, I shall be pleased to dance with you again, but perhaps a bit later. I feel the need to freshen up a bit."

"I have not frightened you off," he scowled.

"No, truly. I just need a few moments to collect myself."

I excused myself and as inconspicuously as possible, made my way through the dancers to the front hall. Realizing that I could not simply stand there, I gathered my skirts and crossed quickly over to the library, relieved as I entered that I had found myself alone.

Why did everything have to seem so complicated? Why could I not go back to those days at Mayfair when I could ride free on my mare down to the lake behind the house and gather wildflowers in the fields? When I was a child, I had always longed for the day when I would be grown, and now all I longed for was to return to those days of innocence.

I was angered at myself as tears welled in my eyes. Here I was at the most beautiful ball of the season—our ball—escaping off by myself, overwrought by my own emotions. I had to compose myself. I was just about to retire to my room, thinking that what I needed most was a cool splash of water on my face to refresh myself before returning to the ball, when I started at a sound by the fireplace. There was a pounding within me as I tiptoed gingerly forward. I had taken but four or five steps when suddenly the bookcase wall opened towards me. I knew that I should run, but I stood transfixed, seemingly unable to move.

A man's hand reached about, grasping the wood molding at the side of the false wall.

"Good Lord, what are you doing here, Daphne?" the voice demanded as instant recognition caused my eyes to widen.

"What am *I* doing here?" I whispered, disbelieving what I saw. "I should think it I who should be demanding that of you."

Before I could make any move to retreat, his arm thrust out and grasped mine.

"Unhand me or I shall scream," I said, trying to wrench from his grasp.

"Daphne, the last thing I expected was to find you here," he argued, "but now that I have, we cannot stay here and talk like this."

"Count de la Brocher, I do not know what it will take to have you understand that we have nothing to say to each other."

His grasp tightened on my arm, and pulling me towards him, he pushed me onto the top steps of the passageway, pulling the bookcase closed behind us.

"You *are* mad," I cried. "By God, have you not caused me enough pain?"

"Keep your voice down," he cautioned. "We cannot risk being discovered. It is too dangerous. And stop fighting me. These steps are treacherous; you could hurt yourself if you were to fall."

I was powerless against his grasp, and though I thought of screaming, I knew it was senseless, for none would hear me over the music and milling guests.

"There, just one more step but go no further, for 'tis damp and I should not want you to spoil your gown."

"Chivalry does not become you," I spat back in retort.

"You are not as clever as I suspected," he murmured.

"How did you manage to get down here unnoticed?" I demanded. "Were you not afraid that someone might follow you? I am amazed that you should let Constance out of your sight for even a few moments."

"Daphne, stop it; you do not know what you are saying," he commanded.

"How dare you tell me what to do," I challenged. "There was a time, I admit, when you could instill fear in me, but what more do I have to fear from you? You thought you could intimidate me by extracting a promise that I would not reveal knowledge of this place. I do not know how I could have been so foolish. Perhaps I was too humiliated by what you had done. I now think it likely that it is you my father has to fear, if there is even an inkling of truth in that warning."

"Daphne . . ."

"No, let me finish," I insisted. "I do not know what you are about here, but I intend to find out. You accept my family's hospitality when you know full well what you have done to me. And now you have the nerve to flaunt a seduction of my cousin. You brazenly flirt with her, and yet I know in my heart you have no intentions other than to satisfy your own prurient interests."

He laughed. "In that you are correct, my dear Miss Barkham. I have no intentions when it comes to your cousin."

"Then why can you not let her be?" I pleaded. "What drives you to destroy this family? Will you not be satisfied until you have brought some harm to each one of us? What must I do to get you to stop this vengeance, or whatever it is, against us?"

"Daphne, look at me," he said, bringing the flame of the candle near where we stood to his face. "Do you not see things as they really are? I cannot believe that you have not sensed the truth. After all I have said to you, do you truly think I am carrying on with Constance? That I wish you harm? I think I fell in love with you that first moment we met."

"How can you stand there before me and have the nerve to say that? The gall. Well, you shall play me the fool no longer. On my life I promise you that I shall retaliate."

He shook his head. "Do you not see that your anger is blinding you from the truth? I know I have hurt you. I never meant for that to happen, but it is not the end of the world. We all make mistakes, but out of those can grow good things."

"Stop it," I demanded. "The only good thing that has

come from our journey here to Channing Hall is that I have met one who truly cares for me . . ."

"I expect you are referring to Lord Sanderson."

"Yes, not that it is any of your business. As despicable as you are, he is a man of caring, of honor, but then you would not understand decency."

"Someday you shall regret saying that, Daphne. I suspect Lord Sanderson is a decent sort, though I should advise you that if you are contemplating it, he will never make you happy. There is no passion about the man. He will take a wife and coop her up in his family's castle, satisfied with the required number of children who will insure the continuance of his small dynasty."

"How dare you even discuss Peter," I cried.

"There is not the time to do so now, even if I wanted to. I must get you back to the ball before suspicion arises. That you do not see things as they are I cannot explain to you right now, but I swear to you it will all come clear to you very soon. In the interim, I cannot impress upon you how important it is that you keep silent about knowledge of this passageway. Contrary to your suspicions, I am not the enemy. I know not that you care that my life would be in grave jeopardy if you should speak of this, but I know your caring for your father. Justin and others that are close to you can only be safe if you guarantee your silence. If you break it, I cannot guarantee their safety."

I had challenged him that I no longer feared him, but I could not dismiss his ability to frighten me. Could it be that there was indeed some truth to his warnings?

"If, as you warn, my father is in danger, why cannot you tell me what it is all about? You have called me a fool, but I am far from that. If I am to consider that there may be some validity in your heedings, you then owe me any explanation."

"Not now," he whispered, taking my arm and propelling me back up the stairs. "Too much time has been wasted already. Only know I swear to you that as soon as I feel that I can, I shall come to you and explain this deception fully."

We reached the top of the landing, and I heard the latch that opened the bookcase click. He peered out and, seemingly relieved, said, "Go quickly while we shall not be discovered. But I repeat again, be forewarned in matters you do not understand. And that includes any thoughts you have about Lord Sanderson.''

I felt as though I were in a daze as I stood in that space between the fireplace mantle and the bookcase. I looked down and realized with horror that the hem of my dress had become soiled by the must of the passageway. I could not return to the ball looking like this. There would be questions, and though I was uncertain that I might not be able to feign answers, I would not do so this evening.

Taking a deep breath I crossed the floor of the library and, waiting until several of the maids disappeared from the front hall, scurried up the stairs to my room. When at last seated before my dressing table, I was shocked at my appearance, for beyond the soilage to the gown one cheek was smudged with dirt. I went to the basin, startled at first by the cool of the water that I splashed freely on my face. My hands shook as I tried to reapply rouging to my lips and cheeks. Fortunately, my hair had suffered none from the experience, and it was within ten minutes after toweling the hem of my gown that I had readied myself to return to the ball.

I knew not how long I had been absent, but it was sufficient time to know that my absence would be questioned, if not by Mother, certainly by Peter. As I made my way down the stairs, I concocted an excuse.

It was fortuitous that I had thought ahead, for I had no more than reached the doors to the drawing room than I encountered the two together.

"Well, there you are," Mother exclaimed. "I was just coming in search of you."

"I fear that is my fault, Daphne," Peter suggested. "I became concerned when you did not reappear."

"Nothing to be concerned about," I advised. "It was so silly of me. The heel of my slipper caught in my hem, and I had to have one of the maids assist me. I cannot think how I might have been so clumsy."

"You could never be that," Peter replied.

My mother smiled. "Actually, I am the one to have benefited from the mishap, for Peter here has been most gallant in dancing with me."

" 'Twas my pleasure, Lady Barkham."

"I have never refused compliments, Lord Sanderson, but I am also wise enough to suspect that it is my daughter on whom you would prefer to bestow your flattery. So I shall leave you two together."

"What did you say to my mother?" I demanded, as she moved off.

"Goodness, such vehemence, Daphne."

"Well?" I pursued.

"If you are asking whether I spoke to her of my intentions, I will admit to you that I did. Was there something wrong with that?"

"I just wish you had not done it. I told you earlier that I needed time. I do not think you had the right, Peter. This is between us."

"I regret you feel that way, Daphne. Frankly, I do not think your mother was so displeased, though I sense that it came as no surprise to her. She is a woman of great perspicacity, and though I wish I were less the type to wear my heart on my sleeve, I suspect that she had known of my intentions ever since that first day that I came to call."

"I still say you had no right," I insisted, my voice cracking suddenly.

"Daphne, pardon me for saying this, but you do not seem yourself. I saw no harm. Certainly my intention was not to anger you so."

I took a deep breath. " 'Tis not you, Peter. Let us not talk of this any longer. I promised you a dance, and that is what we shall have."

He guided me out to the dance floor, and as he did, I just missed brushing elbows with Count de la Brocher, who was deep in conversation with Constance.

She twirled about, a wreath of smiles. "I could not think where you had gone to," she offered. "Are you feeling unwell?"

"Perhaps you should ask your friend," I challenged.

If she looked puzzled, I could not read the expression on Count de la Brocher's face.

As Peter led me to the dance floor, I could not think of how the count could be so uncommonly calm, so blasé after what had happened earlier. He was, I decided, the consummate actor. There was nothing in his countenance, nothing in his demeanor that would give suspicion to our earlier encounter. He was polite if abject and remote. At least to me. How he could lie the way he did was beyond my fathoming. Not that I would ever believe him, but how could be profess what he did to me and yet shower these attentions upon Constance? There had been a second, one single fraction of time when I had not exactly believed, but wondered if I might not have been mistaken about him. What a fool I had been. He was intent on using Constance in the same way he had done with me. Well, he would not be successful. Not if I were to have any measure in it.

Blessedly, Peter did not press me for an answer to his question for the rest of the evening, sensing, I believe, that I would not respond well to pressure. Hard as I tried to reenter into the festivities, I could not dismiss the events of earlier. Though to my amazement I appeared solitary in this, for Count de la Brocher, if anything, appeared to be enjoying himself thoroughly, continuing to give his undivided attention to Constance, who, when our eyes met, communicated a smugness over what she deemed her obvious conquest.

I suspect that they would have preoccupied me totally save for my concern about Mother. It was only natural that she should appear tired, but I knew that the tenseness in her carriage and frown stemmed from more than mere fatigue. It was not that Father was avoiding her, one could never accuse him of that. But one could not deny that he appeared preoccupied. Earlier with Monique and now with Oliver. It seemed odd that he should seek him out this night, since indeed the two had spent the past weeks together, but I supposed that business would always supersede social pleasures for them both.

29

serena

WHAT I HAD suspected, Daphne confirmed to me, when, upon seeing the last of the guests depart, she asked if we might have a brief talk before retiring. Had Justin been about I might have suggested that we make this a family discussion, but he had retired to the library some time earlier with Oliver, assuring me that he would be to bed shortly.

The hour was late, and after seeing to it that the maids would take care to darken the candles and be certain that the screens were in place to protect the fires that still burned brightly in the open rooms, I found my way to the second-floor landing and Daphne's room.

She had already changed from her gown into her nightdress and was brushing her hair, now freed of combs, down the nape of her neck.

"If it is too late . . ." she ventured, "we could . . ."

"Nonsense," I insisted, sinking down on the edge of the bed. "Though I admit freely that my feet are welcoming this respite."

"It was a beautiful ball, Mother," Daphne offered, turning to me. "I want you and Father to know how much I appreciate it. And I am certain Constance feels the same."

I smiled. "Might I venture to ask whether 'twas Lord Sanderson's presence that made it a bit more special for you? I noticed that he would scarce let you out of his sight."

She paused, fidgeting with the ribbons on the gown. "Do you like Peter, Mother?"

"I am surprised that you should even ask that," I replied. "He is a charming young man. Though I cannot say I know him all that well, I would be very surprised if one might uncover anything unsavory in his nature."

She drew a deep breath. "Peter has asked that he might commence calling on me with intentions, well, with the intention that I . . ."

"What I suspect you are trying to tell me is that Lord Sanderson would like to take you as his bride."

She nodded.

"And you, how do you feel about this?" I pursued.

She shrugged. "I am very fond of Peter, very fond indeed. He is very sweet and ever so kind. But . . ."

"But what?" I pressed.

"How did you know that Father was the right one for you?" she queried. "How does one ever know?"

I thought for a moment before responding. "You know I have told you, Daphne, that ours was a rather uncommon union. There was a time when I thought that your father was the last man I would ever marry."

"And what caused you to change your mind?"

"I expect I finally realized, or perhaps I should say he forced me to realize, that I had loved him from the first."

"But you had not perceived that for yourself, Mother?"

I shook my head. "I was not without reason, Daphne. I thought myself to be ever so reasonable, and in many ways I was. But I was not experienced in matters of passion or love. I have oft thought that if I had not gone to Camberleigh and met your father, I might well have settled for some peaceable existence with one of the lads from Cornwall, though in my dreams I always envisioned being pirated away by some dashing sea captain. I shall assure you of one thing, however. If anyone would have told me in those early days that I was in love with Justin Barkham, I would have thought them to be mad. In any event, that is not what we are discussing here. Now it is time for you, my darling daughter."

"Oh, Mother, I do not know why I should be feeling so miserable about all of this," Daphne exclaimed. "It would be so much simpler if Peter had not spoken now. Perhaps in time. He is so decent, so honorable, and I do not think I could live with myself if I were to deceive him so, and yet, then, what would I do with my life?''

I sat forward, troubled by the passion of her outburst. I expected her to be giddy with excitement, confused perhaps, but scarcely self-deprecating at a moment such as this.

"Daphne, forgive me, but you are not making any sense. Why would you talk of deception? Why in heaven's name do you even think you would deceive Peter by accepting his intentions?"

The room was hauntingly silent.

"Darling," I pursued, "the only way you could deceive Peter would be by encouraging him when, indeed, you have no intent of one day becoming Lady Sanderson. I need not, I am certain, explain that to you. You will learn that no matter how sensitive, the male ego is large and does not take affront easily."

"I do not want to hurt Peter," Daphne murmured.

"Of course you do not, darling," I replied. "But I should be more concerned if I felt you were hurting yourself."

"What do you mean by that?"

"Only that I do not want you to feel obligated in any way to Peter," I replied in earnest. "Not, of course, unless you tell me that you do love him and wish to commit your life to him. Daphne, Peter is the first man who has declared himself to you. I should venture to say that if you were to permit it, he would be one of countless gentlemen who would pursue you. But I know your father would join me in saying that I should rather see you a maiden woman than trapped in some loveless marriage."

"I fear Constance should be miffed with me were I to fall out of the season."

"My dear, it is kind of you to consider her, but I should not fret that matter," I advised. "I say to you that I wish that Count de la Brocher did not continue to show her attention, for I fear that there is no future for Constance there. As long as he flatters her, she will not even consider the interest of another."

"If I were you, Mother, I would forbid her seeing him," Daphne replied vehemently.

"You really do not care for the man," I suggested, shocked by the passion in her demeanor.

She shook her head.

"I must admit," I pursued, "that there was a time when I suspected that you were more interested in Count de la Brocher than you cared admit."

"Well, you could not have been more mistaken, Mother."

There was a part of me that wanted to pursue the subject of Count de la Brocher with Daphne, but the hour was late and nothing decisive would be accomplished at this hour. I rose and kissed her good night, begging her not to muddle her dilemma any further this evening. Though I understood Peter's motivation, I wished that his ardor was not accompanied by such an ultimatum, such pressure. As I crossed the long hallway to our bedroom, I feared that I had been of little assistance to Daphne. I understood her turmoil, but I knew not how to counsel her. Finally, what I thought of Peter was of little consequence. I could guide, suggest, get her to perhaps look deeper into her own mind and heart, but the final answer lay within Daphne herself.

I was not surprised to find the bedroom empty. I had come to expect that over these past months. Pluck, who was stretched out before the fireplace, bounded forth to greet me as a long-lost friend.

My body ached with exhaustion, and it seemed a consummate effort to extricate myself from my gown. When at last I had removed the combs from my hair and donned my robe, I nearly collapsed into bed. This night it was almost with relief that my arm crossed into the empty space beside me. That I would have to face Justin was abundantly clear, and though I had come to the point that I could no longer escape from the reality of a confrontation, tonight was scarcely the time to broach things like "where had we come in our lives."

Why is it that when one yearns for sleep it seems that it never comes? I expect it was, if only subliminally, my need to escape the painful hours that stretched before me. I had lain awake, I suspect, for a full hour staring into the shadowed ceiling trying to will away the questions and fears that obsessed my thoughts when I heard footsteps and then the handle to the door turning softly. I shut my eyes quickly and consciously tried to breathe normally as Justin strode over to the bed. I did not stir as he whispered my name and soon, seemingly satisfied that I was fast asleep, moved off and commenced to undress.

As he climbed in next to me, tucking the covers up about my shoulders, I bit the corners of my mouth, prayerful that he would not uncover my deception.

"Serena, are you awake?" he whispered, his hand finding mine. "Darling, I know it is late and you must be exhausted, but I do not want us to fall asleep like this. Not tonight. I know that I have been less than fair to you these past weeks—months, if truth be known. You do not know how many times I have wanted to come to you to explain, but I could not risk that. I still cannot. You simply must trust me. Lord knows I do not know what I would do were I to lose that."

I did not know how I was able to remain motionless. I tried desperately to shut out Justin's words. I could not permit myself to respond, not now. I was far too vulnerable, and though an anger burned within me, I suspected that if Justin were to beg my forgiveness, to take me in his arms with assurances that his love for me had not waned, I would delude myself into thinking that all would be well once again. As painful as it was at that very moment to remain impassive to his words and his touch, I knew that I could not allow myself to submit to his entreatments. I had let far too much time to pass before speaking out, and were I to weaken now I would never fully speak my mind.

Whether I had indeed duped him into believing that I was asleep or whether he simply was frustrated by my lack of response, I knew not, but finally, as his breathing took on a regular rhythm, I knew that sleep had overtaken him.

Sleep for me came fitfully, and thus I sat bolt upright when, I knew not how much later, a knock came at the door. It had startled me so that it took a moment for me to comprehend what had awakened me. The light of the moon was still full beyond the window as I jostled Justin, murmuring to him that there was someone at the door. I was amazed that instead of expressing any surprise, he simply threw his robe about him and went instantly to the door.

I sat up, unable to see who it could be who would be awakening us at this hour. It was with some relief that I distinguished Oliver's voice, for I was loathe to think that something might be amiss with one of the girls.

I could not discern what the two were saying, but the exchange took only a moment, and once Justin had reclosed the door, he crossed immediately over to his armoire and hurriedly began to dress.

"What on earth is the problem?" I demanded.

"Darling, it is nothing to trouble yourself about," he replied as he pulled his britches on. "You go back to sleep."

I did not know whether to be frightened or angry as I blurted out, "Go to sleep? How can you expect me to go to sleep when Oliver comes to the door at who knows what hour, and without a word you scurry about to dress?"

"Serena, I told you it is nothing for you to trouble yourself about," he insisted.

I pulled myself further up in bed, my initial fear turning quickly to frustration and anger.

"No," I blurted out, painfully aware of the stress in my voice. "You are not leaving this room without telling me where you are going and what this is all about."

"Serena, for God's sake, do not start something now," he snapped as he thrust his arm into his waistcoat. "I have told you I must go out for a spell, and even were I to have the inclination, I should not have the time at present to explain. Please, darling, just be a good girl and go back to sleep. I do not expect to be long."

I grabbed the covers and threw them off me. "Do not patronize me, Justin."

He strode over to me. "Serena, lower your voice. You shall awaken the entire household."

"And what if I do?" I challenged. "I suspect there is not one who would be surprised. Even the servants must think me a fool. Well, I shall not be played the idiot any longer, Justin. You take off for weeks on end and return expecting that I shall continue to play the role of the loving wife. You disappear in the middle of the night for another of these secret meetings with Oliver, or is that really just a cover for one of your little trysts?"

I was sobbing now, uncontrollably, as Justin strode over to me and grasped my shoulders. "Serena, I do not know what you are talking about. I know I have been less than husbandly these past weeks and we must talk, but not now. This simply is not the time. You simply must trust me for the moment."

I looked up at him, frantically wiping away the tears, which continued to fall. "You cannot keep asking me to do that, Justin, when you have given me nothing to cling to, nothing to trust. If this is but another ruse to go off to your lover, have the decency to be honest with me. Yes, you will hurt me, but you are hurting me far more with these incessant lies, these mysterious disappearances."

Even in the dark I could feel Justin's eyes boring into me.

"What is this talk of a lover? My God, if that is what you suspect, Serena, it could not be further from the truth. Would that it were that simple. I cannot think what has provoked you to this nonsense."

"Nonsense?" I challenged, shaking my head. "No, Justin, for the first time in months I am making sense. I am sorry that I do not have a grasp on myself at this moment, for I had not planned, not wanted it to turn to this, but . . ."

Justin's hands pressed into my shoulders so firmly that I winced in pain. "Darling, I beg of you to try and calm down. I shall return quickly as I can, and then, I swear to you, no matter what the hour we will talk and resolve all of this. I know I have given you cause for concern, but it is not what you think or appear to be thinking. I swear it."

He released me, mumbling that he had to leave. As he did I reached down to the end of my bed and grabbed my robe. I flung it about me, my feet searching for the slippers I had left at the end of the bed.

"What are you doing?" Justin demanded, as my fingers sought desperately to close the velvet frogs across the bodice.

"I am going with you," I replied.

"No," he insisted.

"Justin, if, as you say, I am mistaken, then prove it to me," I demanded. "If you think I am going to lie abed here while you and Oliver go off to who knows where, you are sadly mistaken."

Another knock came at the door. "Serena, I must go, and I am going alone. You could only be an encumbrance."

I drew myself to my full height. "Well, then you shall have to be encumbered, for with or without your permission I am going with you."

He grabbed the candle that he had lighted from the fire. "This is a grave mistake, Serena, but if you cannot trust me, I cannot force you to stay here. Not like this. You have a stubborn streak, and if you think on it, it has never served you well. I fear that this is one of those times."

"Let me be the judge of that, Justin," I countered, following directly on his heels.

As he opened the door, I spied Oliver in the shadows beyond. "What is she doing here?" he whispered to Justin as my silhouette came into view.

"There is no time to discuss it," Justin retorted.

"But surely you are not going to allow, you cannot be

thinking of letting Serena accompany us?"

"It is *my* decision, Oliver," I interrupted. "And do not think that you can dissuade me from this."

"How much time do we have?" Justin murmured.

"Not much," I heard Oliver reply.

"Then lead the way. Serena, since you insist in this matter, follow closely and for heaven's sake be silent. All I can afford to chance is this candle, so take care in your step."

Justin led the way, and as the two moved at a swift pace through the hallway and down the staircase, I clasped at the skirt of my robe, wishing that I had had the time to change into something more practical for whatever lay ahead.

Not a word passed between us as I followed Justin and Oliver over to the library. I do not know what or whom I expected to find there, but I know I experienced surprise at finding it empty. I had only moved by steps into the room when I watched Justin stride purposefully over to the bookcase and withdraw a volume that I could in no way identify in the darkness of the room.

I watched transfixed as the bookcase wall swung forward. "What in heaven's name?" I murmured as I moved towards the fireplace to where Justin stood.

"Serena, this is your chance. If you follow us, I cannot promise you what lies ahead, but I can tell you it shall not be a pretty sight. You can stay here. You will be safe until we return and then . . ."

"No," I insisted in a whisper.

"Then hear me out," he replied. "Beyond the bookcase there are steps. They are stone and can be slippery, so you will have to guard your steps well. Stay close to Oliver, and no matter what, do not utter a word."

Until this moment I had followed in a state of blind confusion, but now as my slipper searched for the depth of the first step, I experienced my first sensation of fear. The air was damp and I fought back an instinct to cough as I moved with trepidation down the cold stone steps, wondering as I did how this passageway could have existed without my knowledge. Who other than Oliver and Justin knew of this place, I wondered, and where did it lead, if indeed I was to find light at the other end of the tunnel?

What were we doing down here? What secrets lay buried in the bowels of this place? I shivered as my foot hit against something sharp, almost causing me to lose my balance. I had no idea of time or distance, my one priority being to stay as much as possible within the light of the one candle that Justin carried and to keep in close pace with Oliver.

We stopped suddenly, and Oliver, pressing his head close to my ear, whispered, "There are steps ahead. You go ahead of me, but keep your hand to the rail, for they are narrow."

I was silent as he guided me in front of him and taking my hand clasped it firmly about a small iron rail. I had counted six steps when I realized that Justin had paused. He extinguished the candle, and I heard him knock once and pause and then strike three short knocks against what I assumed was a door.

I waited and suddenly I heard what sounded like a latch being turned. Within seconds I felt a flush of air and saw a narrow stream of light bear down to where my slippers balanced delicately on the stairs.

Justin turned back to me, saying, "Serena, take my hand and take care, the last step 'tis almost double in height of the rest."

I did as he instructed, and it was but seconds later that I was drawn to the end of our destination. I covered my eyes quickly with my hands as the light of the room beyond struck me suddenly, causing everything to momentarily blur. Before I could regain focus, I heard a low male voice murmur, "Mon dieu, what is she doing here?"

"Do not ask," I heard Justin reply as I tenuously tried to let my eyes adjust to the change.

As I did I was aware that a man was standing close to me. He went to step forward, and I instinctively withdrew, my eyes rising to meet his as I did. "Count de la Brocher," I gasped, looking quickly from him to the surroundings about me. "We are—this is your library."

Justin's hand was at my elbow. "Serena, since you have insisted yourself on us, you will do as I have cautioned and remain silent."

I did not argue, for though my head was spinning with the events of these past minutes, Justin's tone was, at the least, intimidating.

Justin whirled about and demanded of the count, "Where is she?"

"Upstairs. *Tranquille maintenant,* but as you know that can change."

Oliver muttered something that I could not discern, and I

struggled to imagine whom they might be talking about.

"What happened?" Justin pursued.

The count shook his head. "I do not know, save that these spells according to Maria are increasing in frequency. The medicines seem to take little effect."

"You *have* given her laudanum," Oliver demanded.

"*Naturellement*," the count affirmed. "But there is a point."

Justin, who had commenced to pace about the room, stopped suddenly. "Gaston, where is he?"

The count shrugged. "After the ball, he returned for only a moment. Then left. I thought I heard DeMarcier's voice, *mais* I could not be certain. I wanted to follow. *J'espère* that Vautielle will do that. *Tu comprends* I could not leave. We must move quickly, however, my friend, for I cannot be certain when he shall return."

My eyes shot to Justin, who even in this light looked troubled. He rubbed his brow as he replied. "We cannot risk keeping her here any longer. It is too dangerous. There is too much to lose."

"But where?" Oliver asked.

"I do not know," Justin retorted. "At present we must move quickly."

If I had been confused before, I was now completely befuddled. I could not begin to fathom who the people were that they talked about with such intensity. It dawned on me that I must have struck an awkward figure standing there in my robe, my hair falling in unruly masses about my shoulders. That I was unwelcome had been made inordinately clear by the count's greeting. I had sworn silence to Justin, and I was keeping to my word, though there seemed a thousand questions that needed answers. Who was this poor creature who troubled them so? Was I mistaken interpreting their parlance as concern, or was this woman being kept ferreted away against her own wishes? I was shocked that I could even consider such, for though I had no inkling of what transpired here, of one thing I was certain; Justin might be impetuous, complicated, but his nature was not evil. Nor Oliver's, for that matter. Count de la Brocher had taken an odd place in our lives since our arrival in London. I felt a fool at this moment for having allowed myself to be so preoccupied with the count's interaction with Constance that I had missed what seemed a far more ominous reality. I chastised myself for not having been more perceptive. That night at Monique's when Justin had disappeared and I had been certain that I had heard him talking to the count in the garden, I should have known then that something was amiss.

"Serena, are you listening?" Justin demanded.

I nodded.

"I cannot chance leaving you here, so follow closely. No matter what happens, stay with me. You must trust whatever I tell you to do. Do not challenge me."

I followed mutely as Count de la Brocher opened the library door and, after peering out into the hallway, signalled for us to follow. I was grateful to Oliver, who took my hand and guided me to the staircase, for my heart was beating so fast that my legs felt less than steady.

We reached the second-floor landing, but without pause the count moved us down the hallway to a back staircase, which led to the third floor. I was finding myself winded when we finally reached the doorway to what appeared to be a room tucked under the eaves. Oliver's hand tightened about mine as he guided me into the room, which was lighted only by a single candle on a nightstand. Though it was dark I noticed that the room was small and very sparsely furnished, moreover that it showed no signs of having been occupied for some time.

I pulled the neck of my robe about me as the chill from the room pervaded my bones. Count de la Brocher had in the meantime picked up the candlestick and, handing it to Justin, moved to where a miniature armoire stood. I watched as he drew it back from the wall and, running his hand across the molding beyond, unlocked what appeared to be another secret passageway. In the space of less than what could have been no more than thirty minutes, that there were two spaces that had always been unbeknownst to me seemed uncommon. I had known that some of these old houses had been constructed with rooms where gentlemen of questionable report were said to have ferreted themselves away to entertain their varied proclivities, but what I had seen tonight was scarce that.

I moved forward as I felt Oliver tug at my hand. "Serena, you must steel yourself for a shock," he whispered. "But now is not the time to be faint of heart or mind. Do as Justin says, and all will be well."

I squeezed his hand in response, trying as I did to steady my

nerves. I had known real fear before in my life, and though I
had survived it, one never outlives the experience of terror.
Something told me that what I would find on the other side of
that archway would cause me to recollect some nightmarish
portion of my past.

The room that we moved into was dark, and though larger
than the last, the furnishings here, too, were spare, and this
one, too, was windowless. There was, I noticed immediately, a
strange scent in the room, a pungent floral smell, which for
some reason seemed strangely familiar. The figures of Justin
and Count de la Brocher had blocked my complete view of the
room, and it was not until Justin moved forward that my eyes
scanned across the bed and focused on the chair beyond.

Justin had already knelt beside the chair and was whispering
to the frail figure, who seemed to take the form of the chair
itself. That it was a woman I knew instinctively, even though
her head seemed to have been shorn in a style more suiting a
man. I watched, transfixed, as Justin pulled the shawl up
about her shoulders. It was tenderness that he was bestowing
on this woman, whoever she was. Buried off here in this
fashion, one would sense that she was likely more an unwilling
captive, but she made no move to rail against Justin. Indeed,
she seemed, if anything, unaware of his presence.

I moved closer, freeing my hand from Oliver's clasp. As I
did, Justin moved the candlestick from where he sat, up to the
bedstand beside the chair.

"I have brought someone to see you," Justin murmured as
I moved closer to the seemingly inanimate figure.

As I knelt down opposite Justin, I once again could not dismiss the cloying scent, which I now knew emanated from this
woman. It stirred some memory that I could not place.

"Justin, who *is* this?" I whispered.

He looked into my eyes and very gently cupped his hand
under her chin, bringing her profile into focus as he did.

"Oh, my Lord," I gasped, shrinking back from the figure
before me.

"Steady yourself, Serena," Justin advised, placing a hand
on my shoulder. "Here, take a few deep breaths."

I did as he advised before looking up again to study the
blank face before me.

"How?" I moaned. "How could this be? Clarissa? I
thought you told me she was dead."

"I know."

"This *is* Clarissa?"

"Yes."

I looked in horror at this broken, pathetic figure before me. She had always been diminutive, as was Constance, her daughter. But there were no vestiges of the porcelain prettiness that had been there in her youth. The halo of blond curls was now a mat of grey. She was so thin that the skin about her face gave an almost skull-like appearance to her head, her once blue eyes sunken and nonexpressive, even in this light.

"Clarissa?" I murmured, taking her bony hand in mine. "It is Serena, your cousin."

Justin shook his head. "I expect it should be futile, Serena. She is beyond recognition, I fear. Maria has said that she has thought there were moments when there has been some lucidity, but, in all honesty, I pray that is not true, for I would be loathe to think that she should have any awareness of herself in this state."

"Who is Maria?" I murmured.

"A godsend," Justin replied. "Doubtless you will not remember her, but she was in Clarissa's employ those last years after her husband's death. I cannot fathom why, for I suspect that Clarissa was less than charitable with her, but Maria seemed to have developed a certain fondness for her. She has lived with her, cared for her as she would her own child these past two years."

"Two years?" I gasped. "Do you mean to tell me that Clarissa has been like this, lived here like this for two years?"

Oliver moved forward and put his arm about me. "Serena, were it not for Justin, I do not know what we would have done."

"You have known about this as well?" I murmured disbelievingly.

"Yes," Oliver acknowledged.

"Am I the only one *not* to know?" I pursued. "What of Anne, Richard?"

"Of course not," Justin advised.

"But what does Count de la Brocher have to do with all this?"

"That is long to explain. I can only tell you that he has been of invaluable assistance to me."

I turned back to the count, who had been silent through all this. "I do not understand, Count de la Brocher, but I expect I owe you my gratitude for that."

"There is no need," he replied.

"Does she hear what we are saying, Justin?"

He shrugged. "That is difficult to perceive. If she does, she has not the faculties or desire to respond."

I smoothed the hair back from her brow, disbelieving that it was indeed Clarissa before me.

"What happened, Justin?" I beseeched. "How can this be?"

"It was a progressive thing," he sighed. "You likely will not remember, but shortly after Clarissa's husband died, I journeyed to London. Richard was concerned. He had received a rather odd letter. He asked me to see her, ostensibly to inquire of her financial needs. To say that I was shocked when I visited there would be to understate. You know how Clarissa always was about her appearance. She was obsessed with her looks. You can imagine my dismay when I found instead this dishevelled woman, painted as some harlot. The house was in chaos. Most of the staff had departed, whether by their own volition I never knew."

"But she was ill," I interrupted.

He nodded. "That is true. Though the nature of the disease, I shun to conjecture. Her body was racked by coughing spells, her hands shook often and seemingly uncontrollably. But the most terrifying thing about her demeanor was her nature, which, though never comely, had become spiteful, unruly. Though she had scarce been the model wife, I thought at first that the shock of Harold's death might have plunged her into some strange state of bereavement."

"What of Constance?" I pursued.

"The poor child was bereft. And frightened, naturally. She had lost her father, and now she was witnessing her mother's degeneration. It was pathetic."

I waited as Justin paused, aware that this was not easy for him, aware of the burden that he had carried unbeknownst to me these past years.

"I tell you true I knew not where to turn. When I left there that day, I did so with a dreaded thought in my heart, one that history could not dismiss."

"You mean Maura," I ventured.

"I was loathe to think that it could happen again. Clarissa was never a favorite of mine, but to think that she was being plunged into the same abyss as her mother was almost inconceivable. And yet there it was. Madness had taken Maura, and though disease of a physical nature was apparent, so, I feared, was some twisting, some torment of the brain."

I leaned forward and placed my hand over his.

"Unwilling to trust my own reaction, for I could not have my actions colored by the past, I called on Monique. I took her into my confidence, entreating her to visit Clarissa and then to come to me forthwith and tell me of her findings. If I had any doubts, she laid them to rest."

"But what of a doctor?" I pursued. "Surely you sought assistance, some professional opinion?"

Justin withdrew his hand. "My God, Serena, what kind of fool do you take me for? Though I assure you it was not an easy task; Clarissa would hear nothing of doctors. I suspect, if there were lucid moments even then, that she knew that she might have something to fear as much as to gain from professional help."

"So how did you arrange it?"

"Through Monique. She had a doctor, one that she was certain we could trust. She took him with her to Clarissa's a week later, taking care not to mention, of course, that he was a physician. I think that I hoped, I wanted to be proven wrong, but when I met with him later that evening, he left room only for despair. It would be progressive. Where it would all end he could not say, save that he suspected that the day would come when she could no longer care for herself. And, as you can see, that indeed happened. And quickly. This state you see her in now is not a sudden turn."

"But how does she come to be here, in this house?"

"I had to take action, Serena. If only for Richard's sake, I could not abandon her there in that house waiting for some disaster to befall her or, worse yet, Constance. The doctor advised . . ."

"Yes, he advised?" I pressed.

"He felt we had no option but to commit her."

I gasped. "Not to some asylum?"

He nodded. "He swore to me that she would likely not even know where she was. But he could not guarantee that, as this, this disease progressed, she might not become violent."

"But not some asylum," I moaned. "The filth, the people. My Lord, I used to shudder in despair when I read our friend Cobbett's treatises on the subject."

"Exactly, which is why I had to find some other way, some alternative. At first I considered installing a nurse, a team of them if necessary, at Clarissa's. But Monique was quick to advise me that that was not a solution, for there was Constance to consider."

"But she thinks her mother is dead," I moaned.

"I know, and you must believe that that was not a decision that came easily. But it was finally the choice of the lesser evil. Look at her, Serena. Can you not tell me that this is a living death? I do not know that she would even know her own daughter. And what would it do to Constance seeing her mother like this? Can you imagine what her prospects would be if it was known that her mother was a madwoman?"

"Justin, I have never known you to succumb to gossip."

"But it was not I whom I had to be concerned about, Serena. You know how cruel people can be. Was Constance to suffer all her life for something that had befallen her mother? Even under our care and tutelage, you know full well that she would always carry the onus of suspicion with her."

Loathe as I was, I had to acknowledge that what he said was true.

"I came back to Channing Hall one night so distraught that I knew not where to turn. By some odd turn of fate it was on that very evening that I had a caller. A gentleman who turned out to be Viscount Penberthy's solicitor. The viscount had died, as you know, without heirs. The house was to be sold, and he thought, I suspect, due to its proximity to Channing Hall that I might wish to make an investment."

"You mean you own this house?"

"Precisely. At first I was off put, for I thought it indeed the last thing I needed to concern myself with, but that evening, after he departed, a plan started to take form in my mind. I penned a note the following morning saying that I should like the transfer of the property to take place with haste. If those conditions would be met, I would arrange for the money to be placed immediately in an account the viscount had established for charitable funding. The next steps, I fear, were far more complex. First, I had to devise a way to remove Constance from the house. It was Monique who came up with that solution. She went to Clarissa and suggested that it might prove refreshing for Constance to accompany her for a spell in the country, to Kelston Manor."

"But did Clarissa not think that odd?" I queried. "After all she and Monique were never close."

"That is true, Serena, but you must understand that

Clarissa was not herself. I think somewhere deep inside she knew that she could no longer continue to care for Constance. In any event she appeared to embrace the idea. Thus, it was but two days later that I saw Monique and Constance embark on their journey to the country.''

"And that was the last time Constance ever saw her mother?''

Justin nodded in acknowledgment. "The only thing that gave me strength during that period was that Clarissa had embraced Constance warmly before her departure. In all those hours during those fateful weeks I had never seen Clarissa more responsive. I shall always be grateful that it was that image that Constance took with her at the last.''

"The final step was removing Clarissa from her home and ensconcing her here. It was Maria and the doctor who helped me there.''

I started as Clarissa emitted a low moan. "Justin, do you think she is all right?''

"As right as she can be, Serena.''

"I just feel it is macabre sitting here discussing her life as though she was not there.''

"You will come to see, Serena, that for the most part she is not.''

"But why, allowing that she must remain here, why here in this room? Surely there is no need to keep her in these spartan surroundings.''

"For the time there is, but that is a matter of a far different nature.''

I looked up at Count de la Brocher, who had remained silent during all of this. "You will forgive me, Count, but how have you come to live here?''

"I fear, Lady Barkham, that this is neither the time nor the place. You will forgive me, Justin, but we have allowed too much time to elapse already.''

Justin pulled himself up to his full height. "You are right. Fetch Maria and tell her to be swift.''

Oliver came over to me and, helping me up, guided me to the edge of the bed. "You had best rest for a moment, Serena. I am certain this has been a great shock for you.''

"I tried to spare you,'' Justin advised.

My head was pounding, and I took my fingers to my temples, hoping to ease the pressure. "I know, but I had no idea, but then even Richard and Anne have been duped.''

"I prefer to think of it as protection, Serena. Richard has not been well. Do you really think telling him the truth would have best served his interest?"

As difficult as it was, I knew that I could not fault Justin for his decision.

"You know, now, so many things seem to take form," I murmured.

"Like what, Serena?" Oliver asked.

"Daphne's gown," I mumbled. "Constance swore that it was not she who destroyed it. And then that bizarre evening where she was carrying on about her mother."

"Are you suggesting that Clarissa was in Channing Hall?"

"I do not know, the coincidences . . ."

"Serena, I think it highly unlikely," Justin advised. "Beyond the fact that she is always under watch, you can see for yourself she is scarce in any state to be meandering about."

It was indeed hard to imagine, for she indeed looked too frail even to stand, much less venture forth from this house.

"But what of the incident with the figurines, not to mention the ransacking of the library."

"I know nothing of these figurines you refer to, Serena, but of one thing I am certain, the library was not disturbed by Clarissa. Beyond her lack of strength, she has no motive."

I had no longer to debate the issue, for the count returned with Maria in tow. I moved quickly to her, saying as I did, "I understand that we owe you a debt of gratitude."

She bowed her head and murmured, "That is not necessary. I could not leave her. In her own way she had been good to me."

Justin was at my elbow. "Serena, we must go, and I beg you once again follow close and not a word until we are back at Channing Hall."

I did as he obeyed but not without myriad questions that plagued my mind. What was the need for all this secrecy? The hidden passageways, the silence? Whom did they fear returning? Now that I knew of Clarissa's existence, why was there need to go skulking about with some unknown threat hanging over us?

I did not relish the prospect of returning through the dark cavernous area that I now knew connected the two houses, but it was without incident that we found ourselves moments later back in the library at Channing Hall. I had been surprised that Count de la Brocher had followed us back but also pleased.

for I sensed that I might now press for answers to what appeared an ever increasing mystery.

"Oliver, be a good fellow and get us all a spot of brandy, would you?" Justin asked as he began to stoke the fire.

"Not for me," I said, moving toward the renewed warmth.

"Nonsense, Serena, most specifically for you. This experience has likely taken its toll."

I was not about to deny that, though I could scarce sleep at this point, I was indeed overwhelmed by feelings of exhaustion. Justin downed the first brandy and quickly partook of another. I could not blame him. How he could have carried this burden for these past years, it was incomprehensible for me to imagine. Poor Clarissa. For all her innocuousness, all her jealousies, all the times in the past that she had brought disquiet to my life, what a sorrowful end it was to it all. To have seen her there, a shrunken disfigurement of what she once had been was almost too horrible to accept. Justin had suggested that perhaps it was an indelicacy that had brought her to this state, which he had so aptly deemed a living death. Would we ever know? Or did it make a difference. We never really knew with Maura, and in that instance, too, would it have made a difference? The one thing that I had to be grateful for was that Clarissa had not, as Maura had, brought bodily harm to herself and others.

One thing I now understood was why Justin had been so tentative about embracing Constance into our family. How difficult it must have been to see her each day knowing what he had done. Even in this early dawning I knew it was what he had to do, but Justin was a man of great feeling. The guilt he must have experienced must have been agonizing at times.

And then there had been Monique. She had been against it from the first. And subsequently when we would meet, she would always inquire, always exhibit caution on the subject of Constance. She had always been protective, but at the same time there had been an underlying tenuousness.

They feared perhaps. No, I could not let myself even consider it. Not Constance as well. It would be too cruel to even imagine. I thought of her spinning about the floor earlier with Count de la Brocher. So young, so vibrant. Was she too to be robbed of life before her time?

I turned to study Count de la Brocher, who was speaking in muffled tones to Justin. How, I wondered, did he figure in all of this? With all that he knew, certainly his attentions toward

Constance could not have been of any consequence. There, you see, I was doing it already, writing off poor Constance for something that was totally out of her control. Justin had been right. People would judge, wrongly, but there would always be a hesitancy, a suspicion that would surround her if people knew.

I felt a certain jealousy that it was to Monique that Justin had turned in crisis. True, it was she who had been here, and I was indeed thankful that she had been. But that Justin had never shared this with me did little for my already questioned confidence. Had he thought me so weak, so faint of heart that I should not have been able to share this burden with him? I suspected that it was less that than a desire to protect me. I knew that I would have taken Constance even if I had known the full truth about Clarissa, but it might have unwittingly put additional stress on our relationship. I prayed that I would have the strength not to allow my emotions to give rise to any suspicion from Constance or Daphne.

My mind drifted back to Monique. Could I have been so mistaken in my suspicions? The note, the conversations overheard between Justin and Oliver, could it have been that the only intent was to keep this dark truth from me? But what of the ring and Justin's disappearances? There was much I did not know, of that I was certain.

I felt myself relax as the amber liquid warmed my veins.

Oliver, who had come to sit beside me, leaned over and asked, "Are you feeling better, Serena?"

I nodded. "Though I shall tell you it will be some time before I am fully able to comprehend it all. The anxiety that this must have caused you all," I said, tears filling my eyes.

"It is Justin who has borne the brunt of it, Serena. I had no idea until I came to London this time. For a variety of reasons he simply had to tell me. Clarissa and I were less than fond siblings, but to see her thus today, it is more than one should have to endure, though Justin is convinced she is in no pain."

"What I still do not know is how Count de la Brocher comes to be involved in all this," I murmured.

Justin, who had overheard me, said, "Very little, and for the moment I would prefer to let that rest."

The count turned to him suddenly, saying, "Justin, I do not agree. Your wife is owed an explanation."

Justin shook his head. "It is too dangerous."

"*Non, mon ami, maintenant* it is too dangerous *not* to tell her. I suspect she may be of assistance to us in the future."

"Damnation, I do not want her involved," Justin insisted.

"Gentlemen, I fear I know not of what you talk, but let it suffice that I know enough to know that something is afoot. You know me well enough, Justin, to know that I shall not let it rest here. It is not that I have not known danger before in my life. I have faced it more times than I care to recall. If my husband is in some sort of trouble, some danger as you imply, then I shall stand by him in that."

Count de la Brocher turned to Justin, saying, "She is a brave woman, your wife, Justin. Even if we were want to keep this from her, *mon ami*, I fear it is too late."

"He is right, Justin," Oliver counselled.

Justin looked more than a bit exasperated. "Then proceed, but I swear to you if anything happens, I shall have your neck for this."

Count de la Brocher came and took the chair opposite me. "It is difficult to know where to commence, Serena, but if you have patience I shall try."

I nodded.

"As you know I am French. My family is an old one, having settled in what to you is a little-known area called the Ariege in the Pyrenees. My father, though we occupied this small area, was a member of the aristocracy. He amassed great fortunes in land and farming, much like your family.

"You know perhaps of the revolution in France this past *Juillet*?"

"Very little," I admitted. "Save that Charles the Tenth has fled."

"*Exactement.* What our partners on the Continent do not fully realize, however, is that the Revolution was in large part precipitated by *un petit* sector of the population far from Paris itself.

"For years now in the Ariege there has been a struggle between the peasant communities and their antagonists, the state, which is also to say the landowners."

"And you have been opposed, you have said, to these peasants."

He waved me off. "*Non, non,* you do not understand. Let me finish.

"The peasants, frustrated by their lot, formed a resistance. It is called the War of the Demoiselles. You see, the main profit from the Ariege are the forests—some 175,000 hectares

are in the department. Many communities in the arron-
dissements of areas like St. Girons are totally dependent upon
access to the forests for survival.''

"There is no agriculture?" I posed.

"*Un peu*, the pasturing of cattle and sheep mostly, but they
depend totally on the wood from the forests for fuel. Winters
are harsh there, not to mention the need for building houses.
For many years the seigneurs and the crown owned these
lands, and since there appeared an abundance of wood, the
peasants were permitted to take of it freely.''

"That changed a year ago when Marrot, a wealthy property
owner and lawyer from St. Girons, complained. When he tried
to stop the peasants, they rose up against him. This was but
one incident. Others followed. *Malheureusement* the uprisings
took form against the aristocracy—Laffont-Sentenae and
Trinqué, names that will mean little to you, but they, believe
me, are men of both wealth and power. Blood was shed.''

"By these demoiselles you refer to?"

"Yes. Named such because they are men, men disguised as
women. These disguises, they served to give form to these
bands. Though spread through the various communes, they
finally had some solidarity. I prayed that insurrection would
not take place, for, alas, it was to serve none of us. The gov-
ernment made temporary concessions to the peasants, but
there were restrictions. They would not abide. The prefect
began to tax—he demanded that reparation be made to families like Trinqué, not to mention my own.''

"But surely they cannot afford to pay?" I murmured.

"Of course not. To make matters worse, the prefect, Baron
de Montareus, issued a proclamation on the part of the king.
Troops were sent.''

"The peasants capitulated?"

"*Non.* The people, they fight for survival, but now also for
liberty. It will be some time, I fear, before tranquility comes to
the Ariege again.''

"This still does not explain my husband. What does Justin
have to do with this?"

He smiled. "Ah, that is far more difficult, but it is Monique
to be credited for that.''

"Monique Kelston?" I whispered.

"The same. Monique's late husband and my father were
best of friends. Monique's family was originally from the
Ariege as well. My father was in Paris when she married Lord

Kelston. The two became close. Though of different nationalities they had much in common. In fact, Monique is my godmother.

"When the uprisings broke out, I had to find a way to help. For many reasons it was dangerous staying there at the château. I was watched, my actions were under suspicion. I had to find a way to help the peasants, but with my name, my family, you understand that I could not do so openly. Money was needed for food, fuel to continue the insurrections."

"And Justin gave you that money," I concluded.

He shook his head. "You have a most generous husband, Serena, but it was not money that I needed. What I did have need of was a way to funnel the money out of France to England, where, once it reentered, it could not be traced to me or to my family. It was Monique who came up with the idea. She had offered to do it herself, but I could not risk that. Though she has lived here in England these many years, there are many who know of her whereabouts, her sympathies. I understand that you would have ordinarily been in the country, but when Monique knew you would be here at Channing Hall, she arranged it all. He is an uncommon man, Serena. I know of few who would have taken the risk. And Oliver, of course, has proved of great assist."

Justin, who had not taken his eyes from me this long while, came over to me. "Are you beginning to understand?" he said, placing a kiss on my brow.

"You will forgive me if it takes a while for me to absorb all this. I feel such a fool. Justin, you have no idea how worried I have been," I choked. "I thought, I thought you and Monique. . . ."

Justin put his arms about me. "I do not know what has been going on in that silly head of yours, darling, but whatever you have been thinking, you are sorely mistaken. In any event we shall talk of all that in private."

I flushed at how foolish, how vulnerable I must appear.

"Count de la Brocher, there is one thing that I do not understand," I pursued. "Admittedly there have been times when I have been confused as to, let us say, your political and social leanings, but you have made it very clear, as have your friends on occasion, that you are less than a sympathizer with the common man. And yet you sit here and would have me believe that you are instrumental in helping these peasants? I do not wish to be rude, but you have to admit that there are some major contradictions here."

"Serena, you must not judge," Justin cautioned. "Truly, there is much you do not understand."

"That is not unexpected, Justin," the count argued. "Serena has every right to be confused."

"Then at the ball earlier, when you made a comment in passing about the peasants as marauders who should be eliminated, am I to believe that that was not what you intended, Count de la Brocher?"

I was surprised to see him smiling. "Ah, but those were not my words, Serena."

"What do you mean?"

"Serena, the man at the ball tonight," Justin interrupted, "was Gaston de la Brocher."

"I do not understand."

"The man you see before you is Luke de la Brocher. Gaston is his identical twin."

"Your twin?" I gasped, unable to take my eyes from the count. "But it is uncanny. Do you mean to tell me that it was not you who was at the ball this evening?"

"Not this evening and a number of others, I fear."

I shook my head in disbelief. "I fear I repeat myself, but it is uncanny. Why, one would never be able to tell you apart. Even your voice."

The count laughed. "Actually, there is one way to physically part us, but I feel 'twould be indelicate to reveal the location of this birthmark. Our similarities, however allied physically, could not be more disparate in character or sympathies.

"It is a very long story, but there has always been bad blood between us. I do not know how, growing up in the same house, under the same circumstances as we did, our sentiments could be in such opposition, but there it is. Gaston is obsessed with money, with power. He has contributed nothing to the de la Brocher estates, and yet his preoccupation is that we shall not have to part with one measure of them. I suppose I cannot fault his obsession, for I too am possessed. But in my case I cannot be still while hordes of people about us go hungry and cold. I am not such a philanthropist that I would give it all away. I have not the right for that, but I cannot, will not, remain silent, not when the lives of so many of my countrymen are at stake.

"Gaston discovered that I was helping in the resistance.

Had sides not been drawn before, they were then. He vowed to stop me, to reveal me to the crown if need be. I knew that these were not veiled threats. The logical thing might have been simply to continue to counter him as I had been doing, but I could not risk it. I cared not what Gaston tried to do to me, but there were many others. Innoncents who might well have been harmed, their families as well.

"So I lied to Gaston, telling him that I should wash my hands of it if he did the same. For a time I thought he believed me, but I know now that that very night he instructed his supporters to shadow my every move. I conceived the plan to come to England. Truly I did not think he would go to such measures as to follow me here. The mistake I have made with him is to underestimate how far his greed will take him.

"But how on earth could Count de la Brocher, I mean Gaston, come here and other places impersonating you?" I puzzled. "Surely he had to know he would be discovered?"

"Not to give insult, but *you* did not suspect, did you, Serena?"

"Never," I sighed. "But Justin, surely he could not have taken the risk."

"We are almost certain that he does not know of the risk, Serena," Justin advised. "Though I cannot guarantee that it shall stay that way. He suspects Monique, of that we are certain. But thus far I do not think he knows of my involvement."

"You must be mad," I said, incredulous at Justin's seeming naiveté. "Think on it; the man has entertained us, or perhaps that was you, Luke. I am so confused I do not know what I am saying."

"Calm down, Serena, and hear me out," Justin pleaded. "I ensconced Luke in the house. It was perfect, since no one would suspect. I even arranged to have the papers transferred to his name. I could watch his comings and goings, and though this passageway has not been used for years, it made our encounters far less difficult. What we never suspected would happen was that Gaston would not only discover the whereabouts of the house but go so far as to assume Luke's identity. It was very clever really. When Luke would leave and return to France, Gaston would move in. The servants, save Maria, are new, and it was not difficult to continue the disguise. It was by happenstance that early on I learned the truth. If you shall recall, the first time I left London I returned only to have you tell me of the dinner party at the count's. What you could not know was that rather than being in Northallerton, I had gone to France with Luke, who, by way of being the eldest brother, though only by moments, is the only real Count de la Brocher.''

"But why did you not tell me then?" I pleaded.

"And have you regard him suspiciously every time you encountered him? Forgive me, Serena, but your very lack of knowledge served us well with Gaston. He has been welcomed into our home. Surely, this night of all others he must have taken great confidence in this ruse."

"But what of Clarissa? How have you been able to keep that from him?"

"We could not have done it save for Maria," the count replied. "But she is ensconced there in that room because of Gaston. Justin could not chance moving her, though Monique offered to shelter her for a time."

"Do you think she is safe?" I asked.

"As long as Maria is with her, Serena, I do not worry for her safety," Justin assured. "It has been increasingly difficult to sedate her, which is what happened tonight."

I felt I could stay still no longer and, rising, went over to the fireplace. There was another issue here, one which I had not considered before. If it indeed had been Gaston who had been present at the ball tonight, then it was Gaston who showered his attention on Constance. I shuddered at the thought. His own brother was standing before me talking of the evil of this man. I could only be thankful that things had not progressed any further than they already had. Or had they? Had those encounters been less than innocent? Constance would be devastated, for I knew that she was infatuated. But what was I to do? I obviously could not say anything to her, though I wondered how long this ruse was to continue, but I could not in full conscience give her room to hope that there was a promise of a permanent relationship.

"What are you thinking, Serena?" Justin asked.

"Unless you have not noticed, Constance seems to have been quite taken with Count de la Brocher, I mean Gaston. Though he is indeed deceptive, for there were times when I could have sworn it was Daphne who had caught his eye."

"Ah, but there you are correct, Serena," the count advised. "Except that it was *my* eye Daphne caught. From the first time I saw her, chasing your little spaniel in the garden, I believe, I was smitten, though I could not chance telling her of that meeting. She is so exquisite, so like her mother, if you will permit me to say, and yet so seemingly unaware of her own beauty. You can imagine my dismay when I learned that she was your and Justin's daughter. In truth, even if she were not, given my plight I would scarce have the time to pursue her."

"It is almost incredible to believe," I sighed. "But now I understand. Perhaps, if things had been different."

"What do you mean?"

"I do not fully understand it, but Daphne has formed a particular dislike for Count de la Brocher, or the man she believes is the count."

I noticed that a deep flush had crept into his face. "I am aware of that, but you must understand that that is in part to me as well. It was not always Gaston. There were many times, Monique's notwithstanding, when it was I who appeared to provoke her."

"My husband, I fear, did not help your cause. He made it very clear at the inception that he did not want any Frenchmen trifling with either Daphne or Constance."

"I must apologize for that," Justin conceded, "but you must understand it was too dangerous. I do not know about Constance, but Daphne's no fool. In close proximity over a time, she would undoubtedly have become suspicious."

"*Malheureusement pour moi ce n'est pas vrai*," the count concluded. "I admit to you that I had come to the point where I would almost welcome her discovery. Can you know the frustration of seeing that Lord Sanderson shadow her every move?"

Justin strode over to him, patting him on the shoulder. "I should not let that be of concern to you, my friend. When this all settles down, we shall return to Mayfair. You will visit us there. And then we shall see. Daphne is stubborn, like her mother, and I forewarn you, you shall likely have a fight on your hands. I survived it and likely you shall too."

"I do not wish to interrupt," I said, "but while you two are here plotting Daphne's existence, I should offer that she is deciding her own future. Peter, Lord Sanderson, has spoken to Daphne of his intentions this very night, and though I admit that she has not embraced the proposal without question, I suspect that Daphne is going to accept."

"What nonsense is this?" Justin demanded.

Oliver, who had been silent, spoke up. " 'Tis a rotten blow,

I know, for you, Luke, but I do know something about the chap, and he is a rather decent sort."

"I suspect he is," Justin admitted, "but he is not the right man for my daughter."

"*Our* daughter," I corrected, "and I do not think you have spent enough time with Peter to form any conclusion. I am sorry, Luke, but I must speak my mind on this."

"Mark my words, she would tire of him quickly," Justin advised. "Daphne needs a man of strength, of passion."

"I suspect my husband means a son-in-law carved in his own image," I demurred.

"I know I have not the right to ask, but if you could find it in your heart, Serena, to forestall this somehow. Just, of course, until the time and conditions might be right for me to speak to Daphne—I would be ever in your debt."

"Even if I were to do as you bid," I advised, "how could I be certain that that is what my daughter would wish. Justin has come to know you, Luke, and he must have great regard for you, if he is encouraging you to pursue her. But until a few hours ago we were indeed strangers. I have been dealing with two men who, by birth, happen to have an identical appearance. Of that I know little else, save what you have told me here this evening."

Oliver rose suddenly, saying, "None of this is going to be resolved here tonight, and unless you have forgotten, we have far more pressing issues at hand."

I turned to Justin, who appeared suddenly remote, and wondered what thoughts darkened his mind.

"Oliver is right," Luke concurred. "There is trouble again in the communes of Montgailhard. Though small, it is impoverished. The people, they cannot continue without assistance."

"You are returning then?" Oliver inquired.

The count nodded. "I must. I had hoped to wait, but I cannot chance it. For the time Gaston seems content to lend his support from here in London. He will take many risks, but I suspect not with his own life, and there are many who would not welcome him back at the château."

"You cannot go alone, Luke, not with the fighting as it is. I do not trust Trinqué," Justin said gravely.

The count shook his head. "I have asked too much of you already, *mon ami.*"

"You are not going away again, Justin?" I beseeched.

"Serena, I cannot turn my back on this, not now."

I shook my head. "I regret the plight of those people, Justin, but this is not your war, it is not *your* fight."

"There you are wrong," he scowled. "It has become so. Even were it not for Luke, I would owe it to Monique. One repays one's debts, Serena."

"I fear I am in concert with Justin," Oliver agreed. "Luke stands not a chance on his own, but with Justin and myself . . ."

"I would not blame you, Serena, if you were to disallow this. Justin and Oliver have already given more than my countrymen could expect. I know Monique would agree."

I sank back into the chair, the exhaustion of the past hours impacting every fiber of my being. Justin had sworn to me after that diabolical year when we had all suffered at the hands of Philip Taggart that he would never leave my side again. He had been true to his promise for the most part these past ten years, and though I would never forget, I had come to feel safe again. I wondered now if I had been just in this, for I suspected that while Justin felt compelled to keep me in some cocoonlike existence, he had, in so doing, compromised that passionate, involved part of his nature. But how could he ask me to release him when I knew that danger would surround him? He was not a man of small measure. I had always thought his name suited him well, for he never was one to tolerate injustices. And Oliver? He worshipped him. Even as a child, to him Justin represented everything good and strong in life. But as I had my own fears, I had to carry those unknown fears for Rebecca and their unborn child as well. If it were a fight to save the Mayfair-Camberleigh estates, I knew that I would take up arms if need be to protect our people and our lands. But that was one's own. I could not dismiss, on the other hand, our indebtedness to Monique. I felt at once embarrassed and guilty at the thoughts of her that had plagued me these last months. She had been a better friend to us than I had ever suspected. Even if I were able to turn my back on her, I knew that Justin could not.

Justin had come and placed his hands on my shoulders.

"How long?" I whispered.

"*Trois, quatre semaines,*" Luke replied, "if all goes well."

"I do not know if I could trust my sanity for that long," I

admitted. "And what of Gaston, of Clarissa?"

"You can be of help on both issues," Justin confided.
"Gaston is suspicious, but as long as DeMarcier and his
friends are here, we can gain the time we need. He likes you
and is obviously amused by Constance. And he is curious
about me. You could serve us well by inviting him to dinner.
Encourage him to speak of his homeland, naturally appearing
to be in sympathy with his sentiments."

"I warn you," Luke interjected. "Gaston is clever. You
shall have to be very careful. Were he to suspect your involvement in this in any way, I could not swear to what he might
do."

"You do not think he would harm Serena?" Justin demanded.

"*Mon dieu*, he is my own brother, but even I, who is of the
same blood, could not say for certainty. But bodily harm? No,
though he is not a man to be crossed, he would find some
vengeance."

"Do you think you can carry off this deception, Serena?"
Justin asked. "If you had even the slightest hesitancy, there
are other ways that we could keep watch on him."

I shook my head. "There are only two fears I have. First,
what of Clarissa? He cannot know you are harboring her
there."

"He will not," Justin replied with confidence. "Not as long
as Maria is there. He thinks her to be the housekeeper, which
is to our advantage, since, in that capacity, she has full juris-
diction of the house. Clarissa is sedated. Most times she is
much as you saw her tonight. She became unruly earlier, but I
suspect that was because the dosage the doctor prescribed is no
longer strong enough."

"But what if this were to happen again?"

"Then Maria would arrange to take her to Monique's. At
all costs, it is Constance who must be protected in all of this. I
cannot think what the shock would do to her."

"It is precisely Constance who is my other worry. This infatuation she has with Gaston. If I encourage his presence
here, I shall be inviting trouble. Even if you were to permit me
to take her into my confidence, I could not trust what she
might do. First off, I do not think she would believe me.
Doubtless she would be convinced that 'twas some invention
to discourage the relationship."

"Constance is a pretty little thing and not without charms," Luke replied, "but if I know my brother, this is a mere dalliance. He is French to the core and has had his sights set for years on Marisol d'Epagnee, a young woman whose sharp tongue is surpassed only by her wealth. Gaston is not beyond indiscretions, but if Constance is under your tutelage, I truly believe no harm would come to her."

"Then, when should you leave?"

"This very morning," Luke replied. "That is if Justin and Oliver have no objection."

"What should I tell the girls?"

"Exactly what you have in the past, Serena. Simply say that there is more trouble with the railroad."

"You will not tell them yourself?"

"I think not. Dawn will be upon us in two hours, and I should want to be under way before Gaston is up and about. Among his other vices he is known to frequent the gaming tables, which is where I suspect he is at this moment. But we cannot risk his noting any disturbance from this house."

"I shall ready things with Luke, Justin," Oliver said. "We shall meet here at the strike of six—'tis not much time but the staff will be moving about shortly thereafter."

Justin pulled me to my feet. Oliver came forward and embraced me, assuring that all would be well. I turned to the count, saying, "Save for my son, these are the two most important men in my life. I am entrusting them to your care."

"I shall not do anything to cause you to regret this decision, Serena," the count replied. "I shall guard them with my very being, if it proves necessary. Let us pray that it shall not."

We uttered not a word as Justin led me from the library upstairs to our bedroom, where Pluck had happily settled back to sleep. Closing the door without a word, he picked me up in his arms and carried me over to the bed.

"You must be exhausted," he murmured as he unfastened the frog closings on my gown.

"I cannot deny it, though you are daft if you think I could sleep after all this."

Justin laughed. "I was hoping you would say that," he whispered as he commenced removing his clothing.

It was only moments later when his lean, strong body was pressed next to mine. "Can you fathom how much I have missed you, how I have ached for you?"

"You cannot begin to know the torment I have endurd these past months. Justin, I thought you and Monique . . . I thought you no longer wanted me."

"Why did you not come to me, Serena?"

"At first I thought I was imagining things, and then I suppose I was loathe to hear something that would confirm my fears. Not to mention that you have scarce been about these past months. If only you had been truthful with me."

"I cannot say that Oliver did not advise me to do so. But I, obviously wrongly, thought it would put a cloud over the girls' season. To have had you worry each day seemed cruel, and knowing you, you would not have been able to dismiss your concerns for a moment."

There was veracity in what he said, for though my earlier fears were now dispelled, they had now been replaced by new ones.

I shivered as Justin's hand traced my collarbone and cupped my breast. "There could never be another for me, my darling."

My body arched to his as his lips covered mine. Our need was great, and neither of us needed to tempt the other into lovemaking this night. Our bodies united as one, and when Justin, assured that he had carried me beyond my very being, spent himself in me, we lay together, each unwilling to release the other.

We lay in the night's stillness, words no longer necessary, until it seemed but moments later when Justin whispered, "Darling, it is time."

I clung to him and moaned. "It does not seem just. Not when I have just gotten you back, to lose you again."

"You never lost me before, Serena, and you are not about to lose me now. When I have you to return to? No. I assure you there is far too much to lose."

I watched him as he got up and scooped Pluck, who had come to the edge of the bed, and placed him beside me.

"You shall have to watch over your mistress while I am gone, little fellow."

I wrapped my arm about him as his head nestled against my breast. "Well, he cannot occupy his father's place, but he is a comfort."

Seeing that Justin was only packing a small valise, I took encouragement that he indeed intended to keep his journey short.

"I just hope that I can manage to keep this from the girls," I said as Justin, now dressed, strode over to me.

"You will do what you must," he said. "The important thing is that if you suspect that anything is awry, you will send word immediately to Monique. She will know where and how to alert us. The slightest thing, Serena—you must promise me. Now that I have gotten you involved in this as well, I should never forgive myself if anything were to happen."

"You really do believe that Gaston de la Brocher is evil," I offered.

"There is so much that you do not know, Serena. Evil is perhaps too harsh, but the man is involved with—that is another matter. Gaston is simply a man obsessed with money, with power. Luke believes that DeMarcier has him duped into believing that if his allegiance is with the aristocracy, it will be to his financial and political gain. Gaston has always been jealous of Luke, and if he were to meet some unfortunate end, there would be no remorse."

He took me in his arms. "God knows I love you, Serena."

"And I you," I said, swearing at the tears that started to flow.

"Serena, there is something I want you to have," Justin murmured as he pressed what felt like a small box in my hand. "I have been saving it for the right moment. I had it all planned, a romantic evening with just the two of us, but temporarily as that is not to be, I want you to have it now."

"Oh, Justin," I choked as my eyes focused on the ring, the very one I had found in his dresser.

"I know it hardly makes up for my stupidity these past months, but I would take heart if you would wear it while I am gone."

I watched as he slid it on my finger, expectant of my reactions. I had felt sick at heart when I had found it. Perhaps it was wrong of me, but I knew that I would never tell Justin of my suspicions.

"It is beautiful," I whispered as his lips brushed mine.

The distant chimes of the front hallway clock struck six, and I knew that our time together has passed.

"I shall come to see you off."

"No, I cannot allow it. We cannot raise suspicions. You remain here, get some much needed sleep. I suspect the girls will not be about for hours."

How I struggled to keep my composure as I watched Justin

leave. I did not know how I would bear the hours until he returned. If only Anne were here, I thought. She would be of
great comfort, I knew. She had such a level head, such a positive outlook, and though I was certain that she would chastise
her brother for his involvement in this scheme, she would
scarce be surprised.

I wondered how I could go about my days with the knowledge not only that Justin might be in danger but also that
Clarissa lay but steps from me in some sort of living nightmare. I did not think I would have had the strength to do what
Justin had, and yet one realizes that somehow one is able to
call up hidden responses in times of need. He had done what
only could be done. I wondered if she had any lucid moments.
The woman I had seen there this night, I had to admit, seemed
incapable of any action, but I could not dismiss the events that
had occurred in this house. What if Clarissa were stronger
than one suspected? Maria was not at her side at every given
moment. Might she have managed to wander out somehow?
That made no sense. How could she have gotten out, down the
stairs, out the door without anyone seeing her? That is, unless
she somehow knew of the secret passageway. Could Luke or
Justin have mentioned it in her presence? Even if she knew,
she would not have had the strength. I could not bring any
sense to it, but I knew that I would seek to, for in my heart I
desperately wished to absolve Constance of any guilt.

30

daphne

"ARE MY PARENTS awake?" I asked as Charlotte took the brush to my hair."

"Yer mother is still abed," she replied. "She said she 'twould rise after luncheon. Poor thing, she's like exhausted from the ball."

"And my father?"

"I expect I shouldn't be the one to be tellin' ye, but yer father an' Oliver had te leave agin. Must o' been early this mornin', fer even Sidney did not know."

"He is scarcely about the house anymore," I replied. "I was hoping to talk to him."

"I fear 'twill have to wait fer a spell, Daphne. Yer mother tells me there is trouble agin on the railroad. She's not real certain when they kin return."

"But he just came home," I moaned.

" 'Tis a disappointment I know, but ye've got te keep a brave face fer yer mother. Shall I 'ave Cook prepare luncheon fer ye downstairs, or will ye want te take a tray?"

"Just a tray," I said. "I have not been very good about corresponding with Alexander, and a bit of quiet can serve me well."

"I fear ye'll 'ave little o' that since Miss Constance was askin' if ye were up an' about."

I thanked Charlotte as she took her leave, my spirits dropping as Constance flounced in as she left.

"To what do I owe this unexpected call?" I asked, taking the velvet sash on the dress and wrapping it about my waist.

"Well, that is scarcely a welcome," she snapped as she plunked herself down on a chair. "Particularly when I came here with the very purpose of calling a truce."

"Am I to believe that you have come to see my point on the subject of Count de la Brocher?"

"Of course not. But I do not know why you must persist in this nonsense. You have Lord Sanderson; there is no need to be jealous."

I swirled about to look at her. "We have nothing to discuss, Constance, as long as you persist in this infatuation. You may not believe this, but you are my cousin and I do not want to see you hurt. One of us should at least come away unscathed."

She eyed me warily. "What do you mean by that?"

"Oh, nothing," I said, waving her off.

"I do wish we could just talk," she begged. "I thought there would be more to do here. But with Serena so determined to keep us under lock and key, the days seem dreadfully long."

"You could read; it shouldn't hurt your mind, you know."

"You only say that because Lord Sanderson calls almost daily. I must say that he indeed looked serious last evening. He *is* ever so handsome. Not my type but, then, that is of no consequence. Tell me, has he spoken to you? If he has not already, I suspect he will. Miss Foxcroft will be furious."

"What has she to do with this?"

"Well, you must know that she is terribly interested in Peter."

"Why would you say that?" I pursued.

"Oh, you *are* such a silly goose, Daphne. For all your brains, I do wonder at times. Surely you know of that liaison."

The last thing I wanted was for Constance to goad my curiosity, but I could not simply let her implications lie unexplored.

"Ah, you see," she continued, "you feign a lack of interest, but in truth you are just dying to know. Well, I am surprised at you. In any event, the Foxcrofts and the Sandersons have homes in the same county. I would not say that she was promised to Peter, but the scuttlebutt is that there was an arrangement of sorts."

"Well, I suspect that once again you are misinformed, Constance, for since you were pressing earlier, I shall tell you that Peter has indeed spoken of his intentions, and my present sentiment is to accept."

I was indeed distracted as she jumped up and, almost tripping over her gown, ran forth to embrace me.

"You see, I knew it," she effused. "Oh, I am pleased for you, Daphne. Though I hardly like the thought that you should abandon the season, 'tis indeed thrilling. I truly would have thought that I should be the first but . . ."

I grasped her hand. "Constance, I only told you that Peter had spoken his mind. I did not say I had definitely decided to accept."

"Well, of course you will," she replied, pursing her lips. "I do believe he has oodles of money. Though you scarce need concern of that. Though the Foxcrofts are hardly without funds, your dowry would far outweigh hers."

I could feel myself growing tense. "And so you suggest that Peter would marry me for my money," I posed.

"Well, I think we should be realistic, Daphne," she demurred. "The Barkham name *is* something to be reckoned with."

"That may be so," I admitted, "but Peter does not seem the fortune hunter. In all the time that I have known him, I cannot recall once when he even mentioned money."

"Of course not. There was no need. One can be quite well assured of the Barkham name alone. In any event, you have not said definitely—I mean, when will it be announced?"

It was odd. Last night I had been searching for some reason that I might delay an answer to Peter. That my father and Oliver had departed this morning gave me the very space I had been seeking, for I could never commit to Peter without first seeking Father's approval. Although it was Mother who had always been my confidante over the years, it was Father's counsel that I sought now. Some would say it was obligatory, for indeed the daughter of a Barkham was expected to fulfill a certain trust, a certain right of inheritance. But for me it went beyond that. I had great respect for my father. He was an imposing figure but sensitive and wise. His acceptance of Peter would be tantamount.

"Daphne, I do believe you have not heard a word I have said," Constance pouted.

"No, I was simply thinking that with Father gone I cannot give my decision to Peter. So, you see, I shall not fall out of the season after all."

Constance toyed with a tendril of her flaxen hair. "Do you not think it odd that Justin keeps disappearing?"

"I cannot say I do not find it disappointing," I acknowledged, "but you know of Father's work. He has always been consumed by it."

"Perhaps, but I suspect there is more to this than anyone knows. When Justin *is* here, he appears totally preoccupied, and certainly you have seen the change in Serena these past weeks."

I had to admit that I too had been troubled. Had Count de la Brocher not threatened that danger might follow my father, I suspect that I would have dismissed Constance's remark out of hand.

"You have an overactive imagination," I retorted, not wishing her to sense my own discomfort. "I am certain that Mother is simply weary. These balls do not present themselves."

Constance shrugged. "Perhaps, but I would suggest to you that there is unrest here at Channing Hall. You mark my . . ."

Her retort was interrupted by the arrival of Mary.

"Ye'll be pardonin' me, Miss Daphne, but Lord Sanderson has come to call on ye. Shall I be tellin' 'im ye'll be down shortly?"

"Oh, I was hoping we might visit the shops," Constance whined. "Serena is so stodgy about letting me go on my own."

"Though I must admit I would have wished that I could have spent the day in some quiet, I expect 'twould be rude if I refused his call. Mary, tell him I shall be down momentarily."

"What a bore," Constance sighed, smoothing her skirts as she rose to leave. "If I were you, cousin dear, I should remember what I said. I do not think you can afford to be too blasé about Lord Sanderson's intentions."

As she left, I turned to study myself in the mirror. I added a bit of rouge to my lips, wishing as I did that I could dismiss the flutters in my stomach. It annoyed me that I had allowed Constance's warnings to disarm me so. Likely, it was exactly her intent to cause me disquiet, but I was annoyed with myself for taking anything she had said to heart.

Mary had put Peter in the library since, I assumed, it would take the staff the full day to put the drawing rooms to right. He jumped to his feet as I entered, nearly throwing the tea service on the table before him to the floor.

"I expect my legs are still wobbly from last evening," he admitted as he strode forth and took my hands in his.

"I cannot say that I have fully recovered either," I admitted. "Perhaps some tea—might I offer you some?"

He agreed.

I poured the tea, wishing as I did that Peter would not study me too closely, for my anxiety displayed itself, I knew, in my hands.

"I am surprised not to see Oliver about," he ventured as I handed him the cup.

"I fear you shall not," I replied, settling back into the arch of the sofa. "I have just learned that he and my father were called away again unexpectedly."

"Goodness, it appears that your father is indeed a busy man. Not that I am surprised, for he indeed has holdings that I suspect are even beyond comprehension."

I stiffened suddenly at his remark. "I did not know, Peter, that you were aware of same."

He studied me, his crooked smile playing about his lips. "Surely you jest, Daphne. There is not a man in England who does not know of your father's position."

"I suspect what you say is true," I acknowledged, "though you must understand that to me Justin Barkham is quite simply my father. I shall not pretend that I do not realize that he has amassed responsibility and property, but 'tis simply not something I give much thought to."

"And with good reason," he agreed. "As the daughter, one would scarce expect . . . 'tis your brother on whom the responsibility shall fall. You need only reap the rewards."

"Rewards?" I posed. "That is an odd thing to say."

"Just a poor choice of words," he obliged. "A case of semantics."

I lifted my cup and took a sip of the tea, which had a strong, almost pungent flavor. I could feel myself becoming agitated, and yet I knew that in great part it was caused by the innocuous conversation with Constance earlier. She had planted seeds—of what? Of doubt, of caution, like it or not, and it was now giving rise to suspicion of Peter's every remark.

"I know what you said last evening, Daphne," he pursued eagerly, "but I have not been able to quiet my thoughts since then. Having declared myself, I am not wont to wait for your reply. You can chastise me for my impatience, but if you think well on it, perhaps you will applaud me for my perseverance."

I wished, like Constance, that I had the ability to conjure coyness, for it would have given me the ability to dance about his comments. Mother had been correct; you could not fault him for pressing for an answer, but if I had thought myself to vacillate last night, I was doing so even more today.

"Peter," I commenced slowly, "even if I were ready to give you my answer, I would not be able to do so."

His face darkened as he demanded an explanation.

"My father and Oliver, as I have explained, departed this very morning. It may seem uncommon to you, but I would not make a move without his approval."

His eyes narrowed as he studied me. "Are you suggesting that he would not find me a suitable son-in-law?"

I flushed at his statement, which had suddenly removed the obscurity of our conversation. "I did not say that, Peter. You know, as long as I have known you, I truly have little sense of your own family. Ours is a very close one. Perhaps if you were to inform your parents of your intentions, they should have comment as well."

"Why do you say that?" he demanded, his tone becoming shockingly abrupt.

"For one thing, it has come to my attention that I am not the first who has captured your interest."

In all the weeks and days I had known him I had never seen Peter become so agitated. "And what is that supposed to mean?"

"Oh, Peter, let us not enter into this," I advised, not wanting to create a scene.

He stood up suddenly, pacing towards the fireplace. "No, Daphne. If there is anything I loathe, 'tis inference. If you have something to say, then say it."

"Peter, beyond the fact that I cannot give you any response until I have spoken to my father *and* at greater length to my mother, I will admit to you that certain things have come to light."

"Specifically?"

"Specifically your relationship with Kathryn Foxcroft."

I knew that I was not mistaken. Try as he did, I had struck a chord of imbalance by the very mention of her name.

"What is it that you want to know?" I pursued. "Perhaps better said, what is it that you want to tell me?"

"I never thought you the jealous sort," he retorted, his tone clearly exasperated. "I should suspect that of your cousin, Constance, but not you."

"Leave her out of it," I said defensively.

"Fine, though I suspect she is at root of all this. In any event, since you have asked, yes, I shall admit to you that Miss Foxcroft is no stranger to me."

I had commenced this, but now I began to regret it. The last thing I had intended was that we should find ourselves having a discussion of a girl I had only met socially, of whom I had little or no knowledge, save finding her sweet and pretty.

"You do not owe me any explanation," I said quietly. "As we both acknowledged early on, we are both tired. I should not like this to reduce to something we should both regret."

"There you are very wrong, Daphne," Peter advised. "Since it has been brought up, we might as well see this to some resolve. Kathryn Foxcroft is the daughter of dear friends of my family. Though they are far more civilized than to think that I would comply to some sort of arrangement, I will not deny that it is true that the families have always hoped . . ."

"But, then, what right do you have to speak to me?" I demanded.

"As much right as any," he insisted. "I am not Miss Foxcroft's intended. Certainly not in my mind. If I were, do you believe that I would ever have spoken to you?"

I had to admit that it did seem illogical. But though Peter had been very specific about denying any arrangement, he had also been careful not to comment on how he felt about Miss Foxcroft. Why did that not surprise me? It had not occurred to me before, but though Peter had certainly declared a fondness for me, he had never uttered the one word that I expected to hear. Was I naive to expect that a declaration of one's intentions would also be accompanied by a declaration of love?

But with that, would I not have felt even more pressure than I did today?

Underlying this question there lay yet another that, though I suspected it had been there all along, now pricked at my conscience for the first time. Peter had never, even in his most impassioned moments, ever made any physical move towards me. I suspected that I had indeed been relieved, for after that unspeakable incident with Count de la Brocher, a part of me indeed believed that I should never be able to tolerate intimacy with any man. I no longer scrubbed myself raw in the mornings as I took my toilette, but in my heart I never thought that I should ever recover from the devastation not only of my body but also of my mind. I was still daily amazed that one did not perceive some change in my countenance. Surely I studied myself in secret in the privacy of my room, looking for some evidence of the changes I felt deep within me. How could I, I wondered, be questioning why Peter had displayed no physical communication when it was the one thing that I feared most?

How could I even have these questions when I did not feel worthy of Peter's attentions? He had not admitted to any dalliance with Kathryn Foxcroft, and I had no right to inquire. But how could I deceive him? What he had done was not for discussion. An indiscretion, even meanderings would be forgiven. He was a man. A gentleman of breeding. Even my father would not expect him to come to the marriage bed a virgin.

"I have, if you will pardon me, never seen you so contemplative, Daphne," Peter mused as he came to sit opposite me.

"You know, Peter, I do not seem myself today," I apologized. "Perhaps 'twould be wiser to continue this another day."

Peter, who had looked increasingly uncomfortable, surprised me by agreeing. "I should have had the sense to wait," he demurred. "You must indeed be fatigued. 'Twas indelicate of me to call this morning, though I do hope that you will not dismiss my intent."

"Of course not," I agreed with great relief.

"Then you should allow me to call tomorrow?"

"Should you wish."

"I admit I might welcome more enthusiasm, but I will be wise enough to accept it for that," Peter concluded.

As I saw him to the front hall, I was embarrassed by the

relief I felt at his departure. Cook, I knew, would have luncheon ready at any moment, and perhaps it was rude not to have invited him to join me, but unlike the other days when Peter had come to call, I felt no compelling reason to encourage him to stay.

By the time I returned to my room, I was at once distraught and angered. Why did I feel that the world was crashing down about me? I was young, I had been spoken for by a man whom many would envy. I had every comfort, the promise of a long and secure future. But why, then, was I living in this torment, trusting nothing of others and worse yet trusting nothing of myself?

There were none to whom I could turn. I could not visit the darkness that I harbored in my soul with Mother, for I could not, would not burden her with same. Constance, though I suspected a rapt audience, would never be an ally, not to mention that she would not understand. I wanted to think that Father would be the one to whom I turned, but, again, how could I be truthful with him? Damnation, why could I not dismiss the threats of Count de la Brocher? Would that I could, life would seem so much less complicated.

There had been a time, though I knew 'twas in actual time less than six months ago, when life had seemed so simple. I recalled my mother advising me to cherish that time, for I would be fortunate to ever experience it again.

And while she had talked of calm and simplicity in my life, I had believed that I should never be so troubled again. Oh, I had not been unhappy. How could one be, cloaked in the perfection of life at Mayfair? But the quiet acceptance I had always known and felt had changed in these past months. I was still content to take my mare and ride to the depths of the land, luxuriating in its verdant stillness. But for the first time in my life I had looked beyond, been desperate to know what lay beyond the seemingly never-ending vastness of Mayfair.

Was I looking back on that now as my age of innocence? There was a dreaded fear within me that I might never return to that time of gay abandon. How happy we had all been. Confident with the protection that had always been mine, surrounded by my loved ones, it had all seemed so simple then. For Alexander it had always been different. He had never embraced it with the abandon that I had. But, then, he had suffered more, I suspected, from that odious experience with

Philip Taggart. Though two years younger he had never fully recovered. I could not say that the news of Father's death and Mother's subsequent marriage to Philip had not had its own impact on me. It would always be an indelible memory in my life. But for Alexander it had gone deeper. It had left him with, what was it? A suspicious nature? Certainly an inability to trust. Perhaps I would have done well to have been like him. For now I certainly found myself confused. Perhaps if I too had been more hardened by my past, I should not have found myself so vulnerable in my present.

But that was not what Peter was addressing. He was asking me to journey into the future. A future that, try as I did, I could not fathom. Was that because I could not fathom that I had a future with Peter or any other man, or because Peter had given no clarity to how he deemed our future together?

I recalled the first time a young man had expressed interest in me. He had been the son of a family who my own regarded with care, though I was always aware that they were not, as the servants would call, of "our class." I had thought Charles to be such an amusement until we had ridden out beyond the lake one day. He had dismounted, and on the guise of helping me from my mare, had pulled me down, causing me to fall on him and the grassy softness of the banks.

I could still recall my embarrassment, and yet that had not been the only feelings I had experienced. As we had lain there, his body awkwardly straddling mine, his hands at first groping, I thought, to right himself, there had been another sensibility that had seemed to run through my very being. As I had struggled to pull myself up from my awkwardness, I had suddenly felt his breath close to mine. I remember distinctly that I had not withdrawn as his lips pressed against mine. As he had drawn back from me, I recall thinking how curious that what I had physically experienced on my mouth, I felt not, but I had been terribly aware of a knot in my stomach.

I know that I must have frightened him, for he pulled back with such a fierceness that he toppled back over himself, regarding me with an expression of shock or awe, I knew not which.

I had pulled my cloak tighter about me, though in retrospect I wondered why, for though dishevelled I was scarcely disrobed. 'Twas odd that I should think back on that experience now. It had been my only experience and seemed such a trifling by contrast to what I had experienced under the hands of Count de la Brocher, yet I recalled it today as if it were totally fresh in my mind.

Certainly 'twas not out of a searching memory of Charles, for after that one incident I expected that I had little thought about him until now. Indeed the only recollection that survived was of the incident and not the man.

Why, indeed, was I having these thoughts?

Mary had had one of the maids bring my luncheon by tray to my room. I picked at the flaky crust filled with a creamed fish, which I did not recognize, with disinterest. Why did everything appear so complicated? I had thought, dreamed of this day when I would be embraced by one other than my family with whom I should build a new life. But finding myself on the verge of same, I experienced none of the joy that I had so long fantasized about.

In its stead I felt uncertainty, even a certain dread, which marred any possibility of joy.

I threw the napkin against my plate, startled by my own outburst of anger. How could I even ask a normal reaction of myself after what had been foisted on me? And therefore, how could I ever respond normally to another man? When I could not accept this violation, would I not always feel violated?

My trepidation would, by necessity, remain my own. And yet I wished so desperately that I might share my thoughts and fears with another, for it seemed the only way that I would finally be free.

31

serena

I COULD NOT believe the hour.

Charlotte had entered hours earlier obviously distressed that I lay abed alone. I loathed lying to her, but I had to grow accustomed to these deceptions, I realized, if I were to prove of any service to Justin and Luke de la Brocher.

If she had been suspect, she did not reveal it, choosing instead to encourage me to remain abed and indulge in much-needed rest. On awakening hours later I was amazed that I had been able to succumb to fatigue. Fortunately, my body had controlled my mind, for I expected that I should never have been able to face the day without the rest that I had forgone the evening before.

I felt guilty that I had not been about to receive Lord Sanderson earlier. Certainly I did not believe that I needed to chaperone Daphne, but this was a most important time for her, and I did not want to sacrifice my support due to the events and revelations of the past evening.

Unknowingly, Justin had provided the excuse Daphne had been seeking, for with her father's absence, she could scarce give Peter the answer he sought. I was not certain that I could agree with Justin's conviction that this would be less than a perfect match. As I had reminded him, he had not truly had the opportunity to get to know Peter. In so doing he might well discover that he had more verve than he now imagined.

Of one thing I was certain. If Luke de la Brocher was serious about wishing to pursue Daphne, he was going to have a fight on his hands. At first I had thought that if she discovered that much of her interaction had been with Gaston, it might soften her reaction, but Luke had alluded to the fact that she had not exactly warmed to him.

I had been amazed that Justin was so supportive of his fascination with Daphne. Granted he had come to know him these past months, but I had never thought that Justin would ever champion any man's interest in his only daughter.

For myself I could form no judgement. That he was attractive and had command of his presence I had thought from the first. Justin obviously believed in his cause, and though I had to admire his loyalty to his countrymen, I truly knew little of the man's character.

By the time one of the maids had returned Pluck from his constitutional and placed a small luncheon tray on the table by the window, I had concluded that I would never survive these weeks ahead unless I plunged into some activity. I could not simply sit about letting my thoughts control my days.

The first thing I determined to do was to call on Monique. She was the one person to whom I could turn, the one person who might not only give me more insight about the dangers that Justin was facing, but also advise me about how I myself might be of help.

I dressed quickly, asking the maid who removed the tray to request Sidney to ready the carriage. The girls would likely be disappointed when I did not include them, but the conversation I hoped to have with Monique would, by necessity, be private.

The skies were laden with dark, heavy clouds as Sidney guided the carriage to Monique's. Constance, as I had feared, was outraged at being left behind, and I did have to be sympathetic, for she did not amuse herself easily, and it had to be difficult for her these past weeks with Daphne occupied daily with Peter.

I worried that I should have sent word to Monique of my arrival, for I was so intent on seeing her that I would be heartily disappointed to find her not at home.

When we had arrived, I instructed Sidney to wait for me but not to hesitate going to the kitchens and asking Monique's cook for some warm broth or tea. I pulled my cloak tightly

about me, taking care as I moved up the walkway not to let my
boots slip against the icy surface of brick.

Her man opened the door in answer to my knock, exclaiming as he did, "Lady Barkham, come in, 'tis bitter to be out in
this chill."

I smiled, assuring him that I was fortunate to have a hearty
constitution and inquiring if Monique was at home.

He informed me that she was and, taking my cloak, guided
me to the drawing room where Monique was at work on some
embroidery.

"Serena," she gasped upon seeing me. "Zere eez nothing
wrong I hope."

I shook my head. "Forgive me if I startled you," I apologized. "I should have forewarned you, but it seemed important that we talk this very day."

"Of course, come sit by me, *mon amie*," she said quickly.
"Therese has just brought me some tea."

"I am not intruding?"

"Zere eez nothing I like more than seeing you," she assured, "besides eet gives me an excuse not to make myself
folle with this. I do not know why I even attempt it, I have
never taken pleasure from these things."

I accepted the cup of tea, wondering as I did where I should
commence.

"Serena," she said. "I have never been one to, how do you
say, mince one's words, zo let me tell you that I know zat you
know everything. And believe me, I am zo relieved."

"You know?" I amazed.

She nodded. "I will explain zat *après* you tell me what
brings you here."

"I expect many things. I am so confused, Monique. And
admittedly, I am frightened as well. The last hours, well you
can imagine."

"You poor child," she said, patting my cheek. "Zees ees
exactement why I wanted Justin to tell you. Zo you must not
be too harsh with him, for he wanted *seulement* to protect
you. He made me swear zat I should never break my confidence. *C'est nécessaire tu comprends* eet was ze only way. You
know zere are some men who would not have cared. Zey
would have put her off in one of zose places. *Mon dieu*, I
could not imagine it."

"I know that, but I cannot rid myself of the sight of her
before me. Oh, Monique, it was dreadful."

"*C'est vrai, mais* think of the alternatives, Serena. She is there in zat grand house with Maria, who cares for her *comme une enfant.* She wants for nothing."

"I wish I could believe that," I argued. "I do not think I could bear it if there were even moments when she knew the state she was in. What, Monique, if somehow in the midst of this daze or whatever she is in, she remembers Constance and wonders where her child is?"

"Serena, *non,* trust me zat does not happen. You forget zat I have seen Clarissa over zese past years. Zere eez no recognition. I suspect if one were to mention Constance's name eet would mean nothing."

"Perhaps," I agreed, "but there have been some occurrences that have been more than a bit disturbing these past months."

I went on to explain the incident with the shredded gown and Constance's vehement denial that she had been responsible. I told her of the ransacking of the library and of the bizarre morning when Constance commenced talking about her mother.

"I did not know, Serena," Monique replied, her expression indeed troubled. "*Mais* zere must be an explanation. You saw her. Can you truly believe zat she is capable?"

"I do not know," I cried, wringing my hands. "But it is even more frightening to think that it was not Clarissa."

"What you mean eez zat if eet was not Clarissa, then eet appears likely zat eet was Constance."

I nodded, a sick feeling in the pit of my stomach.

"Zere eez nothing to prove zat, Serena," she advised. "I am ze first to admit zat I have wished zat you would show some caution with her, *mais* . . ."

"But you find no reason to believe that she will go the same way of her grandmother, her mother," I said finishing her sentence.

"*Exactement,*" she concluded.

I placed the cup on the table and, rising, strode over to the fireplace.

"You are cold, Serena, let me get you a wrap."

"No, I am well, truly, just a bit on edge."

"Eet is not surprising, Serena. Zere was Clarissa and now Justin, eet has not been any easy time for you."

My hand traced along the mantle, coming to rest on the porcelain music box, the duplicate of the one I had seen at the count's and which Justin had given to Daphne. I opened it gently, mesmerized for a moment by the haunting but now familiar tune.

"Eet eez not without significance," Monique murmured as the porcelain bird ceased to revolve, as the music slowed to a stop. "Eet eez *la chanson des Demoiselles.*"

"You mean it has something to do with this trouble in the Ariege?"

"*Exactement.* You must understand zat eet eez *difficile* to know of the loyalty of some of the sympathizers. Some of the forest guards, in order to discover ze identity of ze insurgents, concealed themselves in the bands of ze demoiselles. As they were in disguise, eet was not *toujours* easy to spot them. Count de la Brocher, Luke, conceived a plan zat eef zere was a tune, known only to ze demoiselles, ze intruders who would not know of zees could be caught."

"That explains why the count must have been so upset that evening when Daphne went to play it."

"You mean Gaston?"

"I expect I do," I acknowledged, "though you must understand that even now I would be hard pressed to know whether it was Gaston or Luke whose presence I was in."

"Eet eez not easy," she agreed. "I tell you zat even I could have been duped. You must understand zat eet had been years since I had seen the two. Zey were only *petits enfants.*"

"It just seems incredible to me that the two should be at such odds."

"Ah, *c'est triste.* Jacques, *le père*, he would be devastated to know zat eet had come to this."

"You knew him well?" I pursued.

"Jacques de la Brocher was a wonderful man. My own father worked for him there at the château for many years. He was very good to my family. My own mother died when I was *très jeune*, and he saw to it zat I had many advantages. We remained friends and zen when I married, zey too became friends. Eet was a sad day *pour moi* when he died."

"That still does not explain how the two, Gaston and Luke, could be so dissimilar in character."

Monique regarded me thoughtfully. "Zo he did not intend, Luke was *toujours* the favorite of his father. *Peut-être* because he was ze eldest. But Luke was zo like his father, kind, always generous. Gaston was always in his shadow. Try as he did, he never seemed to keep up with his brother."

I returned to take a seat opposite Monique.

"You know, my friend, I should not be surprised if you are terribly angered with me," Monique offered.

"Good heavens, why?"

"If it were not for me, Justin would not be on his way to France at thees very moment. If I could have done eet on my own, *j'espère que tu sais* zat I never would have involved him. At first I thought his role would be minimal, but zen I should have realized that Justin eez not a man of half measure. Even if I had wanted to, I could not have stopped him."

"You have no cause to apologize to me, Monique," I advised. "If anything, it is I who should apologize to you."

Monique looked at me questioningly.

Slowly I explained, not without some embarrassment, my suspicions of these past months. Though she insisted that I need not continue, I pressed on, feeling that I owed her this honesty if our friendship should endure as it had in these past years.

When I had finished, she looked up at me and said, "If only you had come to me. Justin Barkham has only had one love in his life and zat ees you, *mon amie*. Never doubt zat again."

I leaned forward and embraced her, noting as I did that her cheeks were damp as well. When she pulled away, she did so saying, "Enough of zat, zere are *plus important* matters we must discuss."

"Much has changed *depuis ce matin*," she advised. "Oliver did not go to France with Luke and Justin."

"What?" I gasped. "Why not? Where is he?"

"Someone had to stay behind to watch DeMarcier and his men."

"But I agreed that I would do my best with Gaston."

"I know and zat will continue to be important. But you cannot be gallivanting around town surreptitiously trying to keep an eye on DeMarcier as well. Surely you see zat."

"So where is Oliver now?"

"*Je ne connais pas*, but he shall return here after dark."

"Then he is remaining here with you?"

"*Oui, mais j'espère* not for too long a time. If you think you are up to it, we should like you to try and arrange a small dinner party *demain soir*, if it is possible."

"And you want me to invite the count? I mean, Gaston."

"Precisely. I should want to be there as well, but eet eez too dangerous. I think he knows zat I am involved. Eet eez imperative zat he not suspect you as well."

"What of Oliver?"

"Ah. Once you tell me when you have been able to arrange zees, Oliver shall return to Channing Hall, saying zat he had felt unwell on ze journey to Northallerton and zat Justin had insisted upon his return. He will naturally be much improved and able to join you for dinner."

"But what is to be accomplished by this?" I pursued.

"Gaston must not suspect Justin's involvement. We need time for zere return to St. Girons. If you invite him to dinner, I think Gaston will believe zat you would never take ze chance if zere was something to hide."

"I see."

"Do not be fooled, Serena, eet will not be easy. You must seem sympathetic but not overly so. Eet will be a masquerade, *mais* the masks can never be removed."

"I understand."

"*Bon*! If anyone can do thees, *c'est toi.*"

I rose to take my leave, assuring Monique that I should send word via Sidney the moment I knew if and when he had accepted my invitation. As the carriage commenced its return to Channing Hall, I determined that I should invite Peter Sanderson as well. Daphne would likely put up a fuss about my inviting the count to dinner, but Peter seemed to have a calming influence on her. Oliver's presence would help. I had to admit that I would feel more at ease in his presence.

Charlotte was in the front hall with Pluck when I arrived.

"Goodness," she cried, "ye best get out o' those clothes right off."

"I am all right," I assured her as Pluck jumped up against my leg, taking my wrist in his mouth.

"Oh, love bites," I laughed, ruffling his ears.

"The little one's been beside himself since ye left," Charlotte advised.

"I am certain he is confused. He watched Justin pack his valises this morning. You know how bereft he becomes at the thought of being left behind."

Charlotte laughed, displaying her toothy smile. "Indeed I do. Now ye let me take that cloak to the kitchen to dry an' I'll be fetchin' ye a spot o' hot tea."

"Not for me, Charlotte. I have just had more than I should have at Monique Kelston's. I fear I would float away with any more."

"Fine, but ye be gettin' yerself in the library. There's a big fire roarin', just the thing te warm yer bones. An' look on the desk, there be a letter from Alexander an' one from me Robbie I thought ye'd like to see."

I thanked her and went eagerly, Pluck at my heels, to find the correspondence. Gathering both letters, I settled peacefully in front of the fire.

Alexander's clean even strokes told me that he was doing well and thankfully still enjoying his experience at Camberleigh. I had worried that he might be lonely. Not that Anne and Richard were by any means dull, but their lives had quieted greatly by necessity since Richard's stroke. It was discouraging to read that there had been no improvement on that score, but the doctors had forewarned Anne that this condition would only weaken over the years. As winter was upon us, the work load had lessened, though this was no less an important time, as all the ledgers were to be balanced and new machines ordered in preparation for spring planting.

Only the close of his letter was troublesome. In my own correspondence to him I had made note of Justin's need to travel to Northallerton due to problems on the railways. He expressed surprise that his father had not pressed on to Camberleigh, if only for a brief visit. I suspected that these were not his sentiments alone, for he hinted that Rebecca, Oliver's wife, was more than a wee miffed that he had chosen to remain apart for this extension of time.

I felt badly that I might not share the truth with him, but I had promised to keep the secret, and to share it would only do a disservice to all.

Robbie's letter was of a far more ebullient tone, not unlike the nature of the man himself. He took such pride in his accomplishments with the estates and continued to champion the way Alexander had taken hold. His letter was not without traces of sadness, for two of our tenants had died since we had departed. They had been there as long as I could remember, and indeed each became, in their own way, a part of our family. We knew their children, their grandchildren, and as the estates had grown, so had they reaped the rewards. There were many who chastised Justin for his beneficent attitude with the tenants, decrying his opposition to taxation, but he had, over the years, proven them wrong. There was a thread of dedication shared by them all. Certainly in those first years after we had seen near financial ruin at the hands of Philip Taggart, I do not think we could have moved forward without their support. And together we had not only made it back but also reestablished the estates as the most powerful in the county, with few others in England to rival them.

I replaced the tissue in the envelope and moved over to the desk, withdrawing numerous sheafs of paper from within. I would respond to Alexander and Robbie, but the pressing issue was to pen an invitation to Gaston de la Brocher.

I did as Monique had suggested, inviting him for the evening next but allowing that if that proved inconvenient, he should apprise me of another date. I had just closed the envelope with reddened wax, stamping the Barkham seal, when Charlotte entered bringing a tray of tea and scones.

"I know ye told me not, but Cook would not have it. Says ye've been lookin' peaked o' late and I cannot disagree."

I thanked her and instructed her to give the sealed envelope at once to Sidney, who should wait for a response before returning.

"Yer not plannin' another party, Serena?" she queried. "Lord knows I've barely bin able te get the girls te finish from the last."

"Only a small dinner party, Charlotte," I assured.

"I know 'tis none o' my business, Serena, but are we goin' te 'ave a weddin' in the future? I know 'ow ye hate gossip, but the staff, well, ye cannot help but notice that Lord Sanderson there has been paying' court to our Daphne."

I turned to look at Charlotte, who regarded me expectantly, realizing as I did that I had been less than fair to her these past months. I had always shared fears, even intimacies with her, and yet since we had been back at Channing Hall, we had scarce talked, certainly not shared the thoughts and intimacies as we used to at Mayfair.

"Of course, it is your business," I assured. "Lord Sanderson has indeed declared himself to Daphne, though I cannot say with any assurance what will come of it."

" 'E seems nice enough. A little quiet fer my taste but then 'twould not be me that would be marryin' 'im."

I smiled, thinking that Charlotte had never been one to mince her words. "You do not like him then," I concluded.

"Now, I not bin sayin' that, Serena. 'Tis only that Miss Daphne, she reminds me so much o' ye. 'Tis like seein' life go round agin. Sometimes I'm there doin' 'er hair an' it's like time fell away an' tis ye that is before me."

"Has she talked to you, said anything about Lord Sanderson?" As soon as I had asked it, I was embarrassed, for I loathed prying, and whatever had transpired between Daphne and Charlotte was a private matter.

"Ye know, Serena, I would never talk out o' turn. Even if she told me, well, I'd be hard pressed. But fer a lass who is bein' romanced, well, if ye want my opinion, she's too quiet 'bout it all. I can't put me finger on it, but ye mark my words, there 'tis more there than meets the eye. Were she in love with Lord Sanderson, she'd be shoutin' it from the roof tops. 'Cept fer the most part she's blue."

"You are really worried about her," I broached.

"There I go with my big mouth."

"Charlotte," I assured. "I would not press you unless I had absolute trust. There have been countless times when you have guided me well."

"Lord Sanderson seems a nice enough chap. I just think Miss Daphne . . . te tell ye the truth, Serena, I wish I knew."

"Well, with Justin away I very much doubt that she will jump to her decision. Perhaps for that we should be thankful."

Charlotte left to take the envelope to Sidney, and I set about penning responses to Alexander and Robbie, asking Charlotte to have Sidney inform me the moment he returned. I had completed the one letter when Sidney brought me his reply. My hands were shaking as I slid the letter opener into the side and withdrew the manilla sheath.

Lady Barkham," *I read.*

> A matter of some urgency precludes my accepting your kind invitation the night next, but if I may avail myself of your generosity, I will be most pleased to join you the night following.
>
> If this is no longer convenient, simply have your man inform mine, and I will hope our paths to cross some evening in the near future.
>
> Otherwise, I shall greatly look forward to being with you and Lord Barkham Wednesday eve at the hour of six you suggested.
>
> I remain,
> Count de la Brocher.

It had not struck me until this moment that both Luke and

Gaston never had used their given name, save perhaps once in my presence. I had always assumed it to be a formality of the French, but since last evening I realized there was far more to it than that.

I was disappointed that our meeting would be delayed an evening, for though it meant putting additional pressure on the staff, I knew that I should suffer the anxiety of anticipation.

Quickly I took another envelope and, carefully folding the count's note within, put Monique's name to the face. I moved quickly to find Sidney, wanting him to deliver the note before nightfall. Informing Cook that I should like dinner served in the small dining room, I went upstairs in search of Daphne.

Pluck bounded forward, instinctively seeming to know that I was heading for Daphne's room. I regretted that I had disturbed her, for she had obviously been resting before I entered.

"You are not feeling unwell?" I pressed as I moved forward into the dim light of the room.

"Just a headache, but I think it has passed."

"How was your visit with Peter?" I explored. "One can certainly not accuse him of a lack of eagerness."

"I fear it was not terribly pleasant, but 'tis likely my own fault. I do not think he warmed to the fact that with Father gone I could certainly not give him my decision."

"Daphne, he has to respect that," I advised. "It was not of your doing."

"Oh, I think he knows that, Mother. I was just tired from last evening. If you do not mind, I would rather not discuss it."

"I saw Monique today," I offered, changing the subject. "She sent her love to you."

"That was nice," she replied flatly.

Her response puzzled me. Daphne adored Monique and usually would have wanted me to share the news of our meeting. Since she had been at the ball the prior evening, I dismissed it, thinking that Daphne had likely spoken to her at length and her lack of curiosity was not surprising.

"Do you expect Peter to call tomorrow?" I pursued.

"I truly do not know, Mother."

"I see. Well, I am planning a small dinner on Wednesday, and I should very much like to include Peter, unless you have some objection."

"There truly is no need to do that," Daphne argued.

"Ah, but it is not out of need that I am suggesting it. I like Lord Sanderson, and in honesty, if he is one day to become a member of our family, I should be pleased to know him better. I really know very little about his family, and I do not have much opportunity at these balls to have more than casual palaver with anyone."

Daphne rose up in the bed and embraced me. "Forgive me, I know you are only thinking of me. Indeed, invite Peter if you wish. It is a very thoughtful gesture."

I hugged her and pulled back. "Before you give me too much credit, I should advise you that I have already invited another guest, one whom you have made it very clear you have no fondness for."

"Not Count de la Brocher," she exclaimed. "Oh, Mother, please do not ask me to sit through one more evening with that man. Have your dinner party if you want, but make some excuse. Say that I am ill, anything, but please do not ask this of me."

I studied her through the darkened light. This vehement dislike she displayed was simply not natural. Daphne had always had a conciliatory nature. I had always admired her ability to look beyond and find some good in another. There had been a time when I had suspected that Daphne was fighting feelings that she did not fully comprehend. That she, like myself years before with Justin, was either too stubborn or too inexperienced to recognize the stirrings that he might create within her. But now that seemed far less likely.

"Daphne, I rarely ask anything of you, but this is important to me."

"When have you formed such an attachment to Count de la Brocher?' she challenged.

"An attachment? It is scarcely that. But surely you cannot be without compassion for Constance. It cannot be pleasant for her knowing that Peter calls on you, it seems daily, while she is relegated to her room. I think she is lonely, Daphne, and unlike you she is not content to amuse herself."

" 'Tis her fault, Mother. There have been many gentlemen who have shown interest in her, certainly you have noticed it as well as I. But she is so enamored with that man that she has discouraged any other interest."

I could not disagree with what she said.

"If you invite Count de la Brocher here, you will just be

compounding the issue. His intentions are less than honorable. I cannot know why you do not see that. The longer you allow her to persist with these fantasies, 'twill be far more cruel in the end.''

How I loathed this deception, I thought, as I replied, "Perhaps. But though Constance is of a frivolous nature, I do not think she is a fool. The count is attentive at these social festivities, but he has made no effort to seek her company elsewhere. I think you should trust my instincts. This fascination will pass. Forbidding it will only serve to heighten her interest.''

"It really is that important to you, Mother?"

"Yes."

"Then I shall attend," she agreed after a pause. "But do not expect me to be civil.''

I embraced her and we both laughed as Pluck tried to wriggle between us.

"I hope you are up to a light dinner in the small dining room," I offered. "I would welcome some company this evening.''

"Of course," she agreed. "I shall tell Constance."

Though I had indeed not wished to be alone that evening, I found that it took an inordinate effort on my part to keep my mind from wandering. With every chime of the hall clock I wondered where Justin and Luke were at that moment. Had they indeed been able to leave London unnoticed, or were they in danger at this very moment? If Daphne eyed me somewhat suspiciously, Constance was so ebullient at the prospect of the dinner two evenings hence that she aptly filled the voids I created. Though the tension between the two had not fully abated, Daphne seemed to be making a conscious effort to check her tongue.

We were all still weary from the evening prior, and none of us needed any encouragement to retire early. Though I had lain alone many nights since we had come to Channing Hall, the bed seemed particularly empty to me now. I did not think I could bear it if Justin were to be lost to me again. I suspected that the real reason Oliver remained behind was on Justin's insistence that he watch over me, but I would have felt more comely if he were there watching over him. Justin was not reckless, nor was he a man of caution, putting right before his own safety. Blood had been shed, according to Luke, before in the Ariege, and there as no readon to believe it would not happen again.

Sun was streaming through the windows when I awakened the next morning. I hoped it was an omen that things would be bright in our future. Though visiting the shops had never been something I regarded as an entertainment, I was aware that I had not ventured out for feminine frivolity with the girls since our arrival in London.

The days were ever dark and tended to be dreary during the winters, and I determined to take advantage of this respite and invite Constance and Daphne to venture out with me.

Not surprisingly, Constance was elated and even Daphne was enthused, causing me to suspect that she was relieved to avoid the chance of Lord Sanderson's arrival. As I had sent an invitation to him via Sidney earlier that morning and had received an immediate, if florid, acceptance, I doubted that he would call today.

When at last we gathered in the front hall, I could not help but think that we looked a smart set. Even Constance, who always had a tendency to overdress, had chosen a most becoming deep blue gown, trim but elegant with its velvet cuffs, sash and trim collar.

That the streets of London were filled surprised me, until I realized that the eve of St. Nicholas was upon us. Only five weeks left, I amazed. Surely Justin would be long back in London by then. He simply had to be, for though the season would scarce be at an end, we had agreed from the first to return to Mayfair to celebrate the Yuletide. Each year there was the cutting of the tree taken from the land north beyond the lake and the ceremonious trimming of same on Christmas eve. There was no time at Mayfair that I loved more. The welcoming rooms were draped with roping of garland and nothing was spared to keep the candles continuously ablaze. All the tenants and their families were invited to partake of the feasting that had been in preparation for weeks before. And after gifts and well wishes were exchanged and toasts made all around, we would gather in the drawing room, our voices melding in familiar carols.

I prayed that both Richard and Oliver's Rebecca would have the stamina to endure the trip from Camberleigh to Mayfair, for it was important to me that all our family be together for as long as we might.

I shut my eyes, thinking that I must not let myself lapse into maudlin fears.

"Are you quite well, Mother?" Daphne inquired.

"Quite. You must forgive me. I was just thinking of the holidays and realizing that our outing today is of more necessity than I had imagined. If your father and I are going to have anything to lay under the tree this year, I had best use this day wisely."

As the carriage made its way through the cobblestone streets, we chatted gaily about what might be inventive and appropriate gifts for our varied friends and family.

Our first stop was to be the cobbler, for I had realized that my boots were approaching a sorry state. Sadly, I had completely forgotten that to get there we would have to pass Clarissa's old house where Constance had been raised.

As if reading my mind, Constance murmured, "There it is, on the left."

Daphne, who had been there perhaps once as a child, sat forward peering out the window.

It was not a house that one could not take notice of—certainly when it had been built it had been one of the most imposing in all of London. For my taste I thought the architect, likely goaded by Clarissa, had sacrificed style and grace for size. But though not deemed one of the notable dwellings by the small coterie that judged these things, it still had been Constance's home, and I knew that those places ever occupied a special corner of one's heart.

"I *do* wish Justin had not sold it," she said wistfully. "I might have lived there one day."

I said nothing, for though I wished I could share it with her now, we had agreed that she would not be told until the eve of her twenty-first birthday. Though Clarissa had left the house to Constance, the property was so indebted that it indeed would have to have been sold if Justin and I had not agreed to assume responsibility for it. The house would be held in trust for Constance until then.

"For myself I should prefer to live in the country," Daphne mused. "I do not think I could stand being parted from the land."

"Well, if you marry Lord Sanderson, I expect you shall reside in London," Constance retorted, tucking her blond curls into the crown of her bonnet.

"What causes you to say that?" Daphne pursued.

"Only that he seems to prefer the city. I think he has little care for the family estates, and I cannot say I blame him. 'Tis so much smarter being here where there is activity. I should think one would grow quite dowdy and stale living forever in the country."

I could not keep myself from laughing. "So it is dowdy and stale that you find me."

She flushed deeply. "You know what I mean, Serena. I expect you thrive on it, but it does seem provincial."

Dear Constance, she thought herself such the sophisticate. Indeed, I hoped that when she did marry, it would be to one who would ensconce her in a city house. Not that I concurred that it offered more excitement, but I feared that she would have neither the stamina nor the sensitivity to be mistress of a country estate. She had little compassion for staff, much less the tenants, and the responsibility would likely overwhelm her.

Once fitted with new boots, and each girl with new slippers, we left the cobbler's, and I directed Sidney to take us on to a small curio shop that I knew Monique frequented when in London.

I soon discovered that one could spend days in this shop, for there was not a corner that was not crammed with a hodge-podge of everything from fancy buttons and buckles to Chinese vases.

It took me only a moment to spot what I deemed the perfect gift for Anne—a large fan of ostrich feathers with a handle of heavily inlaid mother-of-pearl. Richard, who had a penchant for sporting paintings, I deemed would be pleased with a painting by John Wooton showing a gentleman on a blue-roan horse, with his hounds and a dead stag. For Rebecca I unearthed a fine example of Elizabethan blackwork, a linen pillow case embroidered in silk thread in a continuous pattern of trailing vines, and for Monique a pair of Venetian ice pails decorated with sprigs of flowers.

Two hours later I was amazed at how I could have amassed as many items and still not found one thing for Justin. The girls had been very secretive about their own purchases, and though I suspected that I would be the recipient of one of the silver combs that we had earlier admired, I said nothing.

My pocket was well depleted as we left the shop, with Sidney struggling with our countless purchases. When I suggested that we take luncheon at a small establishment near the opera house, my offering was met with great enthusiasm. We had no sooner been escorted to a table than I sorely repretted my decision, for directly opposite us sat Monsieur DeMarcier. He was deeply engrossed in conversation with two men, and though I hoped that we might pass unnoticed, I knew that some sort of acknowledgement was inevitable.

Constance, it appeared, had seen him simultaneously, and finally I had to advise her not to gape so. We had just commenced our meal when, having completed theirs, he spied us and moved towards our table.

"Lady Barkham and the Misses Constance and Daphne, is it not? What a pleasure to see you looking so well," he effused.

I tried to muster my brightest smile. "Thank you, Monsieur DeMarcier," I replied. "We are taking a bit of a respite from our shopping."

"Ah, well, do not let me disturb you," he said quickly. "Do have a pleasant luncheon."

"Well, that was certainly brusque," Daphne murmured as he moved off. "Not that I had any interest in meeting his companions, but he appeared quite to avoid the issue."

"He seemed perfectly pleasant to me," Constance interjected. "I swear, Daphne, that you react to anything or anyone that has to do with Count de la Brocher."

"What?" Daphne exclaimed. "You know, Constance . . ."

"Stop it, both of you," I demanded. "This has been a most pleasant day. Please let us not let it be diminished by silly bickering."

Try as I did to restore our earlier mood, I was not the least bit successful, and thus when we had finished our luncheon, I suggested that we return to Channing Hall.

We had no longer entered the house than Charlotte greeted us with the news that Oliver had returned but hours before, explaining that he was feeling poorly and that Justin had insisted that he return to London lest it be something of a more serious nature.

I registered what I considered the appropriate amount of surprise, thinking as I did that I was growing into quite the consummate actress. After the girls had retired to their rooms and I had shown Sidney where to place the parcels, I went immediately to the chamber Oliver occupied.

"Has anything happened?" I whispered as he embraced me

warmly. "I did not expect you until tomorrow."

"I know, but the more I thought about it, the more sense it made to return today. I could not simply appear tomorrow on the notion that I was ill and appear at your dinner party in fine fettle."

"I see."

"Besides, I feel better being here. This must be tremendously stressful to you, Serena, and I thought I might be able to give you some moral support."

"I am fine," I assured him. "At least as well as I can be under the circumstances."

"I fear I have no news, save that with Gaston coming here tomorrow night we at least must suspect that though they may be marshaling forces, they have no immediate intent to leave London."

"Charlotte undoubtedly told you that we were out shopping. I decided it might be amusing to take luncheon out, and who should we encounter but DeMarcier."

"He was alone?"

"No. He was with two men whom he rather conspicuously avoided introducing."

"Can you describe them?"

I tried as best I could to recollect the faces I had seen earlier.

"Did the taller one wear a monocle, by chance?"

"Yes, yes he did," I replied quickly. "Do you know him?"

"Only by sight and, unfortunately, by reputation. I believe the gentleman you describe to be Astrie de Gudanes."

"Who is he?"

"An aristocrat who is in particular disfavor with the peasants. He owns a large château in the Ariege and has been known to take the peasants to court for violations of the forest code and fining them francs for pasturing in permitted areas. It is well known that he is a friend of the Minister of War and was instrumental in getting troops sent into the Ariege last year."

"I expect it will take me some time before I understand it all," I admitted.

"What is astounding, Serena, is the impact that this trouble in the Ariege had on the whole of the revolution in France. The cry for liberty rings through these provinces even louder than it does in Paris itself."

We agreed that it would be wisest to have Oliver keep to his room for the remainder of the day. I returned to my own room determined to take a small nap before dinner. I was far more fatigued than I had thought, for when Mary came to ask what I might wish for dinner, it was almost seven o'clock. As the girls had opted for trays in their rooms, I decided to follow suit. Pluck reaped the rewards of my lack of appetite, for though Cook had prepared a saddle of lamb, which she knew was a favorite of mine, I was mentally too preoccupied to partake of much sustenance.

When I finally retired, after spending some time reviewing the purchases I had made earlier in the day, I found myself wondering what the following evening would hold in store. Though a part of me wished that Oliver had accompanied Justin and Luke, I knew that I would appreciate his presence at dinner.

The following day started off poorly, and I prayed that it would not be an omen of things to come. Charlotte had taken ill at some time during the night, and though she insisted it was nothing serious, she was feverish and in a weakened state. Typical of her, her greatest concern was that she would not be able to help with the preparations for the evening, but with Mary's assist I had everything in hand by early afternoon.

As the clock struck six we had all assembled in the library. Oliver's presence had indeed proved helpful with Daphne, who, I suspected, would have fussed most of the day, had her cousin not been about to uplift her spirits. I did not think that I had ever seen Constance look more fetching. Her gown of a pale rose taffeta heightened her creamy complexion and shimmer of her flaxen hair. Though I regretted that her chatty enthusiasm was indeed caused by anticipation of the count's arrival, admittedly I appreciated her animation.

Lord Sanderson was the first arrive. I watched the interaction between him and Daphne. It as clear to me that though he was clearly enamored of her, there was still some question in Daphne's mind. She was scarcely cool, but there was a reticence there that one did not expect to find in a woman in love. It caused me to wonder if Luke de la Brocher might not have his chance after all.

I had become more than a bit nervous when, by seven, there had been no sign of the count. I suspected that Oliver shared my agitation, for though he was on the surface being the consummate host, his eyes, too, wandered often to the library doors.

Constance, who was decidedly bored by our conversation of current literature, turned to me, asking, "Serena, are you certain that you told the count the proper time?"

As if on cue I heard a knock at the front door, and within minutes Sidney had escorted the count into the library.

I took a deep breath as he strode over to me, taking my hand, his lips barely touching it.

"I cannot tell you how honored I am that you extended the invitation for this evening," he said. "Though I have more than an adequate cook, it does get lonely at times ambling about that big house by myself."

"We are delighted that you could come," I replied. "You, of course, know Constance and Daphne, my cousin Oliver Camberleigh and Lord Sanderson."

He made his greetings all around, being particularly effusive to Constance, who I wished would hide her responsiveness if only for decorum.

"I must apologize for the lateness of my arrival," the count apologized as he accepted a glass of port from Oliver.

"Likely you must be very busy with business meetings," I said, studying him closely.

"Ah, I fear nothing so productive, Lady Barkham."

"I thought we were on a first-name basis, count," I replied, "though, do you know that after all this time I do not even know yours, but then you French, you simply interchange your given names with your titles."

"Yes, I suspect we do," he replied quietly.

"I am certain my husband must have mentioned it, but I must be getting forgetful."

"And where is Justin, if I might ask?" he said, studiously avoiding my question.

Oliver, who had clearly been growing uneasy at the turn of the conversation, said, "Justin is off to Northallerton. More problems with the railroad, I fear. I was on my way with him, but unfortunately I was struck with a bout of fever and Justin insisted I return here to Channing Hall. Foolish, for as you can see, I am perfectly recovered."

I could have blessed Sidney, for before the count could retort, he arrived to announce that dinner would be served. I had purposefully seated the count to my right, placing Daphne at the far opposite side of the table, since tonight, of all nights, I did not want any conflagrations.

"We were out shopping yesterday, and you cannot guess

who we encountered," Constance effused as the first course of stuffed pike was served.

The count laughed. "No, I cannot, but I suspect you shall tell me."

" 'Twas Monsieur DeMarcier. He was with two gentlemen."

"Whom he studiously avoided introducing us to," Daphne added.

"I am certain it was just an oversight," I said, trying to lighten the conversation.

"DeMarcier can be a bit absentminded at times," he said quickly. "I am certain he meant no offense."

"In truth I was surprised to see him, for some reason I should have thought that he would have returned to France by now."

"And what would cause you to say that, Lady—I mean, Serena?"

"Well, he seemed so passionately concerned about that trouble in the Ariege. Of course, I scarce understand all of that," I added quickly.

He took a sip of the champagne that had been poured. "Excellent, but then we French are partial to vintage wines, as you must know."

"You must miss your homeland," I pursued. "Have you plans to return there in the near future?"

"Oh, I expect," he replied.

"It must prove troublesome to you, all the insurgencies in the communes."

The count placed his fork down. "Might I say that for one who professes so little knowledge of the Ariege, your interest seems particularly keen."

Oliver, who I knew had not missed a word of our conversation, said quickly, "You will learn, count, that my cousin has a most inquisitive nature."

I flushed. "I only meant that the count must be troubled, if only about his château. I know how I would feel were it to be Mayfair."

"You are sympathetic then," he replied. "*Malheureusement*, it does not cease, this madness. The last word is that the peasants, nearly eight hundred, came to Massat armed with hatchets, scythes and guns. They have burned properties in nearby Boussenac, but I have taken measure to guard the family estates. One must take arms against these people. They are the scourge of our land. It is not easy to be an aristocrat in France these days. But it is our measure. Like you, we were born to it, and I shall not see my family robbed of our inherited right. It is a sacred trust. But then I am certain you know how it can be to deal with these commoners. If I had my way, the ministry would imprison them all in some quarter of our land."

The entrée had been served. I knew from Oliver's expression that he had grown anxious, and I tried to acknowledge with my eyes that I knew he feared that I might press too hard.

What I had not anticipated was that Daphne, who had been quietly contained during this repartee, would bring challenge to it.

"You will pardon my saying, Count de la Brocher, but I find that you speak with a forked tongue."

"Daphne," I gasped.

"I do not know how you, of all people, can sit there and listen to this," she pursued. "The count seems not to know which side of the issue he is committed to. Or perhaps he does. If my father were present, I suspect that his tone would likely be very different."

"I regret if I have said something to distress you, Miss Barkham," the count replied carefully, "though I assure you I should scarce change my attitude if your father were present. You suggest that he would be of dissimilar sentiment. Admittedly, as an Englishman born and bred, I should be surprised if he shared any of my passion about my homeland. That is not to say that he is not versed in the ways of my country, but surely he has no holdings; there is nothing to give him reason to take cause."

"My Lord, what a hypocrite," she cried out. "In that one sense you amaze me, Count de la Brocher. You sit here speaking openly against the very people my father supports yet feign only cursory knowledge of him. Yet from your past implications you have intimated cognizance of his every move. Do you truly expect me to sit here like this while you continue to delude everyone here?"

A deathly hush had fallen across the room. Peter, who had been quiet during the dinner hour, looked to be crestfallen or shocked, I knew not which.

"My fiancée, I am certain, means no affront, Count. Naturally these matters are alien to us."

I gasped as Daphne near threw the chair out from behind her.

"Your fiancée?" she demanded. "If that were but true, you would support me now. You sit there, all of you, as though mesmerized. How can you?"

By this point Peter had risen and run round to Daphne, suggesting that they leave the dining room for a spell.

Under different circumstances I might have been embarrassed but this night I was concerned.

"Daphne, sit down," Oliver instructed.

"So you are against me, too," Daphne charged.

"I think I must agree with Peter," he said quietly. "Perhaps 'twould be best that you excused yourself for a moment."

Count de la Brocher commenced to rise, apologizing profusely for anything that he might have said that was untoward.

"I must apologize for my daughter," I said quickly. "There is no need. Please feel free to remain."

"Ah, so the onus is on me," Daphne said. "That is right, forget Daphne, remove her, then she shall not say anything untoward. But none of you understand. Perhaps if Father were here . . . I am sorry, Mother, but how can you sit there listening to this diatribe? I trusted you, believed in you."

I had put my hand out to stop the count from his apparent exodus.

"Lady Barkham, I apologize, but it is clear that my presence here is causing unrest, to say the least."

"Count, I beg of you," I insisted. "This is just a passing thing."

"Perhaps all of you can sit there and draw on false pretenses, but I cannot."

"Your daughter seems well concerned with my interaction with your husband, Lady Barkham, and though I admit that I find him a charming gentleman, I cannot think why I should be challenged so."

"Oh, you cannot?" Daphne challenged. "Are you not going to warn me again? Or was that like the rest of it? Was it all a ruse? The warnings, the challenges—were they as I suspected simply to cover your dastardly deed? How can you sit there and lie so blatantly? What *is* the truth, Count de la Brocher? Which is the verity? That you are an intimate of my father's, that he truly is in danger, perhaps of your own betrayal, or as you now claim, that he is scarce but an acquaintance?''

"Daphne, please, I beg of you," I beseeched. Oliver had already jumped up and was at her side pleading with her to leave the room.

"Let me go with her," Peter said quickly. "I am certain we can straighten all this out."

Daphne jumped to her feet, plying Oliver's hand from her arm. I was terrified by the look on her face as she turned to face the count.

"Again you are clever," she spat. "I suspect my family believes that I am quite daft, and you sit there masking composure when you must be feeling some terror that I should expose you for what you are. Or are you beyond fear as well?''

"Daphne, I . . ."

"No, Mother, let me finish," she insisted. "I shall leave the room, but I want you to follow me. There is something I should have done a long time ago. I suspect you all think that I am unbalanced, but I promise you I am as sane as the rest. If there is madness here, it exists before you in the form of Count de la Brocher."

Constance, who, up until now, had been shocked into silence, suddenly cried out, "Daphne, why are you doing this? Serena, stop her."

Somehow I knew I could not. This was a scenario that was going to be played out no matter what my protestations. Daphne was hysterical, but it was anger, pure hatred, that was driving her forward. She accused the count of being two-faced, of lying, but I wondered suddenly if she were dealing with more than suspicion. Did she know? Had she somehow unearthed the secret? And if she had, how far would she go?

Flinging her napkin on the table, she turned to Count de la Brocher again, saying, "If you have nothing to fear, then you will do as I suggest and follow me. But I warn you, I am going to expose you fully. And if you think my pride will silence me, you are seriously mistaken."

The count drew to his feet. "Miss Barkham, I warn you you are making a grave mistake, but I shall rise to your challenge, if only to prove that you are suffering from delusions of sorts."

"Peter, would you please remain here with Constance?" I pleaded as I rose to follow Daphne.

She had just reached the door and she spun about. "No, I want Constance to hear this as well. I regret it has come to this, but since you have chosen not to heed my warnings, Constance, I think you had best hear what I have to say first-hand."

With that she left the dining room, leaving a dreadful silence amongst those of us who remained.

"Count de la Brocher," I said, trying to steady myself. "Perhaps it would be best if you were to leave. This has been less than pleasant for all of us and a terrible affront, I know, to your sensibilities."

His regard was steely as he replied, "*Au contraire,* Lady Barkham. If I am to be accused of some misdeed, I should prefer to face my accuser, and in this case it is your daughter, Daphne. I suggest we follow her as she has demanded. I have no doubt that this is going to prove embarrassing to her, but I do have a right to protect my honor."

I marvelled at his composure. He had to know that he was threatened with exposure of some sort and yet his countenance was defiant in the face of danger. But, as I read in Oliver's eyes, it was likely that the danger was far greater to Luke and Justin than to Gaston himself. He must know that, I thought, and must be willing to gamble, whatever Daphne's challenge, on the prospect of gaining information.

I took my cue from Oliver, who said, "Well, then, I expect we should find where Daphne has gone, too."

Although I could not believe that he was going to allow this to be played out, I gleaned that he must have determined that to protest would give rise to greater suspicion.

Oliver led the way instinctively, I thought, with some dread, following Daphne to the library. My head was pounding as I crossed the marble flooring in the front hall. Peter, who had gone ahead of me, went immediately to Daphne as he entered the library. I could not hear what he said to her, but I could not help but notice that where anger had possessed her moments before, it now seemed to have been replaced with a certain sadness. I had felt moments of helplessness before but never like this. There was nothing of good, I felt, that would come of this night. Little could Daphne know that what she had been somehow driven to do could bode ill for us all.

I watched in horror as Daphne walked deliberately over to the fireplace wall and, standing before it, challenged, "Would you like to do the honors, Count, or shall I?''

My God, she knows, I thought, praying that Oliver would do something to stop her.

"Though you seem incapable of comprehending, Miss Barkham, you have me at a disadvantage, for I do not have the slightest idea what you are talking about.''

Was he telling the truth, I wondered, or was he, as Daphne suggested, a clever actor? I had no reason to believe that Gaston de la Brocher knew of this hidden passageway, but once revealed, if he had not already surmised Justin's involvement with his brother Luke, there would be no doubt in his mind.

How had Daphne discovered this? And when? And why had Luke made no mention of it to me? I dismissed immediately that he did not know, for Daphne linked knowledge of the passageway to the count.

As her hand reached for the volume and the bookcase sprung open, I noticed a look of puzzlement cross Gaston's face, leading me to believe that this was indeed a revelation to him.

"I must admit I, too, am surprised," Oliver said quickly. "Did you know about this, Serena?''

"I fear not," I replied, trusting that denial was my only choice. "Though this house was built by my husband's father, this is the first that I have known of it.''

"Likely he used it to store a cache of wines," Oliver said smoothly. "He did love his port, from what I have been told.''

"Well, it is scarcely a wine cellar today," Daphne said quickly. "But, then, perhaps Count de la Brocher would care to expound on its uses today.''

Gaston moved forward and, swinging the bookcase back another foot, peered down below. Oliver gave me a quick shake of his head, bidding me to remain silent.

"What is down there?" Constance murmured.

"It looks to me to be naught but a dark cellar," the count replied. "And one not oft in use by the dankness of the air.''

"Daphne, what is this about?" Peter demanded, looking less the ardent suitor than an agitated bystander. "Is there a point to all this?''

Gaston pushed the bookcase wall back. "I must join Lord Sanderson in requesting some explanation.''

"How can you stand there and deny knowledge of this?"

Daphne demanded, "when you have been using this very passageway to spy on my family, likely since we arrived here in London."

The count's laugh was one of obvious disgust. "I have been accused of many things in my life, Miss Barkham, but spying has never been one of them. Even if it were true, how can you possibly fathom that, even if I had miraculously gained knowledge to this hidden cellar, I might gain access to it. Are you now going to suggest that somehow I gained entry to Channing Hall and spent my days or nights in that damp hole? If you are, I would apprise you that you know me not at all, for I am man who likes his creature comforts. And though I mean no insult, why would I have want or need to spy, as you term it, on the Barkham family? Certainly all in England know of the respect your charming mother and your father command. Are you now going to tell me that the Mayfair and Camberleigh estates are but a foil for some deviousness that they are involved with, some suberfuge that would be so compelling as to drive me to darken their very moves? I would suggest to you, Lady Barkham, that your daughter had perhaps take too much to heart those romantic novels that the ladies seem to be so taken with."

"Do not believe a word he says," Daphne cried out. "I do not know why, but that Count de la Brocher has been watching us is the absolute truth. You see, he needs not gain entry to Channing Hall by any other manner than through that passageway. At first I did not understand it, but the more I puzzled it, the more I realized that there are two accesses to this space you see. One obviously is here and the other is somewhere in the home of Count de la Brocher."

"You say that with such certainty, Miss Barkham, but yet you admit that if indeed the passageway leads somewhere, you know not where. So 'tis speculation at best."

"I never reached the other end, and you know it," Daphne retorted. "When I had discovered you, you had to insure that I would keep my silence. There was only one way, or so you thought, to do that. And so there in that dark abyss you violated me with no guilt, no remorse, simply with the deliberate intent of protecting yourself."

"Daphne, my God, what are you saying?" Peter choked.

"I am so sorry," she murmured, wiping the tears that now covered her cheeks.

I felt as though I had received a blow to the small of my back as I grasped the back of the chair before me.

Oliver rushed forward to her, but she pushed him back, saying, "No, let me finish."

"I swore then that I would reveal him for what he was, and I must have shaken him, for he concocted some story that, if I spoke of this indiscretion, I would put Father in danger."

"Serena, what is she saying?" Constance, who looked ashen, demanded.

"You would not listen to me, Constance," Daphne said.

Constance, who was now also overcome by tears, demanded, "Why must you be so hateful?"

"My only remorse is that I have not spoken sooner."

Oliver turned to face Gaston. "Count de la Brocher, I must apologize for my cousin's outburst. Too much has happened here to permit me to sort any of this, save to say that my cousin is obviously disturbed. I beg your forgiveness in her stead, but I would suggest that at the moment there can be nothing gained by your remaining here."

"You are not going to tell me that you are to take his side in this?" Daphne gasped. "What do I need to say? That he took me wantonly, that he violated my very being, professing undying love throughout it all? But that was not enough, for when I warned him, threatened him with exposure, he blatantly sought the affections of Constance, who was the innocent in all of this. Do you not care that unwittingly she might have been his next victim?"

"You shush this very moment, Daphne Barkham," Constance cried out. "I will not remain here one second longer and listen to your outrageous lies." And with that she gathered her skirts and ran from the room.

Daphne simultaneously stepped forward and, turning to Lord Sanderson, entreated, "Peter, I beg of you to get me out of here. There is nothing more to be said and obviously nothing to be gained here."

I longed to run forward and embrace her, to take this flesh and blood of mine in my arms and assure her that all would be well, that no matter the pain she was feeling at this moment, it would disappear, but I stood still, realizing that it was to Peter that she had turned.

I watched in disbelief as instead of welcoming her, enfolding her as she needed, he shied from her approach, his normally boyish crooked smile now drawn in a regard of total disdain.

"Peter?" she cried out.

"Lady Barkham, you will excuse me, but I fear my presence here is only—well, I think it would be best if I took my leave."

"I cannot say that I lay blame, Lord Sanderson," the count said quickly, "though I feel it is incumbent upon me to assure you that Miss Barkham is suffering from delusions of sorts. I cannot think what would have provoked this, but I assure you that these, these ramblings of hers are totally unfounded."

"I expect we are all overwrought," Peter replied.

I watched in disbelief as he left the library without another word. As the door closed with what seemed an auspicious finality, I heart Daphne mutter, "It is true that certain things are to be expected, but why is it that we never fully expect them?"

"Count de la Brocher," Oliver commenced.

"You need not say another word," Gaston replied. "Save to say that I share the despair that you and Lady Barkham must now be feeling. I will see my way out."

I could not take my eyes from Daphne, who, I thought, looked near the edge of collapse. "You have not won, Count de la Brocher," she threatened.

As soon as he had closed the door to the library, Oliver turned to me, saying quickly, "You see to Daphne, I had best go to Constance."

"But he knows, he must," I said, barely able to raise my voice above a whisper.

He nodded. "Assuredly, but we will deal with that later."

32
daphne

MY EYES HAD found one small square on the rug on which I focused. I could not allow myself to look up from it, for I knew that I could not bear to meet my mother's gaze. What had I done? By trying to expose Count de la Brocher, I had brought ruin not only to myself but also to my family. What had possessed me? Was I, as they must all think, taken by some demon? I should never have attempted this evening no matter what the entreatment. It had seemed so important to Mother that I partake in this evening, and I had agreed against my better judgement. As Oliver and Peter were to be present, I had hoped that they would provide a balance. Why could I not have kept silent? What good had been served by what I had done? He had denied everything—the threats, the violation —but what had I expected, that once confronted he would have admitted his heinous crimes?

I was incredulous that he could have stood there, as he had, seemingly unabashed by my confrontation. The man indeed possessed more cunning than I had imagined.

I felt my mother's hand on my arm as she said, "Come, Daphne, you must sit down and drink this."

"I am all right," I insisted.

She guided me to a chair and pressed the glass into my hand. "I beg to differ with you. But this will help. Sip it slowly until you have regained your composure."

I could not bear to look at her as she pulled a chair up near mine and leaned forward to brush a lock of hair framing my face. "We need not talk unless you want to."

Putting the glass to my lips, I did as she had bid and took small sips of the liquid, which left a hot, burning sensation at the back of my throat.

"If you are up to it, Daphne, I think you should try to go up to bed. We can talk there if you wish."

I nodded. I was indeed exhausted, my senses further dulled by the brandy. I prayed that Mother would not press any conversation, for I did not think I could bear her inquisitions or, even worse, kindly ministerings.

Mother crooked her arm under mine and led me slowly up the stairs past Sidney, who looked more than a mite troubled.

"Shall I lock up the house, Lady Barkham?"

"Please, Sidney," Mother replied. "Though keep a fire going in the library. I shall likely be down later."

We had but reached the second floor landing when I heard shouts coming from Constance's room.

"You would defend her no matter what," I heard her accuse. "She has been jealous of me from the very first. How could you and Serena let her do this? Why did you not stop her before she made fools of us all?"

Oliver's reply was unintelligible.

"Well, you know as certainly as I that she will never see Lord Sanderson again. Even if he disbelieves her drivel, he will scarce want to be involved with some hysterical woman. I hope she knows that she has dashed her chances."

Mother tightened her hold on my arm as she guided me down the hall. "Do not listen to that, Daphne. She is upset. I would not give any quarter to what she says."

We entered my bedroom and I turned to her, responding, "Unfortunately, I think what Constance says about Peter is well founded."

"I think not," Mother assured. "But if he did prove to be so shallow of character as to judge you without understanding fully the circumstances, then he is far less the man that I had hoped. In any event, fretting over that will not serve any purpose this evening. You will feel much better when you get into bed."

I turned to her, saying, "I will be all right, Mother, but

though I expect you feel that you are owed an explanation, I need to be alone right now."

She studied me at length in the dim candlelight. "I will not press, Daphne, but I want you to know that I am here for you no matter what the hour. I know you think that I am full of advice, but I am a good listener as well."

I could feel the tears cascade with abandon down my cheeks. "How can you be so calm when I have caused you such humiliation?"

She pulled me to her, holding me close. "What I feel is not your concern, Daphne, but hear well when I tell you that it is not humiliation. I am confused and concerned for reasons that you do not know, but I have more of a sense of who my daughter is than to experience humiliation over what happened here tonight."

I watched as she turned to leave, saying as she did, "Remember, I am here for you, darling."

I knew I should shed my clothes, but even that seemed an effort of overwhelming proportion. I passed by my dressing table, studiously avoiding the mirror above. I could not stand to look at myself, not now.

As I fell onto the bed and pulled my legs and skirts up onto the downy soft comforter, I began to experience a dizziness that gave me the sense that everything in the room was whirling about me. I clutched at the bedclothes, praying that it would stop, lest I be physically ill.

I tried to tell myself that it was the effect of the brandy that I was having an uncommon reaction to, but I knew that far more it was the range of emotions from shame to guilt to anger that tortured my very being.

The torment that welled within me I could not suppress. The worst of it was that I could find no forgiveness. None for what had happened these weeks before and none for what had happened here tonight. All this time I had kept silent. When even in the darkest moments I had thought I could not bear the pain, the violation, I had been able to muster some strength within myself to go on.

Why now, when the awful truth might have been buried in the past, had I made it part of all our present. Was I, as Constance accused, so selfish that I was driven to use my own destruction to destroy the lives of others?

No, as harsh as I deserved to be on myself, it was not self-ishness that had caused this. Perhaps it was inevitable. Obviously, what I had thought I could control, could somehow purge from my mind, was stronger than I.

Nothing made any sense to me these days. I thought I knew my mother and Oliver. We had always been so close. But sitting there at dinner I felt that I was sitting with strangers. Was I the only one who could see through Count de la Brocher? More than with any instruction of our youth, Alexander and I had been ingrained with the teachings that though we were born to privilege, we had to have compassion for those less fortunate. Father had always been known as a champion of the common man. For years he had opposed heavy taxation, fought the corn laws, not to mention believing, against all opposition, in the railways, which he was convinced would bring commerce and employment to a beleaguered north. It was an acknowledged fact that Mother and Father had been great friends with William Cobbett, whose treatises championed the poor and maligned. Upon Cobbett's death, Mother even established a fund to see that his works would continue to be published and distributed throughout England.

Then, how could she have sat there at dinner listening to the convictions of a man whose principles were in total opposition to her own? Mother had always been one to speak her mind, yet tonight she had almost appeared to encourage the count's diatribe on the place of the aristocracy. Oliver, admittedly, had been less than loquacious, but why had neither spoken, given some challenge to the count? If Father had been there, nothing less than a row would have ensued, but, then, I suspected that if he had been present, the count would have couched his words well. He had tried to convince me that Father was in danger, but it was he who had clearly been deceptive about his real commitments and motives.

I was about to get up to claim a damp cloth to place on my head when the door swung open suddenly.

"I do not care if you are asleep or not, Daphne Barkham," Constance cried out as her rustling skirts moved towards my bed. "Oliver and Serena may be charitable about this but not I."

"Constance, please . . ." I beseeched.

"No, Daphne. For months now I have had to tolerate your

innuendos, your warnings. But you were not successful, were you? So you concocted this, this madness. Well, let me tell you, cousin, you have only succeeded in destroying yourself. I would not be surprised if Oliver and Serena are at this very moment planning how to send you back to Mayfair and what story to concoct to cover the, shall we say, mysterious circumstances.''

I tried to pull myself up in bed, still plagued by the dizziness. "Constance, listen to me," I whispered. "I am not capable of discussing this now, but I beg you not to judge me, not to hate me as you seem to, until I have had a chance to explain. I owe you that, but in the interim do not delude yourself about what you heard earlier. I swear to you it is the truth.''

"Do you really expect me to believe that Count de la Brocher enticed you into that cellar, whatever it is, and then seduced you against all protestation? Please, Daphne, give me more respect than that. If I were so foolhardy to believe that there was indeed any seduction, it would not be the count who I would think to be the aggressor. But, you see, I do not believe that *anything* happened. Not that you would not have wished it. I saw you that night at the Foxcroft ball. You feigned loathing, but it was not loathing that I saw.''

"Constance, you do not know what you are saying," I argued. "Do you think I dragged you all into the library and there confronted you, Peter, and the count for some bizarre ulterior motive? As I have already overheard you declare to Oliver, it is likely that this is the last I should ever see of Peter. Does it not strike you that I have lost more than I could ever have hoped to have gained?''

"You are truly quite remarkable, Daphne. I really think you expect me to show pity for what you have done. All you can hope is that Peter will experience such mystification from your performance this evening that he will never breathe a word of it to another.''

I lay very still, caught between a desperation to convince Constance that I had indeed spoken the truth and the realization that she was so angered and distraught that she would give no credence to my words.

"Then sleep if you can, though if you have any conscience, you will lie awake this night and think of what you have wrought. Believe me, Daphne, this is not the end of it. Serena, once the shock has passed, will likely rise to protect her darling daughter, but I am not going to forget.''

I heard her move towards the door. "Oh, and another thing: though things look bleak at the moment, I have no intention of giving up on Count de la Brocher. Simply because you have ruined your own life, I have no intention of ruining my own.''

33

serena

I HAD LEFT Daphne's room and somehow found my way to my own. I had to find Oliver; we had to talk, but not before I could regain some composure. I had never resorted to anything medicinal to steady my nerves, but I wished at this moment that something was available to me.

My mind was so flooded with the events of earlier that I could not sort one occurrence from another long enough to give focus. Of one thing I was certain. Though Justin's safety had been my first priority, Daphne had now to be my immediate concern.

I longed to be with her now, cradling her in my arms as I had when she had experienced some moment of pain. But I also knew that my daughter was no longer a child who could be coddled into belief that all would right itself again.

Why had I not sensed the truth? But how could I have ever suspected that Luke had defiled her I wondered as I paced the floor, feeling that I would near explode from the anger and frustration of it all. She had called him odious. At this moment that seemed too kind. He had inveigled Justin into this web of intrigue and danger, putting us at risk, and then had dared to violate us all in the worst possible way. God only knew that Justin would likely kill him were he to discover this dastardly deed.

Or would he? Life was in its own way repeating itself. Had I not been but Daphne's age when Justin had taken me there that night at Camberleigh? I tried to think that that was different. He had been fully inebriated. I had not even known the identity of my attacker. But that had not lessened my shame, nor eased the darkness in my soul.

When I had discovered that it was Justin who had robbed me of my virginity, leaving me not in the marital bed but alone and frightened, I recalled, even though it had been lo' these many years, the hatred I felt. He had been contrite, and in my heart I now knew that he regretted this assault to my being. Though I could never have admitted it then, a part of my anger was directed at myself, for in the recesses of my mind I could not deny that he had awakened new and disturbing feelings within me.

Could it be that Daphne too was experiencing the same conflict of emotions? What did it matter, for at this moment I knew that all she must feel was broken and humiliated. The terrible irony was that whether her outbursts had been involuntary or whether she had mustered the courage to expose Count de la Brocher, she had unknowingly accused the wrong man. Only Oliver and I knew that the man who had taken her that night in the passageway was Luke de la Brocher and not Gaston, who stood before her tonight.

That she did not know, had not suspected, seemed incredible, and yet had I myself not been duped? Even tonight I had had to keep myself from staring, for the resemblance truly was uncanny. The trained ear might have discerned the small differences in inflection, but whether Gaston was the consummate thespian or not, even the mannerisms were indistinguishable.

I had been amazed that Gaston had spoken so freely of his political sympathies. And admittedly relieved, for it gave hope that he indeed did not suspect Justin's involvement. Of course, that had all changed now. It had not been difficult for Gaston to deny Daphne's accusations, for he was indeed innocent of the violations and threats, but what she could not have known was that instead of exposing him, she had exposed her own father.

What was I to do? A part of me wanted to return at this very moment to Daphne and tell her everything. Not that it would absolve the devastation she was now feeling, but perhaps it would somehow explain. Explain what? That the man who had violated her was not the man she thought? What would it matter to her, save that if I revealed the full truth, she could not help but realize the danger that she had placed Justin in. If she was not already devastated, would that revelation not burden her to a breaking point?

It was all so clear now. Her protestations, her inability to hear Count de la Brocher's name without reacting. Those days that she had been ill, ferreting herself off in her room the way she had, insisting that I not call for the doctor. My heart broke at the thought that she had endured this alone without the comfort of one who might have given her comfort. Why had she not come to me? For myself I had had none to whom I could turn, but Daphne and I had always been so close. Likely she had kept it to herself with the thought of protecting me. She had sensed, I knew, that I was distressed over Justin's absences. Perhaps she simply could not bear to bring further burden to me or the family. If only she had come to me, at least then I might have borne some of the pain she was now feeling.

These meanderings were doing little good to anyone. I had not the luxury of time, and pacing here alone was not helping Daphne or Justin. I gathered my shawl about me and left the confines of my bedroom to go in search of Oliver, who I knew would likely be frantic with worry.

I knocked at the door to his room and, hearing no response, determined that he must have returned downstairs. The door to the library was open, and I gathered my skirts and moved swiftly towards it.

"Thank God you are here," Oliver exclaimed as I entered, bidding me to close the door behind me.

"I did not realize how late it had gotten to," I apologized. "I must admit I am not thinking clearly."

I sank into a chair near the fireplace. "I simply do not know what to do, Oliver. I feel so utterly helpless."

He came to me and put his arms about me. "I wish I could give you comfort, Serena, but I fear that all is much worse than you imagine."

"Justin?" I choked, grasping his arms. "Something has happened to him."

"No, no, as far as I know he is all right."

"Then what?" I beseeched.

"When I did not seem to be making any headway with Constance, I came down here to try and think what our next move should be. I wish there was some other way, Serena, but I need your help.''

"Help in what, what are you saying, Oliver?"

"I had just come downstairs when there was a knock at the door."

"Not Gaston?" I murmured.

"I fear in some ways it was worse. It was Maria."

"Maria?" I gasped. "Is something wrong with Clarissa? My God, what has happened?"

"She was frantic. It seems that Clarissa is missing."

"Missing? How can she be missing?"

Oliver rose and, striding over to the fireplace, picked up a half empty glass he had left on the mantle.

"After Gaston left to come over here, Maria went to see Clarissa. She was anxious because he had kept her occupied most of the day and she could not risk disappearing if only for moments at a time."

"But how could Clarissa have disappeared, Oliver? I saw her myself. Even if she somehow could have mustered the energy, that door was bolted shut."

"Maria went to the room. She remembers little from there, for Clarissa must have knocked her out the minute she entered. When she came to, she was gone. Fortunately, Clarissa did not think to take the key, for though the door was closed, it was not locked."

I shook my head in disbelief. "Oliver, how can this be? You and Justin led me to understand that she, that she was just vegetating, that all reason, all awareness as we know it had long since disappeared."

"Serena, Justin did not lie to you. I have talked to the doctor. There has been little change in Clarissa over these past years. Save that other night when, well, you know what happened. Justin had been warned that in cases like these there might be outbreaks of irrational, even violent behavior."

"But why of a sudden, why now?"

"Believe me, you know as much as I, Serena, excepting that because Maria was not able to reach her, she was not able to administer the laudanum."

"So, conceivably, without this sedation she has far more of a mental and physical presence than one might suspect?"

Oliver shrugged. "Nothing points to that, for, you see,

Clarissa was ministering to herself long before her illness. Indeed one might have triggered the other. In any event, what we are left with at the moment is that Clarissa is missing and not only do we not know where she is but also we have no idea of the state she is in."

"Oliver, she must be in the house," I insisted.

"If she is, she is far more clever than we suspect. Maria claims she looked everywhere. There was no sign of her."

"Maria, how did she manage to come here?" I pressed, realizing that she risked being discovered by Gaston.

"It appears that Gaston left within moments of returning to the house. Unfortunately, I suspect he went straightaway to DeMarcier to inform him of the events of this evening."

"What will they do?" I whispered.

"Serena, I know you are worried, and I will not lie to you. I am more than a bit troubled, but I know that Justin would be the first to advise us that Clarissa must take precedence to all else."

I nodded. "What do you intend?"

"I have to believe that she could not have gone far. Though Maria insists she has combed the house thoroughly, I think that is where we must start."

"How can you chance it, Oliver?"

"That is where I need your help, Serena. Gaston has left, which gives me some time to search the house. I know that it is late, and I see the exhaustion in your eyes, but I need you to stay here lest Clarissa might come here."

"Why would you think she might do that?"

He shrugged. "No reason except that if she is lost, confused; it is just a chance."

I nodded. "Then I shall stay put until you return."

"There is one other thing, Serena. I want you to place this candle there in the window. If Clarissa does turn up here, I want you to extinguish the flame. Maria will keep watch and be able to alert me."

"And what if Gaston returns?"

"Maria is trustworthy. Do not worry, he will not find me there. I can always use the passageway if need be."

He embraced me quickly as I bade him to take care. I crossed to the window and, taking the candle, placed it atop a small tea stand, moving the draperies aside so that the flame might glow fully in all the panes of glass. As I strode back to the warmth of the fire, I said a silent prayer that Oliver would find Clarissa there in the house safe and sound. I did not know what I would do if any harm had come to her.

The incessant ticking of the clock was doing little to set my nerves to rest. Each minute felt more like an hour. I do not know how long I had sat when I was startled by a scuffling sound that appeared to emanate from the front hallway. Whether from apprehension or pure fear I sat transfixed for a moment before I could move to investigate. I do not know what I expected to find, but the last thing was Pluck, who I nearly tripped over, as he scurried past me into the library.

"What are you doing here?" I said aloud as I leaned down, trying to calm him.

Realizing that Charlotte must have returned him to my bedroom and that she had likely not closed the door firmly, I took him in hand to where I had been sitting, actually pleased that I now had companionship for my vigil.

I had felt that this day would prove ominous when I had awakened to find that Charlotte had taken to her bed, but never would I have imagined the disasters that would befall us all. I could only pray that the ill turn of fate was restricted to the events here at Channing Hall, for I did not think that I could bear it if harm were to come to Justin.

With every moment that passed, I grew more anxious, for it diminished my hope that Oliver would find Clarissa ensconced somewhere within the count's house. The weather was inclement and had turned particularly cold these past few nights. It was likely that wherever she had gone, she was not protected by proper dress, and I could not even let myself consider what would befall her were she to be wandering out in the streets.

I felt so helpless just sitting here and wondered if I should not have insisted on accompanying Oliver. I considered wakening Sidney, but though I knew he could be trusted to keep this confidence, something told me that the fewer people who knew about this, the safer it would be.

Thankfully, Constance was a sound sleeper. Though I knew not the denouement of Oliver's talk with her, she would likely have chosen to rest than to continue fretting, since there were none about on whom to vent her frustrations. Daphne was another matter, for as clearly as the fire burned before me, I knew that she likely lay abed prayerful that sleep would finally stay her agonizing.

I stifled a yawn, realizing that I had to fight to stay awake. My body was taut with worry, and I closed my eyes, hoping it would ease the pounding in my temples. This would be a long night, and I could not afford to succumb to anxiety or exhaustion. Assuming that Clarissa would be found and that Oliver would return her to safekeeping, we still had to face the fact that Gaston now knew for certain that Justin was involved with his brother. I could not even allow myself to think what he would do, but with time ebbing away our hopes of getting word to Luke and Justin before Gaston could take action diminished.

In desperation I tried to turn my thoughts to pleasanter days. I remembered the afternoon before leaving Mayfair when Justin and I had strolled the grounds, visiting the small chapel, revelling in the quiet simplicity of the sheep grazing the hillsides. Would that I could have foreseen what was to befall us here in London, each of us would have been saved such heartache. Would we ever know the tranquility of Mayfair again? There was not one of us who would return there the same as when we left.

Something was nudging my hand, and my eyes flew open as I realized that I had, if only for moments, drifted off to sleep.

"Good boy," I whispered as Pluck whimpered at my response.

I drew myself up in the chair, and as I did, I started at a sound behind me.

"Oliver, is that you?" I cried out as I swung round in the chair.

For a second I thought I was seeing things for there but ten feet away stood Clarissa. My first instinct was to jump to my feet and run to embrace her, but something told me not to make a sudden move lest I might frighten her.

"Stay, Pluck," I whispered as I rose ever so slowly to my feet, keeping my eyes trained to the pathetic figure before me.

"Why do you not come and sit by me, Clarissa?" I urged. "You must be cold, and we can sit here by the fire and visit for a spell."

She took not one step towards me, though her eyes never left my face. I could not help amaze that she had the strength, for she was indeed a shrunken version of the Clarissa I had once known. Indeed, if I had not seen her there ensconced at the count's house and been assured that it was Clarissa, I would not believe that it could be she before me.

"Clarissa, do you know who I am?" I ventured.

When she did not reply, I continued. "I am Serena. Your cousin, Serena. You remember, we met many years ago at Camberleigh. We were very young then. Scarcely eighteen. We have not seen each other in a very long time."

Her eyes narrowed and she pressed her hand to her temple as though she were trying to recall some recognition from the recesses of her mind.

Her mouth twisted suddenly as if she were trying to form a word. "Serena," she murmured.

"Yes, that is right," I encouraged, watching her carefully as she moved several steps towards me. "Your cousin, Serena. I came to Camberleigh to be with Juliette, our grandmother, after my mother had died. And then we lived there together with Richard, your father, and Oliver—remember Oliver, your little brother?"

Her face contorted suddenly as if by an involuntary spasm, her eyes coming to rest once again on my face.

"Clarissa, please," I entreated. "Please come and sit by me. You need to rest."

"Serena never liked me."

I do not know if I was more shocked by the realization that she was not mute as Oliver had assumed or by what she had said.

"You are mistaken there, Clarissa," I said quietly. "We had our little rifts, but we became friends. You were in my wedding party—do you remember that?"

"Justin, you took Justin away. Serena took Justin. He loved me, you know, before she came. He was going to marry *me*. But then she came and nothing was the same. Not ever again."

I was about to protest but realized that it would be futile. Though I wanted to believe that Clarissa knew who I was, I had to acknowledge that it was doubtful. Perhaps I had been mistaken in recalling the past to her, but I could not talk of the present, a present she had not lived in for years now.

"I loved Justin, you know," she continued, her skeletonlike fingers pushing abjectly at the grey matted hair. "He thought I was pretty. Do you think I am pretty?"

"Very," I lied.

Her eyes narrowed and I shuddered as I felt she was looking

directly through me. "Then why did he marry Serena?"

My eyes suddenly were drawn to the candle flickering in the window. I had promised Oliver that if Clarissa came here, I would extinguish the flame. He had to know that she was safe.

I started to rise, and as I did, Clarissa clenched her fists, slamming them down at her sides. "No," she cried out.

I had been tenuous, watchful, until that moment, but the vehemence emanating from the twisted mask that was now her face now threw terror into me.

"I was just getting up to draw the draperies, Clarissa," I replied, trying to keep my voice as steady as possible.

"I said no," she demanded. "I know what you are going to do. You are going to tell, and then I will go away again, and then you can have Justin. But I am not going to let you. Justin is going to marry me."

"Clarissa, no one is going to hurt you, I promise you that. If you will only come and sit by me, we can talk. You are cold and tired. I will fix you some tea; you always liked tea."

I watched almost spellbound as the darkness that seemed to dwell within her erupted into laughter, which stopped as suddenly as it started.

"Serena never thought I was very clever, but I have fooled them all." She leaned forward suddenly and whispered, "I have a secret."

I stayed quiet, making no further attempt to move.

"Do you want to know my secret?"

"Of course," I replied, hoping that it might preoccupy her long enough for me to move to the window.

She turned suddenly, her eyes following the direction of my gaze. "Why do you keep looking over there?"

"I told you it is drafty in the room, Clarissa. We would be far more comfortable if the draperies were closed."

"I said *no*," she insisted as she moved forward, striding directly past me to the fireplace.

Oliver, where are you? I worried, as I was less and less certain of what my next words or move should be. We did not have the luxury of time. Who knew when Gaston would return to the house, and once he was back, we could no longer hide Clarissa away there again. She could not remain here, for in less than five hours the staff would be up and about, and to try and take her to Monique's at this hour would be a feat, at the least.

Clarissa, I noted, was careful even as she moved to keep me in full sight, but it was only when she had actually reached the fireplace that she spied Pluck, who had luckily stayed quiet, curled by my feet.

Her eyes widened suddenly as she took a step back and murmured, "Jaspar."

I shook my head. "No, this is Pluck, but he does look a great deal like Jaspar," I replied, remembering that Clarissa had never had a great penchant for dogs.

That look of confusion spread again across her face as her fingers pulled at the tassel on the skirt of her dress.

"Clarissa, do you know where you are?"

She looked at me and then let her eyes rove slowly about the room. "This is *my* house, is it not?"

"What would give you cause to think that?"

She paused for a moment. "That is part of the secret," she whispered. "My Constance lives here. They do not know that I know, but I do. I have seen her."

"Here in this house?" I pressed, wondering if it was possible that she spoke the truth.

"You do not believe me," she chastised, "but I am much more clever than they think. I even know where there is a secret passageway. I listen to them, you know. And I will tell you something else. I tore up Serena's dress. I know you will think it naughty of me, but I could not have her look prettier than me, not when she is trying to take Justin away from me."

I was incredulous at what she was saying, for though her mind clearly distorted time and identities, some of what she said bore acceptance. How she knew of the passageway, how in the state she was in she was able to maneuver her way unknown to Maria into Channing Hall was beyond fathoming. Somehow in her mind she was still eighteen and still enamored of Justin, who had never, even before my arrival at Camberleigh, given her any encouragement. It was Daphne's gown that she had mutilated, but in Clarissa's mind it was myself that she had wanted to injure. And yet as much as she was living in the past, she was unquestionably cognizant of Constance's existence.

I knew suddenly that I could no longer sit still, for try as I would, no amount of conversation was to lead to anything positive. She was clearly erratic and beyond reason, and the sooner we could get her to bed and sedate her, the kinder it would be for all. This remembering was colored by the twistings of her mind, and it clearly caused her more grief than was warranted.

I put my hand down to Pluck, instructing him to stay, as I moved to rise from the chair. I had not even drawn myself to my full height when Clarissa whirled about, her hand grasping a poker that lay against the fluted molding of the fireplace.

I gasped as she raised the heavy brass implement high above her head.

"Clarissa, put that down," I beseeched.

"No," she moaned, taking a step towards me. "You sit down."

I was not about to argue, for though it sickened me to think that she was in such a state that she might cause me bodily harm, there was an unbridled fury in her that was clearly evident in her visage.

I sank back into the chair, begging her as I did to place the poker down.

"I mean you no harm, Clarissa, I only thought . . ."

"Stop it," she retorted as her free hand pressed against her head. "It is all Serena's fault. Do you not see, none of this would have happened if she had just gone away. But she . . ."

Her voice broke off suddenly, her eyes widening as if she regarded me for the first time.

"It is *you*," she murmured. "You thought you could trick me, but, you see, I know who you are. You tried to make me think it was the other one, but, you see, I know now."

"Clarissa, listen to me," I begged, my hands gripping the sides of the chair. "I have not tried to deceive you. I told you that it was I, your cousin, Serena. The other one you refer to is Daphne, my daughter, Justin's and my daughter. She is the same age as Constance, your daughter. They are grown women now, Clarissa. We are here at Channing Hall, as they are having their season."

For one split second I thought that I had managed to enter a part of her mind that was still capable of reason, for she looked curiously becalmed. The poker, which she had held in a vicelike grip high above her head, she lowered slowly to her side.

I pushed myself forward in the chair, encouraging her to replace the poker and sit down. When she made no move but continued to stare blankly at me, biting furiously at her lower lip, I determined that if I was going to make my move, I had to risk it at that very moment.

What happened next I could never fully reconstruct. I propelled myself out of the chair, but as I did, the heel of my boot must have caught in the intricate weaving of the rug, for it catapulted me not away but towards where Clarissa stood. I remember seeing the poker rise and shouting some word of warning as she lunged forward, flailing the gleaming brass rod towards me. The knife-edged point of the poker raked against the palm of my hand, which I held out before me, and a sharp pain seared my arm as I fell backward. Almost simultaneously I heard Clarissa cry out and realized that Pluck had lunged at her and must have managed to sink his teeth into the flesh of her leg or ankle.

"Pluck, no," I moaned as I watched his brown and white body tearing at the hem of Clarissa's gown.

The shock of the bite was only momentary, for she moved towards me again, a maniacal expression contorting her face, her arm whipping the poker through the air. I tried to pull myself backwards away from her, but the fullness and weight of my gown, I knew, would prohibit my escape.

I would never know exactly, but I thought Pluck must have gotten a firm enough grasp on her gown so that when she went to advance another step, he pulled her back, causing her to lose her balance and drop the poker. I watched her sway there and then plummet forward, a slight gasp emanating from her as her body toppled onto the poker.

I was frozen there for a moment as I watched the inert form before me. Pluck ran to me whimpering, nudging me for some reaction.

"I am all right, Pluck," I choked out as I dragged myself over to where Clarissa lay. I knew even before I turned her to me that life had in those split seconds ebbed from her body. I covered my mouth to keep myself from retching, as my eyes trained on the blade of the poker, which was still imbedded in her neck. Her mouth was wide open and her eyes still bore the crazed, haunted look that they had in life.

I placed my fingertips across each eyelid, praying fervently as I did that her soul would now be at peace. It was then that I realized that my hand, which had been struck by the poker, was bleeding profusely, and I tore at the hem of my petticoat, taking the fabric and binding it as well as I could about my hand. I could not just sit here, but I could not bear to leave Clarissa. Oliver, I had to reach Oliver, I thought frantically. He would help. He would know what to do. I pulled myself to my feet, realizing as I did that my limbs were shaking. I took a deep breath, trying to calm myself as I maneuvered towards the window. I had only progressed but halfway when I whirled about, hearing a sound by the door.

"Oh, my God," he exclaimed as his eyes moved from me to the crumpled mass but feet away from me.

I commenced to call out Oliver's name when suddenly everything seemed to grow dark and swirl before me. I could feel myself sinking, but I remembered nothing until I heard Oliver repeating my name moments later.

"Lie still, Serena," he whispered as he loosened the buttons about the neck of my jacket.

I did as he bade, accepting a sip of brandy, which he pressed to my lips moments later.

"Oh, Oliver," I cried, tears spilling onto his jacket, "she came here. I did not know what to say, what to do. It was an accident. She came towards me with the poker and then Pluck . . ."

"Hush, Serena," he advised, forcing me to take another swallow of brandy. "This will relax you."

"I must tell you," I entreated. "She lost her balance and she fell. The poker must have risen with the weight of her body. And then she just lay there. I did not know what to do. Oliver, we cannot just let her lie there."

"Of course not," Oliver agreed. "But we must get *you* out of here first. That hand of yours needs attention."

"Do not worry about me," I insisted.

"Serena, listen to me. There is nothing you can do to help me here, certainly not in the state you are in. I shall take care of everything, I swear it to you, but we must move quickly, for it will be light within hours, and it shall be far more difficult to conceal what I must in the morning."

Though initially I insisted that I could manage on my own, I quickly realized that I was depleted of both emotional and physical strength and did not protest when Oliver lifted me up into his arms.

"Do not look, Serena," he commanded as we moved past Clarissa's lifeless form.

"Where is Pluck?"

"He is right here at my heels. Now, do not say a word until we are ensconced in your room. We cannot afford to rouse anyone until I can attend to things."

I did as he bade and was silent until he had laid me on the bed. Seconds later he was unwrapping the now blood-soaked fabric from my hand and placing it into a basin of water.

"This will be cold, but it would be better to have it clean. Do you have any tincture about or fresh bandages?"

I nodded. "There in the second drawer."

I winced as he liberally applied the foul-smelling oil to my palm and then wound the bandages deftly about it.

"I fear this will trouble you for a spell," he advised. " 'Tis a very deep gash you sustained."

"Oliver, that is the last thing on my mind."

"Will you be all right if I leave you here?"

I nodded. "But what will you do?"

"Please, Serena, leave that to me. You stay put. You have sustained a terrible shock. The brandy should help you rest, but promise me you will stay abed. I will come to you the moment I have returned. We will talk then."

"God be with you," I whispered as he embraced me and quickly took his leave.

I was grateful, in a way, that he left when he did, for I could not have borne to have him see me disgrace myself. Thankfully, the basin had been left on the nightstand next to the bed, for in one sense Oliver was correct, I was far weaker than I had dared admit.

Realizing that my body was shaking uncontrollably, I pulled the nightrobe, which had been left at the end of the bed, up about my shoulders. Pluck, who had crawled up onto the bed beside me, would not take his eyes from me. But as much as I knew that it was his gentle brown pools into which I looked, I could not dispel the memory of Clarissa's twisted gaze.

I did not want to believe that Clarissa had truly intended to harm me, for I did not want my final memories of her to be of this night. I had to remind myself that it was not Clarissa who had stood there before me but rather another who had simply occupied her physical presence or what had been left of it. I had spoken the truth to her when I had recalled that though Clarissa and I had had our differences, her passions had bordered on jealousy but not on hatred. I could never be certain that she indeed had even known that it was I whom she had shared those final moments with.

All these years I had always thought that her obsession with Justin had been simply the fancy of a young girl. He was young and dashing, and it was, I suspected, only natural that she had experienced an infatuation of sorts. But I had to wonder now whether it had not rooted deeper than that. Certainly it was misplaced, for Justin, I knew, had never given her encouragement, but I could not dismiss that, for Clarissa, feelings may have run deeper.

Was it foolhardy to try and give reason to the meanderings of her mind at the last? Was I trying to bring an understanding to something that was beyond understanding? It would not change anything. Clarissa was lost to us now. Indeed she had, from Justin and Oliver's claims, been lost to us for years now. I could only pray that at last she had found peace, for the other, as I had witnessed with my own eyes, had to be a living hell.

At all costs, what needed now to be paramount in my mind was that Constance be protected from any knowledge of this night. She had buried her mother once, and no matter what lengths I had to go to, she would never have to endure that again.

The grey light of dawn was visible through the windows as I agonized about when Oliver would return. He had assured me that he would take care of everything, but had he indeed had a plan when he had left me? Where would he take her and how?

Forgetting my injured hand, I pulled myself up against the pillows, wincing as I did. I had to remain alert. I had perhaps but an hour before the staff arose, and if Oliver could not return to me by then, I had to come up with some sort of scheme. Charlotte or one of the maids could not find me lying here like this. Somehow I had to find the strength to disrobe. Gingerly I swung my legs over the side of the bed. I took several deep breaths as a wave of nausea overtook me again. My hand still shook as I fumbled with the buttons of my jacket. I cursed in frustration as what would ordinarily be such a simple task seemed to demand every ounce of energy. When at last I had released the last button and had managed to pull the jacket off, I was bathed in perspiration. How I ever accomplished shedding all my clothes and getting into my nightdress and robe I shall never know. My heart was beating at what seemed twice its normal rate as I struggled to stand. I stretched my arm out, grasping for the night decanter.

I sighed in relief as I brought it to me. Placing it on the edge of the nightstand closest to me, I pulled one of the pillows to the floor. There would be questions about my hand and I needed an explanation. I placed the decanter on the floor, putting the pillow atop it, praying as I did that it would serve to muffle the sound of the shattering glass. Fortunately, it was fashioned of a particularly fine crystal, and I felt a sense of relief as with the one stamp of my foot I felt the form give way.

I had just removed the pillow, cast it aside and returned myself to a prone position when Oliver appeared.

"Good Lord, what has happened here?" he exclaimed, seeing the glass scattered about the floor.

" 'Twas the only scheme I could concoct to explain away my hand. But that is beside the point. How are you?" I demanded, my hand reaching up to touch his face.

"In truth, Serena, I have not had time to consider that."

"Clarissa. Is she . . ."

"Gone. From Channing Hall anyway."

"You did not take her, the body, back to the count's?"

Oliver shook his head. "I could not risk it. I had to find someplace where I could have access again as soon as it was light."

"Then where?" I beseeched.

"Serena, do you really want to know? It is a macabre solution, though only temporary."

"Oliver, I have to know," I insisted. "I am no longer an outsider where Clarissa is, or was, concerned."

"I have placed her body in the compartment of your barouche."

"You mean she is lying there in the carriage?" I gasped.

He nodded. "I warned you that it was not a pretty story, Serena. Believe me, if I could have come up with any other solution, I would have."

"But Sidney or one of the groomers, Oliver, they will find her," I protested. "My God, you must not let that happen."

"Calm yourself, Serena. I assure you I will take care of it, but I must enlist your assistance. It will be light in another hour. As soon as I can change out of these clothes, I will hook up the team and take the carriage out myself. Sidney will likely have questions, and I simply want you to say that there was need for me to take something to Monique by daybreak and that you did not want to disturb him.''

'' 'Tis less than a feeble alibi,'' I murmured.

''I know, but 'tis all we have.''

''But where shall you go, what do you intend?''

''I shall go direct to the doctor who has cared for Clarissa these past years. There is no reason to believe that he will not continue to honor this confidence. There is a gravesite, a head-stone is already there, the death certificate already exists. If all goes as planned, Clarissa's body will finally be laid to rest there by nightfall.''

''You cannot tell me that you intend to go and dig the grave?'' I murmured, shuddering at the thought.

''If I have to, I will, but there are many who live impover-ished on the streets of this city who would gladly do my bid-ding for a few pence in their pocket.''

It all seemed so cold, so heartless, but I could not see that there was any other way.

''Part of what you will be telling Sidney will be truthful,'' Oliver pursued, ''for as soon as I have tended to these matters, I indeed intend to go to Monique.''

''To tell her about last night?''

''She must know, Serena.''

''You think she can do something?''

''Let us say I am hopeful. Monique has friends in the resis-tance. Luke and Justin must be warned. If my suspicions are correct, Gaston and his men will not remain here in England, not now. We must somehow get word to them before they can set forth in the Ariege again.''

''You really think that Gaston would bring harm to his own brother?''

''Gaston is beset by the fruits of power and wealth, Serena. I do not mean to frighten you, but if Luke is not in the picture, Gaston stands to inherit it all, the title, the château. The men he surrounds himself with have a great influence on Gaston. I am not certain that he is not used by them for their own ul-terior motives, which complicates matters even further.''

''You must understand, Oliver, when I say that my first thought must be Justin's safety, but with the revelations that you were privy to last evening, I have less than positive sen-timents about Luke de la Brocher.''

''How is Daphne?''

I shrugged. "I do not know. She did not want to discuss it, and she was in no emotional state for me to press. At this very moment I suspect life looks very bleak to her."

"You did not tell her about Luke and Gaston, I gather."

"No. I wanted to but it did not seem advisable. I do not know whether at this juncture it would serve any purpose."

"I swear to you, Serena, I knew nothing of this, save that I know that Luke is totally enamored of Daphne. You heard him admit that yourself. And though I suspect how you must be feeling about him at this moment, I can only tell you that I have found him to be a chap of extraordinary character. The best thing I can say of him is that he reminds me of Justin. He is passionate about his principles."

"Obviously his passions are unbridled, at least in some quarters," I replied coolly.

"Serena, Daphne has more sense, more character than to allow this incident to destroy her. Frankly, though Peter is an acquaintance of mine, I have always questioned that he would be a proper match for her."

"You think that is the last we will hear of Lord Sanderson, I gather."

"I did not say that. I am certain he is shocked. Much will depend on how much false pride he has."

"Daphne is convinced that that is the last of him. I would hope that is not the case, but if his caring of her is not more fervent than that, then she is best off without him. I only hope that I am able to get *her* to see that."

"I fear 'tis not only Daphne who is going to need your ministering, Serena. Constance is bound to be problematic as well."

"If it were not for Justin, I believe I would take the girls and return to Mayfair forthwith," I admitted. "We intended, as you know, to spend the holidays there anyway, and they are in truth but weeks away. I am certain that would not set well with Constance, but perhaps Daphne, once back in familiar surroundings, would be able to heal the wounds that are deep within her."

"I was going to suggest it myself, but I did not think you would consider it."

"I cannot," I admitted. "I know it is selfish on my part but until I know that Justin is returned to me safe and sound and that all this nonsense with the Ariege is behind us, I cannot leave Channing Hall."

Oliver took my good hand between his. "I know that you are likely embittered by all this, Serena, but I beg you not to dismiss it as nonsense. Of one thing I am certain and that is that none of us can afford to be insular in our endeavors or commitments these days. We are Englishmen first, but if we blind ourselves to the plights of those who are not our countrymen, it will come back to visit us at some point. Perhaps it is that Rebecca's family lives afar from us in America and I am, through their letters, ever cognizant that strife and deprivation and a struggle for right are not limited to the boundaries of this land. We simply cannot deny the problems in France. Justin is correct in what he is doing, and though I fear too for his safety, I will have you believe that he is not only justified but should be applauded for what he is trying to do."

"You really believe that?"

"I do, Serena. When things calm and I can give you more detail, I am certain, knowing you, that you will agree. This is not one man who has decided to be altruistic about those who are less fortunate about him. It is the future of hundreds, thousands of people, Serena, who will starve or freeze this very winter if people like Luke and Justin do not come to their aid. I cannot ask you to understand, only to keep an open mind. Unless I am wrong, it shall not be without merit."

I assured him that I would try and then pressed him to move quickly, for light now filtered more fully into the room and we could not risk any more time. I bade Oliver to take care and to return at the earliest possible moment to Channing Hall. I knew that I should not rest until Clarissa had found dignity in her final resting place and until Monique would see to it that warnings were dispatched immediately to Justin and Luke.

Though I longed for the oblivion that only sleep would bring, my head was too filled to give way to exhaustion. I prayed that Daphne had been able to succumb to sleep, for lack of it, I knew, would only serve to compound the turmoil she must be experiencing.

If only I knew the right thing to say to her. Would anything be served by my sharing the privacies of my own experience with Justin with her? Some day perhaps, but, I thought, not at this juncture. She only felt violated, humiliated by her experience. Were I to reveal to her that hers was not the first, that I too had lain as she did now, wondering if I could ever make myself clean again, ever be able to live with the humiliation, the guilt that, try as I did to dispel, seemed to obsess me, would that becalm her? I thought not, for, then the father that she had always seen as a pillar of strength, an example of all that was right and good, she would likely doubt. I could not risk that.

It was perhaps two hours later when Jane came to ask me if I should care to take breakfast in my room or downstairs. I asked whether any were about in the household and when she informed me that the girls had chosen to take trays in their rooms, I suggested that I should like to do the same.

"Ye know, Lady Barkham, I went te Lord Oliver's room but 'e was gone. 'As he left us fer a spell?"

I shook my head. "He shall return later today, but I am pleased you mentioned it, for you can do me a great favor by informing Sidney that I had an errand that I inveigled Oliver to do and he has taken the barouche."

"By 'imself?" she murmured incredulously.

"Oh, in the country we are quite accustomed," I explained. "In any event, 'tis nothing to worry about, but I would feel better if you told Sidney forthwith."

She nodded.

"Thank you, Jane. Before you go, let me ask you how Charlotte is this morning."

"I just took 'er some toast an' porridge, but I think she still feels poorly, me lady. Ye know Charlotte, she won't be complainin', but she looks under the weather, she does."

"I will look in on her shortly," I replied, troubled that she seemed not to have gained strength from the day prior.

"Kin I be doin' anything else?"

"You can," I said quickly. "I fear I did not sleep as well as I might have last night and it would be of great assist if you would ask Sidney to tend to Pluck."

I put my good hand against him as he instinctively seemed to dig his haunches in against me. "Go with Jane, now," I bade. "I expect Cook can find you something delectable in the kitchen before your outing."

Jane giggled, I knew, because it was no surprise that the two had never decided whether to be friends or enemies, though

I suspected even with Cook's protestations that it was the former.

Up to now I had been trying to hide my bandaged hand, but without thinking I withdrew it from the covers as I tried once again to encourage Pluck to move from the space he commanded.

Jane's eyes widened as she moved towards me. "Ye've hurt yerself, Lady Barkham," she exclaimed.

" 'Tis nothing, truly," I assured, "but I fear I created quite a mess. Be careful where you walk, for the glass is shattered just before you there."

"I'll come back with the pan an' broom," she said quickly.

"Before you do, promise me that you will talk to Sidney first."

Jane returned but fifteen minutes later with my tray in hand, and though I surprised myself at my appetite, I ate hungrily as she proceeded to sweep up the seemingly endless fragments of shattered glass.

The sustenance had seemed to give me a renewed strength, and though I moved tenuously, I was relieved that I was steady enough to rise and dress myself without incident. That Jane had tended to me this morning was of some relief, for she had been more than circumspect upon finding my basin, which visited the devastation of the night prior. Had it been Charlotte, explanations would have been demanded and ministrations applied, thus I was relieved not to have to explain away this morning.

I moved from habit that morning, compelled to keep things as much within the norm as I could. It would be a long day and I needed to muster all sense of strength and equilibrium that I could.

34
daphne

How was I to face this day, I wondered as Jane departed after leaving my basin. I had slept perhaps an hour the whole of the night, my mind too active to permit the rest I knew I needed.

Mother had not pressed me last night, but I could not expect that she would not demand that we talk today. I had heard some distant commotion in the middle of the night and suspected that she and Oliver were ruminating about what to do with me now that any hopes they had had for me had been dashed.

I tried to tell myself that I did not care, that the important thing was that Count de la Brocher had been exposed and that he would no longer threaten any member of the Barkham family, but I was not wholly that altruistic.

It was ironic, I thought, that I had begged Peter for time before making a commitment to him. Father's unexpected absence had served me well. Though I had been truthful that I could not consider giving him an answer without first discussing it with both parents, I realized now that the larger issue was that I myself had needed time. My hesitancy had been less concerned with my feelings about Peter than my own turmoil over whether I could become affianced to Peter or any man while I harbored this secret within me.

Well, the truth was out, and now I had the answer to the

question that I had posed over and over to myself these past weeks. Had I truly thought that if I were to have discussed this openly with Peter, albeit in calmer circumstances, he would have enfolded me to him, assuring me that he would love me, that he wanted me, no matter what?

I could not blame him for walking out. Though I was clearly overwrought, I was certain in retrospect that the sight of me shouting accusations at the count had frightened, likely even disgusted, him. But though I could not fault him for being shocked, there was a part of me that I now acknowledged had hoped that he would show some sensitivity to my plight. I could not dismiss the look on his face when he had taken his leave. His regard was one of total disdain, not, as was warranted, for Count de la Brocher, but for me. Could he not see that it was I who was the victim?

Sometime in the middle of the night I had determined that the best, no, perhaps the only option I had now was to return to Mayfair. I could not remain here at Channing Hall trying to pretend that none of this had happened. Certainly Mother would not ask that I suffer the embarrassment of continuing the season. Would Peter be circumspect about what had been revealed here last night, I wondered? Even if he were, what did it matter? No, there was no alternative. I had to return to Mayfair. If Mother would not return with me, I would travel there on my own. She would never permit it, I thought suddenly, not with everyone gone from the house. Charlotte— that was it. If Charlotte accompanied me, she might consider my plea.

Even if I were able to convince her that Mayfair would prove the best solace for me, it would be days before, I suspected, I might leave. With Charlotte ill, there was no way that she could be asked to endure the long journey until she was fully recovered. That meant days here in the house with Constance, who would continue to berate me at every opportunity. While Peter had clearly known that my ravings were born of truth, Constance's recourse was denial. I found her unwillingness to see things as they really were unfathomable. She had been angered with me, but to think that I would invent this tale out of some misplaced jealousy was not reasonable.

Perhaps in the light of day things would look different to

her, though I doubted it. Constance would not be easily assuaged. Not until Count de la Brocher was but a distant memory in all our lives.

I tensed as there was a knock at the door. "Who is it?"

"It is I, darling. Might I come in for a moment?"

I took a deep breath. "The door is not locked, Mother," I replied.

I pulled myself up in bed as I watched her move towards me. I knew that she was managing a smile for my benefit, for I thought that I had never seen her look so drawn or tired.

"What has happened to your hand?"

" 'Tis nothing, just a cut. I fear I was a bit clumsy," she replied. "Might I sit down?"

I nodded and moved my leg aside so that she might be near me on the bed.

"Mother, I am so sorry," I whispered. "Truly, I never meant to hurt you."

Her eyes widened as she leaned forward and smoothed the weight of my hair to the back of my shoulder. "The last thing I want you to feel, Daphne, is that you owe me or anyone an apology."

"How can you sit there and say that, Mother?" I beseeched. "I have humiliated you, Constance hates me, who knows what Oliver thinks."

"Daphne, listen to me," she insisted. "The only one that matters at this moment is you. If you think that your mother is so faint of heart or mind that I should suffer such embarrassment for something that is, well, that is in the past, then I have not shown you the best of me. Constance is upset, we all are, but I can tell you with absolute conviction that Oliver and I are only preoccupied with your well-being."

"Then permit me to return to Mayfair, Mother," I pleaded.

"Would that I could, Daphne," she replied, "but you know as well as I that the house, save the staff, is empty. I could not in full conscience send you back there, not feeling as you do now."

"I have thought of that," I answered quickly. "Charlotte could accompany me, as soon as she is well. I would only be there a few weeks before the rest of you return for the holidays. Oh, I beg you to consider it, for I do not think I could bear remaining here, not now."

"Daphne, do not ask this of me," she replied. "I know that

the last thing you may want at this moment is to have people about, but running off to Mayfair is not an answer. Shuttering yourself off is no solution. To hide yourself away from me, from those who love you, cannot solve anything.''

I felt tears welling in my eyes. "You do not understand, Mother. You cannot, you cannot know how I feel, here inside me,'' I choked.

"Yes, I can,'' she replied in a voice so faint that I asked her to repeat herself.

"I said, yes, I can understand, Daphne,'' she replied. "Curiously, when I came here this morning, this was the last thing that I thought I would say to you. Frankly, in the middle of the night I had determined that sharing what I am about to with you would prove more damaging than restorative. But now I am not certain.''

"Tell me what?'' I encouraged, accepting the handkerchief she handed me.

"When I say to you that I understand, it is more than just motherly compassion. Years ago, when I was just your age, as you well know, I travelled to Camberleigh to be with your great grandmother after my own parents had died.''

"What does that have to do with this?'' I demanded.

"Like you, Daphne, I was young, inexperienced,'' she continued. "I am certain that you remember our speaking of Thomas Masters, Oliver's tutor at the time.''

I shuddered at the thought, for I remembered far too well the day that my parents had told Alexander and myself of the heinous crimes committed at Camberleigh and Thomas Masters's involvement in it all.

"One night,'' she continued, "before we knew—about Thomas, that is—he had invited me to dine with him down at the cottage. When I returned, it was dark. I took the back stairs. Before I could reach the landing where my bedroom was, I was, well, let us say, I was overcome. That I am telling you this is sufficient without giving you any details. Let me simply tell you that when I came round, I was in a strange room. There were times in the weeks, months that followed that I thought I could never go on. But I did, somehow I did.''

I could not believe what I was hearing. "Mother, do you mean to tell me that, that Thomas Masters, that he and Count de la Brocher . . .''

She lowered her eyes. "No, it was not Thomas.''

"Then who?" I beseeched, putting my hand on her shoulder.

I waited, wondering if she was going to respond. I knew how painful this must be for her, for I imagined that though nearly twenty years had passed, one would never forget the violation of such an experience. Was she telling me this in hopes that I would perceive that it needed not signal the end of a full, rich life? Was she suggesting that one day I would find a man as wonderful as my father, who would not shy from something that had been, as with myself, out of her control, or was this a secret that she had harbored unto herself until this moment?

"Did you ever tell Father?" I ventured.

She looked up, her eyes meeting mine squarely. "I did not need to."

"He knew then? But how?"

"Because he was the man on the stairs."

I knew that I had heard her correctly, but instinctively I wanted to deny what she was saying. My father was the kindest, gentlest man I had ever known. He was not capable of such baseness. He adored Mother, or so I had always believed, until Constance had recently planted seeds of doubt about his relationship with Monique. If Mother had indeed been so brutalized by him, how could she ever have married him, unless there was more to be revealed.

"You were not with—you were not?" I forced myself to ask.

"With child?" she replied. "No, no, Daphne, you were indeed born a full year after our marriage."

I felt as though I was going to be ill. My own father, whom I adored, that he would have been capable of ravaging my mother as Count de la Brocher had done to me was inconceivable.

"Daphne, listen to me," Mother entreated, "and listen well. I have not told you this for any other reason than to try and reach out to you not, for once, as your mother, but as a woman and a friend. Unlike you, I did not know that it was Justin that night. Not until much later did I discover the truth. And when I did, I was shocked, mortified, angered. Surely your father was the most despicable man I thought I should ever know. He was contrite. Indeed, I believe that he regretted the act. He had been intoxicated. I say that not in terms of apology, but simply to offer an explanation."

"How could you forgive him?" I cried.

"Because despite what had happened, I knew that I loved him. I suspect I always had, but it took a long time for me to see it. In any event, my telling you this in no way condones what has happened to you. And I would not try to mollify you now by telling you that these feelings that you now have shall pass. But it is not the end of the earth. You have a whole lifetime to discover the passion and caring and joy that I have experienced with your father. You must never think less of him for what I have imparted to you. He is a good husband, Daphne, and a good father."

"You are not suggesting that Count de la Brocher, that he is other than a malevolent being?" I amazed.

She shook her head. "I am not defending Count de la Brocher. But there are things unknown to you, Daphne. If they were known, perhaps . . ."

"Perhaps what?" I retorted with some annoyance. "There is nothing I could know that would ever change my mind about that man. I do not know what his intent is, but he means harm to our family, Mother. He has done with me, but I suspect I was merely a convenience. He concocted this clever ruse so that I might keep silent. Foolishly that is what I did, but he was so threatening about dangers that might befall Father that I was frightened."

"What did he say to you exactly?" Mother asked.

I tried to think. I could not reconstruct it totally in my mind, save recalling the threats. "He said that if I told anyone about the passageway, Father's very life would be in danger."

"But he did not say why?"

I shook my head.

"Then I suspect there is no cause for concern," she replied. "In any event, I do not think Count de la Brocher will prove troublesome to us in the immediate future. Your father is away, and I do not think after last evening that we will be seeing or hearing from the count in the near future, and then we shall be returning to Mayfair for the holidays."

"I will not come back here again, Mother," I said firmly. "You will obviously not abide my returning now, but you cannot force me to return to Channing Hall. You and Constance do what you will, but I do not care if I ever see London or this house again."

"Darling, that is a long way off," Mother sighed. "I would caution you not to be so decisive this very moment. You are distressed, not uncommonly so, but things will look brighter with time. I promise you that. I must believe that myself. And you know there is something, or I should say someone, whom you appear to have overlooked in all this."

"If you are referring to Peter, I will remind you, Mother, of the mood he left here in last evening. I suspect that the very thought of me is distasteful to him now."

"Daphne, if that is true, then I can only be thankful that this relationship progressed no further than it already has," she replied. "It is only natural that he would be confused, at the very least, but I would hope that he has enough gumption to discuss this matter with you in person. Once he has time to sort this out, I suspect he will come round."

"And if he does not?"

"Then he is clearly not a gentleman and certainly not the man to whom I would see you commit yourself."

Mother leaned forward and kissed my forehead. "We will talk again soon, but for now I would suggest that you get some rest. If you like, I shall ask Jane to have a tray brought to you later."

I nodded and settled back against the pillows as she left the room. I marvelled that she could have sat before me and shared with me what she had. It still seemed inconceivable to me that she had undergone the same torment as I at the hands of my father. How could she have married a man who had debased her so? Her answer was that she loved him, but how could she care for a man who had shown so little regard? He had apparently shown remorse, but was that then sufficient? I could not fathom how she had been able to find such forgiveness within herself. I had not and suspected I never would have the capacity for same.

Of course, I had to remind myself that the situations were different. Mother loved Father, whereas I felt loathing and contempt for the count. Though it was true that she had not said that she loved him when he had violated her. But, then, if I were to believe what she had told me she had not even known who it was. At least not at that moment.

Could it have been that Mother had married Father because she had felt as I did now, that she would never again be worthy for any other man? No, another woman perhaps, but not

Mother. She was too strong, too aware to have punished herself so.

But was that not what I was doing, chastising myself for something that, as Mother pointed out, was not only past but out of my control? What had she meant when she had said there were things I did not understand? No, that was not it. She had suggested that there were things that were unknown to me. But what were they? I wished now that I had not been so quick to interrupt, for I sensed that there was indeed something else that she harbored. Some other secret, but, if so, what and what, if anything, did it have to do with Father or Count de la Brocher?

serena

I SAID A silent prayer, as I returned to my bedroom, that I had done the right thing by sharing what I had with Daphne. She had always worshipped Justin, and the last thing I wanted was to shatter her image of him. It was a gamble but one I felt I had to take. I knew how alone she felt at this moment, how tempting it was to let embarrassment or shame, false as though they might be, cause one to retreat from life itself.

If she knew the truth about Luke and Gaston, would it make a difference to her? Perhaps, but at this moment I knew not how any of this would end. Daphne longed for the sanctity of Mayfair. What she could not suspect was how passionately I shared her longing.

I had near worn a path in the rug by the time Oliver returned to Channing Hall.

"Serena, you had best sit down before you fall down," he said as he closed the door quickly behind him.

I nodded. "I must look a fright, though I think you could do with some rest yourself, Oliver."

"There will be time enough for that," he replied.

"Is everything, did everything go smoothly?"

"Thankfully yes, though I am not certain that Sidney is not suspicious about my driving off myself at that hour."

"He did not question you?" I posed. "You do not think he saw anything?"

He shook his head. "No, no, I am certain not."

"You saw the doctor?"

"I fear he was less than pleased at being roused at that hour, but he awakened quickly when I explained the nature of my call."

"He was cooperative then?" I ventured.

"Let us say he is being compensated to be cooperative."

"I wish I could rid myself of the image of Clarissa lying there. It is all so cold it seems so heartless."

Oliver put his arms about me. "I know," he murmured. "All morning I have had to tell myself over and over that there was no other option. I felt like some sort of monster hiring out these blackguards to dispose of the body. But she is buried now, and what we must both try to do is to think that Clarissa left us years ago. The doctor said she could not have survived as she was for much longer. I prefer to think that some higher being protected her from that torture she endured."

"And Monique? Have you seen her?"

"Only briefly. She was shocked naturally. She is terribly worried about you, Serena."

"What of Justin and Luke? Will she get word to them?"

"Immediately, though she expects as I do that Gaston and his men will move quickly."

"Does she think they are still here in London?"

He nodded. "She is certain of it. There is a man, a sympathizer with the resistance, his name is Charles Jullier, who keeps watch on DeMarcier. The moment he would make a move to leave, Jullier would notify Monique."

"But why could we not stop them, keep them from returning to France?"

"Serena, there is no authority for that. These men, at least to our knowledge, have committed no crime against England."

As loathe as I was to admit it, I knew that Oliver was right.

"I do not think I can just sit here, Oliver, hour after hour not knowing if Justin is safe."

"Serena, I am as frustrated as you, but I fear we have no choice. If I thought that by following them I could help, I would, but you know my French is less than fluent. My presence in the Ariege might well cause suspicion. Justin and Luke will be far better served by Monique."

"Do you think she is in any danger?"

"Let me say I think she is vulnerable. But while she is here in London, I do not think that they would make a move against her. Monique is fearless on that score. Justin had suggested some time back that he station a guard by her house until all danger had passed, but she refused. It is likely that her movements are being shadowed, but Monique is clever. I would not have left her if I had any cause to suspect that she would come to bodily harm."

"I spoke with Daphne at length this morning," I offered.

"How does she appear today?" Oliver inquired anxiously.

"Troubled, tired. I have tried to reach her as best I could. She wants desperately to return to Mayfair, and I cannot say that I blame her."

"Are you considering it? You know, Serena, it might prove the best solution for all of you."

I shook my head. "I cannot leave here, Oliver, not while Justin's fate hangs in the balance. If anyone should return north, it ought to be you. Rebecca is alone and with child. She must be frantic by now of when you shall return."

"I expect she is anxious, Serena, I cannot deny that, but she is not alone. Anne and Richard are there and Alexander, of course, not to mention John and Emma, and you know what handfuls they are. And like you, I could not think of leaving Channing Hall until we have seen this thing through. Besides that, I could not imagine Justin's wrath if he thought that I would have abandoned you here. Not after everything that has happened."

"He will be devastated about Clarissa," I ventured. "Not that they were close, but oddly, of any of us, he knew her best. After all he went through to protect her and Constance, 'tis such an unseemly end. I cannot dismiss the thought that I might have done something, said something that might have changed the course of things."

"Serena, you cannot, must not, question yourself. You saw Clarissa only once before last night. I must say I am amazed that she had moments of strength or lucidity beyond my wildest imagination, but these were, they had to be, few and far between. I am only grateful that you have come away from this relatively unscathed. When I think that the body lying there might have been your own. I cannot even think of it. As it is, she can only be pitied, but if things had turned out differently—I do not even want to think of what I might have done."

"I try to tell myself that it is for the best, Oliver, but I cannot. At least not now. Do you know that after I saw Daphne this morning, I thought of going to Constance, but I could not. It would be like looking at Clarissa two decades past. How am I to face her, how can I pretend that none of this has happened?"

Oliver studied me. "Serena, you will, because you must. For Constance, the preoccupation of the moment is her obsession with Gaston. She truly fancies that he is enamored of her."

"Do you believe that?" I ventured.

"Oh, I suspect he finds her pretty, amusing—who would not? But if you are asking whether he has more than a passing fancy, I cannot answer that, save to say that Gaston's preoccupation is with himself. He is French to the quick, and though he might entertain some amusements, shall we say, with Constance, I am dubious that it would ever amount to more than a trifling."

"I hate myself for lying to Daphne," I admitted. "I know she must wonder how I can be so circumspect about Count de la Brocher after she thought by her admission that she had exposed him."

"You cannot tell her the truth," Oliver entreated.

"What harm would come of it at this point? Luke and Justin are in France by now. Gaston knows. And by now so does his entourage. I see more to be lost than gained, Oliver, by keeping silent. Not only from Daphne but Constance as well."

"It is not that I do not understand whereof you speak, Serena," Oliver confided, "but I gave Luke and Justin my vow that we would keep this sacrosanct between us. You ask what harm it would bring; well, think well on it, for what do you think Daphne would do if she were to know that her own revelations might well have put Justin in danger? If you find her confused at this moment, think of how bereft she might be were she to know the truth."

"But what am I to do, Oliver?" I beseeched. "Do you expect me to sit here as though naught has happened? For how long? Am I to recommence the season as if nothing has transpired?"

"Yes," Oliver replied bluntly. "I wish that I could give you the answer, the solution you seek, Serena, but I cannot. I am charged with the safekeeping of you and Daphne and Constance. And that is paramount to all else. Do not ask me to counter my promise to Justin. For though much has changed since then, I must believe that this is what he still intends."

I looked upon this man who I had known and grown to love as a child. A child for whom I knew I represented strength and love. I was ever amazed these days how circular life really was. He desperately was trying to instill in me so much of what I had needed to impart to him in those early days at Camberleigh. He had become the man I had always prayed that he would, and I was ever grateful that he was here with me now.

In fact, it was indeed Oliver who gave me the strength to see it through the endless days and nights that followed.

It was on the fourth day after that disastrous evening that Monique arrived late morning at Channing Hall. We had had no further word since Oliver had apprised her that Gaston now knew of Justin's involvement. Oliver was certain that Gaston had remained in London at least until the night prior, for Maria, who was still ensconced in his house, had managed to get word to him as often as possible.

I knew the moment she entered the library that the news was not good.

"Your hands are like ice," I murmured as we embraced. "Come by the fire and take some tea."

"*Oui, c'est froid,*" she agreed as she removed her broad-brimmed black bonnet and handed it to Oliver, whom Sidney had fetched to join us.

"We are alone?" she murmured as I anxiously poured tea for us all.

"If you are referring to Daphne or Constance, they are in their rooms."

"*Bon,*" she replied.

"I gather you have news," Oliver ventured.

"*Malheureusement.*"

I sat forward on my chair. "It is not Justin—something has not happened to him?"

"I do not know, Serena. We must hope zat he and Luke are safe. *Non,* my news eez of Gaston. Charles came *ce matin.* Gaston *et* DeMarcier have left *pour* France."

"Where are they headed, Monique? Does Jullier know?" Oliver inquired.

She shook her head. "Eez likely zat zey will go to the château first."

"But that is likely where Justin and Luke will be," I cried.

"*Peut-être*, but eet eez possible zat zey will be in Engomer."

"Where is that? Why would they be there?"

"*Ce n'est pas loin de St. Girons.* Zere eez a forge zere which ze peasants resent. But ze mayor we believe eez sympathetic about revising ze forest code."

My despair must have shown in my face, for Oliver said quickly, "Serena, you must not give up hope, not now. We must believe that word will reach them before Gaston or DeMarcier arrive. Luke, you know, is not alone in this plight. I am certain that he will have ensconced a protectorate at the château."

"Oliver eez correct, Serena. And zere eez other cause for hope. We have reason to believe that ze Minister of War à Paris will appoint General Lafitte as commander of ze department."

"Who is he?" I pursued.

"A local hero who has remained influential even after ze new prefect assumed authority. He eez *sympathique* with ze peasants."

"Would this appointment be imminent?" Oliver pressed.

Monique nodded. "Ze troops ze department sent to ze Ariege months ago have not been a success. I expect if Lafitte eez to be named, one could hope zat eet has happened already."

"Then that would put an end to all this?" I asked.

"Oh, eet will take time but certainly eet will mean ze end of power by men like Trinqué. And with the fall of ze aristocrats Gaston and his men would have no support. Indeed eet would be Luke to whom Lafitte would turn first."

"What do we do now?" Oliver inquired of Monique.

"*Rien*," she replied. "We can only wait."

"I think I should go mad," I choked as my eyes filled with tears.

Monique rose and came to me murmuring to Oliver, "*Peut-être* you can tell my driver zat I will be a while longer."

She sat down next to me, saying, "Zees has not been an easy

time for you, *mon amie.* Things would have been *beaucoup plus* simple eef I had never involved Justin in all this. But, you watch, he will return, both of them, and zey will be victorious. He is too tough, zat husband of yours, and Luke, well, he eez *comme son papa.* Zey will be well."

"I know," I murmured, dabbing my eyes with my handkerchief. "It is simply so many things at once."

"When Oliver told me about Clarissa, eet must have been terrible. But you know, Serena, eet eez better this way. Eet was quick. She was not herself. From what he told me, you are indeed fortunate zat eet was only your hand zat was hurt."

"I just cannot dismiss the thought that I could have done something."

"Serena, you must put theez out of your mind. Clarissa was beyond saving. She eez, I pray, at peace now, and we must be grateful zat Constance knows nothing."

I agreed. "She is distraught enough about the other evening. She has not spoken once to Daphne that I know of, convinced that she has ruined her prospects with the count."

"Zat will change; soon she will know ze truth. And Daphne, how eez she?"

"Remote. All the life seems to have gone out of her. I had hoped that Peter, Lord Sanderson, would call, but as each day has passed, I suspect that Daphne's instincts are correct and that, to put it politely, his interest has waned."

"Merveilleux!" Monique exclaimed. "Lord Sanderson eez not for Daphne, Serena. Oh, he eez pleasant enough but scarcely the debonair *gentilhomme* for ze only daughter of Serena and Justin Barkham. And believe me, you will be spared as well, for his mother—*une grande bête, vraiment,* not a woman you would like."

"Perhaps," I agreed, "but this is still a painful time for Daphne. I had hoped that she would be willing to make an effort to go out, even a small dinner party, but she will not even discuss it."

"And Constance?"

"She is badgering me constantly, and I feel guilty, for it is her season as well. If she were to get out, it might take her mind off the count, but I do not feel that I can leave Daphne here alone."

Monique thought for a moment. "I have ze answer," she exclaimed. "Why do you not let Constance come and stay with me for a spell. I am going to all zees soirees and she can accompany me. Eet would also put a distance *entre les deux filles.*"

I had to admit that the idea appealed to me, and I suspected it would to Constance, for Monique was very popular in London's social circles.

"You are certain you want to do that, Monique? With everything else, and Constance is not the easiest person, you know."

"Zere eez nothing zat I can do now, Serena," she countered. "Same as you, I wait. Eet eez better for me to keep busy."

"If she agreed, when would you want her?" I ventured.

"*Cette après-midi,* if she wants. Zere ees a soiree tonight. *Sûrement* you have an invitation from the Earl of Wentworth?"

I nodded. "Admittedly I have lost track of time. Parties and balls have scarce been my priority these past days."

"Then eet eez settled. I shall expect her by, let us say, four o'clock. Eef she eez unhappy with me, zen she can return at any time."

"It is most generous of you, Monique, and I suspect Constance will be thrilled. She is dying of boredom here, or so she says, and this change will do us all good."

"*Bon,*" Monique replied. "And now I must go. Eet eez important zat I meet with Charles before noon."

Monique took her leave, and I went in search of Constance, who not surprisingly was primping at her dressing table. As I had suspected, she was overjoyed at the prospect of staying with Monique. Another time she might have balked at the idea, but Constance was one who needed to be entertained, and when I gave no encouragement about tending to social commitments in the near future, she was less than enthusiastic about remaining at Channing Hall.

Charlotte was feeling a little bit better, but she was not strong enough for me to ask her to help pack, and so it was young Jane and myself who organized Constance's wardrobe. I had hoped that when finally all was done, she would want to go to Daphne before she left, but she made it more than a little clear that the two had nothing to say to one another. I would have pressed, save that the last thing I wanted was a confrontation between the two.

Sidney helped with the trunk, and it was but hours later that Oliver and I waved Constance off in the carriage.

"Are you by chance going up to see Daphne?" Oliver inquired as I moved towards the staircase.

"Yes, I am," I replied, watching as he withdrew an envelope from his waistcoat and handed it to me.

"What is this?" I murmured, turning it over.

"A communique from Peter."

"He was here? Why did you not let me know?"

"It was not Peter, Serena, simply his driver, but as you can see, the letter is specifically addressed to Daphne."

"You think I should give it to her?"

"I do not see how you cannot. No matter what the contents."

"I gather you do not think it is good news."

Oliver shook his head. "Serena, I have no idea of what Peter is about. But I will tell you, if he upsets Daphne anymore than she already is, he shall have to account to me."

I mounted the stairs and crossed to Daphne's room, knocking softly as I reached it.

"Come in," I heard her call out.

"I hope I am not intruding," I said as she put down the book she was reading.

"Hardly," she replied. "In fact, I think I have not progressed one page in the past hour. There seemed some commotion in the hallway earlier. Is everything all right?"

"Perfectly," I nodded, taking a seat opposite her. "But that is why I am here. I wanted to tell you that Constance has left Channing Hall for a spell."

"Left?" she gasped, her eyes widening. "Why, where has she gone to?"

"Monique was here earlier this morning, and she offered to have Constance visit with her for a while. You know how social Monique is, and Constance, I fear, has felt cooped up here these past days."

"Because I have managed to ruin her season," Daphne suggested.

"Nonsense," I retorted. "But you have not seemed to be enthusiastic about the various upcoming events, and without you there, with your father still absent, I can muster little heart for it myself. It will do Constance good to get out, and hopefully she will meet some nice young man and put Count de la Brocher out of her head."

"I thought we agreed not to mention his name," Daphne murmured.

"That we did," I replied. "Actually, there is another reason I am here."

I withdrew the envelope from my pocket and handed it to her. "Oliver gave it to me. It is from Peter."

"Why do you not just take this and throw it away, Mother? I cannot believe that there is anything he has to say to me."

"You shan't know that until you read it, Daphne," I advised.

She shrugged and, picking up the letter opener, slipped the envelope open.

"Do you want me to leave?" I ventured.

She shook her head. "Whatever the contents, there is no reason that they should be kept secret from you. You have suffered the rest of my embarrassment, Mother; you might as well share this as well."

"Daphne, I have suffered nothing from you," I insisted as her hands, which I noticed shook slightly, unfolded the tissue-weight paper.

I watched her carefully for some change of expression that would give me clue to the tone of the letter, but her face was stony as her eyes scanned the two sheafs of paper. When she had done, she simply handed it to me without a word.

"Are you certain you want me to read this?" I inquired.

"Of course. Perhaps you will find it amusing. I do."

From the bitterness in her voice I sensed the last thing I would discover was humor.

Dear Daphne," *I read.*

I regret that I have not come to call these past few days, but I thought it wisest to let time pass since the other evening.

This is my seventh attempt at penning this letter. Somehow what I feel I must say does not come easily. And so I hope you will forgive my bluntness, but I am of a mind that the only way I shall get this from my writing table to your hands is to worry less about how I say what I must than what I say.

Although I had spoken to you of my intentions, I no longer feel that I can be held to such a commitment. I am indeed fond of you, Daphne, but I hope that you can see that after the revelations of the other evening, any consideration of permanence must be dismissed.

I regret, truly I do, that you allowed yourself to be subjected to such an unseemingly occurrence, but I fear that try as I would, I should never be able forgive you this indiscretion.

I expect I should have guessed it all along, for even with all your denials, one could clearly see that something exists between you and the count.

You know I wish you well, and since our paths are likely to cross again, I hope that you will always consider me a friend. Certainly rest easily that I shall never repeat anything that would cause you further humiliation.

                                        I remain,
                                        Lord Peter
                                        Sanderson

I crumpled the tissue in my hand. "How could he?" I murmured. "The insinuations, they disgust me."

"They should not, Mother. He only speaks the truth."

I jumped up, throwing the letter towards the fireplace as I did. I fell to my knees before Daphne and grasped her shoulders.

"Listen to me, Daphne Barkham, and listen well," I demanded. "What happened to you was not your fault. You did not instigate it, and I will not have you feeling guilty for what happened. If Peter is such a fop that he cannot see that, then he is not in the least deserving of you. You are graced naturally by beauty and intelligence, but how you lead your life, the character you develop, is up to you. You will fall in love one day soon, and all this will be behind you. But I will not have you suffer this deprecating attitude any longer."

I knew that my outburst had shocked her. Indeed, I had been surprised at my own vociferousness, which I expected had been incited by my anger over Peter's letter.

"Where are you going?" she asked as I drew myself to full height and moved towards the door.

"I fear I have shuttered Pluck away for far too long," I said. "And then I shall see what Cook is preparing for dinner. I do hope you will join Oliver and myself this evening. He adores you, you know, and I suspect he has missed seeing you as much as I these past few days."

I left Daphne, wondering how she would react to this latest assault. My demeanor, I knew, had not been charitable, but beyond my sheer anger at Peter I had also begun to sense that I needed to take a firmer stand with my daughter. Something had to shock her out of this malaise she had let herself drift into these past days. Her lack of spirit was worrisome and certainly not healthy for a girl who had always had such an optimistic aura. I did not want to seem heartless. Indeed, my heart went out to her, but I could not allow her to let the events of the past weeks and months destroy her.

I admit I was surprised but also encouraged when she indeed joined Oliver and myself in the dining room that evening. She was pale, but she had taken time with her toilette, even selecting a gown that was particularly becoming. That she was not her effervescent self mattered not. By joining us I knew that she had taken the first step towards mending the emotional wounds she had experienced these past weeks.

I would never have conceded it to another, but I actually relished Constance's absence in the week that followed. It was indeed selfish on my part, for though I knew in my heart that I had to dismiss the memory of what had transpired with Clarissa, closing my mind to the memory was far more difficult.

Monique, without Constance's knowledge, sent daily notes via her driver, assuring me that my cousin was being kept too busy to exhibit any displays of temperament. Indeed, though she had her moments when she continued to accuse Daphne of spoiling her season and her prospects with the count, she appeared pleased by the attention she was receiving from several young eligibles.

There was no news of Justin or Luke, which, though Monique and Oliver were quick to assert was a good sign, left me increasingly uneasy. The nights were always the most difficult, lying there in a bed that I longed to share with Justin with only dear Pluck to comfort me.

As much as they wanted me to take solace in the fact that no word that boded ill had come from France, the not knowing was, I thought, worse. Though I felt increasingly guilty for Oliver's remaining in London, I did not know what I would do if he would actually have done as I encouraged and returned to Camberleigh.

We discussed it daily, but it came particularly at issue one
night when after dinner we retired to the library and I shared
with him a letter I had received from Anne in the morning's
post.

It read, Dear Serena,

The snow is falling here at Camberleigh as I commence this long-overdue epistle. You know well how it
blankets the grounds and gives winter life to this house,
which though part of your heritage, I have, as you
know, long found to be an ominous presence against
our northern sky.

There is not a day that passes that I do not think of
you all. How gay life must be for the girls. You were
dear to write me that my gowns have been a great success—it takes me back so to those days when I was but a
fledgling couturière. That is, of course, until your arrival. But then designing for Daphne is not far different,
for she is indeed a copy of her exquisite mama at her
age.

I shall quite chastise Justin when I see him, for he
has obviously not made this an easy go for you. I have
half expected to see him here at Camberleigh one of
these morns, since Northallerton is not that far. But
then I suspect that he knows that he would have to incur
the wrath of his sister for leaving you there constantly to
run off on these damnable railroad schemes of his. You
know I say that in part in jest, for though he shall never
dissuade Richard in full, I do believe that Justin's passion there is not misplaced.

Since I have raised the subject of Richard, I expect
that I should tell you that he had not been well of late.
'Tis nothing new. We have lived with this for years now,
but there appears a change, a weakening, that I find
unsettling.

Before you panic and abandon all, let me assure
you that nothing drastic has happened to lead me to
suspect that it is not but a part of the deterioration
which we knew would happen.

I do know that you have been planning all along to
return to Mayfair for the holidays, but I shall ask a
special favor of you this year. Richard is truly no longer
well enough to travel to Mayfair, and though I could
easily make the trip, I shall not for fear of leaving him

for too great a time. I know the traditions you celebrate, but I thought, if it was not asking too much, that I would ask you to stop here on your return from Channing Hall. 'Tis only a spell out of your journey, and it would mean so much to me and, I know to Richard, as well. You might then collect Alexander and return to your own festivities. 'Tis a great deed to ask of you both, but I suspect, Serena, that this year shall be the last of it, and it would mean more than I can tell you.

As I am certain you will share this letter with Oliver, please impart that Rebecca is well though uncomfortable as she is particularly full carrying this child. If truth be known, I suspect that twins are in store. The dear child has her hands so full with the other two, who for all the tranquility of their parents, are wee hellions, that I dare not suggest that her lot may double soon.

You will scarce recognize Alexander when you return. I am wont to exaggerate, but I could swear that he has exceeded Justin in height in these past months. It has been such a joy for me to have him here at Camberleigh. He has such a facile mind, far more the intellectual than my brother was at his age, and an astuteness that I find almost uncanny. He has become a great favorite with the tenants, which, as he is such a private person, surprised us all at first, but he is sensitive to their needs and they trust his acumen.

We had a visit two weeks past from Robin and Lilliane Kelston, which admittedly left me a tad unsettled, for Robin was disturbed by the tone of Monique's letters of late. I gather it was more what she did not say than what she revealed that has left him puzzling if his mother may not be out of sorts. I assured him that you would have notified him if there was reason for concern. Likely she is simply preoccupied with the rounds of festivities. Though I would scarce have the energy to keep up with the whirlwind, I confess I envy you just one gala.

Robbie was here for three days of recent to work with Alexander on the ordering of some new machines for the estates. I admit that while he was here I endeavored a bit of matchmaking. We hired on a new maid two months past, a dear child named Caroline

who so reminds me of Charlotte when she was young.
Richard, of course, will have none of what he deems my
foolishness, but I have not grown so long of tooth that I
cannot see romance in the bud. Perhaps you had best
keep this in confidence for the moment, for poor Charlotte would be posting the banns if she suspected that at
long last there was hope that Robbie might give her that
long-hoped-for grandchild.

Though, as you can see, our days here are full, I admit to missing you all dreadfully. Our reunion shall be
none too soon for me. Well, little Emma is tugging at
my sleeve and I expect that means that grandmother has
neglected her for too long.

I pray this finds you all well and happy. My love to
you.

                                        Anne

"You should be there, you know," I ventured.

"It will be soon enough, Serena," Oliver replied. "We have
been through this before. My place is here with you, at least
until Justin returns."

"You mean if and when he returns," I argued.

"No, I do not. I have every confidence that Justin will come
back to us, Serena. You must not lose faith. Not now when we
are nearing the end. News from France is hopeful for the first
time during this whole siege."

I tried, as I did every day, to take heart in Oliver's encouragement, but I was emotionally coming to the end of my
tether. I had always been able to muster a certain resilience in
the face of adversity, but this time I felt as though I could be
tested no further.

There was not one I knew who had not some cross to bear,
but it was oft that some illness, some plight had befallen them
for which they had no control. But Justin did not have to do
this. The thought that he would be martyred for no reason
angered me. Did he care more for this cause than for his own
family?

I knew in my heart that that was far from the truth, that I
should applaud and not damn Justin for what he was doing,
but I could not be as selfless as he. There were times when I
wished that he was more like Robin Kelston. Oh, Robin had
his quirks, he had had his days of philandering, but he and

Lilliane lived a tranquil life by contrast. Justin oft chided that Robin played at being lord of the manor, and I suspected that was true, but he had managed to make a success of it, and Lilliane did not, as I, have to endure these days of fretting and wondering, the endless nights of sleeplessness.

The turn in the weather did not help my emotional state over the next few days. I had never seen such gloom hang over the city of London. The days were so dark that one could barely distinguish them from the nights. Pluck, ever sensitive to my moods, never left my side, his own regard as woebegone as my own. Oliver and Daphne had spent more and more time together since that first night that she had rejoined us for dinner, and though I inquired not of the nature of their discussions, I was encouraged by an apparent lightening of her spirits.

It was on the eve of the eighteenth day since Justin's departure that, after an early dinner, Oliver and I had retired, as had become our pattern, to the library. Daphne had excused herself to pen a letter to Alexander.

Oliver, who had just aloked the fire, turned to me suddenly. "Did you hear that, Serena?" he inquired, stopping suddenly.

I looked up from my embroidery. "I did not hear anything."

"I could have sworn," he mused, walking over to the windows that faced the front of the house.

"Do you see anything?" I inquired.

"The rain is coming in sheets," he replied, "but there seems to be a carriage out front. You are not expecting anyone, are you?"

As he said it, we both looked at each other.

"Oliver, my God, do you think . . ."

He raised his hand halting me. "Serena, stay put, let me go."

He had only crossed halfway across the room when Pluck, who had been curled by my feet, scampered by him and began barking excitedly at the door.

I was already on my feet when Justin, who had thrown the library door open, near careened across the room. It was not until later when he finally pulled away from me that I even realized that we were both soaking wet.

"I suppose I should have removed my cloak, but I could not wait," he laughed as his lips began to cover mine.

I clung to him, beseeching him to hold me, not to let me go.

I was laughing and crying, I could think of nothing except that Justin had come back to me.

"Serena, you are hurt," he murmured as he brought my bandaged hand to his cheek.

" 'Tis nothing," I whispered. "Nothing can hurt me now that you have come back to me."

He looked up as Oliver, who had hung back until now, came forward and placed his arms about the two of us.

"You have given us quite a scare, old chap," Oliver exclaimed.

Justin laughed. "What is this old chap nonsense? They would not say that if they could have seen some of the skirmishes we've been through of late, eh, Luke?"

I pulled away and looked past Justin, seeing for the first time that we were not alone.

"You have quite a husband there, Serena," Luke said with admiration as he stepped forward, I noticed, with some difficulty.

"You are hurt," I exclaimed, aware that his hand clasped the thigh of his left leg.

"Nothing that will not recover with time," he assured.

"Count de la Brocher is modest as well as brave," Justin advised. "I fear he elected a bullet that might well have felled me."

"How?" I pressed. "What happened?"

" 'Tis a long story, Serena, but I do not jest when I say that I owe Luke my life."

Luke waved him off. "Believe me, we are more than even on that score."

"Have you seen Monique?" I asked. "Does she know that you have returned?"

"No, we came directly here," Justin replied.

"I see," I answered, realizing suddenly that Justin could not then know about Clarissa.

"You know, cousin," Justin said, turning to Oliver, "I think you are forgetting yourself. I know I could do with a spot of brandy. How about you, Luke?"

As Oliver commenced pouring the amber liquid into the crystal snifters, he said, "Well, I gather from your ebullience that your mission was successful."

I was looking at Luke at that moment and could not help but notice a dark, troubled look about his eyes. I turned quickly to Justin, who shook his head as if to silence me.

"Please do not tell me that this nightmare has not come to an end, Justin," I beseeched. "I do not think . . ."

I never finished my sentence, for at that moment I heard a gasp and I whirled about to find Daphne framed in the doorway, a look of pure terror on her face. Seemingly unaware of her father's presence, her eyes moved directly from the count to me.

"How could you, Mother, how could you allow that man in this house?" she accused.

"Daphne," Justin exclaimed.

I placed my hand out to stop him. "No, let me," I whispered.

"Have you no care for my feelings?" she raged. "What does one have to say or do to have you see the truth about this man?"

"Darling, you do not understand," I cried, moving towards her.

"Do not touch me," she swore at me as I neared her. "I thought you understood. I thought you were my friend."

I stopped in my tracks as Justin's voice boomed, "What in hell is going on here?"

The thunderous tone of his voice sent shock waves through the whole of the room.

Daphne stared straight ahead, tears cascading down her cheeks. "Father, I. . ."

She went no further but, gathering her skirts, turned and ran from the room. Justin started after her, but I grabbed his wrist as he passed me.

"Let her go," I pleaded. "Luke, if you care as much for her as you profess, this is the time to tell her. I warn you you are going to have a lot of explaining to do. As a woman I am telling you that this is your chance. But as Daphne's mother, I will likely not give you another, no matter what you have braved for my husband."

36
daphne

I COULD BARELY see my way up the stairs as sobs racked my
body. My heel caught suddenly in the hem of my petticoat,
and I grasped the balustrade to prevent a fall. As I did, I heard
my name being called and turned round to see the count moving up the stairs behind me.

"Daphne, wait," he called out. "I must talk to you."

"Stay away from me," I screamed as I fell upwards against
the marble steps. I knew he was right behind me as I gathered
my skirts and ran full tilt towards my bedroom. I flung open
the door and threw the weight of my body against it, pressing
it closed.

"Damnation," I heard him exclaim as I realized with horror
that he had managed to wedge his arm just above the lock of
the door, preventing me from closing it.

"Why are you doing this?" I cried, wondering why no one
had come to my aid.

"Daphne, you might as well stand back," he threatened.
"You cannot possibly hold this door against me, and I do not
want to hurt you."

"That is a good laugh," I accused, as I realized with horror
that the wedge in the door was widening.

"Daphne, for God's sake, let me talk to you. I swear to you
that if, after I have explained, you choose not to see me, I will

344

not bother you, but I cannot leave you now without having you see things as they are."

I could already feel the bruise to my shoulder as I felt the strength ebbing from me. Did no one know that he had followed me up here? Had no one heard my screams?

As I reached out to place my hand against the wall to gain more leverage, I felt his fingers curl about my wrist.

"No," I moaned as he pushed me back into the room. "Have you not done enough? Are you so barbaric that you would take me here with my parents just a floor below?"

"Daphne, I would not take you here again or any place until I had made you my bride," he retorted.

I had been struggling to free myself from his grasp, but I now was stock-still. "Your wife?" I gasped. "You *are* mad."

"If I am mad, Daphne, it is only in my obsession about you. It has been so since the first day I saw you."

"Your obsession, Count de la Brocher," I spat back, "is only with yourself. What must one say or do to have you see that I feel only loathing for you. Was the humiliation of the other evening not enough? Must I proclaim to the world what a despicable character you are?"

"Daphne, listen to me," he demanded, his hand tightening on my wrist. "Let me ask you something. How could you, as you say, have humiliated me if I have not been here to humiliate?"

"What are you saying?" I demanded. "Are you now going to tell me that it was not you whom I revealed there in the library? You have me upset, Count de la Brocher, but you have not yet made me unbalanced."

"I swear to you that I am telling the truth," he replied, his eyes blazing. "I do not know what happened here, but I can suspect. The man you apparently accused was not I. And if you will not take my word for it, then you need only ask your father."

"My father?" I gasped. "You, who are his enemy, believe that I would allow him to defend you? Well, you are well mistaken, for when he learns what you have done, whatever deception you have managed will be no longer."

"Lord, you are stubborn," he murmured, "beautiful but stubborn. If there was one you accused, Daphne, then indeed you accused the wrong man. For, for the last weeks, I have not even been in England. I have been in my homeland in France, and your father, yes, *your* father, has been at my side.''

"I expect now you are going to tell me that you have an identical twin," I scoffed.

He studied me for a moment. "That is exactly what I am going to tell you. Whatever you said, you said it to Gaston de la Brocher, my twin by separation of birth by only minutes. *I* am Luke de la Brocher."

I looked at him in horror. Could it be that he was speaking the truth? It could not be. I would have known.

"I thought you had guessed, Daphne, that night of the ball here at Channing Hall. I could have sworn that you knew. I expect it was my own ego that wanted you to see, to perceive, the difference between. But Gaston was clever. Oddly, one of his greatest mistakes was with you. You see, he did not know, had no way of knowing that I had been enchanted by you from the first. And as our principles and politics differed, so did our taste in women. I expect all that he wanted was a dalliance with your cousin, Constance, but it was clearly she to whom he was drawn. Which may have proved disconcerting at times, for though she was clearly flattered by his attentions, he must have been perplexed at least initially by your hostility."

I was trembling and I begged him to allow me to sit down.

He guided me to a chair and, releasing my wrist, said, "I pray that I did not hurt you. Can I get you a compress?"

I shook my head, wishing that I could quiet my nerves long enough to think clearly. I was aware suddenly of a glass at my lips.

"Drink this," he advised, "but slowly."

I gulped at the water, shuddering at each swallow.

"It is a very long story, Daphne," he said quietly, "one which I hope will take a lifetime in the telling. But before you lash out at me again, I would ask that you hear me out. You deserve to know the truth in all of this no matter what the outcome."

I do not know whether I was too tired or too confused. I knew only that my rage of moments before had changed to a slow numbing. I shut my eyes, thinking that when I opened them I would discover that all this had been a dream. But as I opened them I knew it was not so.

"My family is from an area called the Ariege. For many

reasons we have been under siege for three, almost four years now. It is a beautiful area of France, one I suspect that you would love. In any event five, six months ago we came under crisis. And though you would think us a small part of the country, what happened in the Ariege was to affect the whole of the French revolution.

"My brother, Gaston, and I had grown up like you, with great privilege. Though my father was never the entrepreneur as is your own, he was a good man, Daphne. Like Justin, he loved the land and he gave back to the land what he reaped. My mother died young. Perhaps if she had lived, things would have been different. I was the eldest. And though 'tis hard for me to admit it now, I was always the favored. Perhaps because it was I who would inherit the title. Perhaps because my father and I saw things in the same light.

"It was after his death that things began to change. You must understand that though Gaston did not stand to inherit the title, he would never have wanted for anything. And then the revolution. Though our laws and ways are different, you can, I know, understand that I could not abandon the cry of the people. I am not so altruistic that I was willing to abandon all that my family had built. But we all deserve a life and the ministry was robbing the commoner of any life."

"If you speak the truth, then how does my father—what does he have to do with it?"

As he rose and moved away from me, I marvelled that I made no move to escape him.

"Monique Kelston is my godmother."

"Monique?" I amazed.

He nodded. "For many reasons I had come to the end of my influence. Gaston had made it clear that, blood withstanding, we were of opposing minds. There was money, a great deal of money, needed to support the fight of the peasants, if only for the food and fuel that they could no longer amass."

"So you, or this Gaston, came to my father for money? What did you do? Steal it and then he discovered you?" I accused. "Are you a thief as well?"

"I realize that you prefer to think ill of me, but thievery is not one of my faults. I will not suggest to rival your father's wealth, but let me assure you the de la Brochers are scarcely paupers. No, it was my own money that was used, but I needed someone, a way to filter the funds to the various communes without discovery, which is where Monique and your father come in."

"Do you really expect me to sit here and listen to this preposterous tale?" I exclaimed. "I expect that now you will tell me that it was really Gaston who violated me. That would be convenient for you, would it not? To let your brother take the blame for your misdeeds. Well? Is that what you intend?"

He shook his head. "You know me not at all to even suggest that. And you should be relieved that it was indeed I, Luke de la Brocher, who took you there that night, for things would not have gone so easily for you had it been Gaston. I have hated myself, Daphne, for what happened that night. It should not have happened so, but I have no regrets that I made love to you, because I *do* love you. And if you examine yourself, Daphne Barkham, and rid yourself of this notion that you are the only woman who has ever been the object of a man's unbridled passion, I think you will have to admit that you care for me as well."

"Do you really believe that you can come here and tell me all this, this exaggeration, and that it will change the fact that I detest you?" I demanded. "Well, I have had quite enough of this, Count de la Brocher. I would suggest that you leave Channing Hall this instant, for I intend to leave this room and go downstairs and confront my father with all this. And when he hears this fabrication, I would not want to be in the path of his wrath were I you."

I rose, realizing as I did that I would have to cross to the side of him in order to rach the door. "If you put one hand on me, I shall scream," I warned.

When he made no move, I stepped forward cautiously, infuriated that instead of being intimidated he was actually smiling, appearing to enjoy my fear.

"Do not look at me like that," I threatened.

"I was just thinking that you look like a little girl there with your hair flying about your shoulders," he mused, "but if you are going to present yourself as the pinnacle of prudish chastity, I would suggest that you take time to button the bodice of your gown."

I gasped as I looked down and clutched at the fabric across my breasts. As I did, he sprang forward and pulled me to him.

"You tricked me," I shrieked in accusation, aghast that he was laughing.

" 'Tis an old ploy I admit, but I have never taken such a delight in it before."

I could feel the warmth of his breath against my neck. "Unhand me," I demanded.

"Daphne, do not fight me," he murmured, pulling me to him so tightly that I thought I should lose my breath. " 'Tis such a waste of time and energy. I am not about to let you go. Not now, not ever."

I started to protest, but as I did, his mouth covered mine and whatever breath I had left I felt fully taken away. I felt as though the whole of him was invading me, and though my mind fought to keep a balance, all the venom that I had assaulted him with earlier seemed hard to recall.

"We will have to live in France, you know," he murmured as he nibbled on my earlobe. "The château is large, one of the grandest in the Ariege. But then I suspect that Countess Daphne shall bear me a number of children, so we will need the room. And though I am loathe to think of it, I suspect amongst that brood there will be *une petite fille* with hair like gold, eyes of violet pools and a stubborn streak so like her mama."

"You really are mad," I managed to whisper as his lips covered mine once again. But this time I cared not that he took my breath away.

37
serena

JUSTIN WAS BESIDE himself.

"Perhaps I should leave you alone," Oliver offered.

"No, stay," I pleaded. "There is time enough for that. I really need you here with me. I do not think I can go through this alone."

"What on earth is happening here, Serena?" Justin demanded. "I have never seen Daphne in such a state. Why did you send Luke off after her?"

"Darling, calm yourself," I advised, going to him and putting my arms about him. "I will explain all this to you later. There are other things we must discuss while the three of us are privated here."

Oliver refilled his own and Justin's glasses. "Did you get the message about Gaston?" he inquired of Justin. "Did you know he had left England?"

Justin nodded. "And thank God we did. But I still do not know how he discovered my involvement."

"I would prefer to discuss that with you later," I advised.

"What of DeMarcier?" Oliver inquired. "Where is he now?"

Justin swallowed the brandy full down.

"He is dead," he said somberly.

"Dead?" I gasped, fearing what was to come next.

He nodded. "And I may as well tell you, Gaston is dead, as well."

350

"Oh, no," I moaned, feeling suddenly light-headed.

"What happened?" Oliver entreated. "Luke must be devastated."

Justin's hand rubbed his forehead.

"Are you feeling unwell?" I asked, seeing for the first time the exhaustion in his face.

"I am just tired, Serena, and it is not a pleasant story. Gaston de la Brocher did little to engender sympathy, but he was Luke's brother, and in the end that was a lot to lose."

"You regret that you were ever involved in this, do you not?" I suggested.

Justin looked up and winked at Oliver. "She knows me well, this wife of mine. I admit when I saw Gaston's lifeless body cradled in Luke's arms, it gave me more than a second's pause. It should not have happened. It was a senseless, useless death. But it was as if Gaston invited it. Luke had done everything he could over the years, of that I am certain. It was sheer greed that felled him in the end. He could not bear the fact that Luke had inherited the title, the estates, even though Luke would have shared everything with him. This whole thing in the Ariege, I do not think he cared one iota about it. But he was vulnerable for the likes of DeMarcier and his men. I venture to say that had things gone differently, Gaston would have found himself a puppet of the new regime, being bled by his supposed compatriots."

"I still do not understand where all this took place?" Oliver inquired.

"Luke and I travelled first to Foix in the middle of the Ariege. It was there that a courier from Charles Jullier reached us, warning us that Gaston knew of the conspiracy between Luke and myself. Luke believed, and rightly so, that it would only be a matter of time before Gaston would go to France. DeMarcier would insist on it."

"And so you went to the château?" I encouraged.

"Yes. And frankly, in those first days we were encouraged, for there was rumor that the Minister of War was to name General Lafitte to oversee the region."

"We knew that, from Monique," I advised.

"I had hoped if that might take place before Gaston returned, that it might discourage him from taking a further stand. You must understand that there was much jubilance amongst the peasants in anticipation of this nomination. There was a meeting one night at the base of the Pyrenees near some of the foresting lands that Trinqué had held. Luke insisted on going. I thought it unwise, call it instinct, I know not, but until Gaston and Luke could sit down and discuss their differences and try to reach some common ground, I sensed that there was danger.

"What we could not have known was that DeMarcier, who had deftly managed to put a plant inside the château, had us at a complete disadvantage. We had ridden to this place by horseback, not wanting to arouse more commotion than was necessary. I had tethered the horses down by a stream, as there was quite an incline to where the group had gathered. We had been there an hour, perhaps two, when the rain, which had been just a drizzle at the outset, came upon us in torrents. There was no shelter, and I called to Luke to come down the mountain with me and head back to the château. I expect I should have known that something was awry right away, for the horses were nowhere to be seen. Luke thought that the storm must have frightened them off, but I knew differently. There was no way that they could have escaped unless they had indeed been unleashed.

"I honestly do not know if I was even aware that the first shot had been fired. I truly think in my mind I still heard it as a clap of thunder. The next thing I knew was that Luke, who had been but twenty paces from me, was running towards me full tilt. As I hit the ground, there was a second crack, and I heard him cry out. I knew immediately that he had been hit, and raising myself to my knees I crawled through the mud to where he lay. He murmured to me that we had to get out of there. I knew he was right, but I knew not how badly he had been wounded, and without the horses there seemed no escape.

"I can only thank God that some of the peasants too had decided that to remain in the mountains during the storm was foolhardy, for they being not far from us and hearing the shots had converged near the spot where Luke and I huddled. There is no accurate retelling of what happened next, for the forests became a cacophony of cries and shouts and seemingly endless barrage of pistol shots. When it was all over, some seven had been killed and two were seriously wounded. It was not until it seemed safe to rise and examine the scene of this blood bath did Luke or I even know that it had been DeMarcier and his men. One of the men swore that it had indeed been by the hands of one of DeMarcier's men that Gaston had died.

That, I suspect, we will never know, and finally looking down on him there in Luke's arms, it would not have made a difference."

"I can only thank God you were not hurt," I murmured.

"We returned to the château," he continued, "after what ought to have been a night of victory, but for Luke there was no victory. The cause, it appears, has been won, but it was a high price to pay."

"It seems unbelievable to me still that the two, Luke and Gaston, could be so different."

Justin shrugged. "Perhaps life, circumstances made them so."

"Things are better, then, you intimate in the Ariege," Oliver offered.

Justin nodded. "There is no doubt. Luke has great confidence in Lafitte. This matter will not be rectified overnight, but at least the killing and marauding will stop. People will have food again. Anyway, enough of that. I am certain within the next few days you shall both have had your fill of this. What I want to know is how Clarissa fares. And where is Constance?"

A look exchanged between Oliver and myself.

"Your silence does not give me great encouragement," Justin offered. "I wish one of you would say something."

"Let me handle this, Serena," Oliver insisted. "I know you are going to feel that you should be a part of this, but it will serve no purpose to relive this again."

I drew myself to my feet. "I may surprise you, but I am not going to object." I crossed to Justin and gently placed a kiss on his cheek. "If I am asleep when you retire, please wake me."

He smiled. "If that is a command, you can be certain I shall obey."

I called to Pluck, who seemed torn between following and leaving Justin behind, but he finally trotted after me up the staircase to our bedroom. I had had a moment's pause when I had reached the landing, debating whether I should turn and go down to Daphne's room. The mother in me suggested that I should march down there and demand that any discussions take place in the drawing room, but it was the woman in me who won out. Many things had happened since we had come to Channing Hall and far the least of them was the transition that our daughter had made from the naive purity of innocence to the bittersweet realities of adulthood. I would always love her, be fiercely her champion, but I could no longer protect her. It was she who would have to pattern her life. I only hoped that she would be as fortunate as I in finding one to mold and build those patterns with.

I had no conception of the hour it was when Justin finally climbed into bed beside me, bringing me awake with the tenderest of kisses place at the nape of my neck.

"You see, I follow your instructions well, Lady Barkham," he murmured.

I raised my arm and drew his nakedness to me.

"I wish I could take all this pain from you, Serena. You must believe that if I had had the slightest inkling of what was to happen here, I should never have left you."

I put my fingers to his lips. "None of us could have known, darling. Who is to say if you had been here that it might have been prevented? That is not to say I did not have my moments of anger, of blaming you for something of which I knew in my heart you were blameless. After all, it is you who has borne the worry and responsibility of Clarissa these past years."

"Yes. And can you think, if I feel responsible now, of the guilt I would have felt if she had brought more harm to you than she did?"

"Hush. It is past. She is buried and with that the secret is safe kept. And if God is just, He will see to it that the seed of unbalance carried by Maura and Clarissa has finally been laid to rest."

Justin lay quietly for a moment. "You know, I had almost forgotten that the holidays are near upon us. I do not know about you, but I relish the thought of returning to Mayfair."

"Certainly no more than I," I assured. "I am certainly not superstitious, but this house has never been a happy place for me."

Justin laughed. "You are but a country girl at heart, my love."

"I think once I return there I shall never again leave. Nor shall I permit you to," I replied as he drew me closer.

When he did not respond, I pulled back from him slightly. "There is something you are not telling me, and do not say I am imagining things. I know you too well, Justin Barkham."

"Now, do not be angry, Serena. I swear to you we will have our holidays, but I . . ."

"You what?" I interrupted.

"I promised Luke that in the New Year I would make one more voyage with him. But it will be different this time, Serena, I promise you. The danger will be well past, and we will not be gone long. Truly, it will be far different than before."

"It may be more different than you think," I mused.

"How do you mean?"

"Because this time you may be returning with your future son-in-law."

"Luke?" he amazed. "So that is what all this nonsense is about?"

"I cannot be certain," I advised. "She might at this very moment be throwing him out."

Justin bolted upright in bed. "You mean de la Brocher is in her room still? That, that upstart, I shall have him quartered."

I laughed.

"I thought you liked him," I offered as I grabbed hold of his arm.

"I do," he acknowledged. "A lot better than that Sanderson fellow. I never liked a man who did not like to get his hands dirty. But . . ."

"But what?" I chided, slipping my arm under the crook of his neck.

He lay for some time without responding.

"Justin, what are you thinking?"

"I am thinking that, if this be the case, I better have a talk with Luke in the morning. If that is what he wants, fine, but I had better warn the man that he is going to have his hands full. There will be times when dealing with that woman will seem a high price to pay for happiness."

"Justin Barkham, how can you say that?" I challenged.

He leaned over and brushed his lips against mine. "That is easy, Serena. I should know. I married her mother."

"Why, you . . ."

Once again he never let me finish my sentence. As our legs entwined, I hoped he never would.

Postscript
serena

IT SEEMS HARD to believe that there have been three marriages, two births and one death all in the space of the year since we left Channing Hall to return to Mayfair.

The first betrothal was that of Luke and Daphne. Though the two had tried to be circumspect, I had known the moment that I had laid eyes on her the morning after his return there would be no other man for our daughter than Count de la Brocher. When Justin had invited him to return with us to Mayfair for the holidays, I know that he too was certain of it. But, as close as the two men had grown, Justin was not about to abandon his prerogative as a father by causing the hopeful groom-to-be some anxious moments.

It was on New Year's Eve when Justin finally gave his consent, only after my chastising that it was cruel to keep them both in such a state of anxiety. Actually, I think that Luke knew full well that Justin would embrace him warmly to the family, but I was amused and pleased that he allowed him to play out his once-in-a-lifetime moment as father of the bride-to-be.

For all my understanding in those early days, it was I who put a dampening on their spirits. They had wanted to be married immediately, before Luke and Justin were to return to France. My response, I admit, was selfish, for though the two ached to be together as one, I knew that once they were, it would only be a matter of days, perhaps weeks before they would leave England for France. It was scarce that I should never see them again; we would visit often, but there seemed such a finality to it. I wanted Daphne and I to spend what little extra time to continue to grow together before distance put us apart.

My wishes were met, less thán enthusiastically at first, but as the weeks and months passed I believe that Daphne too saw wisdom in my request.

How gay that time was. She and I were rarely apart during the days. There never seemed enough time to plan or talk. Justin frequently said we were like conspirators always jibbering in hushed tones. Conspirators, I thought, was not the right word. Sisters, friends, soul mates perhaps. I had always loved my daughter, but I delighted in this woman I was coming to know. I was also enormously grateful for her companionship. Though Justin kept his promise and returned from the Ariege, leaving Luke behind to help General Lafitte in the reconstruction, with Richard's passing he scarce had a moment to himself save to spend with me.

We had known that it was inevitable, but it did not preclude the enormity of our loss. I was grateful that we had at least had those few days at Camberleigh before we had returned to Mayfair for the holidays. Richard was clearly unwell, but he had tried to rise to the occasion, taking pleasure in the fact that his family had gathered about him, if be it for the last time.

His death was peaceful, taking him from sleep simply into that deeper sleep. Anne's strength amazed me, but then she had always possessed an uncommon resilience. Richard had always regarded the running of the estates as drudgery; indeed, as his health had failed, he had lost total interest, but there was still the necessity of transition, the burden of which fell on Justin. Thankfully, he had Oliver and Robbie, not to forget Alexander, to assist him, for as the railways continued to take form throughout the county, so did the demands on his time.

Though we had heard tell of Alexander's growing passion for and facility in the management of the estates, it was amazing to see it firsthand. There had been more than a physical change in him, though I must say it still shocked me when we embraced to realize that he now towered over me. He was still an introspective young man, his deepest thoughts and emotions were still privated unto himself. But there was now an eagerness, a relaxation that had not been present before. If I had had any qualms about leaving him behind at Camberleigh during our time at Channing Hall, they were quickly assuaged as I watched him enter each new project with a fervency and enthusiasm that had prior been lacking.

Naturally he was still undergoing a learning process, but he could not have had better teachers than Oliver and Robbie, though the latter was so smitten that his mind, we daily teased, was rarely on his work.

That Robbie had found one to love and share his life with delighted us all but none more than Charlotte. Anne's matchmaking had been fully rewarded when Robbie and little Caroline married in late March. She is indeed the essence of Charlotte when she was young, and in this short time we have all come to be ever so fond of her. For the present she is helping us within the household at Mayfair, but that will not be for long if her mother-in-law has her want. Charlotte has already sewn and crocheted enough clothing for a baby's first year, and if that is not incentive enough, she has inveigled Robbie into building a cradle. Realizing she has far enough encouragement, I have kept silent, but deep down I admit that I too shall look forward to the cries of youth about Mayfair once again.

Constance has only returned to Mayfair twice, the first time for the holidays and the second for her marriage. It had not been an easy task explaining to her the deception she had been an innocent party to. And it was some time before she fully comprehended that it had been Gaston who had trifled with her and not Luke. There was an unmistakable embarrassment involved, and, though wrongly, she continued to harbor resentment towards Daphne.

Therefore, when Monique suggested that it might be best for everyone if Constance returned to London to reside with her and renew her season, I was relieved and grateful. The invitation was met with enthusiasm by Constance, who, obviously jealous of her cousin's happiness, was determined to make a new conquest of her own.

I was not surprised when Monique wrote me to say that a young viscount, whom she described as "decidedly inane but deliciously rich" had begun to pay court after the second ball of the renewed season. In her same letter she had informed me that

Peter Sanderson was betrothed to Kathryn Foxcroft. I had debated sharing the news with Daphne, but when I had, she simply had smiled and said, "Though I wish them well, it frightens me to think it might have been I."

When Constance wrote us that she wanted to be married, I cannot deny that the news was met with wariness by both Justin and myself. As much as I tried to suppress the memory of Clarissa, I could never entirely dismiss the possibility that the horror both she and her mother Maura had endured might repeat itself but once again. But could I knowing this deny her a right to happiness, to the prospect at least of a full life? I knew I could not. Justin, on the surface, at least, appeared to be more concerned with the credentials of this man she wished to marry and why there appeared to be such a rush to accomplish same. My initial fears that she might be with child were quickly dismissed by Monique, who speculated that Constance was simply determined to marry before Daphne. I had finally relented, though I had explained to her that by her unwillingness to wait she would have to sacrifice the size of the wedding. It had amazed me when she had agreed, for I would have thought that she would have gone to any measure to outdo her cousin, but apparently timing took preeminence in her mind.

The viscount, whom Justin described as a bloodless sort, appeared genuinely enchanted by his new bride, and I only prayed that he would continue over the years to find her flighty, coquettish ways a source of amusement. If Pluck were to be regarded as the penultimate judge of the viscount's character, he would not have fared well, for he took an instant dislike to him, clearly disdaining his slightest overture. Though I scarcely thought a dog should be the final arbiter, I suspected that my dear spaniel had instincts more educated than our own.

I truly think none of the preparations for Daphne's wedding might have been accomplished without the help of dear Anne. At first I had insisted that it was too much for her with Richard's recent passing and the household so full now with the birth of Rebecca and Oliver's twins. But she would not hear of my protestations, and Justin finally convinced me that the diversion would be good for her.

I was ever so pleased when Daphne offered that she would like to wear my wedding gown, for I had always thought it the most beautiful I had ever seen. It was not in the mode of the current fashions, which were heavily puffed and crinolined, but the simplicity of the line and elegance of the fabric suited Daphne well. Anne designed a new headdress formed from a tiara of seed pearls from which fell endless yardage of alençon lace, which finally formed a long train at the back.

It had surprised but secretly thrilled me that they had chosen to be married in the chapel at Mayfair. There was a great deal of sentimentality and feeling for both Justin and myself connected with it, and I was pleased that it would once again be witness to another milestone in the Barkham family.

I do not think anything could have marred that day in June. There was not a cloud in the sky as carriages from all over commenced lining the drive to Mayfair. Pluck, who was in full fettle, barking his greetings to the endless guests, regarded me with great disdain when I advised him that the ceremony would, by necessity, proceed without him.

Justin had teased me for being typically female, for I could not keep my handkerchief from my eyes when the pastor pronounced Luke and Daphne man and wife, and though I did not refute it, I noticed that he was scarecely dry-eyed during the ceremony.

Seeing them there kneeling together before the altar, I felt suddenly transported back in time. It was no longer Daphne that I was watching but myself, young, so filled with promise, so expectant of what the future would hold. How would life weave its web for them, I wondered. I prayed that they would be strong enough to endure its rigors and wise enough to rejoice in its gifts. I saw in my daughter's eyes the same hope that I knew my own had reflected as I stood in that very place twenty years prior. And I saw in Luke the same outpouring of love that I had experienced from Justin. If they could but keep that hope and love intact, theirs, I suspected, would be as full and rich a life as Justin and I had shared.

My mother had told me years prior that we all had our destinies. But I had also come to know that for each of us there was also opportunity. Opportunity to reach for and challenge and finally accept what fate or perhaps a higher being had predestined. I had seized my opportunities and been ever grateful for my destiny. As Justin's hand reached out and closed over mine, I prayed that the same would be true for Daphne and Luke.

Highly Acclaimed
Historical Romances From Berkley

_____ 0-425-10006-5 **Roses of Glory**
$3.95 by Mary Pershall

From the author of A Triumph of Roses comes a new novel about
a knight and his lady whose love defied England's destiny.

_____ 0-425-09472-3 **Let No Man Divide**
$4.50 by Elizabeth Kary

An alluring belle and a handsome, wealthy shipbuilder are drawn
together amidst the turbulence of the Civil War's western front.

_____ 0-441-05384-X **Savage Surrender**
$3.95 (on sale Oct. '87) by Cassie Edwards

When forced to live in the savage wilderness, a beautiful
pioneer woman must seek the help—and passion—of a fierce
Indian warrior.

_____ 0-515-09260-6 **Aurora**
$3.95 by Kathryn Atwood

A charming favorite of Queen Elizabeth's court, Lady Aurora
must act as a spy for the dashing nobleman who saved her life—
and stole her heart.

BESTSELLING TALES OF ROMANCE